MARTYN OF FENROSE

Gothic Classics

MARTYN OF FENROSE;

OR,

THE WIZARD AND THE SWORD.

A ROMANCE.

THREE VOLUMES IN ONE.

BY

HENRY SUMMERSETT.

Kansas City:

VALANCOURT BOOKS

2008

Martyn of Fenrose by Henry Summersett
First published by Dutton in 1801
First Valancourt Books edition 2008

Library of Congress Cataloging-in-Publication Data

Summersett, Henry.
Martyn of Fenrose, or, The wizard and the sword : a romance /
by Henry Summersett.
p. cm. – (Gothic classics)
"Three volumes in one."
ISBN 1-934555-39-8 (alk. paper)
I. Title. II. Title: Martyn of Fenrose. III. Title: Wizard and the
sword.
PR5499.S27M37 2008
823'.7–dc22

2008003703

Published by Valancourt Books
Kansas City, Missouri

Composition by James D. Jenkins
Set in Dante MT

10 9 8 7 6 5 4 3 2 1

NOTE ON THE TEXT.

Martyn of Fenrose; or, The Wizard and the Sword was first published in three volumes by Dutton of London in 1801. This Valancourt Books edition is the second edition of the novel. The original edition has become quite rare today, with known copies at the University of Chicago, Cambridge, the New York Public Library, and the Corvey Collection in Germany. An incomplete copy, consisting of only the second and third volumes is presently listed for sale for $1,000. A German translation of the novel seems to have appeared in 1802, published by Unger of Berlin.

Little is known of Henry Summersett's life, other than the fact that he published a number of novels, poems, and plays in the last decade of the eighteenth century and the first decade of the nineteenth. An 1805 review of his *Maurice, the Rustic; and other Poems* in *The Monthly Mirror* informs us that, like Burns and Hogg, Summersett was a self-taught man, or "self-instructed Muse [...] of promising talents," as the reviewer puts it.

There are a couple documents in the National Archives that give clues to Summersett's identity. An 1812 poem, "Happiness in Retirement," is signed "Henry Neville Summersett." It is likely, then, that his parents are Henry Summersett and Hannah Nevill, who the Mormon church's Familysearch.org website states married at Hadleigh, Suffolk on 22 August 1770. According to that same database, Henry Neville Summersett was christened 23 June 1774 at Hadleigh, Suffolk. He would have been 27 years old when *Martyn of Fenrose* was published.

A discharge certificate at the National Archives tells us that a Henry Summersett was born at Kersey, Suffolk, and was discharged from the Suffolk militia at age 68, after having served for 25 years, 1 month. Whether this is the same Henry Summersett is not clear, although it is not improbable.

Following Valancourt's editorial policy, the original text has been reprinted with few changes; only in the case of obvious printer's errors or errors likely to confuse modern readers have alterations been made. A list of the most significant of these alterations can be found below. No attempt has been made to regularize or standardize punctuation or spelling, for example in the alternate spellings of Westmorland/Westmoreland.

JAMES D. JENKINS
Kansas City
November 10, 2008

Editorial Changes:

VOLUME I.

p. 1, line 9: to day] to-day
p. 5, line 3: brows of one his] brows of one of his
p. 25, line 20: till to-morrow. "I blush] till to-morrow. I blush
p. 69, line 4: smiling; but] smiling; "but
p. 135, line 13: horid] horrid
p. 140, line 16: the young warrior."] the young warrior.
p. 141, line 5: acknowlege] acknowledge
p. 142, line 18: and bitterness.] and bitterness."
p. 146, line 14: heard to sob aloud,] heard to sob aloud.
p. 180, line 16: having a suit] having a suite
p. 197, line 9: the king; begone] the king; "begone
p. 217, line 1: gigantic aud lofty] gigantic and lofty

VOLUME II.

p. 2, line 9: rout] route
p. 8, line 21: beir] bier
p. 20, line 14: thro,] thro'
p. 35, line 13: to day] to-day
p. 156, line 14: to night] to-night

VOLUME III.

p. 22, line 9: I have] "I have
p. 32, line 19: attainment."] attainment.'"
p. 43, line 5: aproaching] approaching
p. 43, line 21: it, His] it. His
p. 129, line 8: To night!] To-night!

MARTYN OF FENROSE;

OR,

THE WIZARD AND THE SWORD:

—••••••——

A ROMANCE.

—••••••——

BY HENRY SUMMERSETT,

AUTHOR OF LEOPOLD WARNDORF, JAQUELINE OF
OLZEBURG, &c. &c.

—••••••——

VOL. III.

PRINTED FOR
R. DUTTON, NO. 10, BIRCHIN-LANE, CORNHILL;

AND SOLD BY

COBBETT AND MORGAN, CROWN AND MITRE,
PALL-MALL; MILLER, BOND-STREET;
AND HURST, PATER-NOSTER-ROW,
LONDON.

——

1801.

PREFACE.

WHO is he that starts when a cloud passes over the sun—that walks in dread of earthquakes—that trembles at the serenity of nature, and almost yields himself to annihilation, while viewing the storm which breaks not the sport of children?—FEAR.—His birth is of old; and he has the curse of immortality upon him.

One evening he fled through the gloomy mazes of a forest, and made towards a rude and pitiful dwelling, at the door of which he struck a hand that neither vein warmed, or sinew strengthened.— "Who disturbs my quiet?" was an enquiry made within. "Open your wicket, and admit me instantly; the foul spirits, with lash and brand, pursue me. My body will be lacerated by the cord—my flesh blistered by the flames—and the ever burning pit will gape and swallow me!—Open, open, and shield me from their rage!"

The latch was raised—he rushed forward with wildness, and ploughed the muddy floor with his head. IGNORANCE was the mistress of the hut, and the first object on which the fugitive fixed his eyes. The stupidity of her countenance partly banished his terrors, and at length gave him as much energy as his frail frame had capability to admit.

They lay on one couch till the morning. He sojourned with her during five moons, and on the appearance of the sixth crescent, from her premature womb came a languid bantling, who afterwards took the name of SUPERSTITION. Her mother rocked her cradle on rushes, and her father told her stories of hell. Her body and mind were equally imbecile, still she had an obstinacy of spirit, which the softest persuasion could not divert.

Her parents gave her early to the world; and she traversed every part of it. Wherever the sea washes, and wherever the winds blow, she has been found. All men listened to her wild doctrines, and were amazed; she must however have fallen in her extravagancies, had not priests patronized her follies, and abetted her inconsistencies. But she no longer lifts the scourge, which, throughout many ages, she raised with the hand of a despot; and her antics, though they may amuse, and even for a moment impress, can actually terrify no more.—Nothing can re-establish her power; and all her false lights, compared with the dawning star of REASON, are like the harmless fires of the glow-worm beneath the unclouded moon.

I will not insult the reader's understanding by telling him my motive for prefixing this allegory to my book. The judicious will not need any such confession; and the idler, viewing it as an excrescence, would not compliment my task even with a glance of his eye.

THE AUTHOR.

LONDON,
1800.

MARTYN OF FENROSE,

OR, THE

WIZARD AND THE SWORD.

"WAVE the flag on high," said the bard of Alwynd; "and sing the song of triumph."

> Come, play the merry timbrels,
> Our Lord returns, with glory crown'd;
> Clash, clash the lively cymbals,
> And let the song of joy go round;
> For victory, for victory
> Upon our banners smiles to-day
> And pale defeat and agued fear
> Attend the cowards of the fray.
>
> Bright rose the sun at morning,
> Forth flew our swords, our trumpets bray'd,
> Our heroes, caution scorning,
> And not of danger's threats afraid,
> Rush'd to the fight, rush'd to the fight,
> And battled there most valiantly!
> All seem'd to snatch at fame's high crown,
> All wish'd to triumph, or to die!
>
> O, blue-eyed chief! whose glory
> No living warriors can exceed,
> Thy name shall live in story,
> In many a brave recorded deed;
> And while thy bones, and while thy bones
> With thy forefathers idly rest,
> Thou wilt by every heart be mourned,
> By every tongue thou wilt be blest!

This song came from a company of men and women, who were stationed on the battlements of the castle of Alwynd; a maimed soldier was in the front of them, and, tho' his wounds were bleeding, he joined in the chorus. Several instruments assisted the voices; and on the finishing of the last stanza, a loud shout was sent into the air.

One of the men ran to the highest turret, on which he hung a flag; and the party below requested that he would inform them of the first appearance of their expected Lord. The music again sounded, the shoutings were renewed; and the bloody arm of the soldier was bound up with some of the linen which the females tore from their bosoms.

"Thanks to ye, maidens," cried the hero, "you have touched my hurts with gentle hands; but the joy caused by the success of the day removes all pain, and I can laugh, girls, while I throw my cap in the air, and cry, huzza! glory and long life to the Lord of the castle!"

"Comes he yet?—Comes he yet?" cried the impatient group, turning up their eyes to the man on the turret.

"No, I see nothing of him:—But he will be here anon.—Ha! they are climbing the hill!—I see their banners—their glittering arms—and now, the warrior on the white horse.—He comes!—He comes!—They have gained the brow."

The man immediately joined his friends below; and within a few minutes, Lord Alwynd and his soldiers were seen by all of them. Their joy encreased; and when the noble leader and his brave followers were under the walls, it became tumultuous. As soon as they saw him enter the gate-way, they hurried down, and were ready to receive him as he came into the hall, when the song was once more repeated, and a crown of leaves put upon his head. But he smilingly removed it from thence, and twined it around the brows of one of his poorest vassals; whose enterprizes he had marked, and whose sword had cleft the scull of an enemy that had taken an unfair advantage of his Lord, while he was engaged with another man in the field.

This action of gratitude was highly applauded; and the fame and generosity of Lord Alwynd formed many a deserved panegyric. He was not accompanied by any nobleman. He took off his helmet, and all those who were around him, were desirous of having the honour of disencumbering him. At length his armour was entirely removed; he requested every one to attend to the festivity of the hour, and then retired to the interior of the castle, in quest of objects which he longed to gaze on.

He went quickly through several rooms, and then came to one in which he caught the sounds of childish sport. His heart beat with delight:—Gently opening the door, and without advancing, he cried, "William! Agatha!"—There was a momentary silence—he called again,—"Hark!" said the voices of children within;—he heard them running across the room, and in the next minute they were hanging upon his neck, and kissing his cheeks.

The hero burst into tears; and he who had so lately frowned on death, was dissolved by the tenderness of two children.

"O, my dear Lord!" cried the boy, "how glad, how happy I am to see you!"

"And so is Agatha!" said the little girl, removing her mouth from the cheek to the lips of the warrior, whose emotions still kept him in silence.

"Why do you not speak to us?" said William.

"Dear boy!——"

"And now to me!" cried the girl.

"Sweet Agatha!—Did I not tell you, little ones, that I should soon return to you?—Give me your hand, William; and kiss me again, Agatha. Come with me to my chamber. There will be a feast in the hall this evening, and both of you shall be present, and hear the music."

He then placed Agatha on one of his arms, and led William out of the room. Delighted with their innocent talk, he could not part with them; and when he was summoned to the hall, he took them with him, making the mirthful William his sword-bearer. The warriors smiled when their gallant Lord approached, and he gave his hand to many of them, as he advanced to the table; at the top of which he seated himself on an elevated chair, and the children were placed on each side of him, tho', before the repast was finished, he more than once drew them on his knees.

The feast was sumptuous; and it was eaten with merriment—no cold formalities of state checked the gaiety of the banquet. The

Lord looked not above his guests, but seemed to consider them all as friends and brethren. Mirth was not lost for want of his smile; neither did the song sink for want of his voice. As he was about to retire, he drank a general health to his associates, thanked them for their support and fidelity in the late skirmish; and to the man who had rescued him in the field, he gave his sword, desiring him to hang it under the wreath that had been transferred to him for his valor.

He then rose, and led the smiling children out of the hall; but previously desired that his absence might neither conclude, nor interrupt, the festivity of any of his people.

As he was returning to his apartment he heard a loud altercation; and, looking forward, found that it arose between one of his servants and a stranger. Surprised, he went near, and turned towards them. He demanded of his domestic the cause of the contention; and the fellow was going to reply, when his opponent prevented him, by asking Lord Alwynd, whether the day was not considered as a general festival?

"It is, sir," replied the Baron; "all who enter the castle, are most cordially welcome to whatever fare may be found in it."

"Victory to your arms, and happiness to your heart!" cried the stranger.—"Yet why, my Lord, am I to be treated with scorn, when your hospitality takes in every one?—Why driven from your gate by a barking cur, whom your Lordship's bounty fattens?"

"Use no more angry words, I beseech you stranger; enter and feast."

"My Lord!" cried the servant, "my Lord, is it really your pleasure that this hideous wretch should be entertained at the public table?—He is too frightful an object to be endured!—His eyes are too dreadful to look upon!—Pray, my Lord, desire him to retire, or give orders that he may be driven out of the gates. The sight of him makes me sick—it fills me with fear and astonishment!"

"Are you mad?" cried Lord Alwynd; "or is it the force of wine that makes you talk thus strangely?—This person is not such as you describe. His garments are good and clean—his countenance mild, humane, and respectable—and he bears the best appearances of a gentleman."

"My Lord!—His countenance, did you say?—Hell cannot produce any thing more ugly!"

"Peace, unmannered fellow, or I will chastise you for your insolence. Good sir! drink has destroyed my servant's reason:—Go into
the hall, to which yonder passage leads, and be merry with those
whom you may find there."

"Aye, do, good stranger!" cried young William; "go in and be
merry with the rest."

The man kissed the robe of the Baron, and laid his hands on
the heads of the children; then bowing to Lord Alwynd, whom he
respectfully thanked for his hospitality, he retired from the castle,
instead of going to the feast.

The servant was very severely reprimanded by his Lord, who,
supposing him intoxicated, commanded him to go to bed, in order
that he might not give offence to any other of the guests. But
the man affirmed that he was not, in the least degree, affected by
drinking; and again asserted that the filthiness of the stranger's
garments, and the hideousness of his face, had caused him to act
as he had done.

"Lunatic!" cried Lord Alwynd; "I now perceive that you are not
drunk; but it is evident that your mind is diseased. The person you
speak of has a very good countenance, and he was habited like a
gentleman."

"O, mercy on me!—I protest, my Lord, that the fiercest devil
could not——"

"Be silent!—Your extravagant talk is not to be borne. Did you
ever see the stranger before?"

"Never, my Lord; and I pray Heaven I may never see him
again."

"You cannot, then, possibly suspect who he is?"

"My Lord, I do believe that he is one of the wizards that live
in the forest. It is said that there are several of them, and that they
have resided there an hundred years and upwards; but no person
has ever ventured to go near them. Ha! he is here again, and more
ugly than before!—Look, my Lord!—Look! look!"

"On what?—Compose your mind, or you will certainly grow
distracted.—Why do you shake so violently?—What do you fix
your eyes upon?"

"On that abominable creature!—Ah! he has torn my flesh with
his brutal nails!—He throws his filthy foam at me; and now his

eyes grow more large and red.—Save me, my Lord!—Save me!
save me!"

He was flying towards the Baron, but he fell into a swoon; and
his Lord having called some of his attendants to the assistance
of the distracted wretch, retired with the terrified children. The
heart of Alwynd truly commiserated the state of his domestic, and
the sudden insanity that had affected him; still he was sorry that
any person should have gone from his castle without partaking
his hospitality, and he sent some of his servants in quest of the
stranger, with an entreaty that he would return. But, after an hour
had elapsed, they all came back, and informed him that the object
of their search could not be found.

About two hours later, and as the sun was declining, he parted
from the children for the night, and took himself to a wood at some
little distance from the castle. Tho' he was skilled in the science of
war, still he was a lover of nature; and he had often wandered amid
her scenes with the purest delight. He was no promoter of broils
and contentions; and he never sought the field of battle, when false
honour held out a lure for him. But in a true and justifiable cause,
he would prowl among the ranks like a determined lion; the whisperings of peace, however, were always pleasing to his ear, and the
smiles of humanity he regarded as precious.

The mortal that knew and did not love him, with only one
exception, was not to be found; still among those who esteemed
him most, there were some who called him a strange, good man.
His fortune was noble, and his adherents were numerous and loyal;
the thirtieth summer was coming over his head, and his manly
beauties were then in their richest blossom.

He lived but in the castle and in the field. The court of his
prince, tho' he wanted neither favours, nor respect, he absented
himself from; but his services were granted as soon as they were
commanded, and no noble of the realm was more firm in his loyalty, or more ardent in his exploits. Peace and retirement, however,
were his favourites; and in the summer evenings, the villagers generally saw him either wandering thro' the meadows, with the playful children, or roving alone, with an air of melancholy, among the
shades of the forest.

Tho' his was not a confirmed sadness, yet many were surprised by the temporary gloom that often hung on his brows; and tho' he smiled on those who unexpectedly accosted him in his reveries, still they wondered at the dejection of his faded countenance.

It was known that he had never been married; and there was no probability that he would enter into the state of wedlock. The two children that have been mentioned, were reported to be the offspring of a deceased friend; they were twins, and Alwynd had brought them, about three years before, and when they were only two years old, to the castle, where he desired that they might be treated with all possible tenderness and respect.

This love for the orphans was of a paternal nature; and every person who resided in the castle, not only praised the benevolence of his heart, but also, in different degrees, and according to his station, strove to imitate the Baron's example.

He had, within a few hours, come smiling and victorious to his home, and afterwards joined in the revelry of his friends and followers, and also in the fancy sports of the children. But in his evening walk, all mirth seemed to be forgotten—every splendid and lovely image to fade. He moved slowly among the trees—he paused—he sighed, and his eyes were raised to the summit of a hill, from behind which the moon was coming, with a devout and strong expression, as if he were expecting the appearance of a spirit of Heaven.—Man! thou shalt exult thy hour; but look for nought of joy beyond it.

The mutterings of two hoarse voices, and the approach of feet, disturbed the ruminations of Alwynd, who, looking towards the spot from whence the noise proceeded, saw two objects which caused him to start, and filled him with surprise. One of them was designed for a man, but nature had strangely sported with his form, and compounded him of ugliness. His body was misshapen, and his face brutal; one of his eyes was fierce as fire, the other seemed a lump of senseless matter, and was dull and rayless.

Alwynd, not without a fearful emotion, turned towards the woman, whose deformities nearly corresponded with those of the man. But she was naked almost to the waist; and some of her greasy hair was pulled partly over her breasts, which seemed to contain nutriment for, and also to have been swayed by the eager jaws of a tribe of imps.

Alwynd grasped his sword, fearing that the monsters would attack him; but each of them made a respectful motion, and wished the blessings of the new moon upon him. Ashamed of his fears and rashness, he sheathed his half-drawn sword, and enquired who they were, and from whence they came.

"We are beggars, my Lord," replied the man; "we are compelled to rove about the world, and to subsist by charity. You have seen the lightnings fly, while lying on a bed of down; we then have been unhoused and unsheltered. You have heard the fierce spirits of the rigorous season—you have heard the wind howling in the nights of December, and the hail rattling against the window of your well-warmed chamber; aye, then we have been shivering in a ditch, covered only by a blanket that was supported by a leafless hawthorn."

"With twenty thousand agues on us," said the wild looking woman; "our bones ready to crack with the frost, and our very marrow to freeze."

"Pinched by want, I have said to many whose purses have been overstocked, give me something to buy food with, lest I perish; some of them cursed me, others baited me with their cries, and there were among them those who passed me with unopened eyes."

"Aye, and the time has been, when I have begged the herdsman's wife to give me a few grains, which she was carrying to her swine.—But I have had them not.—Get thee to hell, beldame, she has said, get thee to hell, and gape for the steams of sulphur."

"You have been victorious in battle," said the male beggar, "and, in consequence of it, have given a feast to-day. I asked one of your servants for some food to appease my hungry bowels; but he cursed and drove me away."

"For which may fire from the clouds turn him into a cinder!" exclaimed his dreadful companion.

"Had I been there," said Alwynd, "you should have had it; go back again, and I will order provision to be placed before you."

"No, no, we have since made our meal:—A dead lamb came down the river; we pulled it to the bank, and feasted daintily. But we were not alone refused admittance to the castle; for I met a knight, who said that the Lord might be honourable, but his servants were villainous."

"I am sorry for the misconduct of my people. Here is money for you both. But tell me how you came to be so misshapen?"

"Ask that of Him who furnished the Heavens:—I refer you to the highest authority. There is a design in every thing—in monsters, as well as in angels. Whatever you see, dare not to call it abominable, for it comes from the hands of One, whose ever active eye loaths it not, and whose works none should venture to blame. Good night, noble Lord!—We shall travel till the stars are lost in the clouds of morning."

They went forward, and Alwynd noticed their strange limpings till they disappeared. At first he had thought them supernatural, but in the parting speech of the man, he found some forcible truths, which made him blush at his own weakness.

The ravings of the servant were now accounted for; it was evident that he was labouring under the impressions of terror, when the knight demanded admission into the hall; and, indeed, the wildness and deformities of the beggars, were sufficient to affect even a strong and unprejudiced mind.

Alwynd's fears decreasing, he rambled still further; and about a quarter of an hour after the wanderers had left him, and while it was yet light, he saw the gentleman that had been repulsed by the servant, riding along the forest on a beautiful steed. He was accompanied by a lady, who also rode a handsome horse. She was uncommonly lovely and graceful in her person; and tho' they travelled very fast, her eyes were fixed, with an expression of affection, on the face of her companion, who checked his steed on being accosted by the surprised Alwynd.

"Return to the castle, gentleman," cried the Baron, "and sojourn with me till to-morrow. I blush for the manners of my servant, whose distraction can alone excuse him. Several of my fellows have since been in quest of you; but now I have the pleasure of seeing you again, I entreat you to go back with me, and to partake the hospitality of a willing host."

It was with difficulty that the travellers restrained their steeds, which were as beautiful, and apparently as capable as those of the charioteer of the Heavens. They appeared as light as æther; and while they disdained the curb, their hoofs scarcely imprinted the forest turf.

The stranger placed his hand on the back of his horse, and gracefully turned towards Alwynd, to whom he said,—"I must decline your invitation, but I most cordially thank you for it.—I judge not of a chief by the manners of his vassal. Prosperity attend your Lordship, till we meet again, for ere long, perhaps, I shall be within the walls of your castle. We are bound to the north:—We have an hundred miles to ride to-night, and the moon will not live till the morning. Our coursers will not be held any longer.—Away, ye fiery spirits!—Farewel, Lord Alwynd!—Farewel, gallant and hospitable chief!"

"Good night, sir.—Adieu, fair lady!"

"Health to the Lord of Alwynd; success to his sword, and repose to his pillow!" said the lovely traveller, smiling like a cherubim. The reins were given, unlimited, to the horses; they began not their course by degrees, for no archer could send an arrow with so much swiftness as they commenced their journey.

The riders sat firmly—they even turned and saluted Alwynd with their hands. There were graces in the horseman which could not be excelled; and the long and glossy locks of his companion, were raised from her fair neck, and sported with by the winds. They soon lessened—in a few minutes they were on the verge of the wide forest, and the wondering eye that had followed saw them no more.

"Is this a reality?" cried Alwynd, rubbing his brows with his hand.—"Have mortals these powers?—Have I seen and conversed with corporeal things, or been cheated by visions?—I have beheld strange objects to-night, which will excuse my doubts; yet the beggars, tho' monstrous to the sight, wanted neither faculties nor reason; and these mysterious travellers—these meteors of human form—Pshaw! the strangeness is in my eye, or in my imagination. My blood has been heated in battle, and my spirits have been roused into confusion—I feel a giddiness in my head, and to that I attribute these seeming wonders. I have foolishly made phantoms of substance, and grossly perverted the plain truths of nature."

Convinced of the temporary defects of his own faculties, he returned to the castle. The remainder of the inferior guests were then departing, the others having gone before; he wished them a general good night, and retiring himself soon after to his chamber, the comforts of a soft repose came upon him.

On his rising in the morning he was saluted by the sun, and afterwards by his merry little fairies; they all went forth to breathe the air of the forest, from whence they returned, enlivened and refreshed by the breezes that had blown on them. It gave great pain to Alwynd, to find that the servant still laboured under his fears, and that his wits were still disordered. On the third day, however, he became more calm; and his Lord advised him to think no more of the beggars, and also not to alarm his superstitious fellows, by talking of the strange object that had presented itself to him, and caused his short derangement.

Peace! thou wert ever, and ever wilt be, loved by the good, the gentle and humane. He is no hero who scorns thee—he is not noble who would turn his eyes from thy fair face, to gaze upon the glaring and bloated countenance of war. The lord and the peasant must love thee; and the venerable matron, the tender wife, and all her little progeny, ever bless thy name. How cheerful and bounteous art thou in cities, where a thousand smiles in every moment are created by thee!—How mild in the temples of religion, where it is held to be no longer necessary to implore Heaven to rout our opposers, and deluge their blood!—How beautiful and serene in meadows and in groves, where thou givest rich rewards to industry, and crown'st the heads of youthful innocence and virtue, with garlands of long living flowers!

Three years passed away, during which the hand of Alwynd was never incumbered with an instrument of war; neither national broils, nor private contentions, interrupted his tranquillity, and the piled arms were not resorted to, for the chastisement of either a public or domestic foe.

The servants of the castle still loved and revered its Lord; and they were pleased to observe, that he was less subject to those fits of melancholy, and to those seemingly bitter ruminations, which had previously robbed his face of half its beauties. They now saw him generally cheerful, he smiled upon them in the hall, and frequently went blithesome to the chase. A quick recollection, however, would sometimes strike his mind; and once or twice he retired abruptly from the feast, and also turned, dejectedly, from the steed that was to convey him to the forest sports. But the infrequency of these actions made them less noticed, and they were attributed to the indisposition of the body, rather than to the more serious and inveterate malady of the mind.

The children still continued the principal objects of his happiness and delight. His care over them was exemplary; whenever they smiled he was never sad—he encouraged them in their sports, they attended him every where, and frequently partook his bed. If they ever complained of illness, his face shewed nothing but anxiety, till they again gambolled around him, and by their sportiveness assured him that they were no longer afflicted by pain.

Many idle stories, respecting these children, had long been abroad; but none of them reached the ears of Alwynd. No person, except Lord Celwold, ever importuned him in regard to their birth and origin, which he had never thought proper to explain; and it was not in every season that even Celwold, who was the cousin of Alwynd, ventured to touch upon the subject.

Living at a small distance only from his relation, he was almost every day at the castle; and he frequently came accompanied by a boy, to whom he was an appointed guardian, and who was two or three years older than the adopted children of Alwynd. Edward was considered, by the young ones of the castle, as a dear companion; and at their solicitation, he frequently abided with them for the course of a week, at the expiration of which time, he always left his associates with regret.

This youth was of high birth and fortune; his father had been dead nearly two years, but his mother was still living. Owing to some peculiar matrimonial disagreements, to the extreme caution of the one parent, and to the implacable temper and violent passions of the other, the boy was, by the mutual consent of the authors of his being, made the ward of Lord Celwold. As his mother had withdrawn herself to France, without thinking it proper to account for her motives, Edward was taught to look to his guardian as his dearest and only friend.

Lord Celwold had intimately known his father, and not unreadily became his guardian. Perhaps it was neither true friendship, nor true affection, that caused him to assume the character; but having taken it on him, he was indulgent to the youth, and his conduct, tho' injudicious, was not untender.

At the time his guardianship commenced, he had an infant

daughter, and he entertained a hope, that, in a later season, a connection might be formed between her and his ward, whose alliance would greatly honour his family, and whose wealth would munificently enrich it. Within a twelvemonth, however, his expectations were for ever blasted, for the little object of his ambition was destroyed by a consumption; and in the course of the ensuing year, the parent from whom she had come, also went down into the grave.

These events had a very serious effect on Celwold, he felt to the full force of his nature; but, perhaps, he suffered as much from disappointment and foiled ambition, as from the afflictions of a father and a husband. Baffled and chagrined, he shut himself awhile from society; Edward was sent from him for a few months, and his visits to the castle became less frequent. At length, however, he recalled the boy, his mind recurred not so often to the departed, and he renewed, with an unclouding brow, his attendance on Alwynd; who, long as he had known and conversed with his specious kinsman, was still very ignorant of his well-disguised character.

With suspicion no one was less acquainted than Alwynd; he never put on any disguises himself, and was not fortunate in discovering them on those who made them their frequent habits. He generally judged of man by his exterior; and respected and applauded his good traits, without searching for, or prying into his bad ones. The smiles of Celwold's face, therefore, and the mildness of his tongue, were favourably regarded; and he who could so smile and speak, was not to be suspected of either artifice or depravity. How far Celwold merited the good opinion of Alwynd will soon be shewn; and his character must be judged by his actions, not by a superfluous description of the tenor of his mind and past pursuits.

While Alwynd was in tranquillity, Celwold seemed, by an almost daily intercourse, by a countenance which was always pleasing, and by the never deviating words of affection, to make the life of his kinsman still more happy. The children of Alwynd's love and bounty, and the young ward of Celwold, sported together in the forest, and often gambolled before their guardians, while they, pleased by their actions, followed them with smiles.

"How delightful are the hours of youth!" said Alwynd, one evening as he was sitting on the turf, by the side of Celwold.—"How delightful are the hours of youth!—Mark the faces, the bodies of these children; how joyful, how elastic and animated!—They seem to be mounting on the wind that wafts the glossy ringlets of their hair. I hope they will ever be happy; but no moments can be more precious to them than the present. O, I hope they will ever be happy!"

"Heaven grant it, my dear cousin!" cried Celwold, with apparent feeling and tenderness.

"Yet, whatever portion of felicity may, after a few more years shall have gone by, be awarded to them, it must be comparatively poor. Surely that must be the happiest state, when the human mind has still to make its first calculations of joys and sorrows. The man who has attained his full strength of reason, the sage, the poet, nay even the impetuous warrior, will often for a while neglect their studies, and forego their soberer pleasures and serious occupations, to turn a wistful eye upon the gaities and sportiveness of youth. It is the knowledge of the utter impossibility of recal, that makes us say we wish not our days to come back again; otherwise we should willingly hazard the chances of life, willingly start again from the goal of childhood, to hunt the gossamer and butterfly, and to run, with outstretched hands, after the distant rainbow."

Celwold assented to this opinion with a significant motion.

"What a charming little group!" continued Alwynd, with his eyes still fixed on the children.—"The figure and actions of William are truly graceful; and those of Edward are equally so. They may be heroes while I shall yet live. I would not check the spirit of valor, but were I to see my boy mown by the scythe of war, I should perish ere I could draw my eyes from his bleeding body. Observe the lightness of the fairy Agatha! the flowers scarcely bend under the pressure of her feet. Perhaps Providence will ordain that, I shall not only see her grow up to a beautiful maturity, but also that, in the days of my age, my ears shall be delighted by the prattlings of her innocent offspring!"

"My dear Lord! you speak with all the tenderness of a father."

"Suppose I do," answered Alwynd, after a pause evidently occasioned by his emotions.

"And yet, such you are not."

"You are deceived:—Such, I confess, I am."

"My Lord—you—this confession agrees not——"

"It agrees, cousin, with every thing that I have ever spoken on the subject. The world has many tenants, of various qualities; and all among men who are virtuous, and free from crime, I can esteem as much as if they bore my name, and were of the loins of my father. I rejoice in their prosperities—I can mourn for their adversities; and when they die, after the final departure of their wives, I can say to their progeny,—'Come hither, poor orphans! and I will be a father to you, you shall dwell with me, and share my superfluous riches; and in return, I shall expect that you will love me, and also perform the duties of children, as willingly as I shall those of a parent."

William and Agatha came up to him, as he was concluding his speech. They ran into his arms, and his head fell upon the shoulder of the boy; in the next minute, however, they flew again to their sports, when the uncovered face of Alwynd, shewed to Celwold the tears which had risen from a quick emotion. He was conscious of his weakness being observed, but he pretended to smile at it himself, and immediately addressed Celwold in a lively manner.

"Your Edward and my Agatha," he cried, "appear to be dear companions. It is not improbable, but that their youthful attachment may grow with their years, that the love of youth may ripen into perfection; and that, in the course of time, my adopted daughter may——"

"What, my Lord?"

"Become the wife of Edward, of your ward, my good cousin."

"Is your Lordship serious?—Do you not know that the family of that boy is illustrious—that his fortune, when maturity shall allow him to possess it, will be immense; and that it will consequently be my duty either to select for him, or guide his choice towards, a woman who shall have some nobility to speak of, and also a dowry suitable to his wealth?"

"Well—Suppose I admit it."

"Then, my Lord, the connection can no longer be thought of. You have veiled the little Agatha in obscurity, from which it may be inferred, that there is no great degree of dignity in her ancestry; and as she and her brother confessedly are claimants on your bounty, every person must acknowledge, that her alliance could neither be solicited for, nor, with any degree of propriety, accepted by one of the descendants of the Earls of Mercia."

"Indeed!" cried Alwynd, with a blushing face.—"I confess that you are a most cautious guardian; yet one whom I believe to be somewhat too hasty in his conclusions. If ever the heir of Mercia shall lead Agatha to the altar, his bride may, if she chooses, boast of a descent *nobler* than his own, and also of a fortune which the most venal would not look on indifferently."

"You astonish me, my Lord. But you look displeased; if I have incautiously offended you, I entreat your pardon. Were your Lordship to entrust the secret with me——"

"I cannot, cousin, therefore, do not ask me. I spoke more than I intended, and that perhaps too warmly. But it is time to return:—I shall keep you at the castle to-night; and as the dew is falling thick, we will go back with the children."

They all took the path leading towards the castle, where the remainder of the evening was spent by them with apparent cheerfulness; and the hour was rather late when the kinsmen separated for the night.

Lord Celwold, on entering his chamber, did not immediately go to his bed, for there was business in his mind which strongly claimed inspection. He was the nearest relation of Alwynd; and in their ages there was a difference of only two or three years. Alwynd had never been married; he had assured his cousin, very frequently, that he should ever continue in his present state, and also that he believed it not to be in the power of any woman to lead him from his determination.

This had been welcome intelligence to Celwold, tho' he always concealed the satisfaction arising from it. The title and riches of Alwynd, he thought might, in an after season, devolve on him; and as his wife had left him no children, it was his wish to marry again, in order that he might raise an heir for the envied possessions, in case he should not live to take them to himself. He had always looked with an eye of displeasure on the children that Alwynd had brought to the castle; and he secretly hated the good deeds which he openly extolled.

At first he had supposed them to be the natural offspring of

Alwynd; nothing, however, warranted the suspicion, and many things went against it. The idea of a secret marriage afterwards gave him considerable disturbance; but the declaration of Alwynd, that Agatha was of birth superior to Edward, convinced him that he was not her father, for the name of Alwynd, tho' nearly allied to honour, and greatly distant from obscurity, still required a very considerable encrease of fame to rank with that of Mercia.

Pleased as he was, with the self-assurance of the children not having any of the closer claims of nature, yet he was not perfectly satisfied; and tho' he presumed to think that there were no ties of consanguinity, still he was discontented, as well as alarmed, by the unbounded affection of Alwynd for William and Agatha, who, in the end, might greatly impair the fortune for which he was greedy and craving. Avarice was not one of the least vices of his nature; but he had craft enough to put a specious disguise on it, which was perceived only by those who were nearest to, and had daily intercourse with him, and which also concealed his niggardliness, even from many of those who were inmates of his own dwelling.

He was seldom the creature he appeared to be; the gems of honour sometimes seemed to throw their beauteous rays around his head, even while all the different corruptions of human nature were mingling together in his breast.

He indulged his mind, during the greater part of the night, with many suggestions and selfish calculations;—in the morning he hailed Alwynd, with a seemingly generous smile, and a few hours afterwards returned with Edward to his home.

In retirement and happiness, Alwynd lived till the children had arrived at the age of fifteen years. They promised to repay their guardian and instructor for his care and tenderness. The roses of health and beauty bloomed every day anew upon their cheeks; and the comeliness and form of the boy, were equal to the sweetness and gracefulness of the girl. They both delighted in exercise and activity. The sun had seldom long dawned on the forest trees, before they were wandering among them; and at early morning they often mounted their horses, and spurred them on, in order to meet their friend Edward, who was as dear to them as they were to him.

The charge of Celwold was now a noble looking youth; he was also enterprising, generous, and humane—dignified without vanity, great without pride, and sensitive without affectation. On many occasions, he bore himself in a manner which seemed to import a more advanced age; but there were times when mirth had not a lighter-footed follower, nor wit a more sportive or merrier child.

Lord Alwynd, agreeably to his vow, still continued unmarried; and Celwold remained a widower, without the desired heir. He had, indeed, been almost on the eve of marriage with a woman of distinguished rank and fortune, but his superciliousness towards one of her nearest relations, had caused a misunderstanding, of which an hasty dismissal was the consequence. This circumstance affected him strongly; the little amiability there was in his disposition, was considerably lessened by it, and his dependants had to witness no inconsiderable degree of gloom upon his brow, or of spleen and petulance in his temper.

His reason had ever been subordinate to his passions, which, from his childhood, had had an uncontrouled sway; and as even trifles had the power of irritating him, the effect produced by matters more weighty, was generally to be seriously dreaded by those who stood in fear of him.

The second failure of his project, which has been alluded to, made him inconsistent and extravagant; and his ill-humour arising from it had nearly once fallen even on Edward, whom he had ever previously treated with respect. But the nature of the youth would brook no insult, and he spurned at that which, in this season, was offered to him. His resistance and unrestrained retorts, brought to the mind of Celwold a sense of his impropriety; but the apology he made on the occasion, was accepted somewhat coldly by Edward, who had for some time past commented with privacy on the character of his guardian, which often appeared to him spotted and discoloured.

Another year went over, and preparations were made for the annual celebration of the birth day of William and Agatha, which had never passed unnoticed. It was generally distinguished by a rural *fête*, in which the Lord of the Castle, his domestics, and tenants, always joined. On this anniversary, however, the entertainments were more numerous, the hospitality more diffusive, and a general joy was on the faces of those, who saluted the young people, whose calling into life was thus commemorated.

Celwold, hypocritically, wished health and happiness to be showered on those, whose deaths would have excited neither sorrow nor regret. Edward embraced his young friend with great warmth and sincerity; and the kiss that his lips imprinted on the cheek of Agatha, tho' preceded by those of her protector and her brother, raised on her face a fine suffusion, which afterwards spread over his own.

Alwynd caused his favourite girl to be drest in the most splendid manner. Her robe was rich and elegant; and her dark locks were confined by a wreath of the most beautiful gems that had ever been seen in the castle. The eyes of almost every person, particularly those of Mercia, were fascinated by her charms; but envy checked the admiration of Celwold, who secretly cursed the folly and profuseness of the infatuated Alwynd, for such he was pleased to think his happy kinsman.

The splendor of Agatha dazzled not her reason, which shone brighter than the jewels that studded her crisped locks. She moved with her accustomed ease—wore her native smiles—was affable to all the dependants—loving to her brother and his admiring friend—and most tenderly affectionate to Lord Alwynd, around whose neck she many times threw her delicate arms, in order that she might, more freely, give those kisses, which flew from her lips towards his smiling face.

The song and the instruments of music inspired mirth and harmony. The sunny forest was made the spot of their pleasures during the day; but, at length, they retired to the hall, to eat the evening feast, and to renew the enlivening dance.

Alwynd was seated at the head of the table, and William and Agatha were placed on each side of him. The viands had been taken, and the goblet passed around the board, from which the whole party was rising, when a stranger presented himself before the Lord of the Castle, craving leave to speak to him either in public, or in private.

"I am surrounded by my best friends," replied Alwynd, "therefore be pleased to use your words freely and without ceremony."

"The Lord of Bartonmere once received succour from your arms. Your Lordship fought bravely—even bled for him; and he, in return, afterwards fought and bled for you. I am commissioned by him again to entreat your aid."

"He shall have it, sir."

"My dear Lord!" cried Agatha, in a low voice, and moving nearer to him.

"What! pale in the cause of friendship and of honour, my girl?" cried Alwynd. "Pray explain further, sir, and tell what services may be required of me."

"The haughty Baron of de Stacey, the old and inveterate enemy of my noble Lord, has again demanded tribute, which has been openly refused. In consequence of this he has, we learn, been making preparations for an excursion to our castle; and from a man, who broke his allegiance with the Baron, and came over to us, we are informed, that within two days an attack will be made by our imperious foe."

"I'll meet him there myself," cried Alwynd; "so inform your Lord. The distance from hence is trifling. This is a night of festivity; but to-morrow we will put on our arms, and go forward to subdue avarice and pride. This tell the Baron of Bartonmere, whom I would have you greet in my name. Partake of our cheer, sir, before you depart.—The night promises to be fair, and your Lord is doubtless anxious for your return, I will not therefore ask you to sojourn till the morning."

The messenger bowed and smiled; and in the course of an hour he went from the castle.

Lord Alwynd attended him to the gate, and stood by him while he mounted his horse. Retiring afterwards to a private room, he conversed some considerable time with Celwold, and then went towards the hall, at the entrance of which he met Agatha in tears. The festivity of the evening was clouded by her sorrow. Alwynd took her hand from William, and led her to her chamber, where he endeavoured, by tenderness and by precept, to sooth and fortify her mind. But she declined returning to the hall, in which it was necessary he should be present, he therefore embraced and left her. He then went back to his friends; he conversed with them for a length of time, on the subject of the expedition which he had been summoned to make; and every man that was present, without a single exception, offered his arm and his sword to the cause.

Among the rest was heard the voice of Celwold, who would have been silent had not his honour been at stake. William also wished to go forth with the warriors; and Edward spoke firmly of his design of joining them. But the former was immediately denied by Alwynd; and the peremptory commands of Celwold were placed on the latter youth, who received them in a manner which evinced his mortification and disappointment.

It was with pleasure that Celwold heard Lord Alwynd declare he must not accompany him, but stay at the castle till his return. To this arrangement he acquiesced without a single scruple; for, ready as he had seemed to go to the succour of Bartonmere, he was better pleased to remain within unmolested walls, than to undergo the fatigues of the march, and risk the dangers of the skirmish.

Agatha enjoyed but little repose during the night; at early morning she went to the chamber of Alwynd, and gently opened the door.—She saw that he was writing. Tho' the light of day was growing strong, his lamp was unextinguished—his habit remained as it had been in the preceding night; his bed was unpressed, and it was evident that he had taken no rest since they parted.

There was a great degree of expression in his countenance; he wrote—paused—sighed—and wrote again. The name of Agatha was more than once repeated in the tenderest strain. He saw her not.—She felt inclined to rush upon his neck, and to return affection for affection; but thinking that he might not wish to be disturbed, she walked softly away, and went to her chamber.

She met his Lordship again about seven o'clock—her eyes were thrown eagerly upon his face; she feared that she should see him distressed and agitated, but serenity sat on his brows. She could scarcely believe, by his countenance, that he had been waking all the night; and never had his smiles appeared to her more precious, or more beautiful.

The three next hours were spent by Alwynd and his men, in preparing themselves for their route: within that time all his vassalage had attended, they immediately equipt themselves in an armoury, and the chief and his followers were soon ready for their march to the Castle of Bartonmere, in which they meant to pass the coming night, in order that they might be refreshed, and sit to meet the expected assailants on the following day.

Alwynd had another private interview with Celwold, with

whom he was closeted upwards of half an hour; he then came forth, and summoned William and Agatha to take his farewel. This was a tender and truly affecting period! The hero himself melted. Had he been inclined to speak he would have been unable. He silently pressed the hand of the youth; kissed the cheek of his sister; strained them both affectionately to his breast; and, having put them into the arms of Celwold, he vaulted on his horse, and proceeded at the head of the warriors.

He knew that this was not a proper season for the indulgence of the weaknesses of human nature; he therefore endeavoured to recal his energies, and, within a few minutes after the separation, turned his face, on which appeared a noble fortitude, towards his vigorous and determined followers, whose love and loyalty closely attended their gallant leader.

They had gone about a mile across the forest, which was of great extent, when Alwynd perceived a horseman approaching him. Soon afterwards he was saluted by the person whom he had, several years before that period, seen, with a lady on that very spot, and who had been refused by the distracted servant, to partake of the feast which he had given on his former victorious return to the castle.

Alwynd immediately recognised him, for he was mounted on the same beautiful steed; and time had not in any degree impaired his personal graces. The warrior instantly checked his horse, and held forth his hand, to meet that which the stranger smilingly tendered him,

"Health to your Lordship!" cried the latter; "and your countenance assures me that you enjoy it. Believe me, my Lord, I am glad to see you well!"

"I thank you, noble sir," replied Alwynd. "Your present kindness is not necessary to bring you back to my memory, for since I last saw you, I have many times thought of you, and I am concerned that it is not in my power to go back with you to the castle, and offer you the hospitality which, at our former meeting, I could not prevail on you to accept."

"I cannot wish you to return; yet I am loath to part from you. Let me not impede your march, I will ride to the border of the forest with you."

The troop that had halted with the leader, now went forward again; and Alwynd's horse walked by the side of that of the
stranger, who continued—"I know your designs, Lord Alwynd,
and applaud them too. This morning, for my journey since sun-
rise has not been short, I saw the hostile preparations which were
making by de Stacey, who, I doubt not, will be at the Castle of Bartonmere early in the morning of to-morrow. I afterwards passed
the place of his destination, where, I am assured, a gallant defence
will be made by the insulted chief; a defence which you, and this
excellent troop, will serve greatly to strengthen. Bartonmere merits your assistance, de Stacey deserves to be scourged. The one is a
good man, with a fair name; the other an earthly devil, who shall
hereafter be known in hell."

"I hope we shall succeed in chastising him," cried Alwynd.

"The dangers of the contest," replied his companion, "will be
many; and your life is precious."

"As that of any other individual, sir; I know how it should be
estimated."

"You speak with too much modesty. I would not have you fall
for the world's united riches; by yonder sun, and by the power that
governs it, I swear I would not!"

"My thanks are greatly due to you: but, from a stranger, I could
not have expected so much feeling and concern. Your countenance
beams with sincerity; and I can readily believe what you profess."

"And yet," said the traveller, abstractedly,—"And yet, perchance,
Alwynd may be the mark of fate. Ha! See you not that black cloud,
to the west, my Lord?—It is an omen which I like not."

"I believe not in omens, I draw no fears from them; madmen
and children only consult and tremble at them."

"He who is too secure, is not less faulty than he who is too
apprehensive. It is true that you breathe, my Lord, and so true it is
that yonder cloud portends much evil. It enlarges—it grows more
black—Shall Alwynd conquer, or be conquered?—Indeed!—Jug-
gling fiend!"

"Sir!" exclaimed the amazed Alwynd; "to whom did you speak;
On whom do you look so angrily?"

"Pardon me, my Lord," he replied, with a smile which beauty
could not excel—"Pardon me, my fancy was sporting with my rea-

son: I was, indeed, strangely bewildered. But I would entreat you not to go forward to the battle."

"You must entreat in vain, then. Besides, did you not, a few minutes ago, spur me on; commend and applaud the expedition?"

"True, but in every moment man may have cause to shift his opinions. Wisdom never whispers, but we may learn something, however often she has spoken to us, or however long we may have listened to her. I have some sudden apprehensions for your safety. I conjure you to appoint a leader to the troop, and to let your soldiers go on without you."

"You, indeed, speak earnestly," said Alwynd, smiling; "but I cannot make your prejudices my own. I perceive that you are governed by some strong and peculiar opinions, by which I never was directed, and which I must ever reject. Still your kindness—it appears to me almost that of a brother."

"I love you like a brother, Lord Alwynd; and would guard you from every peril with my every mean."

"I am grateful, noble sir; but every human voice, directed towards me at one time, should not make me turn from the succour of so excellent a friend as Bartonmere,—from the menaces of his wolfish and sanguinary oppressor."

"Then go, my Lord," said the stranger, after a pause, during which his eyes had been fixed, with a strange expression, on the earth,—"then go, my Lord—meet the proud barbarian, and crush him, if you can. But first accept this gift; and be not incredulous to what I say.—Here is a sword, which I offer to you for your preservation, for it has a magic power that nothing can resist. The ore of which it was formed, was once millions of fathoms below the surface of the earth:—The feet of the miner that walked towards it, trod a horrid and dangerous path:—The fire that melted it was elemental:—The hand that tempered and fashioned it, the property of no mortal:—The man that could avert its point has never yet been created; and the blood it has shed, would crimson all the waters that are around the globe. Nay, it can even fascinate with its rays:—I'll prove the truth of this. See here, my Lord."

He unsheathed the weapon, and held its point towards one of the soldiers, whose eyes instantly assumed a wild and terrific expression. The fellow, apparently propelled by an instinct which was irresistible, left his companions—he rushed forward to his destruction, and his breast seemed to court the instrument that was to slay him.

"Forbear!" cried Alwynd, stricken with horror and amazement, "forbear! forbear!"

The stranger immediately dropt his sword. The willing victim stood for a moment in wonder before him, and then returned to his unobserving companions, looking like one that had been cheated by a vision, and was ashamed of his folly and idle superstition.

"Take it—use it," said the stranger, again presenting the instrument to Alwynd: "You can no longer doubt what I have said. Let it be your companion till the fray is over, when I shall claim it again."

"Replace it in your scabbard, and wear it yourself," the warrior replied. "I had no belief in these matters before; and will not now become an agent in sorcery. I am going forth in the cause of justice, not of murder. I will not turn from my opponent, whoever he may be, while I can lift my arm; but I will not attempt to cut him off by means so devilish as those which you advise."

"Meet the true warrior, with the spirit of a warrior; but be not falsely merciful to him who pants for the blood that is in your veins. Under the banners of de Stacey there will be many who delight in butchery. I have examined the body, and discovered its corruption. De Stacey knows that Bartonmere has claimed your succour, and believes that it will be given, in consequence of which he bears you a most deadly enmity; and he who shall bring to him your head, or trunk, is promised a reward which all the felons wish to grasp. They will pounce upon you like a flock of kites. This I swear to be true, as I swear my friendship to be sincere. I shall make you only one more tender. Think not ill of me for being the possessor of this strange instrument; employ it in your defence—be sure you part not with it, even for a moment, and return it to me when I shall claim it of you. Decide, my friend, decide instantly, for I can go with you no further."

The intelligence of de Stacey's stratagem and villainy had a considerable effect on Alwynd. He took the sword, and placing it by his side, vowed to give it back again to the stranger, if he should ever return.

"Of that there can be no doubt," said his companion, "if you retain it as I have directed; but should you part with it even for the smallest measure of time, I would not stake the most trifling thing on earth against your life. Adieu!—You shall see me again ere long; I will then explain to you my name and circumstances, which the pressure of the present moment will not allow."

"Go to the castle, and continue there during your pleasure:— My kinsman takes the government of it while I am absent, and he will receive and entertain you hospitably."

"He is unworthy of the trust, tho' he so kindly, so modestly accepted it.—Celwold would be the master, not the deputy. I know him—his heart is before me. You have not been sufficiently observing of his nature. When you have tamed the savage de Stacey, let your first action be to take all power from Celwold—your next to dismiss the hypocrite."

"You speak too freely, sir.—Celwold's ancestors have ever been virtuous, and he is nearly allied to me."

"And what of that?—Virtue is not hereditary; and where there is much honour, there may be an ugly speck, which, tho' not absolutely contaminating, should, for the sake of fair appearances, be removed. Farewell! farewell! I reverence the known merits of Lord Alwynd, but detest the corrupted heart of Celwold."

The stranger placed his spur to the side of his horse, which, with an almost incredible swiftness, bore him from the astonished chief. Alwynd continued his march with his men, who had moved at too great a distance to hear any of the foregoing conversation.

The forest friend appear'd to him a singular being—more than once he thought strangely of him; and he was tempted to throw from his side the mysterious weapon, that was to atchieve the wonders which had been spoken of. His own mind, however, soon accused him of ingratitude and injustice; he was not long in bringing back his belief that the stranger was honest—and he girded the loosened sword again round his loins, while he entered into converse with those who were at the head of his troop.

The shadows of night were resting on the towers of Barton-mere Castle, when the assisting warriors arrived at its gates. They were received with acclamations of joy by those who were in the walls; the men grasped the hands of each other like brothers—and the chiefs, as soon as they met, placed together those breasts in which honour and heroic friendship were, in an equal degree, to be found.

The enemy was expected on the following morning; and before the Barons separated for the night, it was determined that they should not remain coolly defending themselves within the walls, but quit them on the approach of de Stacey, and give him immediate battle, in case the inequality of their numbers was not great.

It was near the hour of midnight, when Alwynd retired to a chamber appropriated to his use, and even at that late season he was little inclined to repose. His mind was too busy to be speedily lulled; the images set upon it were many and various, and each of them had its peculiar interest. The events and concerns of the day were neither unaffecting nor without interest. He had risen in the morning, and perhaps would be incapable of rising ere the sun should shine and again disappear.—He had embraced those dear, those beloved children, whom his arms might never more infold,—his Agatha!—His William!—And he had, in case of his death, explained a long concealed mystery to, and reposed the most precious of all trusts, in a man, whom he had ever thought most honest; but who had been denounced, by one to whom all things seemed to be known and familiar, an enemy to his house, and an artful foe to himself.

"The falsehoods of hell," cried Alwynd, "were in the accusation!—Celwold is tender, honest, and virtuous."

"The falsehoods of hell," returned a voice, sounding like that of the stranger in the forest, "are in the heart of Celwold; and he is cruel, deceitful, and full of vice."

"Come forth!" exclaimed the astonished chief; "I know thee— we have met before since the morning, therefore come forth. I have some things to demand of thee."

"When the battle is over, my Lord, ask of me what you will. I am not what I seemed—but trust me not the less for it. My sword will lead you through a thousand dangers; remember, however, not to part with it till I shall hail you in your quiet castle. I have now no time for converse, as I am a busy agent in concerns which are innumerous. Forget not the perfidious intentions of de Stacey; forget not your lovely children—the children of Matilda."

"The children of Matilda!—Mysterious being!—Surely nothing can be concealed from you. Matilda!—Oh, there is agony in my heart!"

"There shall, if my advice be followed, hereafter be in it an immense store of joy. Remember the offspring of the dead—and that Celwold is unworthy. But see, I place before you a silent monitor. Adieu!—Matilda must go with me a space untraversable by mortals in a thousand years, before the lark soars, or the clouds grow grey."

A lovely spirit rose at some little distance from the warrior. She bore the smiles of heaven on her cheeks; affection shone from her dove-like eyes; her bright hair dispersed itself on her snowy bosom; her white and naked feet were visible beneath her spotless robe; and her whiter arm, and extended finger, pointed towards those regions, in which virtue is crowned with unfading bliss. In the centre of her cestus beamed a small, but matchless star; and on her head was placed another of nearly equal radiance, serving as unextinguishable lamps in the paths of immortality.

A secret dread was mixed with the rapture of Alwynd, who slowly strove to approach the beauteous shade of Matilda. But, smiling still more strongly, and waving to him her hand, she retired as he advanced; and, when he had reached the window, he found that the essence had burst through the walls, and saw the spirit mounting in the air, and hailing him from the moon-light plains of heaven. At some small distance from her appeared the being of the forest, mounted on his curbed courser, from whose nostrils a pale blue fire seemed to issue, and whose hoofs had nothing more solid than the air to press. The looks of the rider were turned towards the female shade; and he summoned her by his motions and gestures. The rapidity of the spirits then encreased; the appearance of the steed became more fiery; and within a few minutes, the mysterious group pierced through a cloud, which previously began to over-shadow the moon.

The eyes of Alwynd closed. Astonishment affected his breathing; and his head fell on the stone casement, from which, for a considerable length of time, he had not power to remove it. The window fronted the ramparts, and when he awoke from his trance, at no great distance he perceived a soldier pacing on his guard, and called on him to advance, which he did as near as was possible.

There was no small portion of dread mingled with his wonder; and at an hour like that, it was comfortable to speak to a human being.

"Have you had no disturbance, friend?" enquired the chief: "and are our foes yet distant?"

"All is quiet, my Lord," replied the soldier; "not a single enemy has dared to approach the walls."

"And have you heard no noise near your post? Have you observed the clouds, and seen nothing strange in their appearance?"

"No, my Lord. The moon has been smiling ever since I took my station, and the sky calm and cloudless."

"Did you not see a meteor in the air, and hear the wild neighing of a horse, or some most strange sound?"

"No, in truth, my Lord."

"You have not slumbered, friend?"—

"If my eyes have closed since the morning, may they instantly shut, and never open again."

"Good night, soldier. Make yourself known to me in the morning, and I will give you something for your wife, if you are married; and for your children, if you are a father, in case you should not return to them from the expected battle."

"Good night, my noble lord. My infants and their mother shall bless your Lordship, and pray for the happiness of those who are most dear to you."

The soldier retired, but Alwynd remained at the window, looking towards that part of the heavens in which Matilda had faded. It was not long, however, before the first rays of morning began to appear; expectation was no more to be indulged, and he turned towards the still burning lamp, by the side of which lay the sword that had been lent to him in the forest. He viewed it with fear and suspicion, for he was now assured that the giver was no mortal; nor did it seem unlikely to him, but that the vision and the weapon were effected and presented by the arch fiend, to whom man's misery is pleasure, for the purpose of bringing him into that horrid snare, from which there can be no extrication.

Much, indeed, had been protested and sworn: But he might have merely listened to the wily speeches, and feigned assurances of the devil, or one of his principal agents. Yet had he not, for many years, believed Matilda to be a spirit of heaven, over which hell could have no domination? That idea still added to his perplexities: But ruminating farther, his better opinions returned, and he resolved to bear himself as he had been instructed.

Shortly after he laid himself down, and, though his agitation had been so great, for three hours enjoyed a tranquil sleep; he then arose, and sought Lord Bartonmere, whom he found in the court yard, inspecting a body of his adherents. But the expected enemy had not appeared. All, however, were in preparation, and every man in the castle was eager to grapple with the clan of de Stacey.

Impressed as Alwynd was, by the mysteries of the past night, he strove to conceal the effect of them from Bartonmere, and succeeded in doing it. He did not forget the promise he had made to the man on the ramparts, who privately presented himself before the chief, from whom he received a gift, which was to be transferred to the partner of his breast, for the succour of herself and her innocent progeny.

The Castle of Bartonmere was a scene of busy preparation; that of Alwynd of sorrow and apprehension; excepting one man that it contained, who wanted every virtue which he imposed on his observers. Agatha's fears were almost insupportable; and when her following eye could no longer distinguish Lord Alwynd on his departure, she hastened to her chamber, from which she debarred all intrusion; and after the tumult of her grief had partly subsided, on her knees she implored the aid and protection of the God she adored, in behalf of him who was next in her love.

"Spare him, Eternal Providence!" she cried; "let the sword be lifted against him in vain, arrows fly around him, and wound not. Guard him, power of my adoration—oh! return him to me in safety, that my sorrows may fade while I hang on his neck, and my fears vanish, while I press my kisses on his lips!"

She wished not for society, not even for that of those beloved friends who were still near to her, her William, and young Mercia; they, however, succeeded in drawing her from her retirement, and induced her to attend the evening repast, though the appetite of sorrow alone was craving. Celwold, with great tenderness, endeavoured to soothe her, nor was she insensible of the kindness of his

efforts; her brother's voice also assisted the intentions of his Lordship, and the eyes of Mercia strove to cheer her spirits, and lessen
her despondency.

Still her heart could not recal its fortitude; there was langour
in her countenance, and tremor in her speech, and it was difficult
to check the tide that was so strong and impetuous in its course.
She looked at the chair in which Celwold was seated, and thought
of him who was accustomed to fill it; of him who had been to her
tender and loving as a thousand fathers; of him who, perhaps, was
on the eve of destruction, and fated to the butchery of the merci-
less and savage.

The repast being over, she was glad to hear Celwold speak of
the necessity of his retiring for the evening; and when he was gone,
she agreed to walk awhile with her brother and Mercia. After an
hour's ramble in the moon-light forest, she returned with them,
somewhat benefited and enlivened by the exercise and the air.

During their walk, the expedition of Alwynd was the chief
subject on which they talked. William lamented that he had been
forbidden to go with his Lordship; and Mercia more vehemently
exclaimed against the prohibition of his guardian. His dissatisfaction increased every moment, he seemed to consider the conduct
of Celwold as too scrupulous and arbitrary, and his own submission as tame and dishonourable. William strove to change the
tenor of his friend's thoughts, though his own in some measure
accorded; and Agatha entreated him to appear tranquil and satisfied, and also to believe that the caution of Celwold arose from
tender, good, and generous motives.

Mercia listened with greater pleasure and respect to her voice,
than to that of her brother; and when she was about to retire
to her chamber, he arose also, and having wished William good
night, he walked across the hall, and ascended the stair-case with
Agatha. There was in his countenance a strange expression, which
she could not fail to notice; and his mind was evidently labouring
with something which he feared to disclose.

When he came to the end of the gallery he stopt, and took hold
of her hand. His lips were in motion, but his voice was not heard.
He paused—gazed on her still more carefully, and with greater
affection—a smile was on his cheek, and a tear in each of his eyes,

which fell from him in sadness, and over which he placed his agitated hand.

"Dear Mercia!" she cried, "whence arises this sudden distress?—What is the cause of it, my Lord?"

"I dare not tell you, sweet Agatha!" he replied; "but you shall know it when we meet again—probably you will hear of it in the morning, before you see me. Angels protect you, Agatha!—Good night, dear girl!—My foolish emotions must not keep you from your pillow; nor can I now with propriety speak to you as my wishes prompt me. Good night."

He then walked hastily out of the gallery, and Agatha went into her chamber, greatly surprised by the agitation of Mercia, and wondering at the unexplained cause of it. She was acquainted with the nobleness of his mind, and also well assured that his fortitude was not to be shaken by trifles; for she had seen him, on many great occasions, bear himself with heroic firmness, and rise above those things which threatened him with vexation and disquiet.

His extreme perturbation gave her a considerable degree of concern, as it seemed to arise from something difficult to conceal, and distressing to speak of. She had reason to believe that the cause of it had been kept from her brother, and she hoped in the morning to gain the confidence of Mercia, and to see his anxieties greatly diminished. The fears which she entertained for Alwynd, and the serious interest that Mercia's behaviour had created, kept her mind long and actively employed; and the pillow which she prest scarcely afforded her any repose or refreshment.

While she was turning on the bed of disquiet, Celwold was still walking and ruminating in his chamber. Since the departure of Alwynd, there had been a restlessness in his spirit, which he could scarcely conceal; and had he not risen immediately after supper, he feared it would have discovered itself to the eyes of some of those who were around him.

When his kinsman, previous to his leaving the castle, took him to his closet, an interesting conversation had ensued; but it was of a mixed nature, and the most important part of it related to the youth William, and his sister Agatha.—It has been said that, Lord Alwynd employed himself in writing the whole night that came after the summons of Bartonmere. On the following day he signed and placed his seal upon the papers, and afterwards put them into the hands of Celwold, whom he took apart for that purpose.

"I am going," he cried, "where there will be some danger:—My fall may be ordained, and I may perhaps be fated never more to enter these walls, tho' I have spoken so confidently of my return to my adopted children. Celwold, I commit these papers to your hands. Should I come back in safety, you will return them to me in the state you now receive them; but should the sword of de Stacey, or any of his men, cut me off in battle, I charge you to break the seals, to peruse the papers attentively, and, as you shall respect my memory, implicitly to obey the directions they contain. My will is among them, and also a written particular concerning the birth of William and Agatha.—Love those children, Celwold, as well as I have done, and be to them a tender guardian, if, owing to my loss, they shall stand in need of one."

"I will, dear my Lord!"

"Heaven bless you, Celwold, for the promise!—If I live, I will make my friendship better known to you; and if I die, you will find that I have not been neglectful of you, tho' there were prior claims on me."

The last words cooled the blood of the new appointed guardian. He contrived, however, to keep his countenance smooth, while Alwynd continued before him; on his departure the effects of hypocrisy were still more strengthened, and tho' he looked softly throughout the day on the favourites of the warrior, yet he almost wished some mischance would remove them from his sight before the morrow; and it was with a considerable degree of satisfaction that he could escape from them so early in the evening.

Celwold felt the power with which he had been invested, and strongly wished that it might be long and permanently continued in him; though it could only be so, by means of the death of the amiable Alwynd, whose merits made him more precious to the world, and to society, than a thousand such men as his fawning and disguised enemy. Celwold was full of his own greatness; and as he passed by the menials of the castle, he was inclined to think himself their arbitrary lord. Pride raised his brows, and vanity swelled his heart; yet he knew that it would not be politic, in that uncertain season, to let them be visible, difficult as it was to him to wear his false appearance undetected.

As he walked through the apartments he looked on their costliness and worth; he regarded them as things that would be more dear to him thereafter, and went to his chamber, musing on the probability and means of his succession. He afterwards opened a cabinet, and took from thence the papers which Alwynd had deposited with him. They were sealed with great care and exactness; and it was impossible to unfold the packet, and again to secure it, without discovering the action. The silken cord that fastened it was, in several parts, covered with wax, and stampt with a private seal, which Alwynd had not left behind.

Celwold's curiosity was so powerful, that it almost made him dangerously incautious; for he was strongly tempted to lay all open before him, and the impossibility of disguise could scarcely restrain the impulse. But as he was about to raise the cord, the impressive words of Alwynd returned to his memory—"Should I come back in safety, you will return them to me in the state you now receive them."—Disappointment and vexation unnerved his arm, and the packet dropt from his hand to the floor.

Having, of late, considered himself as the destined heir of Alwynd, his desire to peruse the will may be conceived to be strong; especially as Alwynd's parting words had turned towards a *prior claim*, which seemed to frustrate the designs of ambition, and to shift from its eyes the brightest of those prospects, on which it had long and anxiously dwelt. The history of the favourites, too, he longed to possess himself of; for they had, during several years, been objects of great pain and concern to him. Should any disaster befal their benefactor, which the prayers of his false friend and relation would not strive to avert, obscurity would no longer hang over them; the narrative would be resorted to, and explain to whom they belonged, and in what proportion they would decrease the envied fortune of Celwold.

He could not conceive that the prior claim rested with them, nor trace it in any other person; and he endeavoured to persuade himself, that he had either misunderstood, or strangely misconstrued the words of Alwynd. His principal motive for leaving the young people so early in the evening, was, in order that he might again inspect the packet, which he hoped he should be able to look into. The expectation however faded, an anxious and seemingly lengthened night succeeded, and in the morning he met William and Agatha with such smiles on his face as villains teach themselves to wear.

His hypocrisy was not discovered either by the youth or his sister, they both conceived that he was intitled to their respect and gratitude, and the one was as willing as the other to offer them to him.

They all met at one time, and it was not long before the eyes of Agatha began to look for Mercia, whose recent agitation had greatly interested her. But, after waiting a considerable time, he did not appear, and Celwold, wondering at his absence, sent a servant in search of him. The messenger, however, soon returned, and informed them, that Lord Mercia left the castle just at the break of day, having previously commanded the man who let him pass the gates, to cause a letter, which he had given to him, to be delivered to Lord Celwold, but not before the hour of nine.

Celwold started at the intelligence, and took the paper hastily. The eye of William became suspicious; and Agatha's face grew still more pale and painfully expressive. Celwold's countenance shewed immediate anger, and his hand trembled as he unfolded the letter, the contents of which he made known to his companions, by reading it aloud to them. It was brief, but resolute—

"The struggle to obey your Lordship's commands," it said, "I find myself unequal to; nor do I think, in this instance, the duty that might be owing even to a parent, could fix me here at a time like the present. Before this will reach Lord Celwold, I shall be near, and perhaps giving assistance to his noble, his gallant kinsman; for whose preservation I would brave the most imminent dangers of the field, and encounter the most daring of his enemies. My inclination is not to be baffled. I am not emulous of staining my virgin sword with blood, merely to gaze on it when my eyes shall be stretched by ambition, or by false glory.—No!—I would aid the persecuted, and side with the meritorious and valiant. Adieu, my Lord. I will not be recalled. What you would impose on the boy, the growing spirit of manhood cannot brook. I take the chance of the warrior. Conquest may send me back to you, smiling, and bearing her ensigns; and death may drain the vessels of my body, and shut me from all further pursuits in the tomb. Health to your Lordship. To William and Agatha, friendship and love.

Mercia."

"Perverse and obstinate!" cried Celwold. "I little expected this ingratitude from Mercia. Should danger befal him, he alone will be accountable for it; for in this letter he scorns my advice, contemns my power, and frees himself from my guardianship. Should his blood therefore be spilt"—

"Gracious God, preserve him!" cried Agatha, with much energy; "his agitation when I saw him last was great indeed, and the cause of it is now explained. Our father and our friend may both fall; if so, peace will never thereafter be known to me."

"Did he confide in neither of you," said Celwold; "and did neither of you know of his intentions?"

"I had no suspicion of them," replied Agatha; "my mind was as free in that respect as your Lordship's."

"But why are you, sir, silent?" said Celwold, turning to William. "You were doubtless in his confidence, and probably aided him in his designs. Young man, I should have viewed you more kindly, if you had not judged of Mercia by yourself; and also if you had balanced my disappointments against your own romantic friendship."

"My Lord, your attack commences sharply. What if my ignorance of the affair amounted to that of my sister?"

"O, I am not easily to be persuaded to believe that. Edward and you corresponded in every thing; indiscretion was your tutor, and vain-glory your mistress. It is not likely that Mercia should leave you a stranger to his important project, in the execution of which, I could almost wish his vanity to receive a check, that might for a long period mortify and gall him."

"He is too noble to deserve mortification, too spirited to receive it from those who would ungenerously impose it; and too wise to take it to himself on slight occasions."

"You are a champion with your tongue, sir, tho' not with your sword."

"My tongue, my Lord, may at present assert its freedom; so

should my sword, by the side of my heroic friend, were it not restrained by him to whom I owe an equal love, joined with a true and honest duty."

"But why do you evade my question?"

"Because it is unfair. Your very suspicion contains a most disgraceful accusation. The beauties of truth are heavenly; but, to preserve her dignity, she may sometimes retain her veil, especially when she is too imperiously commanded to remove it."

William, who had been standing in an easy attitude, slightly bent himself to Celwold, and then, with an air in which there was some dignity, walked out of the room. Agatha had listened with emotion to this conversation; she rose from her seat at the conclusion of it, and followed her brother, whose conduct was such as her free and liberal spirit approved. But she did not then recollect that the deputed Lord of the castle was entitled to her respect, and she hastily retired without offering any to him.

Celwold was mortified and confounded. Mature in years as he was, he wanted that equanimity of temper which had then been shewn to him; and he was conscious that the boy was in the possession of qualities, which the man had never been able to obtain. Wanting admiration for talents, he slighted what most men would have applauded; and he wished to curb, and wholly subdue, the noble spirit that animated the breast, and gave vigour to the tongue of his young opponent.

It was not a fit time for him to vent his spleen, and exercise his resentment. The departure of Alwynd was too recent for his purpose; but his fixed dislike accumulated, and he longed for the arrival of the hour, in which he might set up his power and dignities, and teach the boy to bend to them. Agatha's conduct, bearing a resemblance to that of her brother, also excited his displeasure. Their youthful arrogance, as he termed it, seemed to be alike in their natures; and when he should see them again, he expected to have words more free, and looks more expressive, directed towards him, by the stripling and his assuming sister.

At the hour of dinner he went into the eating-room, but neither of the young people were present; in a few minutes, however, Agatha entered, without a single mark of resentment on her face, and with eyes shewing so much beauty, that even Celwold was fas-

cinated by, and returned her smiles. But his principal enemy was
still to appear. Almost immediately after the entrance of Agatha,
William came in, and, with a face scarcely less interesting than his
sister's, he advanced towards, and respectfully bowed to Celwold,
who had not previously expected any such condescension, or mark
of respect.

"I come a suppliant to you, my Lord," he cried; "and it is for
your Lordship's forgiveness. You were angry with me when I last
parted from you; and it was my impetuosity, perhaps, alone, that
made you so. I have since reflected on the cause of your vexation,
and more seriously thought of your disappointment. My own
warmth, and too spirited retorts, I have also considered; and reason has told me of their impropriety. Take my apology, my Lord,
and give me your pardon."

Celwold was astonished; even his insensible heart was touched
by this unexpected conduct, and he readily took the hand that was
offered to him.

"Now," continued William—"now my heart is lighter, and my
mind more free. But, in some degree, to extenuate my fault, let me
declare to your Lordship, by all that good men reverence, and bad
men dread, that Mercia never told me of, or even hinted his design.
Tho' he spoke against your restrictions, I suspected not that he
meant to break thro' them, and my surprise, when I heard of his
departure, could not fail to be as great as your Lordship's; for, on
our parting last night, he planned an excursion, in which myself
and Agatha were to have joined this morning."

There was a sincerity in the words and countenance of the
speaker, which the most suspicious would not have doubted. Celwold regarded him with eyes more favourable than he had ever
done before. Something told him that he deserved not what was
then offered to him; and after dinner he drank to a forgetfulness of
past anger, and to a reconciliation of friendship.

Agatha was a well-pleased spectator of the scene, and her looks
fully expressed her satisfaction. Joy could not, however, establish
itself in the soft bosom it had entered; apprehension demolished
the throne on which it wished to be erected, and the delight that
was produced by the amity of Celwold and William, the fears
which waited on Alwynd and Mercia were not long in destroying.

The Castle of Bartonmere remained unmolested during the whole of the day on which the enemy had been confidently looked for, and the united nobles began to suspect that the force of de Stacey had been found either incomplete, or unprepared, or that he did not mean to execute what he had so loudly and basely threatened.

Alwynd strongly hoped that he should not withdraw himself, without having performed some serviceable action; for, loving humanity, as a son would love his mother, and averse to the trade of war as he was, he saw in the infamous de Stacey a general enemy to his species, a combination of the darkest villanies, a wretch deserving of the scourge of a powerful hand, and almost unmeriting of mercy, should he even be brought, by any disaster or mischance, to call for it.

Another night came on, and Alwynd, whose thoughts since the morning, had many times wandered widely from the object in which every person around him was so deeply interested, again went towards his chamber. He felt a sensation of awe, when the man who had preceded him placed the lamp on the table, and left the apartment; for the recollection of things recently gone by was powerful, and though he was inclined to wish for a renewal of them, there was a dread combined with the desire, from which he found it not easy to be separated.

He placed his charmed sword by his side, and, partly undressing, laid himself on the bed; for he not only wished to be ready to join Lord Bartonmere, the very moment in which he might be summoned, but also to watch for the re-appearance of the forest wonder, as well as for the pure and angelic form that he had seen, travelling amid the clouds of heaven. He was, however, soon attacked by a drowsiness, from which he could not free himself. His propensity to sleep was not to be resisted; he rubbed his brows, and even sat up on the bed, but he almost immediately sunk on his pillow, and became insensible to all things that were around him.

His slumbers were soft as those of infancy; no dreams disturbed him, and after the morning had been beaming at least two hours, he was still composed and tranquil. But at that time Lord Bartonmere rushed into his chamber, and summoned him to rise, as the enemy was within half an hour's march of the castle. The powers of Alwynd were sufficiently roused by the information. He instantly accoutred himself, and hastened with his gallant friend to the warriors in the castle yard, who were animated by the smiles and liberal praises of the chieftains.

They were all properly arrayed by the time de Stacey was at the gates; when Bartonmere was desired to shew himself on the ramparts, and also to listen to the leader of those who were come against him. He immediately complied, when, below the walls he saw his collected foes, in the front of whom stood the tyrant that had led them thither, smiling with contumely and peculiar arrogance.

"The time is come, Baron," he cried, "and you must listen to me. I am inclined to believe, that you have repented of your obstinacy, and that you will hearken to the terms on which alone peace and amity can be grounded."

"Terms from thee!" exclaimed Lord Bartonmere.—"But speak them—I may reject afterwards."

"You know I am allied to royalty.—Acknowledge me your superior, and give me the annual tribute that I have before demanded; or you shall soon see us proceed in our power, and demolish the castle in which you think to hide yourself."

"Now take my answer," replied Bartonmere.—"Royalty is stained by the alliance of which you so proudly vaunt. Flatter not yourself that you are my superior, for you are much below me. Would the tribute of a single coin appease you, it should be withheld; and your threats, great Lord, alarm me no more than would the same menaces coming from an instructed pye."

"We'll raze your castle!" exclaimed de Stacey, made almost frantic by the galling answer.—"Ere night you shall be buried in its ruins."

"Nay, we wish not to hide ourselves in it," said Bartonmere; "and if you are not dastardly you will withdraw to the heath, and wait for us there. We will attend you soon; and this may convince you, that the incaged lion is not always to be tamed."

"It shall be so.—Follow to the fate that awaits you, Bartonmere."

"To the heath!—to the heath!" cried the clan of de Stacey; and soon afterwards they marched from the castle, towards the place

to which they had been directed. Bartonmere then went down to
Alwynd and the soldiers, whom he apprised of what he had proposed, and found that it corresponded with their wishes.

The leaders retired for a few minutes to the hall, when Alwynd threw his arms around the neck of Bartonmere, to whom he
said—"There is an uncertainty in our ever meeting hereafter; and
tho' we may strongly hope to return hither, when the battle shall
have ceased, yet we cannot expect any assurance of it. We may
come back ere night, and renew our friendship on this very spot,—
and we may travel thro' worlds unknown, before we are allowed
again to hail each other. Bartonmere, God bless you! If providence
lead you thro' the battle, believe me I shall rejoice in your preservation; and if it be ordained that I shall see you fall, while I am assisting in laying you in the tomb of your ancestors, the remembrance
of what you have been, and at this present moment are to me, will
not pass away like common thoughts."

Bartonmere was a hero; but he had a heart of great tenderness
and susceptibility. He repaid the affection of Alwynd, whom he
had long known and truly esteemed, even with a tear; the adieu on
his part was equally kind and impressive—and they immediately
returned to the soldiers, for whose passage the gates of the castle
were widely opened. They began their march; but Alwynd desired
them to halt for a moment, and requested one of the servants to
bring him from his chamber his sword, which he had forgotten.

"Your sword, my Lord!" cried Bartonmere;—"you have it by
your side."

"True, I have one there; but that is to be used only in the
greatest emergency—and indeed I shall be loath to draw it from
the scabbard. It has been lent to me; my own, however, must be
employed before I resort to this."

The servant came back with the sword, which Alwynd carried in
his hand; the warriors then passed over the bridge, and went onward
to the heath, which was scarcely more than a mile distant from the
castle. The men were well prepared for the combat—and the nearer
they approached to the danger, the less they seemed to think of it.—
Their spirits had reached their possible altitude; resolution strongly
shone in every eye, and their swelling chests seemed to brave the
arrows, which the compulsive cords were to put upon the wing.

Alwynd felt the general ardor; but just as they came in view of the power which they were to oppose, a momentary tenderness pervaded his breast—an exquisitely painful thought, hanging upon William and Agatha, took a temporary possession of his mind, and he breathed forth an unheard prayer for those dear objects of his love.

Both Bartonmere and his friend, observed that they had a superior force to contend with, and this they spoke of to their men; but the inequality of numbers robbed not the troops of their valour—and as they had so far advanced, they were determined not to retreat, till they had tried the temper of their swords, as well as the elasticity of their bows.—Indeed the disadvantage served only to inflame them, as it made the baseness and depravity of de Stacey more flagrant; for he had brought only a third part of his men before the castle, tho' it had been considered as his whole force, and kept the remainder in ambush, for those purposes which treachery and cowardice are most apt in inventing.

As the terms of the enemy had been before so peremptorily and scoffingly rejected, they were not repeated in the field. The trumpet of each party soon called them to the attack, and the battle commenced with spirit and bravery. The heroism of Bartonmere shone at the head of his troop; and Alwynd led his men with the greatest gallantry.

At the onset, and for some time afterwards, there was some method, as well as regularity, to be observed in their proceedings; neither of the bands were able to break thro' the other—and tho' determination moved the nerves of every arm, yet, for a while, slaughter had the veins only of a few to fix her lips upon. At length, however, confusion began to prevail—the soldiers were indiscriminately mixed, and Bartonmere and Alwynd widely separated. But the latter, wherever he went, and whatever was the danger that he risked, perceived a soldier, whose face he either saw not, or did not recollect, keeping close to his side. His sword was not merely for himself, it seemed to be designed as a guard to Alwynd; and once it had assuredly saved his life.

"You are a noble fellow!" cried the latter, while he was in pursuit, "but let me warn you to be less unguarded. Your enterprising spirit merits the wreath of glory; if, however, you are not more cautious, you will never live to wear it."

The man replied not.—Nearly half an hour longer he ran and fought by the side of the Baron; they were then separated by a party belonging to de Stacey, who seemed to design Alwynd as their joint victim, and whom they afterwards surrounded.

"Alwynd, we have you now!" cried one of them.—"We ask you not to yield, for it is your death, not your captivity, that will appease the fury of our chief."

"His life," said another, "will bring us nothing; but his head, or his heart, will pass current for a hundred pounds."

"Dispatch him, comrades!—dispatch him!"

"Villains! blood-hounds!" exclaimed Alwynd; "I have heard of you, and also of your tyrant's promised reward. Five opposed to one!—Infamous dastards!—Take my life, if you can, and claim the gift; but you shall find that your prey will not be quietly netted."

He felt within himself the strength of a tyger; and the first man that struck at him soon lay gasping on the earth. The other four, however, closed him in behind, when, as his last resource, he drew forth the sword that had not been before unsheathed; well knowing that if it wanted the promised power, his death must be inevitable. It was instantly proved that the giver of it had not lied, when he described its virtues, for two of the fellows, in the course of a minute, became its victims. The weapon of a third broke upon it as if it had been made of glass; and the fourth ran speedily away, yelling like a fiend that had just slipt from the manacles of hell.

Heated in blood, and made almost mad by their treachery, he pursued the flying soldier, and commanded him to turn. The fellow, tho' he feared for his success, made a struggle for his life; when Alwynd, disdaining all unfair advantage, threw on the ground the sword that was so fatal, and drew forth that with which he might fight only on equal terms. His foe was not without skill, which made the contest long and obstinate, but, at length, the soldier fell; and at that moment a body of nearly fifty men was within a few yards of Alwynd, when he fled towards a party of his own followers, whom he had joined before he recollected that he had left the magic instrument behind him.

It was now too late to attempt to recover it. The loss, however, struck him with pain and apprehension; for, setting aside his personal safety, he knew not what answer he should give to him who was hereafter to demand it. His mind was much harrassed, while he scoured the heath in search of Bartonmere.

The soldier that had displayed so much attachment to Alwynd, was unsuccessful in his attempts of joining him again. He sought him in many places, and asked several soldiers of his party, to direct him to their chief. Disappointment, however, waited on him wherever he turned; and he could neither find the Baron, nor hear any thing of him. He was re-commencing his search, when a man, without any weapon, or means of defence, appeared by his side, and took hold of his arm.

"Lord Mercia," he cried, "is looking for the noble Alwynd, who is in yon corner of the field, and exposed to the greatest danger. He has lost this sword, which I found at some little distance. Hasten to him; replace it in his hand, if you should find him alive,—if dead, let your arm drive it thro' the trunk of de Stacey."

"You know me then," said Mercia; "Lord Alwynd in such danger! I will fly to him instantly. But I leave you stranger, defenceless in the extreme."

"Regard not that. Neither swords nor arrows can give me any injury. Were it in my mind I could turn every blade of grass crimson with human blood, and tear the wolfish de Stacey piecemeal. But vengeance is reserved for you. Away, Mercia, away!"

Edward's feet seemed no heavier than the air; he ran with his sword in his hand, and to his astonishment, he saw soldiers fall before they were attacked. As he went forward nothing resisted him; the power of a divinity was apparently lodged within him, and he trembled at what the stranger had said, and also at what his own arm unconsciously performed.

At the place to which he had been directed, and ere he could wholly reach it, he saw Alwynd and de Stacey engaged in fierce combat. His speed encreased; he raised his voice, in order to attract their notice, and cause them to desist; but before he could come up to them, the heart of Alwynd was pierced by his enemy, and as he sunk into immediate death, the conqueror hastened away exultingly, to boast of the deed to those who were as sanguinary as himself.

Mercia now arrived at the body of Alwynd, threw himself upon it, and mourned the hero's fall with tears, which would not be restrained; and tho' the weapon of de Stacey had made a passage for the bowels, yet Mercia gazed on Alwynd's face, in the earnest hope of seeing some signs of life, and distractedly called on him who was never thereafter to reply. "And art thou gone," he said, "worthiest and best of men, art thou gone!"

"Aye, for ever, for ever!" exclaimed the unarmed stranger, who was now standing by his side.

"You here so soon?" cried Mercia: "See the flower of the field is blasted! He stirs not—he breathes not—the star of human nature shall rise no more. The friend of the good, the protector of the innocent is gone; and, oh! who shall relate this deed, who bear this body to thee, dear William, and to thee, sweet Agatha?"

"You, Mercia. This must be done by you. But the hero shall not be borne to his castle, without the head of him who slew him. You, friend to the dead, shall hew it from his accursed body; or if you refuse, it shall be performed by me. Ask me not now who or what I am. I belong to the globe it is true; but I can go beyond it. The sword you brought hither I lent to Alwynd, and charged him not to part with it; had he been cautious the fury of millions could not have reached him. Now, Mercia, it is your turn to use it."

"I stand in fear of you, stranger!"

"May the flames of hell environ me this instant, if I deceive you. But see, de Stacey returns! Shall he triumph? Shall the wolf again shew his fangs in savage joy? Give me the sword, boy. So many men as there are in the field, into so many pieces will I cut him."

"No!" cried Mercia; "I will be confident; the deed shall be per-formed by me, or my blood shall stream for it. I rise above my nature, my arm is of steel; I feel the growth of my heart within me, and can doubt no longer. He comes, he presses towards me; guard you the body, till I bring you some trophy that may be borne away with it."

"Begone, youth! Away, away!"

He grasped the sword, rushed forward with a degree of swift-ness which he himself wondered at, and within a few minutes stood before the slayer of Alwynd. "You must engage with me," he cried; "villain, it is you whom I seek. The blood of Alwynd cries aloud for vengeance; by you he is sent to heaven; by me you shall be dispatched to hell."

De Stacey replied only with a laugh of contempt; and he raised his weapon against his young opposer. He aimed, however, without success; and it was not long before the sword of Mercia had cut through the very centre of his skull, from which his loosened brains found an immediate passage. The soldiers, seeing the fate of their leader, were struck with dismay; many of them yielded to those who were against them, others scoured over the heath in the greatest confusion, and Mercia dragged the trunk of de Stacey to the spot where he had left the body of Alwynd, over which the bleeding Bartonmere was standing with looks of anguish.

The stranger also was there; he snatched the sword from Mercia, and hurried away with uncommon speed; but by the singular expression of his countenance, it was evident that he wished his interposition, and wonderful assistance, might be kept secret from the surviving hero. The eyes of the astonished Mercia followed him till he disappeared; the young warrior then cast them, moistened by pity, on the breathless body of Alwynd, and with his arms raised it from the earth, and placed it against his breast. In this action he was aided by Bartonmere, whose wounds, though many, were not mortal, and to whom Mercia, unreservedly unfolded himself.

Some soldiers soon joined them, and they proceeded, with the poor remains of valour, towards the castle; leaving the disfigured and horrid corse of de Stacey, to the chance of being either taken away by those who might seek for it, or to be corrupted by the summer heats.

Victory was on the side of Bartonmere, but he thought it dearly gained, while he contemplated the ghastly face and gaping wounds of his fallen friend. The farewel that had preceded the battle afflicted him greatly; and he now grieved that they must, indeed, "travel thro' worlds unknown," before they should meet again. His concern for the fate of his noble ally, made him indifferent to his own wounds, on which it was a considerable time, before he would consent to have any bandages placed; for he felt himself unable to turn his eye from the pale object which it still dwelt on with gloomy sorrow.

Mercia bore not the loss with so much quietness; though, perhaps he felt not more exquisitely. His was the impetuous grief of a young and unfortified heart, which could not call in philosophy to heal its bruises, or teach him how to alleviate the anguish of them. From the indulgence of his passions he was, however, at length roused by prudence; and fearing that some unguarded tongue might pour the intelligence into the ears of his friends, he silently pressed the hand of Bartonmere, mounted his horse, and rode towards the late residence of Alwynd, to be the narrator of the fate that had attended him.

The feet of his horse were swift, but it was evening when he entered the forest, which, tho' decked with all the blushing sweets of summer, seemed not to him more interesting than a blasted desert. Sorrow was in his heart, and tears frequently in his eyes. His heroism was faded, and his fortitude still more shaken by the sight of Agatha and William, who were sitting beneath the branches of a tree, the former half hiding her melancholy face in the bosom of the latter, whose conciliatory smiles she did not seem to heed.

Mercia wished to pass them undiscovered, and attempted to turn his horse into a path, which was screened by a thick row of trees. But this he was not able to effect, for the eye of William had fallen on him, and instantly his friends came running up to him nearly breathless. He hastily dismounted, and took them both into his arms. The face of Agatha shewed a strange expression of happiness and dread; and her brother was scarcely less agitated by this unexpected meeting.

"Praises to Heaven for your safety and return!" he cried, with the accents of the most animated friendship.—"Dear Mercia! the sight of you gladdens my soul. But you come from Bartonmere.— How goes it, friend?—Has the battle been fought?"

"Yes, William. But has no messenger arrived?—Have you heard nothing relating to the event of which you enquire?"

"Nothing.—You are the first from the field. Be quick, dear Mercia, in telling me on which side victory is to be found. Lord Alwynd—how fares he?—Not speak, Edward?—God! what mean your silence and your tears?"

"He has cause for them," said Agatha, almost with a shriek, "and I had cause for all my fears. Ask him no more concerning Lord Alwynd, for there is a horrid meaning in his eyes, which I well understand."

"Dear Agatha!" cried Mercia, "I conjure you to be calm."

"Calm! when I hear that Lord Alwynd, my friend, my protector, oh, I may say my father!—When I hear that he is dead—cut off
by the murdering sword—torn from me for ever, for ever!"

"But this you have not yet heard."

"You cannot say that it is not as I interpret. I read a dreadful
history in your countenance. If I judged wrongly, you would look
into my face and smile; but this you cannot do. Your eyes turn
from me—your cheeks are of a deadly colour—and all your limbs
are quivering. Brother, behold this messenger!—Brother, weep not
for me if I sink into instant death. Mourn with me for Alwynd—
for——" Her eyes closed, her breath was suspended, and she fell at
the feet of William and the young warrior.

"Let us bear her immediately to the castle," cried Mercia; "delay
not a moment, for I am distracted with a thousand fears, lest death
should be still more busy with us."

"Still more busy!" exclaimed William; "there you confess it—
there you acknowledge to be true, what I strongly hoped to be
false. Mercia, my strength is leaving me, and I think I am sinking
into the condition of my sister."

"Rouse, William!—shake off this lethargy. Alwynd has
perished!"

"Oh, world, thou art worthless to me now!"

"He perished, but he died the death of a hero. He fought nobly.
His foe was de Stacey, whose sword, after a sharp contest, pierced
the noblest of hearts. William, the conqueror did not escape—I followed him, and hewed his scull in pieces. His brains even splashed
against my shield."

"Did they?" cried William, roused by a speech which was made
merely to release his mind from torpidity.—"Did you, Mercia,
revenge the death of Alwynd? May the sinews of your arm be
strong for ages. May the action, in centuries to come, be praised
by those who shall point towards your grave. The work of fate
is accomplished, but de Stacey has suffered as he deserved; and
though my grief may be strong, it shall not be foolish. My sister is
yet motionless; help me to raise her, Mercia, and let us carry her
home. Poor Agatha! thou wilt shake off this insensibility with pain
and bitterness."

The young friends took the unconscious girl from the ground, and carried her in their arms to the castle; when Mercia desired William to attend his sister to her chamber, while he should go to relate his painful narrative to the kinsman of Alwynd, who was yet unapprised of his arrival.

Having been informed, by one of the servants, in which apartment he might find his guardian, Mercia, drooping under the sorrows which oppressed him, went towards, and after a moment's hesitation, entered it. Celwold started on seeing him; and before he spoke, his eyes had darted a thousand reproaches. At any other time, Mercia would have either warmly resented, or calmly smiled upon this severity; but he had then no spirit to strengthen him, no resolution to resist the attack.

"The hero is come from the battle!" cried Celwold, in a tone of irony. "Where are your laurels, warrior? Why do you not relate your atchievements?"

"Peace, my Lord!" exclaimed Mercia, stung by this ungenerous speech; "this is no time for scoffing. If I disobeyed your orders, it was for my own gratification; and though I would not wilfully break through the barriers of respect, yet I will never submit to thraldom. I have, indeed, been to the battle."

"And to what purpose, sir?" enquired Celwold, with a sneer. "Where is the blood of your enemies?"

"It is moistening the heath of Bartonmere; it still floats on the surface. But why do you not enquire after the noble Alwynd?—See you these stains upon my arm? Look at the crimson marks.—Oh, spirit of the brave! let my tears, my present agonies, bear witness how much I loved thee!"

"Mercia—What do you say? Has my dear kinsman——"

"He has perished!—He has perished!"

"Do not tell me so, dear youth! forgive my unkindness, and say, I beseech you, that Alwynd still lives; that he is returning to these walls with victory."

"Ere long he will, indeed, be within these walls; but he will be borne hither, only to be consigned to the tomb of his forefathers. His body, gashed and mangled, now lies in the hall of Bartonmere; but his spirit has soared through the regions leading to the high dwelling of his God."

"Oh, Mercia, you have heaped afflictions on my heart!"

"And I, my Lord, have no power to console you; I feel the loss we have sustained, too deeply to sooth the sorrows of another person, with any of those cold speeches, which are called philosophy. I must retire; for weariness, as well as grief, oppresses me. William, is at this time, weighed down by sorrow; and Agatha—poor Agatha!"—He rushed out of the room, and as he passed through the gallery, he was heard to sob aloud.

His absence was a great relief to Celwold, who now uncovered his face, which he had concealed with the skirt of his habit, but on which there was not a line of sorrow to be traced; nor had the tale of Mercia drawn from his eye a single tear. A strange expression was stampt upon his countenance, thro' which ran a wild gleam of unnatural satisfaction; but he seemed half frightened by his own sensations, and the baseness of his pleasure was not altogether unnoticed, while his smiles momentarily faded and returned.

He sat a considerable time confused in his intellects; and his brain almost wanted capacity for his thoughts. At length, however, he was obliged to resume the garb and mask of hypocrisy, for William came to him, and without speaking threw himself into his arms. Few hearts could have resisted the grief of the youth; and few men could have beheld it without sympathy. Celwold, however, was but in a small degree affected, though he professed himself to be feelingly sensible of the calamity which must occasion a general mourning.

From William he learned that Agatha could not possibly be soothed, and that, though her women had succeeded in getting her to bed, no means could be found to prevent her faintings, which had been so numerous, that life was sometimes scarcely to be found in her. Celwold heard this account with apparent concern, and he shewed himself desirous of alleviating the distress of her brother; but after some fruitless efforts on his part, he declared that his own anguish was insupportable, and that it was become necessary for him to retire to his chamber.

Mercia now joined them, but Celwold was anxious to depart; he therefore called one of his attendants to light him to his bedroom, and having tenderly wished the young men good night, he placed his hand over his brows, as if he had legible characters of grief written upon them. He then slowly followed the servant out of the apartment, leaving his ward and the adopted son of Alwynd, to talk over the tale which had before deeply searched their hearts.

As soon as he reached his chamber he dismissed the servant, and prevented all intrusion by locking himself in. His heart was beating with the quickest and most painful motion; he could scarcely believe that his breathings came from his own body, and his knees knocked against each other as he went towards the cabinet in which the explanatory papers of Alwynd had been deposited. Base as he was, he was not totally insensible, but felt the stings of conscious villany. The remembrance of the many virtues, of the numberless kindnesses, and of the ever-lively affection of the departed, came to his mind; and he almost fancied, when he touched the ivory box, that he grasped the death-cold hand of Alwynd.

The first paper he took up was directed, by the fallen hero, to his "dear cousin Celwold." He laid it down hastily; and collected as he had been, when ruminating on the probable issue of the warrior's interference in the cause of Bartonmere, yet he now found it impossible to steel his heart against the puncture of remorse. He continued a considerable time absorbed in reflection. The evening had been sultry, and a storm succeeded; the thunder rolled heavily over his head, and his eyes seemed fearful of being scorched by the lightnings.

Superstition began to work on him, and feeling himself insecure, at such a distance from the inhabitants, he replaced the papers, took up his lamp, and again went to Mercia and William, whom he informed that there was no possibility of obtaining either sleep or repose, while the events of the day so forcibly impressed his mind. The young men were softened by these apparent traits of humanity and affection, and though they stood in need of consolation themselves, there was an equal wish in either of them, to give it to him who actually wanted it not; and also a reciprocal desire to heal the imaginary wounds, that neither pained nor bled.

The generous are ever the tools of hypocrisy; Celwold mourned without affliction, and was sincerely compassionated. He felt himself secure in his deceit, while they remained with him, though Mercia's known discrimination was more to be feared than William's unbounded tenderness.

The chamber of Agatha was often visited by her brother, who returned from it with reports very unfavorable, to Celwold and Mercia; the latter of whom was not less pained by her situation, than if he had stood in an equal degree of kindred to that of his young friend. Sorrow, or the appearances of it, hung upon every countenance; and the servants of the castle were heard to sigh heavily, as they passed from room to room. The tempest at length spent itself, and the morning followed with loveliness, which, however, was regarded neither by the anxious Celwold, nor by any of those with whom affliction claimed acquaintance. The heavens were tinted with beauty; but their imaginations, dark and disturbed, took in none of the rays which glowed in the canopy of creation.

The appearance of day seemed to recal some thoughts into the mind of Celwold; and once more he separated from his companions, and went to his chamber. The coldness of apprehension had passed away; a glow of hope entered his heart, and he again opened the cabinet and broke the seals of Alwynd's packet. He immediately saw, that, among other papers, it contained letters addressed to William and Agatha; that, however, which was directed to himself, he instantly unfolded, when he read, with impatience, the underwritten lines.

"I am summoned to the dangers of the field; and when next I see you, it is my intention to say, that, if I return from it alive, these papers may be delivered to me unperused; but if I fall, that you may read, and at your discretion, act according to the directions contained in them. If they hereafter should meet your eye, mine will be closed for ever, but I can readily believe that you will not look on them without concern; and that my being peremptorily called from hence, never more to come back to those who shall anxiously look for me, will raise a regret within your bosom, which shall not be easily appeased."

At that moment the reader forcibly felt his own unworthiness; his eyes fell from the paper, and he paused for several minutes.

"Your blood is allied to mine, dear Celwold! and our friendship has been of a long date. Our affection has reigned without interruption. I have seen your face grow bright at my happiness; and when sorrow came upon me, I have beheld your concern and dejection. I am assured that you have ever acted with true sincerity, and that assurance, at this moment, greatly distresses me; because I am conscious of having, during many years, borne myself with duplicity.

"But let the motives I shall mention, soften the offence of which I have been guilty. When you shall know them, Celwold, when you shall read the confession that I am now going to make, I dare believe that the unaffected voice of nature will tell you to pity the friend that is dead; and also that you will be even compelled to obey her. From you—my nearest acquaintance—from every person have I concealed the origin of William and Agatha. I have reported them to be the children of a deceased friend—have framed many excuses for withholding the circumstances of their birth, and even declared that they owed not their existence to me. Celwold, forgive me for quitting so long the paths of truth, which it was painful for me to forsake—forgive me, when I confess, that this dear boy, and this lovely girl, are my own beloved and legitimate offspring!"

"Liar! Liar! Execrable liar!" exclaimed Celwold, dashing the paper on the floor.—"Forgive you!—I swear I never will forgive you."

The fairest object that he had ever contemplated, seemed to be changed into a black deformity; and the rich designs of the palace of hope, were strewn disorderedly on the unsolid earth. An envenomed serpent had pleased his eye more than the letter of Alwynd. He spurned it with his foot, and heaped many an impious curse on the soul of him, who was then associating with the spirits of the blessed. After a long and half frenzied rumination he snatched up the hated paper; and followed, with a gloomy eye, the remainder of its contents.

"It would be unfair, and I must appear unworthy indeed, dear Celwold, if I were to withhold my motives after this free confession of facts. No, I will conceal nothing, but put an unbounded confidence in you; and well I know there is not a man on earth more worthy of the precious trust I am about to repose in you.

"But before I proceed to that tender consignment, you shall know who the mother of my children was—for, ah, she is dead!— Why I have spent so many years in retirement; and why I have hitherto wrapped my children in mystery and obscurity. You will pity me, Celwold, not merely in the capacity of a father; for you will also dwell compassionately on the sorrows of an afflicted husband, and grieve that such I have been.

"I could dwell long on the story of my unhappy love. The night, however, will soon be gone, and as I have my principal affairs still to settle, I must abridge a tale, that I should find a melancholy pleasure in lengthening; lest my brave fellows, in the morning, have cause to chide the tardiness of their leader.

"You and I, Celwold, have known each other from the days of childhood. When a youth, you will remember, I was accustomed to be often in the court of our sovereign, with whom I was a favourite, and, after his death, I was equally esteemed, and perhaps regarded more affectionately by his successor. Indeed he was seldom seen from my society. The prince and the subject appeared as brothers; and there were men who beheld me with dislike, merely because they could not catch those smiles, which were so liberally bestowed upon me.

"I held out no lure; I angled not for royal favours; but they came unsolicited from one, in whose heart friendship had firmly established me. In the train of state it was his command that I should be nearest to his person; when he wished to join the chase, he would not mount his steed till he saw me on the back of mine; and in the field of battle, I kept myself almost as close to his side as the armour that incased him. His virtues were many, and his failings by no means conspicuous. He was capable of loving with enthusiasm; but in his resentments, he was more strong than any man of whose nature I ever had any knowledge. That unconquerable passion has for ever alienated me from him. He still lives; and may the crown of England long sit upon his brows, though I have become an object of his displeasure, and fallen from that eminence, on which he was once pleased to place me.

"The smiles of royalty has been compared to a sun-beam; a monarch's praise to the restlessness of the winds and waves. The countenance of my king, however, shone not on me merely for a summer's day, but throughout a long and happy season; and the kindness of his words was not withheld till it was, I am convinced, as painful to him who suppressed, as to him who no longer enjoyed it. You remember his sister, Matilda—You have seen her, Celwold; and he who ever saw, surely never can forget her! She was in point of personal charms so superior to the court, and to women in general, that she impressed even the unwilling heart of envy. Her complexion might have vied with that flower, which we liken to things most fair and delicate; and if she wanted the measured gait, which is denominated dignity, she had the graces of ease, and the sprightliness of joy. Her airy tread was superior to all the formalities which her sex, in their self-important moments, take upon themselves; and the unrestrained smiles, that gave fresh beauties to her face.

"Ah, Celwold! the pencil of affection, while it sketches the charms which were so dear to me, is drawn gratingly over the heart that still mourns for Matilda.

"She was greatly loved by her brother, and I was one of her earliest friends; in our younger days we were often together, and still more often as we advanced in years. I was daily receiving from her marks of esteem, and from the gratitude which rose in my breast, and which I too indulgently nursed, my soul at length took in wishes, which, being considered as fruitless and unattainable, caused anxiety to possess that spot, where ease and happiness had thitherto uninterruptedly reigned. I became more than a simple friend—I was the silent, desponding, and uncomplaining lover of Matilda.

"Honour forbade me to speak to her of a passion which I thought almost criminal; I therefore strove to stifle it, but it even grew under the unequal opposition. I foresaw a thousand evils arising from my misplaced love; still I was unable to change the tenor of my thoughts. I sighed that birth and national custom, should destroy the most charming plan that happiness had ever formed; and never turned my eyes upon a cottager's daughter, without wishing that her and Matilda's pretensions were on a level, and that love might fly as unfettered to the bosom of the one as the other.

"Had Matilda borne herself with the usual dignity of a princess, or with half the importance of many of her attendants, I had broken the chain by which I was enthralled. But neither pride nor consequence could be found in her actions; she was even less restrained in conduct towards me than she was to her brother, who, tho' not devoid of affection, sometimes commanded her to be less indifferent to her elevated birth and rank, and to assimilate her manners to those of the daughter, as well as the sister of a British monarch. She would listen attentively to him, and for a while appear with the desired restraint before her brother; but nature, irresistible nature, broke through the imposition, and shewed her darling child in all her loveliness and unstudied graces.

"I suffered at the heart while my eyes fondly contemplated. I really became indisposed, and retired into the country. But the king soon followed me, and after endeavouring to draw from me the secret of my malady, for such an one he assured himself there was, he took me again to his court, even to the cause of my inquietude and affliction—to Matilda, whose compassionate looks, and soft accents, kept open the wounds which indifference and neglect would probably sooner have closed. Oh, how beautiful were her pitying eyes!—How forcible the accents of her concern!

"She once visited me without attendants as I lay on my couch. I was starting up to meet her, when she stept forward with a quicker motion, put her hands gently upon me, in order to prevent me from rising; and, seating herself by my side, softly asked me how I did. I scarcely answered her with reason, a torrent of joy rushed into my bosom, and caused a temporary suppression of the pain that I had previously endured.

"She saw the varying colours of my cheek, and her own also changed. Her beauty had never before appeared so exquisite, and I gazed on her unconscious of the action. When she again enquired concerning my health, I assured her that I felt a quick amendment; and when she asked me what I supposed to be the occasion of my illness, caution and prudence deserted me on the instant. I threw myself on my knees, and pressing her hand to my glowing lips, exclaimed, "You, dear Princess!—You, Matilda, are the cause of it. I love you—as dear as my life I love you!—But I know that the treasure which my affections covet can never be attained; and that, in consequence of it, the acquaintance already formed between me and misery, must be lasting while I continue to exist."

"She arose hastily—one of those looks which her brother wished her to wear, took possession of her face, but it could not establish itself. Her features were almost immediately governed by the generous instinct of her heart; and tho' she quitted the room abruptly, in her countenance I traced the marks of pity and concern, but not a single line of resentment. Left to myself, I cursed the folly of my tongue, and also the vanity and presumption of my heart. Though no anger had apparently been raised in the bosom of Matilda, I could not assure myself that she would not thereafter shun and contemn me; nay, knowing how loving she was to her brother, I believed it probable, that honour might urge her to repeat to him what I had so inconsiderately uttered; the result of which would have been eternal banishment from the court of my generous and friendly monarch.

"I saw not Matilda again for several days, tho' I left the apartment in which I had confined myself. It was evident that she avoided me. The king spoke of her being very strange and capricious; and about a fortnight afterwards I met her as she was going on a visit to the Countess of Surrey. It was in the court-yard where we encountered each other. Our agitation was equal.—She turned for a moment, as if she was going again into the palace; but recollecting herself she advanced, and when I bowed to her, I saw in her face the smile that never failed to charm. It gave me confidence, and I ventured to speak to her. She was embarrassed, but not displeased. Accompanying her to her horse, I assisted her in mounting it; and on wishing her good day, and a pleasant excursion, "Adieu, my Lord," she cried; "adieu, I am very happy in your recovery."

"I curbed the horse a minute, in order that I might peruse her lovely countenance, after she had uttered these words. I traced in it characters which flattered and delighted me; and then it was I first assured myself, that she felt an affection of the same nature as that which I had declared to her. From that hour my acquaintance with anxiety ceased, and my health amended surprisingly. My friends noticed the sudden alteration, and congratulated me; but when the king expressed his pleasure on the occasion, I felt, for a while, as if I were unworthy of his regard, hypocritical, designing, and cunningly presumptuous. Honour pointed towards a path which my passions would not allow me to tread.

"Matilda continued at Lady Surrey's nearly a month, during

which time, I visited her, and also gained a full assurance of what I had before merely suspected. She loved me—she confessed it—and I was more than happy. Love made us both indiscreet, and though danger stood so glaringly before us, we did not seriously regard it. In the course of the six months which followed our return to the court, and after we had placed a very considerable sum in the hands of a priest, we were privately married. Matilda became the wife of Alwynd, and he the most joyful being that trod the earth, or smiled upon the heavens.

"It was not the falling off, but rather the increase of affection, that called us from joy to apprehension; for our intercourse was dangerous, and our very pleasures were stolen. Matilda started at the sight of her brother; and I found it impossible either to look on, or converse with him, as I had been accustomed, with ease and confidence. My alarmed wife reposed her secret with none of those women who were around her. It rested only with the priest that united us, and with a female attendant of the name of Neville; the former of whom could not reveal it without bringing himself into immediate danger; and the latter loved the princess so truly, that we believed tortures could scarcely have wrested it from her.

"Still Matilda was agitated, sorrowful, and not easily to be consoled. She wept on my breast, and in our nightly intercourse, which was hazardous and full of peril, fear chilled the bosom of either, almost as soon as love had warmed it. These surreptitious meetings were continued for a few months, when Matilda found herself pregnant; and that circumstance, which to most married women is joy, was to her frightful and distracting.

"Now our ruin is complete!" she would exclaim; "now the danger comes upon us indeed. I know my brother well; his virtues will not resist his ambition. Where shall I bring forth my infant? The king will hurl his vengeance on me; and Alwynd will suffer imprisonment and death. He will bleed! My husband will bleed!"

"I shuddered at her expressions! I assumed a fortitude, but did not possess it. My fears grew as strong as those of Matilda, and I was nearly distracted, lest the agitation of her mind, should do a serious injury to her precious health. I knew that confidence would carry us thro' the difficulties by which we were surrounded, rather than timidity; and I vauntingly resolved to act in a manner which my passions would not sanction. To add to my many tortures, my sovereign one day informed me of a most distressful project. He began by speaking of the changed manners of his romantic sister; and concluded with saying that, he hoped the love of the King of Scotland, who had made private overtures which had been accepted, would bring her back to her former habits, and also cause her to resume that character, of which she had so strangely divested herself.

"We were walking in the palace garden when the king thus addressed me; and astonishment nearly bereft me of reason. I could not raise my feet from the ground; I became instantly cold, stiff, and almost as insensible as the walls of the fabric that stood before me. The king regarded me with amazement; he shook me by the arm, as if he would rouse me from the spell of sorcery; and quickly asked what was the occasion of such a frightful attitude and expression of features?

"Have you your senses, Alwynd?" he enquired, "or is your brain seared by witchcraft?"

"My liege!"—My head seemed the sport of an eddy—I could utter no more.

"This is most strange and incomprehensible!" exclaimed my royal companion.—"Tell me, I conjure you, Alwynd, under what influence do you labour?—What are your sensations?—What makes you thus wild in your looks?"

"You have surprised me greatly.—The princess——"

"Well!—What of her?"

"Is young, beautiful, and virtuous.—The King of Scotland——"

"Go on—go on, my Lord."

"Has no youth in his favour—is disagreeable in his person—and known to be most gross and indelicate in his amours."

"You are too free with your pencil, Alwynd," he replied; "yet I will forgive you. The picture you have drawn of Matilda is just; but in respect to her intended husband, you are truly illiberal."

"Do not mention the name of husband—for heaven's sake do not. Never, my liege, never place so sweet a flower in a soil which would not nurture its beauties."

"Silence!" cried the king, in a tone of displeasure,—"you are

as romantic and extravagant as Matilda; nay, I believe more so, for
I cannot think that she will hesitate in ascending to the throne to
which she is invited. You know the dissentions which have long
been between our country and the Scots:—Matilda once their
queen, and I trust our bickerings will cease. This marriage is highly
political; and the King of Scotland has already received our best
assurances.—Matilda will be apprised of the honours which are
awaiting her to-morrow; and it is expected that she will take them
to herself with the satisfaction and pleasure which they ought to
create."

"The king left me in the garden, and filled with terror, I hastened
to the apartments of my wife. None of her women happened at
that time to be with her. Almost bereft of reason I rushed up to
her—I clasped her to my breast, and could not check a womanish
flood of tears that fell into her bosom. My actions were sufficient
to alarm her.—Trembling, she demanded an explanation, which I
gave to her in a disjointed and almost distracted manner, and she
sunk, with her hands bound together by the force of agony, upon
a couch that stood beside her—her eyes shut up in languor and she
fainted in my arms.

"Terrified, lest we should be surprised in this situation, I called
on Matilda, but she was wholly senseless. A footstep was heard in
the passage that led to the room, when I left my insensible wife
alone on the couch, and was hastening out of the apartment by a
door opposite that near which the noise was made.—To abandon
her, however, in a state so distressing I found myself incapable—I
again flew to her, and raising her on my breast, looked anxiously,
yet fearfully, for the person who was approaching.—Fortunately
for us it was our only confidant; and she ran to the assistance of the
princess, whom we immediately conveyed to her bed-chamber,
into which I entreated my female friend to let no person intrude.

"I will obey your Lordship," she replied; "but I entreat you to
retire immediately, for ruin would fasten on us all were you discovered here. Away, my Lord. The princess shall have my best services. Begone, I conjure you. I will contrive to see you again in the
course of a few hours."

"I hid myself from all observance, till I learnt from her that
my wife was more composed and tranquil; but when I stole to the

chamber of Matilda—oh, what an interview ensued!—The night went over, and neither of us closed an eye;—the morning at length dawned, but we were enveloped in the thick clouds of sorrow and despair.

"Rise, and retire, my Alwynd!" cried Matilda.

"I will, my love," I replied; "but let me conjure you to fortify yourself for the trial to which you will be brought to-day. Be collected and resolute in your refusal, and leave the consequences to me. We will abandon all rank and titles—I will search for some secluded spot, where, in summer and in winter, I will love, cherish, and solace you.—For yourself, for Matilda, not for the sister of a king, will I forget my ancestors, fly from my native land, and put on the garb of rusticity."

"All the morning I remained in a state of sickness and trepidation; and towards the evening I saw the king, who was red with anger, and agitated by passion. I could not speak to him till he had disclosed himself to me.

"Matilda is base and worthless," he cried; "she is only fit for a herdsman's wife, and unworthy of being my sister. She will not consent to the alliance—she has asserted a will most strong and obstinate—and on her knees, and in the name of God, sworn never to become the wife of the King of Scotland. But she shall suffer for this."

"Oh, be not severe with so much gentleness!"

"Gentleness, Alwynd!—Obstinacy and cunning are in her nature. To-morrow she shall depart from the palace. She shall retire into the country—she shall live as humble as if she had never heard of royalty; and instead of having a suit to attend her, like a plain housewife, she shall be compelled to administer to her own necessities."

"This design filled me with a secret pleasure; but, knowing his disposition, I ventured to oppose his intention with some warmth, and, by that means strengthened his determination. I did not go to Matilda's chamber, but I saw our friend, and desired her to tell my wife, that I admired and loved her more truly for her conduct; and that I hoped we should, ere long, be intimately acquainted with the wanderer peace.

"Early on the following day the king, with a smile of satisfaction, told me that he had begun to retaliate, by sending Matilda away, as soon as it was light, and without giving her an hour's notice of the journey. I could scarcely bear this stroke, without betraying my weakness; for, tho' I had wished him to remove her from the court, still I hoped to have seen her depart, and also previously to have offered her the consolation of a true and loving heart. I made an effort, however, to recal the fortitude that was shrinking from me; and the king, without reserve or suspicion, informed me that he had sent her to a castle in Kent, and that the old Lady Westmorland, whose splenetic temper was generally known and despised, accompanied her."

"And did the princess take no other attendants?" I enquired, with an affected indifference.

"I allowed Rosamond Neville to go with her," he replied, proudly; "neither the beauty, nor the wisdom of that girl will be missed at court, tho' Lord March says her eyes are all heaven, and her voice all harmony. But enough of this—If Matilda is wise, she will consent in time—If obstinate, by what is most sacred I swear, I will both hate and punish her."

"With all the pangs I suffered, it was still a small consolation, to find that our faithful Rosamond was with her mistress.—The pressure of the time accords with the melancholy remainder of my story. I must briefly say, that, pretending a journey into France, I contrived to see my beloved wife at several different periods. I put a deception on Lady Westmoreland, eluded the eyes of the servants of the castle, and, aided by a large sum of money, procured and also bound to secrecy, a midwife of skill, with whom I found my way, at night, to the chamber of Matilda. Rosamond was every thing to us, without her we should soon have been inclosed by ruin.

"It happened that Lady Westmoreland was confined to her chamber when the princess began to feel the pangs of labour. Rosamond looked pale, and I remained shivering with apprehension in an adjoining chamber, shutting my ears against the stifled cries of my dear Matilda. Neither of the agents came to me for a considerable time; at length, however, the midwife entered, bearing in her hand a basket, which had been previously prepared for the purpose, and in which were laid two innocent babes—my William and Agatha.

"I burst into a flood of agonising tears. The feelings of a father for the first time rose within me. I stood shivering, and with my hands almost growing to my breast, my eyes were fixed on the infants, gazing to the full, fixed, rivetted. The midwife returned to Matilda's chamber, and Rosamond came from it, and took hold of my arm. "My wife!" I exclaimed, "my wife!"

"She lives, my Lord."

"Lives!—Can you say no more than that?"

"I trust in heaven to her recovery," replied my gentle friend, whose voice was changed by her emotions. "But retire instantly, my Lord; for the morning will break ere long, and you cannot too soon place the infants with the woman who is to receive them. The love of your wife attends you. Adieu, my Lord, heaven be your guide and protector!"

"The night was somewhat cold. Rosamond placed a comfortable covering on the pledges of Matilda's love, and I retired unmolested. I scarcely retained my senses, and when I ought to have been calm and collected, my passions made me almost wild. I had left a horse in a wood at some little distance, tied to a tree, but on looking for him, the moon being full and clear, I found that he had broken the bridle and strayed away; consequently I had to walk to the residence of the nurse, which was ten miles distant. Thro' motives of security I had wished to place my offspring at a place rather wide of the castle; but the loss of my horse made me fearful of their safety. Perhaps I should have had no cause for apprehension, had my reason been unruffled; at the faintest noise, however, I trembled, and the wing of a linnet would have agitated me. Still, at intervals, I felt as if my ribs were of iron, and resolution bound within them.

"Fancy that you see a tyger, bearing away its young, when the hunters are thought to be in pursuit; it flies with the cub in its jaws; but what single power would dare to stop it in its course? I would have been hewn in pieces, ere I would have parted from my children. My mind was in its greatest elevation, I seemed not to touch the earth as I went forward; and just as the cottage-woman, who was a childless widow, had risen from her bed and opened her door to the air of morning, speechless and almost breathless I put my infants into her arms. She instantly saw their wants; she had, providentially, a breast for either of them, they clung to it; I sat myself down by her side, I saw my babes imbibe the milk with eagerness. On earth I never can experience a sensation so precious; and heaven itself can never offer a joy more exquisite.

"I had previously told the nurse, whose youth, health, and cleanliness recommended her to my favour, that the child I should bring to her, was the fruit of a true but unmarried love; that its mother had ever been respected in the middle class of society; and that I wished her to perform her duty, without indulging any useless curiosity. As an earnest of my intended liberality, I threw into her lap a purse of some value; and was impressed with pleasure, on seeing that my gift was less noticed than the children whom she lulled on her bosom. I explained to her neither my name nor quality; I wished her to believe me an untitled gentleman; and had appeared before her previously, as I did at this time, in a habit that accorded with the character I adopted.

"I staid till the approach of evening with her, and partook of her humble fare. I had much anxiety in my breast on Matilda's account; but knew that I could not see her, till darkness should favour my clandestine entrance into the castle. When the sun was shining in the western region of the heavens, I kissed my sleeping infants, bade adieu to their nurse, returned to the place from whence I had taken them, and gained the chamber of my wife without detection.

"What a meeting was this!—Our converse was soft as the accents of angels—our joys delicious as heaven. The considerate Rosamond, however, would not allow many words to pass from her mistress; nor would she suffer me to remain more than an hour in the chamber.

"During the following week I was alternately with my wife and children; and I was as blessed in learning from the cottager that my infants thrived, as I was in believing that the strength of Matilda was gradually returning. Our plans had been favoured greatly beyond our expectations. Lady Westmorland was still confined to her bed, by an almost excruciating rheumatic disorder; and Rosamond informed her that the princess, owing to an intense pain in her head and eyes, was obliged to shut herself up in a darkened room. The dowager murmured her complaints without much regarding those of Matilda; and the servants of the castle, who were few in number, and of the inferior order, were only informed that the princess was indisposed, and did not require their attendance.

"Matilda's spirits were still greatly depressed; she pined for her children, and urged me to take her out of the kingdom as soon as possible. A fortnight had elapsed since her delivery, when Lady Westmorland was carried in a chair to her chamber; and she was so much surprised by the alteration of the princess's health, that she proposed to send an immediate account of it to the king. This the terrified Matilda opposed; endeavouring at the same time, to assure Lady Westmorland that her illness was slight, and that she should probably be without cause of complaint before her brother could send her any assistance. She even attempted to be lively while the old lady continued in her apartment; but she afterwards found that her exertions had weakened her nature, and sunk almost breathless on the bosom of Rosamond.

"When I saw her at night I was terrified by her appearance; her eyes seemed to me almost beamless, her cheeks were ashy, and she regarded me with the looks of the departing.

"Death will enforce his claim, my Alwynd," she murmured, while she lay on my breast; "we must part, dear husband! the grave will soon hide me from you for ever. My powers are nearly exhausted, and my brother will ere long be fully satisfied. But never, never divulge the secret of our union—never let the king know the unhappy issue of it. My children would not be safe.—Oh, my little ones, I shall never see you more!—Hide them, Alwynd, from my brother. All will soon be quiet with Matilda."

"I was nearly distracted, and could scarcely persuade myself to retire from the castle at day-break; and when I returned to it again, I was assured that my wife was departing from the world. I threw myself by her side, I groaned with the pangs I endured, and alternately supplicated the aid, and arraigned the decrees of the power that alone could save her. She made an effort to raise herself, when kissing me with her cold lips, and uttering something indistinctly, which related to her children, she pointed to the door.

"Lady Westmoreland and her attendants were then coming to the chamber; the trembling Rosamond hurried me out of it, and I was sent to make my lamentations in the open air, and amid the gloomy shades of the night.

"I never saw my wife again. When I next entered the secret avenue it was with a throbbing head, a sick heart, and enfeebled limbs. Affection hurried me forward, but the hand of despair seemed to draw me back again. I had passed the chapel, and was ascending the stairs with uncovered feet, when several men started from behind, and seized me rudely by the neck. Having no weapon to defend myself, I was obliged to submit to the superior force, and my detainers bore me to a room, in which I beheld Rosamond Neville. She shrieked when she saw me enter.

"Our ruin is now inevitable!" she cried; "now they have you in their power, there can be no hope for us."

"But your mistress—my wife!—I charge you, in the name of heaven, to tell me how it is with her."

"Ah, my God! what can I say, unfortunate Alwynd!"

"At that moment a greater light broke into the room, and to my astonishment I saw the king.

"Alwynd!" he cried, in amazement. "Impostor, villain, traitor!"

"His face crimsoned, his eyes became fiery, and I expected that he would punish me with instant death. He commanded his attendants to withdraw, and haughtily desired Rosamond to accompany them.

"You see, Alwynd," he said, "you see that I am not afraid to trust myself with you, tho' I believe you capable of any baseness. And is it thus you repay my regard, my friendship, and my confidence?—To thwart the wishes of your king—to impose the most artful lies on him—to screen yourself in mean disguises—and to alienate the duty and affections of my unfortunate sister!—You have been as an adder to me, Alwynd; the sting did not merely touch, it even reached the centre of my heart."

"Oh, I do not deserve your hatred!" I cried.—"I was guided by love; and God alone knows how much, how fervently I loved your sister!"

"Arrogant and presumptuous!—How could you dare to step over the barriers that were placed between her and you?—Oh, misguided, but ill-fated Matilda!—Heaven will vouch that I bore for you a most tender affection; but you are become insensible to it, and the current of your heart is stilled for ever."

"Almighty God!" I exclaimed, "is she dead?"

"She is torn from me, and can never be restored!" cried her brother, in a strain of agony.—"Her bosom is icy, her lips are closed, and her sweet eyes sealed for ever!"

"I groaned in agony, while my sinews were relaxing.

"Leave me, Alwynd," continued the king; "begone, and from this hour never let me see your face. Your friendship and loyalty once formed a source of pleasure; but now I throw you from my heart, and swear by my Saviour never to take you to it again. What I have conferred on you, retain; but retire from my court, and dare not hereafter to place yourself before me."

"I believe this was not the conclusion of his speech; but the sickness of my soul overpowered me, my senses fled for a while, and on their return I found myself in another apartment, and Rosamond Neville and a servant of the castle standing by my side. My head had scarcely been raised, or my eyes opened, when the man addressed himself to me.

"I have been commanded, my Lord," he said, "to continue with you till the return of your reason; but now I tell you to begone.—Rise, Lord Alwynd, and instantly depart from the castle; you must not stay in it another minute, for the wrath of the king is not to be appeased.—Rise, rise, and go out at the gates immediately."

"I will not depart," I replied; "I tremble not at the anger of the king, and I will not be forced away till I have once more beheld my——"

"Silence!" cried my tender companion, "as you value your life and mine I charge you to be silent. I feel more on your account than on my own; tho' I am an outcast, and have been treated with severity. Nothing further can be done here, let us away, my Lord, for in my present state, I find it necessary to call on you for protection."

"I knew by her words and actions, that my marriage, and the innocent issue of it, were yet unknown; and tho' I wished once more to look on my departed love—once more to strain her cold bosom to my heart, yet I suffered Rosamond to lead me away, and we both left the castle in public disgrace. Grief, however, lessened the mortification. In the anguish of my heart I regarded not the glances of subordinate scorn; and my poor and faithful associate went forward with me, leaning on my arm, and with her eyes sorrowfully fixed on the earth, as if she were courting a grave to receive her.

"I now learned, that my detection and seisure, had been effected by the wary Lady Westmoreland, whose emissaries had been dispatched to the king, in order to apprise him that the princess had contrived surreptitious meetings with a stranger, (for my disguise had not been seen through,) and enquiring in what manner she should cause the night visitor to be treated. Her sovereign returned with the messengers. That Rosamond was instrumental to our interviews was perfectly clear; and, as she had never stood in the favour of the king, his anger and resentment fell heavy on her.

"Matilda's faculties were nearly gone on the arrival of her brother; and tho' she had spoken distinctly a few minutes before his entrance, yet when he was announced, and afterwards approached her bed, terror destroyed the few remaining powers. Her eyes grew more dim; her tongue became speechless; and in less than two hours she fell a corse into the arms of her anguished and astonished brother. Oh, my wife! Why was I not there to consign thee to thy sister angels!—Fraternal grief soon yielded to the more violent passions; and the rage of the king, and the contempt of Lady Westmoreland, were heaped upon the innocent Rose Neville, who was strictly watched till I had been detected and secured. After the interview between me and Matilda's brother, my agitated and abused friend was commanded to leave the castle, at the time that I should depart from thence.

"This I became acquainted with, as I and my companion went forward; but the voice that told it me, was often indistinct, and my heart was bleeding during the recital. I had turned round to look, once more, at the fabric that contained the breathless form of Matilda, and Rose had done the same, our eyes then met, and made reciprocal confessions; and we trod the path in silence and agony undescribable. It was early morning, and heaven and earth were smiling. Scarcely a wave sported on the sea, the flowers of the field raised their heads amid drooping gems, and the tillers of the earth, russet clad and healthful, went down into the vallies, and ascended the hills; while the indistinctive harmony of thrush and lark, sounded from the thickets and the regions of the air.

"I was wretched, and, I thought, accursed even in a world of seeming happiness. All objects now were to be envied; and I could almost have wished the spirit of animation to fix, to become insensible, and to stand motionless as long as the heavens should hang over the earth. I had so loved my wife that, in losing her, I found myself of neither worth nor importance. But I knew better how to estimate myself, when Rosamond suddenly spoke to me of my children. Matilda had, indeed, nearly made me a bankrupt in happiness; still her progeny were as rubies of the east to me.

"At a farm house, about four miles from the castle, I procured a horse of a countryman, and placed Rosamond on the back of it; the owner of the beast followed her at some little distance, and I walked by her side till we came to the village where I meant to stop, and from whence the rustic returned after I had satisfied him for his trouble. We were now within sight of the dwelling of my children, when I pointed to it, and with great emotion told Rosamond of what it contained.

"Then let me speak to you, my Lord," she cried, "before we go any further. When last you saw the dear and lamented Matilda, you must recollect how many fears she expressed for her helpless little ones. After your departure she continued to talk of them, her apprehensions hastened her death, and the last words she said to me were, "Tell my husband, Rosamond, never to forget what I have said concerning my children; and, in my name, charge him to let them never be known to, or reside near, my offended brother."

"Dear and precious Matilda!" I cried, "you shall be most willingly obeyed."

"We are yet insecure, and fearfully situated," said my companion; "and tho' the king has driven us from him, his vigilance will not sleep. I know his temper, his resentments.—Ah, God! If he should, by any means, discover the precious babes, and wrest them from us."

"He shall not!" I exclaimed; "by the Eternal God I swear, he shall not! See, the cottage is close by; let us hasten to it. Be quick, quick as the emotions of a father's heart. I will tear my children from the arms of their nurse, and plant a poniard in the breast at which they have sucked, should I think she will betray me. For them I would renounce every thing; would live in a desert, amid the damps of a cave, bury myself all the day, and prowl all the night with a heart fierce as the wolf's ere——"

"Hold, hold!" cried Rosamond; "your impetuosity alarms and terrifies me. Let us go to the cottage, but not in the manner you have proposed. Inform the woman that I am the mother of your children; and I will aid the deception, as far as I can. You say, tho' she is poor, she is seemingly honest, and I have no doubt but that she will readily accompany us to some other spot. Make the proposal to her as soon as you can; and, if she consents, remove us to some distant retirement. If you will shelter me from the world, my Lord, I will be to your children————"

"She paused, sobbed, and fell upon my shoulder. Words could not so tenderly have expressed her feelings; and after I had embraced and blessed her, I went with her to the cottage, and was admitted by the simple mistress of it. I shall not describe what I felt when I again fondled the soft pledges of Matilda's love. I followed the advice of my friend, made liberal offers to the nurse, and gained her acquiescence. Rosamond had been worn by watchfulness and distress; her countenance, naturally delicate, became sickly; and the maternal imposition was not suspected.

"Soon after our arrival, we finished the plan that we had previously sketched; and some of our designs we communicated to the cottager. I proposed to take my friend, my children, and their nurse, to a distant part of the kingdom; and on the following day we all left the hamlet, without exciting any particular notice, and removed to the next small town, where I procured a covered carriage and a pair of horses; and during the ensuing twenty-four hours, we travelled nearly fifty miles.

"I knew that great exertion on my part was necessary; but my heart was all grief, and to counterfeit serenity was, indeed, an arduous task. Soon after we halted, I found accommodation for my offspring and companions. It was my wish that they should remain there, till I had been to my castle, and also till I could, on their account, make some further arrangements. To this they assented, and I accordingly departed. It was absolutely necessary, that I should shew myself to my dependents, before the story of my disgrace should be rumoured. I staid, however, only a day or two with them, and having determined on placing the poor fugitives in an ancient manor-house, which stood on one of my estates in another county, I hastened back to them, and by easy stages afterwards conveyed them thither in health and safety.

"It was to this place I so often retired, when I was absent from the castle; and I acquainted no one with the nature or extent of my excursions in order that curiosity might not interrupt, or lessen, the felicity I found with my thriving progeny. The priest that married me to Matilda, I patronised till his death; and I supported the midwife for her fidelity, till she and her secret expired together. I loved them for their honesty and attachment, and sighed over them when they were breathless. But it was no common grief that took possession of my heart, when I grasped the unnerved hand, and closed the rayless eyes of the good, the tender, the sensitive Neville! Peace, dear woman, to thy spirit; and in the invisible world may'st thou and my Matilda dwell everlastingly, in renewed friendship, and with joys unfading! The nurse still lives; but she married respectably, and retired into Scotland, the native country of her husband, to whom she carried a dowry which I proportioned to her merit and virtue.

"You know the rest, Celwold; and I think I have sufficiently explained my motives for the obscurity in which I have hitherto wrapped my children. My love and reverence for Matilda made me observant of her dying request; and oftentimes has the quick eye of imagination, caught her delicate form in the act of approving my caution. If, in adhering to my promise, I have been led beyond the boundaries of truth, I hope, situated as I was, the fault will be considered as venial.

"Many times have I wished to open my breast, and give to you unreservedly its mysteries; for I have ever believed you worthy of my friendship and confidence. Some invisible power, however, has hitherto seemed to divert the impulse; but as I am now about to rush into danger—to take the chance of either conquering, or of being conquered—of mounting the banner of victory, or of being trampled upon by the hoof of the war-horse, to whose care should I, acting on probabilities, consign my beloved children?—To you, to you, dear Celwold!—I believe there is no worthier man within my knowledge. You must be their friend, and, in case I should stretch in death on the plains of Bartonmere, also their father. They have no mother—I no wife—Thou art gone, Matilda, for ever art thou gone!

"Since my separation from her whom in this world I can behold no more, I have only once seen the king. I met him in the field of battle, to which I went without my services being required. He was in extreme danger, and my heart glowed when my falchion rescued him from it.

"Remove your helmet, soldier," he cried, "and let me see the face of my gallant deliverer!"

"I put it aside, and bent myself before him.

"Alwynd!" he exclaimed, "Alwynd the preserver of my life!—I thank you; and tho' our friendship can never be cemented, still from my soul I thank you!"

"He grasped both my hands—he looked earnestly in my face, and as he gazed his eye moistened. He then ran from me, and I never saw him afterwards.

"Part of this narrative has been written many months; and it was designed for your reading, in case any casualty had befallen me. The other part, present circumstances draw from me; and I give the whole of it to you, with a confidence nearly as strong as that with which angels wait for the good works of providence. Oh, children, children! you are in the heart of your father!—Shield them, Celwold, from the brother of Matilda, for even now I am not wholly divested of fear. Tho' I wish them not always to remain ignorant of their descent, yet suffer the reason of William to correct his enthusiasm, before you tell him that the blood of princes runs in his veins, and that his uncle is the beloved monarch of this happy country."

———————

Here concluded the narrative of the fallen warrior. It affected the reader variously and strangely; his heart alternately glowed and sickened—the burning blush of shame was often on his cheeks, and his brows wrapped in disappointment. Tho' he knew himself to be unworthy of the praises which honesty and virtue had bestowed on him, yet his merit grew not; for avarice and pride had taken possession of his breast, and recent circumstances demolished the fabric which had cost him numberless and busy days in erecting.

That which stands between man and his desired attainments, whatever may be its qualities, is generally despised; and those objects which were barriers to Alwynd's wealth, tho' worth, innocence, and beauty attached to them, were contemned and execrated. He threw from him the papers that he had been reading, and snatched at the will which he had not yet perused. The first devise was to the acknowledged son of Alwynd, and it comprised demesnes and accumulations of gold, which princes would have deemed acquisitions. The bequest to Agatha was noble, and would afford a dowry equal to most of the heiresses in the kingdom. Then followed the gift to Celwold—It included the manor-house, to which Rose Neville had been conveyed with Matilda's children, a large tract of land contiguous to it, and many articles of value once esteemed by the ancestors of Alwynd; besides a pecuniary legacy, which none but a most liberal hearted donor would have bestowed on a person who stood only in a distant degree of affinity.

But the latter part of the will was read by Celwold with disgust. He thought of his shorn honours with a gloomy malignity; and comparing his treasure to that of the youth, whom he so envied and uncharitably hated, it seemed no more than a remote star faintly twinkling, while all the gems of the firmament were shewing themselves in extreme lustre and beauty.

He arose from his seat, and after pacing the chamber some little time, went to the window and looked around him. But the prospect added to his mortifications, and encreased his splenetic humour. The view was wide and lovely. The flowery forest, the ample and luxuriant meadows, the groups of cattle and fleecy sheep, and the gigantic and lofty oak trees in all their summer beauty, attracted his eye. The hills that bounded the eastern prospect were distant, and the sun, having long journied over their summits, spread his rich beams on the extensive lawns, and on the rippling waters that coursed between the pendant willows.

But all that he saw were as treasures which had been drawn from his confident grasp.—All that he saw belonged to the newly discovered son of Alwynd, whom he had once beheld as a creature of charity; and who was designed to be the homaged Lord of the castle and domain.

"Even I," exclaimed Celwold, "must bow before the boy, and smile and say, sweet Lord! your servant greets you.—Even I must—No, ruin and perdition overtake me if I do! Alwynd, you might have spared your praises, for I neither profess, nor will strive to deserve them. Had I earlier known what I was reasonably to expect, I might have been different to what I am. But now I will not love your name—I will not reverence your memory; and should your pale spirit, too troubled for repose, haunt me throughout each night, I would not bend to your will, or be diverted from my own purposes. Your fortune and your children are at my disposal; placed absolutely within my power. You confided in me too late; and what I so long and ardently wished for, I will still attain and enjoy. I am your nearest relative; and those papers destroyed, I may boldly step forth, and say aloud to the world, I am the heir of Alwynd! O, I will be no coward in my ventures; my grasp shall be resolute and strong. Not only your riches, cousin, but also your children must be at my command. Tho' the king has many good qualities, he is tenacious of his dignity and jealous of his rights. Tell him only that the lawful issue of his sister stands secretly behind the throne he now sits upon, and to which his darling grandson is to succeed—tell him but this, and where shall the young pretenders fly for shelter? Procrastination will be my surest foe; my operations, therefore, will I begin, by destroying this paper,—this accursed instrument!—which, once divulged, would place me in a state of insignificance that I should despise,—and bring to me an host of undermining plagues, more to be dreaded than the sudden and inevitable attack of death."

He walked quickly towards the table, in order to destroy the will and narrative; but as he was laying his hand on them, a body of air rushed impetuously into the room, and carried them out at the window. His endeavour to catch at them was unavailing; for he saw them sometimes floating on the air, and sometimes blown rapidly over the ground. Greatly alarmed he immediately left the room, and, hastening out of the castle, found the papers still the play-things of the element; and tho' he ran with all his speed, he could not get possession of them.

Half mad with fear and vexation, he continued his pursuit. Several times he thought he had put his hand on them, but when he lifted it from the earth, he found himself deceived; while, as if he were the fool of sport, they curled above his head and frolicked before his eye. What he had at first regarded as a common event, he now looked upon with amazement; they still were hurried over the more open parts of the forest, and still he followed them. At length, however, they were blown beyond the verge of a dark and almost unfathomable quarry; and he watched them from the brink, as they slowly descended.

"They are lost to me," he cried; "and I shall assuredly never regain the possession of them."

"Who complains there?" said a voice near to him; when he turned his head, and found that the enquiry came from a poor traveller, who had apparently been reposing on the sunny turf. His garb was coarse and mean, and his countenance shewed not much of health. His cheeks were pale, his beard neglected, and his eyes beamed with anxieties. A wallet lay by his side, and an ill-fed, but watchful mastiff stood near his head, baying the disturber of his master's slumbers.

The man arose, and, drawing his hand over his brows, walked towards Celwold; who still was looking over the edge of the quarry, and repeating his fears of never recovering the papers from such a dark and dangerous abyss.

"What have you lost, my noble sir?" enquired the stranger.

"Some writings of great concern," replied Celwold, "which, considering the depth, the darkness, and the dangers of this place, I fear will never be restored to me."

"Send some person in search of them," said the traveller.

"But whom should I employ? Who would venture? Who trust himself in a place so unfrequented and dangerous?"

"O, there are many men who will go far for rewards."

"Would I could find one willing on this occasion."

"Behold him here, in me," cried the traveller; "fashion the advantages according to the hazard, and I will not long remain above the surface."

"See this purse," said Celwold, "it is filled with gold. Go down into the cave, bring me the papers, and the money shall be your's; aye, this, and fifty more of equal value, shall be your reward, if you redeem what I have lost."

The man looked into the quarry, drew back, and shuddered.

"What, you will not venture?" asked the fearful Celwold.

"Yes, if it lead to hell I will descend.—And yet how horrid—how dreadfully silent!—Nothing to be heard, nothing seen, except that little ridge of earth which my hand's breadth would mock. God, how dreadful!—Give me the purse, and if I return, observe well your promise. I go—but first let me tell you why I go. At a distance, in the western country, stands a hovel of clay, in which I lately dwelt. Beneath the thatch of it lies my dying wife, and around her bed of straw stand my four children, with faces of the colour of the walls, and with their juices dried up by poverty.—Are you a father?"

"No, I am not."

"I am, I am!—I prove it here—I feel it deep in my heart. Must my wife die, and shall my children perish in want?—You know not the pain arising from the emptiness of stomach and long fasting. Nature is kinder to brutes, to birds, and to reptiles, than to many of the children of man. See what an ample pasturage for the sleek-coated deer. Yon herd of stupid swine revel amid showers of acorns; and the beasts of prey find, beneath the turf of this forest, caves comfortable and suited to their dainties—as are marbled halls and rooms of tapestry to the luxuries of ennobled gluttons. I grow wild and giddy with my thoughts!—The ghost of my wife is before me, and I hear the shrieks of my famished babes!—Nature, I owe thee nothing, nothing but curses, and them will I give to thee unstinted. In my craving mood I should have killed and eaten my dog, had it not been for the well known love he bears for me. I have called him Fidelity. No, Fidelity, thou shalt not die!—Should I hereafter be rich, I will build a temple, and set up thy image in gold. It will be religion in me to worship thee; and I will speak in praise of thy loving instinct, and execrate the savageness of reason. Come to my arms, thou worthier being than man!"

The animal leapt upon the traveller's breast, and seemed to view him with ecstasy. Celwold was astonished and alarmed; he began to suspect that he had been conversing with some lunatic straying from his chains, and was going hastily away from his strange companion.

"Hold!" cried the latter, perceiving his intention; "the cave—I will descend instantly."

"But the peril; the extreme danger——"

"I laugh at it; I see it not. I am assured I shall come up again."

"Should you find the bottom of the cave, how can you, amid so much darkness, discover what I have lost?"

"O, I will cast up my eyes, and gather in such a body of light, that I will describe to you every species of insect that may crawl in the regions beneath. Adieu!—Fidelity! Fidelity!"

He stept forward, no longer dull and slothful, but with vigour in his limbs, and with a strangely altered countenance. The dog followed, growling at Celwold, who laid his head over the cave, in order to mark the descent of the adventurer.

The man passed the first ridge, and leaped lightly on a second, turned up his face, laughed at the observer, and still pursued his course. He was seen for a considerable time, then he lessened to the sight, seemed to grow smaller still; and after space had reduced him, in the eyes of him who looked from the surface, to the size of a pigmy, he was lost in impenetrable darkness.

Celwold did not believe it possible that he could ever return, and, indeed, it was a matter of indifference to him; for he was now convinced that the papers could never be brought again to light, and that he should not have been more secure had he consigned them to the flames, or torn them to atoms. He frequently spoke to the stranger, but was not heard by him; the voice of the latter, however, and the howlings of the dog frequently ascended, in different degrees of strength, sometimes like audible whisperings only, and sometimes like the rumbling of thunder.

He had left the mouth of the cave nearly half an hour, when Celwold, who was still in the act of listening, very distinctly heard himself spoken to.

"I prosper in my undertakings," said the man; "I am now treading a path upon which I could spur forward a courser of the quickest mettle. A little light from above—darkness and no visible bottom beneath. Now the scene changes again, but it is to my discomfiture.—Leave not the cave till I return. The damned can never go into ways more dreadful!"

The first part of this speech was soft as echo, when she replies to the cheerful forester; but the concluding words were hoarse and strange, as if they had been bellowed in pain and agony, by a monster huge as the leviathan, and strong as Atlas. Celwold trembled at the sound; and it was a long time before he heard the voice again. At length a shriek of horror came to his ear.—The stranger had slipped from one of the projections—his screams were dreadful—the noise made by the brute follower loud and terrifying. The one of them, by turns, prayed and execrated; and the other, unvarying in the tones of his distress, yelled like the keeper of the gates of hell.

The uproar continued nearly half an hour, and the wretch, without being deprived of life, was dashed from shelf to shelf. A pause ensued, and afterwards a noise was made by the body dashing into a bed of water, at the bottom of this unfathomable abyss. It was as horrid as if all the seas and rivers had met in silence, and a star had dropped in the midst of them. Tho' the heart of Celwold was roughly fashioned, and had but few qualities of feeling, yet this strange circumstance impressed him most sensibly. His body weakened, and his mind grew feeble. He arose with difficulty, and having walked a few paces, he fell on the roots of an oak tree, and became insensible.

When Celwold awoke to a sense of his situation, it was a satisfaction to find no person near him. From his loneliness he concluded that he had not been observed; and after sitting a while on the turf, in order that his intellects might resume their former capacities, he arose from the spot on which he had fallen. Having looked with dread towards the abyss, in which the adventurous traveller had perished, he returned to the castle.

In the hall he met with Mercia, who cast his eyes upon the face of his guardian, and read with secret comment, the wild characters that were yet stampt upon it, and which no present artifice could disguise. He was assured that the mind of Celwold contained some most strange matter; and the affirmed cause of the visible disorder, tho' he spoke not on the subject, he peremptorily rejected.

Celwold had always found the penetration of his ward unsuited to most of his purposes. He had, for a considerable time, been convinced, that his hypocrisy passed not to Mercia as to other men; and nothing but the pecuniary advantages which his avarice craved, could so long have induced him to retain his charge. He now perceived the glances that came to him indirectly, but, in his apprehensions, he did not venture to chide what he deemed impertinent and found distressing.

He wondered alike at his own present fears, and at the recent consequences of the traveller's disaster. No occurrence had ever so strangely wrought on him, nor had any preceding event ever reduced him to a state of insensibility; and that which he had considered as a womanish and conquerable impulse, he now acknowledged as an irresistible attack on human nature. Having made enquiries concerning William and Agatha, and been told that the youth was in the chamber of his sister, who was still weak and inconsolable, Celwold was retiring, when Mercia stepped before him, and begged that he might be heard for a few minutes.

"I shall not long detain your Lordship," he cried, "for I have only a single request to make. I beg you will allow me to return to Bartonmere, in order that I may bring from thence the body of Lord Alwynd."

"Would it not be more proper if I were to go thither, either alone or in your company?" enquired Celwold. "Why do you, Mercia, wish to engage in the melancholy office?"

"Oh, my Lord, you know not how dearly I loved him! Neither William nor Agatha, could have a warmer affection for him; and having lost him, they cannot feel more acutely than I do, tho' my external appearances of sorrow are so few. I fought by his side—I was near him when he fell. I never knew my father or my mother—had the former, however, died in my arms, grief could not have laid a stronger hold on me; and had the latter——But there no comparison will rest. Her long and shameful neglect of me has made her an object of little concern. Let me go to Bartonmere, let me bring back that beloved, once beautiful, and manly form, in which the spirit of animation shall never more be found."

"Go, Mercia," replied Celwold! "go on the mournful errand whenever you shall think it proper. I own, I feel myself unequal to the office. In the death of Lord Alwynd you have only to lament a friend. I must mourn for him as a relation; as one closely linked to me by the chain of nature, and made most precious by the ties of kindred. When will you depart?"

"With the permission of your Lordship, I will be gone within the present hour. Some of the servants should go with me."

"Command such of them as you best approve to wait on you."

"And William, my dear unhappy friend! He too will accompany me."

"Oh, it will be too much for the gentleness of his nature! Spare him, spare him, Mercia, from a sight so distressing."

"No, my Lord, I have prepared him for the occasion. His grief is such that it should be disturbed. It gathers, it accumulates, and threatens to canker his heart; but when I bring him to the body of Alwynd, and point out his many gashes, the tempest of the soul will vent itself freely, and probably be soon succeeded by a calm of long continuance."

Celwold agreed to what Mercia proposed; and the latter went to make the necessary preparations. He found all the servants desirous of going for the remains of their loved Lord, and allowed many of them so to do. He then sought his friend William, and after a short conversation they both entered the apartment of Agatha, to whom Mercia, who had some knowledge of the human heart, unreservedly spoke of the errand on which he was going.

"Restrain your tears, dear girl," he cried, "and shew not so much sorrow for an event, which was not brought about by mere mortal agency. Every hour, nay every moment is pregnant with death. With our general belief in things hereafter, and estimating future rewards and neglects, we have more cause to sigh for the departure of those, who dwelt among us in the habits of vice, than of those whose time was spent in virtue; and whom we, reserving all the best qualities of our nature, joyfully acknowledge as brothers and fellow-men. Does Alwynd, in his present state, demand the tribute of human tears?—He does not Agatha! sorrow never was where he resides, and earthly pity is not wanted where there is heavenly gratulation."

"Adieu, dear girl! Adieu, dear sister!" cried William, while he pressed her to his breast. The friends then left the room, and soon afterwards the castle, at the gate of which appeared Lord Celwold; who waved his hand in silence, and affected to feel infinitely more than his nature had ever been sensible of.

END OF VOL. I

MARTYN OF FENROSE,

OR, THE

WIZARD AND THE SWORD.

THE young men walked their horses slowly towards the forest, and the servants were left to follow at their leisure. William sighed heavily as he went forward; and Mercia reflected on the difference of his late and present journey. He had then gone forth free as the air, and disencumbered as the feet of liberty; now he moved towards the ways of recent slaughter, in order to view, in death, the hero that had so lately towered with marshal dignity, and shone like the god of battle.

Tho' his thoughts were melancholy, he would not pass them to his companion, whose breast he wished to ease of its pains, not to afflict; he therefore continued his route two or three hours, offering such consolations as his generous mind could devise, when something very forcible came to his memory. Checking his horse he desired William to look before him.

"Yonder was the battle fought," he cried, "yonder de Stacey, Bartonmere, and Alwynd, mingled their forces, and ardently strove for victory."

His companion directed his eyes towards the spot, they moistened, they overflowed, and he spoke not till they came to that part of the heath where broken swords, pikes, and breast-plates told of the past confusion, rout, and carnage. William contemplated and groaned, when Mercia, by halting a second time, interrupted those thoughts which almost distracted the mind they occupied. Mercia leaped from his horse, and looked up to his friend.

"Dismount, William," he cried, "dismount instantly, for this is sacred ground, and it must not be passed unheeded. Look on this spot—here Alwynd received the death-blow of de Stacey."

"Here, Mercia?"

"Even here the hero perished! After he had become still in my arms, after his quiverings ceased, and all that had been mortal sunk into horrid stillness, I laid his body on the turf, and, in the frenzy of my mind, struck the warrior's broken sword into the earth. It has, I find, escaped the notice of the plunderers.—See, here it remains— a small, but bright memento of departed greatness and valour."

"Take it up, Mercia; or rather let my hands remove it. While I have life I will retain it; and to-morrow will I come hither, and in the place of the weapon plant a yew-tree, beneath the branches of which I and Agatha will often lament the fate of our friend, our preserver, and protector."

"The yew!—Let it never appear on a spot like this. Say, rather, the laurel, which here I would see root, flourish, and grow into unusual greatness, that from its branches the noblest of our living heroes may receive unfading circlets for their brows; and that the shades of all those who shall sink under the battle-axe may repair hither, and take from the hands of immortality, unperishable wreaths. But, come, let us be gone. Yonder are the towers of Bartonmere; and near to the holly that grows on your right hand, William, did I mangle the body of de Stacey."

William looked sorrowfully again at the turf, and then languidly on the turrets that rose above the wood; but when his eye met the last spot that Mercia had pointed to, his bosom glowed, and his face crimsoned.

Lord Bartonmere came to them as soon as their arrival was announced; and the meeting was not unaffecting. The early friend of Alwynd took William to his breast, and gave him strong assurances of love and esteem; and also entreated, that, on every future occasion he might be resorted to, and confidently considered as one who would joyfully become, both to the youth and his sister, what Alwynd had so long and truly professed himself to be. He, to whom these words of kindness were addressed, answered them in terms of tenderness and gratitude; which having done, he begged that he might be allowed to see the corse of Lord Alwynd in privacy. Bartonmere at first persuaded him against it, but on his further entreaties, his lordship conducted him to the chamber in which it lay, and afterwards left him to the free indulgence of his sorrows.

He was absent from Mercia and Bartonmere nearly half an hour, during which time he had uncovered the white face of Alwynd, and looked with agony on the wounds of his cold body. He had also renewed his complaints, and spoken them aloud to the insensible, but his passions having reached their climax, philosophy talked to him, and he listened to her voice; and when he returned to his friends, they were pleased by the quietness of his sorrow, as well as by his unruffled deportment.

Mercia and William spent the night with Bartonmere, and on the following morning departed with the body of Alwynd. The servants, who formed the unostentatious cavalcade, retraced the path they had come on the preceding day, with Mercia and his friend at their head; and about noon they reached Alwynd Castle, and bore the late Lord of it in silence to the hall. Celwold met them there; he was habited in black, and the face of grief that he assumed was nearly perfect in its lines.

William, believing the truth of appearances hastened towards him, and throwing himself in his arms, mingled his own actual, with Celwold's affected sorrows. Mercia stood apart, viewing the conduct of his guardian, and alternately believing and doubting his sincerity. His knowledge, however, of past duplicities was not to be easily destroyed, and though his nature was generous, he had seldom cause to tax his credulity.

It was noon, and the season summer, yet Celwold had directed that all things might accord with the solemnity of death. From the stained windows of the hall, the light of day was excluded; tapers were scantily placed around the darkened walls; and a single torch was affixed to the bier on which the corpse had been raised. By Celwold's desire, the pall and the cover of the coffin were removed; and the senseless frame they had concealed was accordingly exposed to view. Celwold bent towards the hand of Alwynd, and kissed it; he then called around him the attendants to do the same; when they approached slowly and in grief, and in following the example they had witnessed, every man, as he retired, left a tear behind him.

The scene was too tender and affecting for the heart of William, who was walking from it, and going towards his chamber. As he opened the door, however, he saw his sister approaching; and though he entreated her to return, he found that she was not to be guided by his direction. She took his arm, and led him to the spot where death invisibly triumphed. Her lips fixed on the cheek of the fallen warrior; her friends almost immediately endeavoured to draw her from him, but she resisted all of them.

"Hold, Lord Celwold," she cried, "dear William and Mercia forbear! Though you would drive me hence, I know none of you suspect that my love was not sincere and equal to your own. Alwynd, friend and father! Ah, God, how dull those eyes in which love and humanity ever shone! How pale those cheeks, where health lately strewed the freshest roses! How still this breast, which, while warm, was ever active with virtue and benevolence! Mercia, you argued weakly. We must, indeed we must mourn for the departed worthy."

"Dear Agatha!" cried Celwold, "I entreat you to remain here no longer. Suffer your brother to lead you from so distressing a scene."

She did not reply, but she prest the hand of Celwold; and having again looked earnestly on the face of the deceased, she returned, accompanied by her brother and his friend.

On the sixth day after the fall of Alwynd on Bartonmere-heath, his body was conveyed to the vault of his ancestors, and there left to moulder. Celwold stood near the priest, in the "suits of woe." Mercia was on his right hand, and William and Agatha hung their heads in anguish on his left. Lord Bartonmere, struggling with his strong and many griefs, was also present; and stifled moans were heard to come from the affectionate servants and honest peasants, who were placed behind.

No scene could be more solemn, and with one exception, no sorrow more sincere. There was not a single person among them who did not join in prayer; but the voices of all the mourners were instinctively suspended, and even the tongue of Celwold faltered, and made his words indistinct. The remainder of the day was spent in silence and retirement. Bartonmere had gone home in heaviness of heart; and Celwold shut himself up, in order to consider of what nature his next operations must necessarily be.

After frequently yielding to the attacks of conscience, and feeling the cowardice of vice, he became somewhat more bold and confident. He resolved, on the ensuing day, to establish his claims to the title and possessions of Alwynd; and to inform both William and Agatha of their dependant state. He knew that a feeble spirit would be unsuited to the business he had to perform; like an apprehensive actor, he therefore, diligently studied his part, and in the morning found himself better skilled in the language he was to use, and also more free and unembarrassed in his deportment.

The night went over, and his resolution grew with the day. He descended into the lower apartments, at his accustomed time; and about noon, sent to request that William, Agatha, and Mercia would come to him. It was not long before they appeared, and he received them with such smiles and tenderness, as made him an object of great estimation in the eyes of those who thought too liberally of his nature. The last person that came before him, was not, however, so warm; for Mercia had long been convinced that the general softness of his guardian's features, was not effected either by any sensitive qualities, or generous impulse.

The kinsman of Alwynd soon explained to them his reason for calling them thither. "I wish you all," he cried, "to be approvers of my conduct, and would have none of you think that I act with precipitancy. He who lately resided among us, diffusing happiness and pleasure, we have deposited in the unrestoring tomb. We were all objects of his love and esteem, even from his first knowledge of us till his latest hour. But why should I mention those things which are generally known? Why speak of his excellent qualities, of which none of you can be insensible?"

Agatha concealed her face in the bosom of her brother, who had turned in tenderness towards her.

"It is the desire of doing what is right and equitable," continued Celwold, "that induces me, in this early season, to speak of those concerns which seldom employ our minds in the hours of sorrow. Think me not rude, dear children of our Alwynd's love! if, desiring to promote your interest, as well as your happiness, I ask that of you, which will encrease your present griefs.—If, at a time like this, I make a strong enquiry of you."

"Proceed, my Lord," said William, "I will answer you."

"Who is your father?"

"Alas, I know not!—I was never informed."

"But your mother, William?—Of her, I presume——"

"There, my Lord, I am equally uninformed. Neither my father, nor my mother, were ever known to me."

"Strange and mysterious! That Lord Alwynd, for so many years, and knowing the dangers he had recently to encounter, should keep you ignorant of that which must appear to every one a matter of importance, is most extraordinary!—Can you recollect no little circumstance leading to the secret? Did you ever importune him on the subject?"

"My Lord, I have frequently spoken to him of my unknown parents; frequently entreated him to declare their names. Not many months ago I urged him on the subject more strongly than at any former time. Oh, had you seen the effect it had on him! He caught me in his arms; I felt his heart beating against my breast; and his tears even dropt upon me. "Now," I cried, "now release me from these difficulties."—"William," he replied, "William, you torture my soul. Your father still lives, but never, tho' he loves you and Agatha as dearly as a parent ever loved his children, never will he dare to acknowledge himself to either of you!"—I groaned, and spoke the name of my mother—"She is dead, William," he cried in inexpressible agony; "she was called from this world soon after you were sent into it. Enquire no further. Your birth is virtuous; and, while I have life, I will stand in the place of the unfortunate parent who wishes to acknowledge you, tho' he is fatally prevented from doing so. I will perform his duties; I will love you nothing short of his affections; and should you survive me, perhaps I may leave that behind which will tell you the story of your unhappy parents."

"Well!" cried Mercia; "he is dead, and where is his promised bequest? Has he deposited it with you, my friend?"

"Oh, I lament that he has not!"

"Then, doubtless, he placed it in your Lordship's hands," said Mercia, turning to Celwold; "or the information may be contained in his will."

"And where is his will, Mercia?" cried Celwold, with eagerness. "That was the enquiry I should have first made, had my love for your friend been less. Do you know in whose hands it has been placed?—Have either of you seen it? I stand the first relation of Lord Alwynd, yet no selfish views—Can the writing be soon produced?"

William and Agatha declared that they knew not of it, and Celwold assured them no confidence was placed in him. Mercia's eyes had been reading the characters of his guardian's face, and he took into his mind some fresh suspicions; which, in one moment, he wished to contemn for their unworthiness, and, in the next, to retain for their justness. He, however, withdrew his attention from the object he contemplated, and looked at his friends, who appeared in grief and disappointment.

"Nay, droop not, William," cried Celwold in a strain of tenderness, "dry up your tears, Agatha. The secresy of Alwynd respecting you I could never break, but, among his papers, may yet be found something that will explain the mystery; and which, in respect to fortune, will independently place you both in ease and elegance. Alwynd never did wrong designedly; and if, thro' inadvertence, he strengthened not your security, look up hereafter to me. I am the heir of his fortune, and his title will also come to me; but all that you have hitherto enjoyed, and all that you can further wish for, you shall most freely command."

William and Agatha thought this speech was fraught with tenderness; but Mercia found in it arrogance and ostentation.

"Two things I would propose," continued Celwold, "and you may either accede to, or reject them. Let us defer the business that must necessarily be performed, till the first day of the ensuing month. During that time, if we can find no writing, explanatory of the circumstances which we are all anxious to be acquainted with, let the supposed intestacy be proclaimed in the castle, and among the tenantry, in order that any person, who may have been entrusted by our lamented Alwynd, may appear, and remove all our doubts and difficulties. Do you agree to this, William?"

"Readily, my Lord.—Your proposal makes me sensible of your worth and integrity. The other thing you desire——"

"Is this.—What I last said, I applied only to the will and fortune of Lord Alwynd; what I would next speak of, is the secret that, perhaps, went with him when he expired. I have a heart capable of judging your feelings—a heart that can sympathise with you too. Who knows but that some person, not very remote from us, is well acquainted with the circumstances of your birth?—Would you not discover that man, if such an one exists?—Would you not willingly know from whence you came, of whom you might claim relationship, and what the name and actions of your ancestors were?"

"I would, indeed I would!"

"Then let your desire form a part of the proclamation that we have agreed shall be made. Offer a reward, great as you please, to him who shall give you information concerning your family, and particularly of the father from whom you sprung."

"Never, never, my Lord!—What my preserver and protector with-held, and ever spoke of with fear and agitation, I will not strive to learn by the proposed means. Eternal ignorance will be better than opposition to my respected friend, who, tho' dead, shall be regarded as sincerely as if he were living. His motives must have been strong indeed, or he would not have resisted my many prayers and entreaties. My father lives—he may be known—the offered reward would probably draw the secret from the breast where avarice is stronger than honour, and bring on my parent, who can be in concealment for no small concerns, such pangs and distresses, as might, after conscience should have attacked me, make me howl in madness on my death-bed."

Agatha afterwards spoke in similar terms. Mercia loved them the more for their filial tenderness and consideration, and Celwold agreed to confine the proclamation entirely to the first point. They soon after separated, when the oldest actor of the scene pondered on his last performance. He had advanced much, but nothing without caution. What he had advised with so much apparent generosity, would, he was assured, be unavailing, for Alwynd's will was where no mortal could ever go in search of it; and the narrative had said, that the secret of Matilda's marriage would be unknown to any second person, at the time of her husband's death, if he should fall in the cause of Bartonmere.

Celwold smiled at his own security, and was, each moment, stretching forth his hands for something vast and magnificent. He laughed, likewise, in secret, at the credulity of those on whose rights he intended to place his own greatness; and tho' the shrewd observance and penetration of Mercia sometimes troubled him, he soon taught himself to contemn what he then deemed boyish impertinence. All that he had promised the children of Alwynd, he immediately, and with seeming disinterestedness performed. The proclamation was made within the castle, and among the most respectable of the yeomanry, but day came after day and brought no intelligence; and the search that had been made by William and his friend, proved of no advantage.

A fortnight passed away, and the appointed day was nearly arrived. William had not a single expectation remaining; and tho' he was neither craving of wealth, nor forgetful of the fair promises he had lately heard, he could not check the sighs that rose in his breast, when he thought that both he and Agatha must become the creatures of Celwold's bounty. On the evening preceding the decisive day, and while he was walking abroad with his sister and Mercia, he spoke to them on the subject that had so greatly troubled him.

"Lord Alwynd," he cried, "always led me to expect a share of his fortune; and I must regret that I shall not be entitled to such a part of it as would, at least, have kept me from the manacles of dependance. How I have missed it I know not, but I am assured it was not occasioned by my becoming unworthy of my dear friend's affections; for, till his last moment, I am convinced he loved me. Happy be his spirit, and ever honoured his name, tho' I have ventured to complain of his forgetfulness."

"Complain no more," said Agatha, "let us remember our past benefits, and be grateful for them as long as we exist."

"I am justly reproved, dear sister, and will speak no more of my disappointments. Why should I brood over these dull thoughts?—I rate the merits of Lord Celwold as they deserve. I am conscious of his generosity and virtues, but cannot take with cheerfulness what he offers; and, therefore, never will take it. What! shall I despond?—Shall I, in the noon, I might almost say the morn of life, possessed of health, and of strength, open my eyes to dull prospects, and anticipate the evils of to-morrow?—No—my poverty shall not extend to my mind; I will rouse myself from this insensibility. I will tell Lord Celwold, that, if he protect my sister, my wishes will be complete; then I will away to the king—become a soldier of fortune, a defender of my country, and a chastiser of its most daring enemies."

"Be not rash, William!" cried Agatha.—"Should you leave me surrounded with wealth and state, I should find myself as comfortless and forlorn as one solitary deer would be in this ample forest. Dear brother, act not precipitately."

"But my fortune, Agatha?"

"Shall be the fortune of your Mercia," cried his generous friend.—"Yes, by heaven, William, you shall be an unconditioned sharer of it. My means, at present, are not scanty; but, ere long, they will serve all our purposes, and gratify all our wishes. How joyful to me will be the day, when I shall go, with you and Agatha, over the demesnes of my father, and say, look at our flowery meads and budding groves. And not less the pleasure, when, with Agatha on one side, and you, William, on the other, I lead you among the noblest and worthiest of my friends; telling them to love my sister, and to respect my brother, not less than myself."

"Generous, excellent Mercia!" exclaimed William, "take the thanks of a grateful and overflowing heart!"

"And refuse not mine," said Agatha. "My Lord, you excite within my bosom feelings of such different qualities, that I am divided between pleasure and pain. I should be loath to decline the services of Lord Celwold, which have been most liberally proposed; yet there is not a man existing of whom I would so willingly ask assistance, as the long tried and inestimable friend of my brother. I now move in the world almost as an unconnected being. My mother is dead; and my mysterious father——"

"Pray, Agatha, I pray you no more of this," said Mercia, with tenderness, "I know what you would say, and judge of what you feel. You are, I confess, unfortunately situated; but compare your condition with mine, and tell me which is the more enviable. While I was in a state of childhood my father died; and not long had I forsaken the breast, and dared to trust myself upon my legs, when my mother—Oh, shame—abandoned, forsook, and turned me over to the care of strangers. I have no recollection of her; and I have taught myself to regard her as one deserving of contempt and indifference. She never could feel the instincts of nature; she never was worthy of bearing a child, or of giving it birth. To leave me when I was so weak and innocent—to fly to other countries, and live in pleasure and dissipation so many years; never, never claiming me as her son, or informing me of her existence. Base, unnatural woman! I told a lie just now. Tho' I love her not, tho' I actually contemn her, she can still move me into sorrow."

Those whom he had been endeavouring to console, now found it necessary to offer him their consolations.

"Nay, do not think," he cried, "that my emotions will exist beyond the moment in which they arise. I could have loved my mother—God!—I feel I could have loved her, as strongly as the most filial sons ever did those women who bore them with hope, and cradled them with joy. But I have a sense of the manner in which I have been treated, and can now answer neglect with neglect. Should I hereafter marry, and my wife should bring me children, if I ever act as my mother has done, may my progeny hate me while I am living. And when I am dead, let them all gather around my grave—all join in cursing me. I do not say that I shall be so fierce in my resentments. I should not have spoken of the hateful subject, had I not wished to convince you both, that my certainties might, were I possessed of your sensibilities and opinions, be equally distressing as your want of knowledge—that, tho' fortune has raised heaps of gold for me, I have been robbed of many of the felicities of nature."

The conversation of the evening had considerably affected all the young friends; and they returned home soon after the departure of the sun.

The day that succeeded was made important by the business that was to be transacted on it; the nature of which every person who resided in the castle was well acquainted with. Celwold left his bed, on which ambition had made him restless, as soon as the morning began to blush. Though no eye observed him, he paced the chamber with a false dignity, speaking to himself of the honours that were awaiting him. Had he been going to take the jewelled ornament that encircles the brows of a king, he could not have been more elated; and so impatient was he for his acquisitions, that he cursed the sloth of those whom sleep made heedless of his expected distinction.

William opened not his eyes to such pleasures. Hope sketched for him no picture; still he was serene in his disappointments, and with calmness he awaited the commands of the heir of Alwynd. About the hour of ten he came to him and his sister. At his request they accompanied him to the hall, where they found a great number of the superior servants, and all the vassalage, in attendance.

Mercia, also, was among them, and he placed himself near to Agatha; who had come thither at the entreaty of her brother, and in order to shew willingness to the accession of Celwold.

Society delights in novelties; and the funeral of a good man is often forgotten, on the appearance of the gaudy retinue of his worthless successor. Alwynd had been beloved by many, and respected by all who served him. His departure had been mourned; and tears had fallen on the earth that was piled on his body. The human heart, however, often shifts its sensibilities. Death is made familiar by its certainty; and man finds that the shortness of his own existence will allow him no long time to lament the dissolution of others. Pleasure is the end of life. Lightness of heart, and freedom of mind, ever constitute happiness; and tho' the ear to-day sadly inclines to the shell of melancholy, it will to-morrow turn with rapture to the viol of joy.

Celwold had not been long seated when he caused the proclamation to be read aloud. There was no person present who had not heard it before; but it was deemed proper that it should precede the business of the day. It invited all those who might possess any knowledge of the concerns which it contained to come openly forward, and speak of them. After the reading of it a long pause ensued. Celwold, who had, with difficulty, curbed his impatience, then rose, and smiling upon all who were present, produced his pedigree, and claimed the fortune, as well as the title, of his deceased relation.

His pretensions were soon acknowledged to be just; his descent fair and honourable; and the hall echoed with shouts and repeated cries of "Long be the life, and happy the days, of our new Lord!" William and Agatha were not backward in shewing him their respects. He put his arms around them both, while the assembly was full, and gently made those promises which he had given to them before.

The looks of Lord Alwynd's favourites accorded not with their sensibilities; but they strove to express an unreal pleasure, and wished it to be believed that they placed in Celwold an unlimited confidence.

Mercia bowed in silence to his guardian. Truth was to him a goddess, and he would not on any occasion violate her chastity, or neglect her precepts. Feeling no pleasure at the elevation of his guardian, he scorned to express any; and he bent before Celwold, merely to remove himself from observation, and to avoid singularity.

Tho' the eyes of the newly acknowledged Earl were courteously directed to every part of the hall, and his countenance was smooth and placid, yet his heart enlarged with pride, and fluttered with vanity. The usual forms of succession were afterwards attended to; the oath of fidelity administered; and Celwold was preparing to dismiss his attendants, and retire from the hall.

"Hold, all of you!" said an approaching voice,—"let not a single man depart till I am fully answered."

This command proceeded from a person, who entered the hall with a quick and bold step. His port was noble and majestic; and obedience must have followed the glances of his eye. He was regarded by every person with surprise; and Celwold wished to be informed why the stranger had spoken so peremptorily, and on what occasion he had come thither.

The unknown seemed to look into the very soul of the enquirer. He bowed gracefully to Mercia, William, and Agatha; and afterwards declared, that he had been brought to the castle by the proclamation which had gone abroad.

"I came not," he cried, "to be a witness of the honours that are springing around the heir of Alwynd, or of any pomp or pageantry. Who now is the Lord of this castle? What is his name, and where is he to be found?"

"Celwold is his name, and by that am I distinguished," replied the guardian of Mercia.

"You!—I should not have suspected it. Did ever greatness before reflect so poor a shadow?—Are you to fill the seat of Alwynd?—O, be tenacious of your honours, or, by my soul, men in their very sport will with-hold them."

"Insolent and presumptuous!" cried Celwold, almost trembling with rage.—"Hence, hence, thou unknown villain."

"Silence! or I will extinguish the few dull sparks of life that are within you!—Silence! or with my breath alone will I blow you to atoms. But let us be more soft with each other.—You may bring my spirits to the gentleness of the avis of summer; and you may make them fierce as the winds that rock your battlements in December. Answer me calmly:—What enables you to take the title and fortune of that most honourable Lord, who lately, and on these very stones, walked like a descended God amid the rays of beauty?—Sir, have the courtesy to reply."

"My consanguinity, and his intestacy."

"What! did he neglect the welfare and prosperity of those who were most dear to him?—Did he consign the creatures of his love, to one who has no love but for himself?—Did he forget what he swore to perform, and willingly leave his name to infamy?—No, no, no!"

"You are a maniac," said Celwold, "and I charge you to depart."

"Send forth your commands to the desert lion, and he will give them my attention. I must have better information. I am called Martyn of Fenrose; and having come from the borders of the third county that lies northward of this, I swear I will not retire unsatisfied. You tell me Alwynd left no testament; and I reply, I put no belief in you."

"No belief in me?—Beware——"

"Of what?—Threaten me again, and I will make you dance before me, to soften the humour your audacity may fret me into. I say it is false!—The blame of the virtuous shall never rest on the memory of Alwynd. I was once the friend of his bosom.—Do you remember the jewel he was accustomed to wear?—I put it on his hand; and he swore, while the gem had lustre, to love the giver of it. He also vowed, that I should be one of the first objects of his affections, as long as he lived; and that, after his death, I should receive a gift that might be retained till his bones should crumble, and his shroud seem to be the produce of the spider's loom. My legacy—I claim my legacy."

"Madman!" exclaimed Celwold.—"Alwynd, I could swear, knew neither your person, nor your name. Turn him out at the gates, my fellows."

"If any one approach me," said Martyn of Fenrose, "his next opponent will be the monarch of hell. The sinews of my arm would enable me to strangle you all like dogs. I tell you, Celwold, I come to claim my legacy, nor am I to be diverted from it. See, you have made me talk so passionately, that the lily which rears itself by your side seems ready to droop. Be not alarmed, sweet lady!— Beauty like your's would tame me, were I even a savage. Frown not on me, favourite of my departed friend, and gallant Mercia, for, tho' I have been wrought into vehemence, I know what degree of respect is due to you. Yet I will stand to my point:—Produce the will, Celwold, and let me have reparation."

"You demand an impossibility, rude sir,—your wishes cannot be complied with."

"Aye, say you so?—Let no man then, aver that your face is honest when you turn it towards him. Look you bloated and corrupt usurper of another's rights, justice *shall* be on my side; and if the will have been blown into the middle regions by the winds——"

"The winds!——"

"Aye; or should it be buried in the very centre of the earth, I will labour with these hands till I have dug it up again."

Celwold hastily quitted the hall, at the door leading to the inner apartments, and Martyn of Fenrose rushed out at the other end of it. The former was followed by William and his sister; and the latter, just as he passed over the bridge, was laid hold of by the hands of Mercia, who had run after him so hastily, that his breath was nearly suspended.

"What would you with me, noble youth?" said Martyn, smiling on his young detainer.

"Tell me," replied Mercia, "for heaven's sake, stranger, tell me why you have been thus open in your suspicions; why so unreserved in your accusations? What cause have you? What grounds to rest upon?"

"Hold, hold, excellent son of the thoughtless Githa! I am, at present, forbidden to answer you. I will hereafter lay every thing open as the face of heaven; but I cannot give greater activity to the wings of time, than that with which he has, for many ages, moved them. You have a friend; a true, a loving friend, around whom dangers are flying as thick as desert sands. His sister, too,——"

"Agatha! What, what of her?"

"You love her, Mercia; tho' you have never confessed it to any mortal, I know you love her with sincerity. She will partake of the perils of her brother. Adieu!"

"Stay, for God's sake stay! You fill me with fear and amazement. Speak to me farther. A few words more I entreat you. Agatha——"

"Stands on a perilous brink. Thunder clouds gather over her head; and threat'ning surges bellow near her feet. Be you as a guardian angel to her, and she may still be saved from destruction. Counteract the plots of a villain. Keep the edge of your sword sharp; and let not your eye often wink when Celwold is in view."

"Shall I ever see you again?" said Mercia, rapidly; "say yes, and be my comforter."

"Nay, I can answer you no further.—But we have met before. On the heath at Bartonmere I gave you a weapon. Do you not remember? "Fly, Mercia," I then said, "fly and let your arm drive this sword thro' the trunk of de Stacey.""

Mercia, in amazement, gazed on the face of Martyn of Fenrose, and saw in it features which he recollected with terror. His head became confused. For several minutes he was incapable of raising it from the trunk of a tree, against which it had fallen, and when he was able to look around him again, he found no person near.

During several succeeding weeks, the mind of Mercia was strongly impressed by this adventure. It slightly affected his health, and greatly damped the ardor of his spirits. In the fray at Bartonmere the giver of the sword appeared to him a most singular being; and after the battle, he had often thought of the stranger's words and actions, till he almost believed that he had been familiar with one who came from the regions of the dead. Martyn of Fenrose had added a thousand doubts and fears to those which had first been ingrafted. The thunder of his voice, the lightnings of his eye, his dreadful prophecies, and his searchings of the unrevealed mind, seemed to Mercia stretches beyond the limitations of human nature.

He wanted to speak of his suspicions, to acknowledge the dread he had been inspired with, and to hear those who were not ignorant, talk of things which he had hitherto derided as weak and fabulous. His former doubts were strengthened, and he thought Celwold more artful and infamous than he had previously supposed man possibly could be. The acknowledged heir of Alwynd was, he believed, the villain whose plots he was enjoined to counteract. The dangers that were crowding about William, alarmed Mercia as much as if he himself was actually surrounded by them; and what had been said of Agatha, caused him alternately to feel the ague of fear, and the fever of rage.

"Yes, Martyn of Fenrose," he cried, "yes, thou seeming man, but suspected spirit, I do, indeed, love the sweet and virtuous Agatha! Let all to whom innocence and beauty are dear, stretch forth their arms when she shall need protection. I am but one,—still to defend her from harm, to snatch her from injury, I would encounter a thousand ruffians, and fly to her, tho' a thousand swords might oppose me. Oh, God! Let the angels of thy confidence never, never forsake her! My affections are not new. They have been growing from my boyish days. Never may I marry, unless the priest shall give Agatha to me. Never may I be called father, if my children's rosy lips fasten not on her soft and delicate cheek."

He was thus speaking to himself, and fearfully ruminating on what had been predicted, when he was interrupted by the approach of Alwynd's successor, whom he avoided, and instantly departed from.

Celwold had been recently much agitated by the uncommon conduct and appearance of the disturber of Mercia's quiet. The vehemence and audacity of Martyn of Fenrose on the day of succession, had somewhat weakened his confidence; and many of Martyn's words seemed particularly to allude to those events, which Celwold had thought unknown to any person save himself. But he soon regained, in a considerable degree, his former ease and tranquillity.

Both William and Agatha spoke of Martyn as a lunatic. The servants believed him to be an idle impostor, and nothing that he had said was credited by any person who had listened to him, except by Mercia, whose eyes had seen most of the prodigy.

Celwold entered into his government with so much mildness and cunning, that wealth, which is often supposed to corrupt, seemed to have amended his heart. William and his sister felt not the dependance they had dreaded; their wishes were complied with, their wants anticipated, and they missed none of the respect that had been shewn to them while Alwynd lived. They thought of him who was gone from them with an unaffected regret, but resignation stilled the sorrows that were once so turbulent.

Peace was returning gradually to their minds; but it was afterwards checked in its progress, by the altered looks and manners of Mercia. They found him often strangely gazing on them. Sometimes he met and left them without speaking, sometimes he was almost incoherent in his words, and his behaviour towards Celwold was not less surprising. William and Agatha frequently spoke of these altered appearances, which both astonished and distressed them; and they resolved to question him so closely, that he would be compelled to acknowledge the occasion of them. This they did one morning when Celwold was not present.

"Tell me, Edward," cried William, "the cause of your late and present behaviour, which appears to me most extraordinary. Have I been so unfortunate, unhappy I might say, as to lose your esteem?"

"You never were dearer to me than you are at this moment," replied Mercia, "I never thought better of you, never regarded you with more affection than I now do."

"Then why must I notice your paleness and dejection? Why see you start and tremble? And tell me, I entreat you, the reason of your frequent sighs and agitations."

"Do, my dear friend!" cried Agatha, pressing his hand, "either confirm, or banish, the conjectures which we have passed to each other. You say my brother has not offended you; and surely I have done nothing to excite your displeasure. Often, of late, have I detected you in the act of gazing on me and my brother, in a manner which nearly frightened me. Reveal to us the cause of your altered conduct; and tell us why you, who were accustomed to sport and joy, have resigned yourself to melancholy and dejection?"

"Oh, William! Oh, Agatha!"

"What would you say? You are in agony! Speak, and ease your heart. Confide in me and my sister, as you have done on every past occasion."

"You urge me, urge me closely, and shall be satisfied. I dare not tell you of all those things which distress and incumber my heart, but of some of them I will speak without reserve or hesitation. I have, indeed, of late been miserable—more wretched than either of you can possibly conceive. I have lived in fear, in the most dreadful state of apprehension!—My days have been without peace, and my nights without rest!—Felons, in their cells, have enjoyed more happiness. You, William, and you, Agatha, have been the disturbers of my quiet."

"Oh, heaven forbid!" they both exclaimed.

"I have been told," continued Mercia, "that around one of you dangers are flying as thick as desert sands; and that thunder clouds gather over the head, and threat'ning surges bellow at the feet of the other. These are the very words that have been spoken to me.—Believing truth to be in them, I have often repeated them. For you, for you, my friends, have I suffered most severely."

Both Agatha and William were stricken with terror; they feared that his intellects were deranged, and entreated him not to think any more of the person who had so idly talked to him.

"Nay, be not too secure," he replied, "for I have listened to no common babbler. I know something of the man who spoke of you, which I should dread to confess.—Nothing is concealed from, nothing unknown to, Martyn of Fenrose."

"Martyn of Fenrose!" cried William, "a maniac!—a lunatic, extravagant as the winds, and wild as the sea."

"Gently, gently—speak not ill of him, for he may hear you."

"Why, where is he?" enquired Agatha, faintly.

"Every where.—I almost believe that he can ride in the air, and gather up the words of a thousand men, without attracting the notice of any one of them. Smile not, William, for, with my love of truth, I swear I could repeat things pertaining to him, that would chill the warm blood of your heart. He has spoken of Lord Celwold——"

"To whom I owe a thousand obligations," said William, "of whom I think most honourably."

"Of whom I charge you to beware," cried Mercia, "for if there be deceit in man, it is in Celwold's breast. He speaks you fair—and his looks are soft and gentle. You *had* a friend—Alwynd, I mean, as much unlike him who has stept into his place, as the supreme Spirit of Heaven is to the governing fiend of hell. I cannot root out my suspicions—cannot forget the prophecies of him who calls himself Martyn of Fenrose—cannot banish the dread of your coming miseries and present insecurity."

"You are disordered, Mercia," said Agatha, bursting into tears, "let me bind this handkerchief around your brows."

"Do you believe, dear girl, that I am mad?—I protest, since I had mind I never had more reason. I have been drawn into this conversation, and will now enlarge it, by telling you further why I am so strongly interested in your cause. William, I have ever considered you as my brother, and now, for the first time, confess my love for your sister; for Agatha, who stands beauteous and blushing before my eyes. Friends of my youth, I am sincere in my professions.—All that I expect of happiness I look for here. How I have so long concealed my strongest affections I scarcely know. But tell me both of you, and tell me without confusion, (for our friendship began not yesterday) whether you will approve of my alliance—and whether one of you will be willing to become my brother, the other my wife?"

"You amaze and confound me!" replied William. Agatha turned her crimsoned face towards the ground, and spoke not.

"After indulging myself," said Mercia, "with those delightful expectations, which, without my explanation you may conceive, are my apprehensions to be wondered at, when the most mysterious of beings talks of the perils and dangers that are about to assail you?—This Martyn of Fenrose—I met him on the heath at Bartonmere, and there——Oh, I dare speak of him no further!—Have I ever shewn myself a rash and illiberal censurer?—Has my disposition ever evinced uncharitableness?"

"May the tongue that shall say that of you, Mercia, become motionless, and remain so eternally!"

"Then here do I declare my strong belief of Celwold's villainy. Start not, doubt not. The confirmation that is coming to you, will, I fear, bring with it curses and sorrows. Be on your guard, William; and oh! how strictly will I watch over our Agatha!—But let me return to the subject on which I was preparing to speak."

"Spare me," cried Agatha, "suffer me to retire!"

"I cannot spare you—I must be both heard and answered. What I have confessed to you, I would, with pride, acknowledge to all the world. William, you are most closely connected with Agatha.—Sanction my affections, I entreat you; and join with me in requesting her to declare, whether she will allow me to hope that we may journey together thro' life in conjugal felicity."

"Hold!" cried William, "I cannot consent to this—I cannot sanction any thing so precipitate. You are a descendant of the Earls of Mercia. You might claim the daughters of our proudest peers; and, within a little while, you will be possessed of a fortune which cannot be equalled. You have honoured me with your friendship, and lived among us without pride. But now you have stooped too low; and God forbid that I should encourage, what you might soon regard with sorrow and repentance.—My Lord, I would have you say thus to yourself,—"Who is this Agatha?—What is her name?—Whence came she?—She is a stranger even to herself. She is simply Agatha, and has no proper appellation. No person owns her. No wealth——"

"Cruel and unjust William!" exclaimed Mercia, "can you suppose that I should ever act so meanly? Agatha is every thing to me, and all the circumstances you have alluded to, I do, and shall always disregard. To every man there is an object in the world, for which he raises his arm in transport. Agatha is the prize that would make me forego all other chances; but in the desired attainment of which I seem to be baffled by indifference."

"I cannot bear that reproach," cried Agatha, "and tho' prudence may tell me I ought not to listen to you, yet indifference—Oh, Mercia! How imperfect is your knowledge of my heart!"

She held forth her hand, and he prest it with ecstacy. William had no controul over the feelings of his friend, who again avowed the sincerity of his love; and protested that, if it should be met by the affections of Agatha, he would declare his sentiments to Lord Celwold, and cherish the hope of soon becoming what he had long since wished to be.

William, whose sense of honour never was inactive, would have expostulated further; but Lord Celwold approaching them, the subject was necessarily suspended. Mercia, considering the temper of his friend, was not displeased by the appearance of his guardian; and Agatha rejoiced at the opportunity she afterwards had of retiring to her chamber.

Her pleasures and pains were nearly equal. Simply as Edward, she had ever loved the man who possessed an unsuspected passion for her; but she had checked every presumptuous hope that wandered to the Earl of Mercia. Tho' his declaration had been heard with joy, and was retained by memory, yet prudence did not depart from her. She had not been less attentive to the language of her brother, than of her lover; and she rated the discretion of the one, as justly as the affections of the other.

"Let us be cautious and honourable in our proceedings, my dear sister," said William, when they were next alone. "The happiness of life rests weightily on self-approbation; and I should be loath to take a present benefit, at the expence of future repentance. Perhaps I do not, on all occasions, act with such nice precision! yet, in a case like this, my sister, I cannot be too thoughtful and deliberate. Mercia is a noble, a generous young man. I implicitly believe in all that he has said, for he is the loving son of Sincerity, and has ever righteously regarded his mother's precepts. I confess I should be most happy to call him brother; and, under different circumstances, to see him, what I will never expect, the husband of my Agatha. But think of his fortune—his ancestors; then of our poverty—our mortifying obscurity. I am sensible of the inequalities, and as no person has ever dared to accuse me with presumption, a scoff, a single reproach of that nature would wound me deeply like the sword of an enemy. Besides, Lord Celwold is our friend. In spite of the uncommon fancies, the prejudices, and, I may add, the strange infatuations of Mercia, I am assured he is our friend. May no imprudencies on our part, therefore, cause him to change his character. Let us, Agatha, regard the noble Mercia as we have been accustomed. Let us aim not at any thing which cannot be honourably acquired, and happily retained."

The affections of Mercia were not to be diverted by the opinions of William; they encreased daily, and Agatha became to him more precious. He had promised not to speak to her alone on the subject of his love; but he never saw her in the company of her brother, without entering into it, with an ardor which was not to be suppressed by either of their counsels. They could scarcely restrain him from avowing his sentiments to Lord Celwold, for he believed that punctilious scruples alone were against him; and that William and Agatha had, tho' they spoke not of it, grown stronger friends to him, since the day on which he made known his attachment.

He stood so firmly on the rock of Hope, that he could not easily be cast down; yet, tho' generally gay in his expectations, he was, for some considerable time, frequently disturbed by the prophecies of Martyn of Fenrose. At length, however, his apprehension of events decreased considerably; for every thing passed in a customary manner, and his threatened friends still lived and smiled unmolested by fate. He wished to believe Martyn the impostor that William had pronounced him, and sometimes nearly brought himself to that opinion.

There were periods, however, in which he reflected on the prophecy with unconquerable dread; and in which his big voice and gleaming eyes were remembered with strong astonishment and fear. William had ever sported with his credulity, of which he was nearly become ashamed; and Lord Celwold conducted himself with so much propriety, that his ward wished to think his suspicions had been too many, and his accusations too bold.

Summer was now yielding to the season of autumn, and Alwynd had been lying three months in the tomb, when Mercia went to see an old nobleman, the former friend of the late Earl, his father, and to whom the son had been accustomed to pay an annual visit.—William accompanied him, and they were absent nearly a fortnight.

On their return, it was with pain that they observed a great alteration in the looks of Agatha, who first hailed them with a wild pleasure, and afterwards sunk into dejection. They questioned her as to the cause, but she would make no answer to either of them. With a feigned composure, she pleaded a slight indisposition; and told them she did not doubt but that, in their society, her health and spirits would speedily be recalled.

William believed all that she said.—Mercia, however, regarded her with truly anxious eyes. He perceived that her cheeks were unusually pale, and her mind restless. He observed her attentively, both alone and in company.—He urged her to lessen his concern, by declaring what had thus affected her; and his returning fears would make him sometimes in private exclaim,—"The predictions of Martyn of Fenrose will yet be fulfilled!"

Her efforts to appear composed and happy he detected. He saw her generous artifice; and, after much watching and discrimination, perceived that when Celwold came near to her she was agitated—and also that she spoke not to him without faltering and blushing.

Mercia's spirits mounted at this evidence, and he could scarcely bridle them. His suspicions grew into belief; and he was almost rash enough to apply to Celwold for that information which he had, without being satisfied, demanded of Agatha. An event, however, happened, which not only deterred him from seeking the explanation, but also caused much surprise and confusion in the castle.

One evening, when Celwold and the young people were looking on the western prospect, which the hour and season made delightful, a distant horn announced the approach of visiters. The sound came on the gales; and at length a party of travellers spurred their coursers down the gentle declivities. The retinue was not small, and it bespoke much grandeur. In the front appeared two females, mounted on beautiful horses; the gilded harness was enriched by the sun, and the liveries of the followers, even at a distance, shewed their costliness.

Celwold left the apartment, and went down into the castle yard. Agatha was unwilling to meet the company for the present; and, attended by Mercia, she retired to the picture gallery, leaving her brother gazing on the unknown travellers. He stood at the window till they had come to the castle gates, and had been admitted. He then saw Lord Celwold, with a strong expression of surprise in his face, assist the elder woman, who appeared like a full summer rose, in dismounting; and afterwards give his hand to the younger, who came to the ground light as a zephyr.

Such beauties as the latter possessed, William had scarcely ever seen. He wished to view them at a smaller distance, he therefore hastened to his guardian, whom he met in the hall, and by whom he was introduced to Lady Githa Mercia and Mary Mortimer.

William was stepping towards the first presented lady, when

her name was spoken by Lord Celwold.—On hearing it, however, he drew back; astonishment nearly overpowered him, and his face crimsoned while he formally bowed to her. But his conduct to Mary was very different. He answered the sweet expressions of her face with smiles, and welcomed her to the castle with a grace that was peculiar to him.

Neither Lady Mercia nor Mary lost any of their beauties by being closely observed. The mother of Edward was possessed of a majestic person and admirable features; and the face of her companion was fair as lilies, and fresh as morning.

Lady Mercia had evidently married very young, for, at this time, she appeared scarcely more than thirty years of age. She walked with such a dignity as royalty generally assumes; and her full and vigorous mind seemed to dawn thro' her large and exquisitely bright eyes. There was little of maternal impatience in her looks.—She smiled on Lord Celwold, as he led her to an interior apartment; and Mary Mortimer gave her hand to William, who gazed on her with pleasure and modest admiration.

William soon discovered, by the language of Lord Celwold, that he had not expected his beautiful visiters, whom he again welcomed with a strong and animated hospitality.

"But I wish," he continued, "that I had been apprised of your coming, in order that I might have received your ladyship in a manner better suited to the rank of Earl Mercia's mother, and to the merits of her young companion."

"Mention it not," replied the Countess. "I shall probably continue your inmate for some considerable time; and the less ceremony I observe in your Lordship, the greater will be my comfort and ease. But Edward, my Lord? My son——"

"He shall be immediately apprised of your arrival," replied Celwold, "which I doubt not, will occasion much surprise and emotion. William, do you inform Lord Mercia of the circumstance. Prepare him by degrees, and bring him with you, to pay his respects to the Countess."

William bowed, and went, with a beating heart in search of his friend, whom he found returning from the gallery, in which he had just parted from Agatha. Mercia smiled, and enquired the names and qualities of the guests; but the question was so abrupt and perplexing to William, that he could not immediately find words to reply to it. Mercia laughed at his confusion, and continued to do so, till he learned that one of the women, whom he had seen approaching the castle, had brought him into the world, and afterwards cast him upon it, a weak and helpless stranger.

He would not believe what he heard, till it was more than once repeated; and even then, the effect of it was such as William had looked for. All the former resentments of Mercia fiercely returned. He was neither inclined to acknowledge his mother, nor to place himself before her.

"Let her away again," he cried, "let her return to France with all her late indifference. She has been so long neglectful of her duties, that she will make herself ridiculous in resuming them. Tell her this—tell it bluntly, and leave her to ruminate on it as she may."

William entreated him to send no such message, and begged that he would go to the Countess. But, for a long time, he urged in vain; and nearly half an hour had elapsed, when Mercia consented to a private interview, in a room which was called the cedar-parlour. William went down to the Countess, whom he conducted to the apartment Mercia had proposed to see her in; and there he left her to wait the appearance of her son.

She found herself neither easy, nor comfortable; for she had wished to meet him in the presence of a third person, and not to hear any reproaches, tho' she was conscious of deserving them. But during the few minutes she was alone, she regained her composure. She expected only the tears and murmurings of a boy, the puny offspring of a man whom she had despised.

Soon afterwards she heard some person entering, and looking towards the door, saw the handsome and finely formed Edward, standing near to it. She had not expected any such person, yet there were features in his face, which, to her shame and confusion, convinced her of his being her son.

His expectations, like her's, had not met the object; but he felt not her embarrassment. His cheeks grew red, his chest swelled, his eyes searched her deeply, and, with a strong voice, he exclaimed, "Do I see the widow of the late Earl, my father?"

"You do," she replied, "and I judge you are Edward, my son."

"How, madam? By what means? be not hasty in your decision.

Has your eye been familiar with my face? Have I features which your memory ever dwelt upon with any pleasure? An object rarely seen may, possibly be mistaken. You have only the report of men to govern your opinion; the instincts of nature direct you not. A woman, of whom I have no knowledge, comes hither, saying she is my mother. I am told of it, and may either believe or discredit the report. To her it has been said, your son shall be sent to you; and any person with whom she casually meets, is supposed to be of that connection which God has made so sweet and tender. Shame! Shame! to rest on such unworthy evidence!"

"Edward!" cried Lady Mercia, "Edward, your attack is cruel and severe. Come near, and take my blessings."

"Be not prodigal; I have not begged them of you. Last night I saw a peasant lad kneel before his mother, who turned her eyes towards Heaven, and placed her gentle hands upon his head. How I envied the boy! My heart has since taken in another set of feelings; and my knees will not bend when my mind approves not. Blessings, say you? Blessings should be spontaneous, growing out of devotion, and issuing on the wings of ecstacy. I like not things of early growth. They cannot stand the changes of seasons."

Lady Mercia sunk on a chair; her nerves vibrated when she heard the energetic tones of her son; and she placed her hand over her eyes.

"I know I have been to blame," she cried, "I confess my conduct has been highly censurable, and am most truly ashamed of it. Mercia, I never loved my husband—it was an unhappy union. I forgot him almost as soon as he was interred; and, tho' it was indeed unnatural, some of those sentiments which I bore for the father, attached to his unoffending child. But now, on my knees—here, at your feet, my son, do I entreat you to pardon me!—Do not throw me from you—do not turn your ears from my supplications.—Forgive, oh forgive me!"

She arose hastily, and sprung upon his neck. He felt her tears rolling into his breast, and they washed away his rage. He heard her sighs, and pitied them. He became what he had never been before; called her mother, and wept upon her bosom.

After conversing together nearly an hour, they went to their friends, who rejoiced at the reunion; when Mercia was introduced

to Mary Mortimer, and Agatha to Lady Mercia. Mary congratulated
the mother and son on their meeting. When her eyes encountered
those of the latter, they at once filled with tears, and glistened with
pleasure. Her joy seemed to be that of a loving sister; and she was
apparently desirous of saying something, which was forbidden by
the brows of Lady Mercia.

The next day Edward made some enquiries respecting the
blooming Mortimer. He was informed that she was the daughter
of an English gentleman, by a French lady of great beauty and
merit; and also that the death, and previous misfortunes of both
her parents, had caused his mother to adopt the young orphan.
Lady Mercia concluded, by speaking, with some degree of commendation, of the daughter of Mortimer; and by charging her son
not to converse with Mary on the subject of her birth and disasters,
which had never failed to occasion much emotion and sorrow.

The protection his mother afforded Mary, was greatly applauded
by the generous Mercia. It shewed that she possessed those excellent feelings of which he had believed her to be destitute; and he
thought less of his own neglect, after finding that the care of his
parent had been directed towards an object so lovely and deserving
as the gentle Mortimer.

Lady Mercia's conduct in regard to her son, was, at first, such
as claimed his filial love. His new created affections were exquisite.
He forgave her for her past, and loved her for her present conduct.
He looked not so deeply into the causes of human actions as he
had been accustomed to do. He admired the strength of his mother's mind, as well as the uncommon beauty of her person; and he
arose every morning, and ran thro' every day, with joy.

Lord Celwold was most attentive and polite to his visiters, and
always desirous of encreasing their pleasures. Agatha and Mary
were become true and tender friends; similar sentiments, affectionate hearts, and corresponding years had cemented their esteem,
and endeared the one of them to the other. William rejoiced at the
improved happiness of Mercia, and was not himself without his
felicities. He talked not so frequently of his dependant state—seldom spoke of his design to go into the world to amend his fortunes—and indulged himself so often in looking at the bright eyes,
and in listening to the voice of Mary Mortimer, that, at length, he

loved her as ardently and sincerely as Mercia did his sister.

His tongue was ever active in praising her, and he suffered not his passion to be checked by discretion. Mercia was a gainer by the captivity of his friend, who could not attempt to rouse any person from slavery, while he continued in it without struggling for his freedom.

Celwold's disposition appeared to have been greatly improved. He studied dress, talked complaisantly, gave feasts and entertainments, and was very sparing of those cant sentiments in which his dealings had previously been so liberal, and for which Mercia had been accustomed to despise him. The first interruption of this general happiness was occasioned by the declaration that Mercia made, of his passion for Agatha, to Lord Celwold; who not only heard him with surprise and displeasure, but immediately protested against the proposed union.

The warmth of the guardian and the minor encreased in equal degrees. The opposition of the one could not lessen the determination of the other; and when Celwold declared that the marriage should never have his sanction, Mercia calmly replied, that he would dispense with it, and yet complete his wishes.

Lady Mercia was apprised of this circumstance by Celwold; and, with all his prejudices, she undertook to talk to her son on his misapplied passion. The cool determination with which he answered, greatly irritated her; and he now discovered some traits of character that had not before been seen.

She spoke still more decidedly than Celwold; alluded, with no great delicacy, to the obscurity, poverty, and supposed demerits of Agatha; and was almost provoked to violent anger by the undisturbed smiles of her son. At length her qualities displayed themselves broadly—she became severe, illiberal, and grossly vindictive. Mercia smiled no longer—he viewed her as his quondam mother, not with his late filial tenderness, and his face crimsoned with displeasure.

"To whom have I been listening?" he cried, "from whom have these words proceeded?—From the Countess of Mercia, once esteemed by our English peers, for her sense and accomplishments, and since praised, for her high breeding and fashion, in the polite and glittering court of France!—Madam, your language is disgraceful; cleanse it of its foul particles, and deal out your words more sparingly, or your late actions will make you, in my eyes, an unworthy impostor. How can you lash misfortune with so much cruelty?—How can you contemn and grossly censure an object so innocent and unoffending as Agatha? If you continue this conduct, my eye may turn with severity again towards your past actions. If you say not,—'Welcome, daughter,' when I shall present Agatha to you as my wife——"

"That I will never do, haughty and presumptuous boy!"

"Then, madam, I will press her with more tenderness to my heart—love her ten-fold—and, with a full assurance of your insincerity, turn from you with indifference for ever."

Mercia immediately left the room; and his mother, whose rage nearly deprived her of her senses, went to Celwold, and repeated the foregoing conversation. It was owing to his advice, and to some projects they then formed, that Lady Mercia, when she again saw her son, seemed not only to have forgotten the late quarrel, but also to regard Agatha in her usual manner.

The disposition of Edward was naturally mild and forgiving; but he was neither a superficial observer of the human passions, nor weakly credulous when fair appearances were placed before him.

He no longer esteemed his mother.—In one little circumstance she had revealed her true character, which, stript of its disguise, he held to be odious, and accordingly contemned. It was principally to secure the peace of Agatha, and of her lovely friend Mary, who was, he observed, treated with a certain degree of severity and unkindness, by her who had vaunted of being a kind protector, that Mercia did not further shew his resentment. Undesirous, however, of promoting strife, he assumed a cool and artificial respect. Tho' his festivity ceased to display itself, he forbore to speak, either publicly or in private, except to the unreserved friend of his bosom, of his recent anger and mortifications. Neither Agatha nor Mary had the least knowledge of them; but from William nothing was with-held, and to him Mercia frequently expressed his disappointments and intentions.

"Would I had never seen this mother," he cried, "for I have strong suspicions, and scruple not to declare, that her tongue and heart do not accord. I will drop my accusations, but persecution shall not reach me. Before God, William, I here declare, that I will never marry any other woman than Agatha.—And let neither the heir of Alwynd, nor the widow of my father, whose past actions add not to their reputation, dare to oppose my just and honourable principles. I am a man, and will not regard their beckonings. We will be brothers, William.—All my desire is to live in happiness among the happy. My fortune may be with-held for some time, but, ere long, it must be resigned to me. Then we will enter into the felicities I have planned; and nothing will I partake but what you enjoy. Agatha shall be my wife; and may the fair Mortimer, whom you so truly love, be also your's. We will dwell in one house, resort to one purse, and thank our God, in an united prayer for his blessings, till we are divided, to meet no more beneath the heavens."

William listened with pleasure to this discourse. Before the appearance of Lady Mercia, he had blamed Edward's passion, and opposed his project; but now his own happiness was materially concerned, and the chance of acquiring the love of Mary, or rather of bringing her to a concession of it, seemed to depend, in part, upon his acquiescence to the sentiments and proposals of his firm and bounteous-minded friend.

Mary had been now nearly five months at the castle, still William never ventured to speak to her of the passion with which he had been inspired. He confessed it to his sister, whom he charged to make no discovery; but both Celwold and Lady Mercia remained as ignorant of it, as Mary herself. Indeed they were only objects of a secondary concern, to the guardian and mother, who, in plotting against the generous and undisguised Edward, had not leisure to think of beings who were rendered insignificant, by the adventitious circumstances of fortune and worldly casualties.

Soon afterwards, however, William made a declaration of his love to Mary, whom he had taken apart for that purpose. He spoke with hesitation and diffidence; and she listened to him with timidity and confusion.

"The affections of a poor man, sweet Mary!" he cried, "are all that I have to offer you. Mine is a naked love, and never can be approved by one who would treat it, as the world expresses it, discreetly. I have merely a heart to offer you; tho' the first hope of my soul is to be united to you, so destitute am I, that I have not a house to shelter you in, or a single jewel to place upon your bosom. Oh, call me not rash and presumptuous! Do not chide those affections that cannot be opposed, without I take upon myself eternal misery. Can you, Mary, esteem a man to whom your happiness is more precious than his own; whom fortune favours not; and who has no other parent or patroness to acknowledge, than nature? Ah, that look confesses it—that exquisite tear speaks a thousand virtues! I thank you Mary—I sincerely thank you!"

"Suffer me to depart," she said, "allow me to go to your sister."

"Evade not my questions, fair Mortimer, but answer them with your accustomed sincerity. If I have inferred too much from your sensibility—if you are not interested for me, in that degree which I flattered myself you were, tell me plainly that I have been deceived, and that my expectations ought to be no longer supported. Say only this to me, and I will fly from you, Mary, and never more place myself before you; in order that, if my own departed happiness should prove irreclaimable, I may not be the disturber of your's."

"You compel me to speak," said Mary, blushing and smiling, "but you must pardon me for being brief. I am your most sincere friend, and fully sensible of your goodness. May your past misfortunes be compensated by years of happiness and content. No man has ever spoken to me as you have done; and many of your wishes are answered by mine——"

"Charming Mortimer! Beloved Mary!"

"Yet hear me further.—Friendship is a barrier beyond which I must not attempt to stray. All that I can perform on this side of it, shall be done willingly and sincerely. I am so situated that I may possibly run into an indiscretion before I am aware of it. Tempt me not, therefore, if honour and virtue be dear to you. Forget me, William—"

"Never, never!—While I have memory you must live in it."

"Then let me dwell there in gentleness.—Look on and love me only as your sister."

"As the partner of my heart!—As my adored wife!"

"Ah, William! in a character like that I can never appear. You bring many sorrows to my heart—many distresses to my mind. Is there not one person in the world in whom I can confide?—Must I, by unnatural force, be restrained from shewing my truest friends, that I possess a heart neither callous nor unfeeling?"

"What do you mean, Mary?—Confide in me."

"Oh, I dare not!—Never ask me again.—You make me shrink from myself. That which torments me must ever be confined to my own bosom. I want to communicate, but am imperiously restrained.—Many times do I find myself flying, with forbidden words upon my tongue, to Mercia——"

"Mercia!"

"When I am stopt by recollection.—I pause, my mind works painfully, tears roll down my heated cheeks, and his mother seems to threaten me. Agatha is happier—you are happier than the creature that now stands before you. I estimate the felicities of human life, and err not when I reckon my own large portion of them. I must retire—my heart is oppressed, and the friendship of Agatha must ease it."

She immediately left the room, and William remained in grief and amazement. Mary was inexplicable, strange, and mysterious. He could not understand her words, which had been spoken rapidly, and with visible pain. For a long time he pondered over them; and at length concluded, that her heart was attached to Mercia, and that she was terrified lest his haughty mother should discover it. The suspicion rushed on his mind, and fixed there; it oppressed, it even tortured him; and the sudden destruction of his hopes, for a few minutes, nearly deprived him of strength and sense.

He repeated the words of Mary till they seemed no longer equivocal; and what she had said was now unambiguous, amounting to a declaration of an unsolicited and apprehensive love. That her affections should arbitrarily resort to an object so amiable, he could not, examining his own feelings, censure her for; but that she should so strongly allude to it, before the brother of a woman, who had prior and allowable pretensions—before him who was then pleading an anxious and sincere passion—seemed an indelicacy, which he had not previously believed to pertain to Mary Mortimer.

Nothing can withstand the force of jealousy; nothing has equal

means of making the actions of man so inconsistent and ungenerous. William looked with fond eyes on what he frequently strove
to regard with indifference; and to the best and truest of friends
he became cold and reserved. Mercia often enquired the cause of
the extraordinary change, but was always answered merely by a
sullen smile. William shunned both him and Mary. In an agonized
moment he fully disclosed his mind to his sister, and, unmindful
of her repose, as well as his own, stimulated her to become a close
observer of Mary's actions.

Agatha trembled and faded at the intelligence. She feared the
loss of something which it was precious to retain, began her obser-
vations with uneasiness, and continued them with apprehension.
Wherever Mary went, she followed; whatever she said or did, was
both noticed and commented on; and it was not long before she
believed that William had not been deceived.

The awe with which Mary had ever regarded Lady Mercia
seemed to have encreased; and that she loved her son was palpable. When he was absent, she was ever wishing for him; in her
impatience she often went in search of him; but on his approach,
her cheeks gathered up their roses, and she appeared desirous of
throwing herself into his arms.

The esteem of the good and virtuous is ever enviable. Mercia
was pleased by the soft accents and enchanting smiles of Mary; he
loved to hear her unaffected talk, and, when the Countess was not
near to observe them, they often came before William and Agatha
in the happiest mood.

At length Mercia was offended by the obstinacy of William,
who would not account for his singular conduct, and also alarmed
by the behaviour of Agatha, whose love seemed of a perishable
nature. Her face no longer had the boast of health. He suspected
that either his mother or Lord Celwold, had been busy with her
quiet; but he perceived that both of them treated her in their
accustomed manner, tho' at intervals, he thought he saw the latter
taking up again some of his former hypocrisy.

The distress of Agatha exceeded that of her brother; that irresistible passion, which is formed out of the tenderest, and partakes
of the deadliest, found a passage into her bosom, which bled while
it opened to the fiend-like stranger. She saw with agony the atten-

tions which Mercia paid to Mary, and accused the latter, who had been in her confidence, with levity and dissimulation. William first communicated his disappointments to her, and she now poured her complaints into his ear, while every new hour brought to her shame and vexation.

One day she found herself alone with Mary Mortimer, who, in order to banish the melancholy of her friend, took up a lute, and played some old gallic tunes with great taste and feeling. She touched the strings with an exquisite finger, flying from the simple and pathetic to the wild and irregular. Agatha, whose heart was but a little vitiated, applauded the talents which she admired; and one of the airs was so expressively composed and charmingly executed, that the tones of the instrument, as well as the accompanying voice of the performer, had a strange effect on Agatha. This Mary saw, and she instantly struck up a lively madrigal; but turning her head towards the window, she perceived Mercia approaching the castle.

She threw aside her instrument, and gazed on him with a strong expression of love. The month was January—the day, however, was remarkably fine and clear. The quick exercise of Mercia made an additional covering unnecessary, his exquisite form was therefore disencumbered, and roses seemed to overspread his cheeks.

"He comes!" cried Mary, "see, Agatha, he comes!—How beautiful he is in person!—How noble in his mind!—Every body must admire, every body esteem him—and oh, Agatha, how dearly do I love him!"

"Love him, Mary?" said Agatha, faintly.

"Life is not dearer to me. Why did I not know him before?—My heart ever springs to be near him; and my arms——Oh, Agatha! Why am I not allowed to say more?"

"Enough—this is enough!" cried Agatha, breaking from her, and running to the other side of the room. At that moment Lady Mercia entered. Mary walked from the window—pleasure fled from her eyes, and she looked at her severe protectress with her usual diffidence.

In the evening of the same day, Agatha imparted the confession of Mary to her brother; and as it affected the happiness of both, it was repeated and heard with reciprocal pain.

"Sister!" cried William, "sister, let us act in the manner I now propose—which is, for you to tell Mary that you will not stand between her love; and for me to assure Mercia, that I will forego all claim, and calmly resign her to him. That his mother will ever consent to his marriage with Mortimer's daughter, is very improbable. Of that, however, we need not think—we have only to perform our duties. To live where Mary is will be impossible, I will, therefore, go from hence; and as a temporary residence elsewhere, may be more pleasant to you than continuing here, I will solicit the hospitality of Lord Bartonmere, and conduct you to him in the early part of the ensuing week. Lady Mercia will be pleased by the removal of two such objects; Lord Celwold will approve our conduct; Mercia, freed from the sister of the humble William, may bear himself according to his wishes; and Mary——Oh, Agatha, what a sacrifice am I making!"

"You are indeed, William!—One of the victims must be torn from my breast!"

Her sighs were heavy, and her pangs severe; but she acceded to his proposals, and promised to conform to his directions.

Within a few hours, they entered into this perplexing business. William took Mercia apart, when he explained to him the cause of his late conduct, and spoke of those things which he had previously mentioned to his sister. He was greatly affected; he prest the hands of Mercia, dropt tears upon them, and wished him eternal happiness.

But he was exceedingly surprised by the reply and actions of his friend, who assured him that his eyes, and all his senses, must have been strangely deceived. Mercia solemnly protested, that he had never regarded or spoken to Mary, only with the allowable kindness of friendship. Agatha, he added, reserved as she had lately been, was never more truly beloved by him; and he protested, that all his happiness rested on the hopes he had long since formed of being united to her.

William was partly relieved from his pangs; yet many of them still oppressed him. He repeated the short conversation, that had passed between his sister and Mary; but Mercia insisted, that such part of it as pertained to the latter had been misunderstood. William was not yet satisfied, tho' Mercia entreated him to leave the paths of jealousy, and return to those of love and friendship.

Agatha began the business that had been assigned to her, with pain and anxiety. The renunciation that she was about to make afflicted her heart, and when she saw Mary, she found her so tender and sweetly disposed, that it was long before she dared to enter into the premeditated subject. Afterwards, growing somewhat more resolute, she recurred to the conversation that had so recently distressed her; and, with a forced and artificial smile, told Mary, that she would voluntarily yield up to her the heart of the changed Mercia. She was heard with astonishment; Mary interrupted her not, while she was speaking, but burst into tears when she became silent.

"Never," she cried, "never have I been more debased and humbled. O, Agatha! I expected not this from you. What have you seen in my looks, what discovered in my actions, to cause you to think meanly and ungenerously of me? I have witnessed your partiality to Mercia—you have even confessed it to me. In your absence he has spoken ardently in your praise, and also told me, that he regarded you as the most precious object in the world. Not an hour has passed since he talked to me, of his love for Agatha;—since he mourned that her affections no longer rested on him. I have ever believed that jealousy makes levity its first criterion; but if aught of that has been discovered in my nature, may the finger of derision point at me for ever."

"Say no more," cried Agatha, in confusion, "you cover me with shame—you make me open my eyes to my own unworthiness."

"I must proceed," said Mary, "I must be fully vindicated. Reputation is my sole inheritance; and, I confess, I would be tenacious in preserving it. Perhaps I have not spoken of Mercia, according to rule and custom; and, indeed, when I talked of him, at the time you have alluded to, it was with a warm, a glowing heart. I again aver that I love him; my affections are boundless; and I would have none of them concealed, except from one person, of whom I must ever stand in fear. I name him in my morning prayers, and, every night, recommend him to the favour of Heaven. Speak not, Agatha—I know that it is that causes the colour of our cheeks to vary. Yet hear my solemn declaration; was the heart of Mercia at liberty, and offered to me in terms of marriage, I should instantly reject it. My sentiments are not such as would lead to an union with him. May I be so happy as to be eternally his friend; but his wife—Agatha, how greatly you have been deceived! In spite of the prejudices of his mother, I still hope to be at the altar, when he shall call you his own. I shall then embrace both of you with joy, and ever after regard you with pleasure and content."

Agatha rushed into Mary's arms, and wept upon her bosom. The painful illusion was over; jealousy left her in shame; and the playful fingers of love plucked out the thorns that so cruelly wounded her.

Before the day had passed, the vexations and concern of all the young people were removed. The general reconciliation was tender and affecting, and not a doubt remained in the mind of any of them. Even the rejected William wore his usual smiles. The conduct and looks of Mary led him to hope that his late disappointments would be forgotten in his future successes; and it was not long before Mary confessed to Agatha, that his assiduities made him appear to her an object of great worth and merit.

The visit of Lady Mercia had been long, and she talked not yet of departing. She and Lord Celwold appeared to possess each other's confidence. She had not ceased to remember the spirit with which her son had lately addressed her, yet she continued to treat him with respect, particularly when any observers were around them.

Her dislike to Agatha encreased—still she secretly demanded the aid of hypocrisy; and not only smiled, while her heart was rancorous, but lied, while she ingeniously fastened on the mask of sincerity. At her command, she could call many beauties to her face; and it was deeply to be regretted, that so much loveliness should pertain to so small a number of virtues.

Mercia was not pleased with her long continuance. Had it not been for the society of Mary Mortimer, he could have wished her to return to France, or to take herself to whatever distant place she might choose.

It was his chief pleasure and consolation to talk with William of those things, on which his mind dwelt at all times and seasons. But he was surprised on seeing that his friend sometimes viewed him strangely, and seemed as if he were anxious to speak on a subject which he feared was unallowable.

Mercia noticed this to him, when he simply enquired,—"Why am I not in your confidence?"

"Respecting what, or whom?" said Mercia.—"I have not a thought, or wish, that I should scruple to make known to you."

"Then why have you been so silent in regard to the condition of your mother?"

"The condition of my mother!—You amaze me!—Pray explain further."

"Nay, I only allude, my friend, to her connection with Lord Cel-wold. If I do wrong, pray pardon me. You may, indeed, think me impertinent for having spoken of it to you."

"What does all this mean, William?—I solemnly declare I know not."

"Are you really unacquainted that Lord Celwold and your mother——I fear I have been too busy. I am surprised at your want of information, and shall say no more. Lady Mercia will never be guilty of an act of dishonour."

"William will never be my sincere friend if he does not explain the mystery he has alluded to. My spirits are up, and your words have roused me. My mother is a woman, who——If you love me, you will speak of her as you think."

"O, I was jesting, Edward, merely jesting. My horse is prepared to carry me over the forest—Will you go with me?"

"No—I can neither accompany nor allow you to go alone. Jest-ing!—Come, come, deal ingenuously, and treat your friend as he deserves. My mother and Lord Celwold!—By the eternal——I implore you, William, to tell me your meaning."

"You rave at trifles—you will not be calm. It is absolutely danger-ous to talk with you, except on the most common of subjects."

"I will bear this reproof, bear any thing with true patience. I will not speak, or even look at you.—Only proceed."

"Remember your promise, then, and keep it. I do not believe there is a heart among us that wants integrity, and will therefore gratify you. You know my chamber is distant from, and that I have seldom any occasion to go near to Lord Celwold's. The other night, however, being little inclined to sleep, I left my room, and went into the picture gallery. My intention was, to look at the resemblance of that excellent man, who must ever live in my heart and memory, and of whom I had been pensively thinking. I had scarcely reached the gallery, when the lamp fell from my hand, and I found myself exceedingly perplexed by being in darkness. Within a few minutes, however, I saw a light in the passage, at the further end, and supposing, by the lateness of the hour, that one of the servants was there, I went forward, and saw——"

"I guess at it!—But, go on.—Whom did you see?"

"Lady Mercia, in her night-dress, at the door of Lord Celwold's apartment. He met her there.—She entered; and I returned in amazement to my chamber."

"Were you awake?—Were you not dreaming?—Did you not mistake the person of the midnight visiter?—Are you sure, perfectly sure it was Mercia's widow?"

"I could swear it. Two nights since have I watched her to the gallery, for I was amazed by such strange appearances."

"May the blood of the harlot stagnate, and the bones of her paramour quickly decay!—May they meet again to-night, and be blasted by lightnings in the very act of wantonness!—No, I will go to them instantly and pierce both bodies with my sword, and find pleasure in accelerating the vengeance of hell!"

"Hold, mad-man!—Desist!—The wretch who foamed and stormed for his legacy, was an hundred times more reasonable than you. Is this my friend Edward?—Oh, recollect yourself, and let me have some marks for remembrance."

"You may detain me now, William, and call me by whatever name you please. But, by the ruler of the world of angels, I will level all my rage and resentment at these smiling devils.—What! commit their impurities while I am almost near enough to hear their breathings?—Oh, I shall go mad, indeed!"

"I will remain with you no longer—I am afraid of you; and your fever may be contagious."

"Stay! for God's sake, stay!—I dare not continue here alone. My thoughts and temptations are horrible. If you would prevent the shedding of human blood, I conjure you not to leave me."

"And who has invested you with the sword of death?—Who delegated you to be such a tremendous judge?—Whence comes your authority?—Recal your reason, banish your presumption, and ask pardon of him from whom you would, impiously, snatch the scourge, which you know not how to exercise."

"You know not what it is to have a polluted mother, smiling under your eyes."

"And dare you say such is the case with you?—Will you heap shame and infamy on a person who may still walk in the paths of integrity?—Mercia, I must severely blame you for your impetuosity and rudeness of speech. Lord Celwold is a man of honour; and Lady Mercia's virtue, whatever appearances may have been, will yet be found unimpeachable. I cannot suppose that you will be inactive in this business; but I charge you to investigate with calmness, to treat your mother with respect, and to let neither your blood heat with passion, nor your uncurbed tongue to become *licentious*."

Mercia was struck with these strong reproaches; he immediately gathered in the meaning of his friend, and blushed at the language he had used.

The remainder of the day, however, was tormenting to him; and he had not been long separated from William before his mind turned again to the most disgusting of subjects. Loving as he did, he scarcely noticed the smiles of Agatha.—The voice of Mary was not attended to; and William's looks of caution were soon disregarded.

His eyes were alternately on Celwold and his mother; he misconstrued even their common civilities, and fancied that he saw guilt in all their actions. He scarcely tasted food at dinner; he raised his goblet merely to glance more secretly at the objects of his hatred; and while they emptied their glasses, he considered them as designedly priming their accursed voluptuousness. The words of Celwold seemed to him as guileful as those of the devil; and the smiles of his mother as odious as the ghastly aspect of death.

In the evening it was proposed, that they should hear music in the hall; and orders were given that the harper should attend on them. Lady Mercia commanded Mary to prepare her lute; and Agatha promised to sing her favourite ballads, accompanied by the instrument of her friend.

"And what part will you, Lord Mercia, take in our amusement?" enquired his mother.

"None, madam," he replied, "when the minstrel is diseased, he

can produce no true melody. The noise would be too much for my
head, in its present state; my eyes could not bear the glare of the
torches; and should your Ladyship be boisterous in your mirth, I
might, perhaps, be rude enough——"

"Sir, that you now are."

"Pardon me, my good mother; I meant not thus to offend you.
My brain seems giddy; were the groom and the chaplain here, I
might, probably, talk to the former on the observance of our reli-
gious duties, and teach the latter the best mode of polishing the skin
of my horse; but I will to bed, and sleep away my pain. Good night,
mother. My Lord and guardian, may your repose be soft and undisturbed. Agatha, God's blessings on you; and on you, too, Mary!
William, we will breathe our horses together in the morning."

"Nay, do not leave us thus early," said Celwold.

"I must, my Lord; but should I, in the way to my chamber,
meet that ingenious gentleman, to whom your Lordship annually
gives, besides other presents, a cap of music, and a stocking of
scarlet, I will send him to take my vacant chair; and then your
Lordship will not even suppose me absent."

Mercia immediately retired, and every person was struck by
the singularity of his temper. Celwold crimsoned with anger on
hearing his last ironic speech, and Lady Mercia, enlarging her
voice, protested that she would no longer bear such spleen and
insolence.

The proposed entertainment was countermanded. Agatha and
Mary retired in concern; and William hastened to the chamber of
Mercia, to whom he spoke in terms of unreserved censure and
displeasure.

"There may, indeed, be justice, in what you say," he replied,
"but, as I cannot bring myself to the belief of it, I am still distant
from conviction. How useless to oppose your feelings to mine!
Of what importance is the nature of facts to you? You are, in this
case, of the multitude only; but I stand an individual, whose fame,
whose honour, and whose peace of mind, rest on an untried and
fearful point. Leave me to myself, William; here will I remain till
to-morrow; and then, should I not find a satisfactory explanation
of the present doubtful circumstances, may the spirit of my father
strangle me in savageness, if I am not amply revenged."

William wished to stay with him, but he would not suffer it. He partly undressed himself, drew the curtains around him, and would neither speak, nor lift up his head again, till William had left the room.

In restlessness and anxiety he lay a long time, and did not rise from his bed till twelve o'clock. He heard no noise whatever, except such as he made himself. He put on his cloaths, opened the door gently, and went towards the chamber of his unreserved mother. His lamp was nearly extinguished, and he could not brighten the flame. The moon, however, shining thro' the windows, was, in many places, serviceable to him; and he gained the station, without making the least disturbance.

He stopt at the door, and applied his ear to it; when he distinctly heard the breathings of some person, who slumbered within. Concluding that it was his mother who slept so soundly, a hope that William had been strangely deceived, entered his mind. But it did not long abide there; and wishing to make every possible discovery, that the season could afford, he crept, with uncovered feet, along the gallery, till he came to the apartment of Celwold.

This place was more silent than that he had left.—"Still my mother may be innocent," he inwardly said, "and I a licentious villain." A few minutes afterwards, however, Lord Celwold spoke, and was answered by some person in his chamber.

It was the voice of a woman. Mercia started, and put his ear still closer to the pannel; but he merely heard his guardian utter some loose and extravagant words, which were answered by his companion only with a partly supprest laugh. Still he had no assurance of its being his mother; and, indeed, there was some small degree of evidence to the contrary.

His heart panted—he wished to break into the room, and at once satisfy all his doubts. But he had still reason enough to estimate the madness of such an action; and, as the unknown wanton and her lover now became silent as inanimation, Mercia softly seated himself near a window in the gallery, he being determined to watch for the breaking up of the clandestine meeting.

He thought the time of darkness very long, and when the morning appeared, his heart almost seemed to leap from his bosom. He praised not heaven for sending of light, and shut his eyes against the mild rays of the rising sun. He was nearly as cold and cheerless as if he had, naked and unhoused, borne the buffetings of a December night.

He heard a noise in the chamber, and sprung lightly upon his legs, tho' he was scarcely sensible of treading on any thing. A bolt was slipped—the door opened, and a woman came out of it, attended by Lord Celwold, who was only slightly covered. Mercia hesitated not a moment longer, but caught the female in his arms. She shrieked aloud. He tore her spread hands from her face, and recognised his guilty mother.

He was now convinced, and dashed her indignantly on the floor. The wild spirit again took possession of him; and tho' he had no weapon, and knew that the chamber contained several instruments of defence, yet he struggled fiercely with Celwold, whom he soon secured under his swelling hands.

Perceiving that his mother was endeavouring to get away, he left his captive for an instant, and shut the door in violence; but before Celwold could rise, he had returned, and doubled his security.

"Never," he cried, "I swear by the God who made me, that you shall never stand erect again, till you have told me, on what authority you entered into this secret intercourse. I will remain here eternally, famish, and moulder, unless I have answers from both of you."

"Attempt not to expose me," cried Lady Mercia, "villain, let me pass to my chamber!"

"No, my virtuous mother! you shall not go beyond the reach of my arm till I am satisfied. Expose you!—O, then you wish to retain the mask of reputation, tho' you so well are known to me. Villain!—Call me so again, and I will proclaim your infamy aloud—speak of it every where—and teach the dirtiest fellows of the stable to crook their fingers at you in derision."

"Release me," cried Celwold, "only release me, and I promise to mitigate these seeming offences."

"Offences!" exclaimed Lady Mercia, "and supplications to that baby champion!—Rise, my Lord,—free yourself. Pluck down the beardless piece of vanity, and chastise the shameful—the unnatural monster, that thus insults and abuses your wife."

"His wife!" cried Mercia.—"And who made you so?"

"May my tongue loosen at the roots if I gratify you!" replied the half frenzied mother.—"Cursed be the hour in which I gave life to such an envenomed serpent!"

"Hold!" cried the prostrate Celwold, "hold, both of you, and let me be heard. Take your hands from me, Mercia, and you shall be satisfied."

"I *will* be satisfied—I have already sworn it. Rise, and be explicit."

"You will repent this violence hereafter, and blush at your own barbarity. My intercourse with your mother is sanctioned—for a month has nearly elapsed since I became her husband."

"Refer me to some person who will speak to the truth of this. Who married you to Earl Mercia's widow?"

"Godfrey Bolingbroke, the chaplain. Now are you satisfied?"

"No, I must see and speak to Godfrey before I enter into other business. But tell me why, being married, your wife should nightly steal, like a harlot, to your bed?—Aye, colour, madam, at the name. And why, in society you live distinctly, and under different names, when the forms of the world, and the actions of the virtuous are ever contrary?"

"I have many reasons for my conduct, of a weighty and most important nature, none of which I can at present explain. Our union has, indeed, been secret, and so, for a while, it must remain."

"Not a single hour.—Having avowed it to me, I will be your herald on this occasion. Madam, you see, by the interest I take in your concerns, that you are not an object of indifference to me. What an odious epithet is sometimes placed on woman!—It shall not rest on my father's widow any longer. Go, and put on some proper covering—smooth your angry brow—and prepare yourself to smile upon those who shall heap their congratulations on you. Tell me not of secrecy, for, in a cause like this, my voice shall be free and unrestrained as the winds."

He ran to the chamber of the chaplain, who was not risen; and placing himself on the bed, asked the surprised man, whether he had not married Lord Celwold to his mother. This Bolingbroke denied; but Mercia informing him of the confession of the parties, he at length acknowledged it.

Mercia, having cursed him for his hypocrisy, hastened to the hall. He tolled a large bell, which was used for no other purpose, than that of assembling the household, on sudden and particular occasions. In less than a quarter of an hour he found all the domestics gathered together, and William standing by his side.

"Such of you," he cried, "as love your Lord, and respect Lady Mercia, remain where you are; and let the others depart. They are coming among you, in new characters—as man and wife. Treat them, therefore, accordingly.—If you have any flowers, maidens, throw them here; and I would have you all observe the usual customs, and spend the time till night in feasting and merriment. William, we will not ride today. Bring hither your sister and Mary, to greet Lord Celwold and his wife."

He then went to the apartment of his mother, and found that her woman had put on her a costly robe; but her face changed its colour alternately, and she closed her eyes, as if in abhorrence, when her son approached her.

"I am come, madam," he cried, "to wait on you and your husband to the hall, where the surprised domestics will pay their duty and respects to you. I can forget all that you have said, and, if you are inclined to bestow it, will ask your forgiveness for what I have done; yet I speak not in extenuation of the business itself; but merely of my passionate conduct, on which alone I would make the least apology. By the holiness of truth, I vow, I should not repent of any thing that I have performed, had it been with somewhat more gentleness. Come, madam, your hand."

She gave it to him, but made no reply; and he led her into the gallery, where they were met by Lord Celwold, who had been apprised of the young enthusiast's last actions. It was vain to oppose so much resolution; they therefore proceeded to the hall, where they were received with acclamations.

Agatha and Mary were there, and with marks of astonishment fixed on both their faces. The latter appeared in extreme confusion, and could scarcely repeat the words which the former addressed to the bride. Lord Celwold heard the wishes of his friends and dependants with a feigned respect and thankfulness. Tho' he detested the son of his acknowledged wife, whose impetuous spirit had vaulted so high, yet he could not bear the irresistible force of his scrutinizing eye.

Githa had to struggle violently with her passions, and to cast her smiles around her, while rage was shut within her breast. She retired as soon as possible; but as she declined, for the present, the attendance of Mary and Agatha, Mercia led her from the hall to her chamber. She then dropt upon a seat, and, for the first time, during a long period, shed a most copious shower of tears. Mercia softened, yet sunk not into weakness.

"Having seen you acknowledged as the wife of Lord Celwold," he cried, "some of my wishes have been gratified. Though I approve not your choice, I would have you live in content and happiness. If you are satisfied, I shall be silent. I have no concern in your affections and opinions, neither have you any in mine. Nature once bound us together; but, I find we must be separate and distinct. Madam, I have been hurried on by honour, and the feelings of a warm heart. Your opposition, and your husband's duplicity, strongly actuated me in my dealings and expressions. But your own words and conduct were equally unreasonable. Forget what passed between us this morning, slight not the common festivity of the day; and let our altercation be known only to ourselves. Truth is a deity, and I will worship her. Lord Celwold's motives for concealing his marriage, I am convinced, are puerile; and should any unpleasant events ensue in consequence of its being divulged, they must be less weighty than foul accusations of the tongues of men, or the obscenity of the watchful and suspicious."

He then went out of the room, leaving her still weeping, with her face concealed by the train of her robe.

William had talked with his sister and Mary on the uncommon event with which they had become acquainted. They knew that Mercia had many antipathies to oppose, and therefore spoke only in general terms, of his mother's marriage, when he appeared among them.

The servants, agreeable to the orders they had received, held the day as a festival; and about noon, Celwold and his wife again shewed themselves. Mercia viewed them at a distance; but the rest of the young people gathered around them. William rejoiced that the mother of his friend still retained her honour. Agatha expressed an uncommon degree of pleasure at the union, tho' she wished the smiles of her lover to go with her own.

Mary Mortimer displayed more surprise than joy; and seemed to entertain a strange dread of the frowns of her protectress. Celwold strove to be free, festive, and amusing. He gave much of his notice to Mercia, whom he frequently addressed by the name of son; and to his fair partner, whose eye was no longer red with passion, he was assiduously kind and tender.

From this day many alterations took place in the castle. The union that had been so curiously concealed, was now made known abroad; and Celwold, who had formerly been distinguished by an œconomy bordering on parsimony, gave frequent and costly entertainments. He filled the hall with nightly visiters, and freely opened his gates to those who sought joy and festivity. His wife went before him in the path of pleasure; and none of her thoughts seemed to dwell on her late mortification.

She formed new friendships, studied dress, entered giddily into many excesses, and sported her wit somewhat too freely with the men. Her son she no longer noticed, except as a person of general acquaintance; for she was too implacable in her resentments to pardon his late actions, and he always appeared to her an object of contempt.

She treated Agatha in a manner which was both intended and found to be mortifying. In speaking of her she was venomously obscure; and the stare of consequence was frequently directed towards the meritorious girl. Agatha's dislike to her encreased every hour; but she would neither confess it to Mercia, nor speak of it to Mary Mortimer, who had infinite cause for complaint; her disposition became more rude and arbitrary.

These matrimonial disputes were not confined to the closet— they were often indelicately carried on when the young people were present; and it was well known that they had forsaken the nuptial bed, and returned to their singleness. Mercia loved them too little to be pained by their infelicities, which arose from their own frailties and absurdities; and he neither reproved, nor attempted to soften their asperities.

The original cause of their bickerings they did not seem willing to explain. It was, however, easily learned, that Celwold's dissatisfaction sprung partly from jealousy, and partly from waste of treasure; and also that his wife contemned him for the poverty of his spirit and narrowness of soul. Mercia talked with his friends on this unpleasant subject, and vowed that he would attempt either to expedite his succession to the property of his father, or to wrest the temporary power from Celwold, and have it placed in some person whom he could more esteem and confide in.

The dissentions of his mother and guardian disturbed, rather than afflicted him; but one night, during supper, their vicious conduct filled him with disgust and rage. They began the conversation with spleen, and continued it with encreasing acrimony. The sarcastic remark gave place to the deep insinuation. Celwold not only wished that he had never seen her, but joined her name so closely to that of a nobleman, whose visits had of late been very frequent at the castle, that honour could find no space to stand between them.

The face of Mercia seemed composed of burning matter; and his mother, wild, and bursting with ire, sprung from her seat, and menaced her husband with fiery eyes. His passions however were not to be checked; and he proceeded in his accusations.

"Villain!" she exclaimed, "mean, abominable villain! I will now strip the mask from you; though I must betray myself I will do it. I loathe, I despise you; and my only consolation is, that I can free myself from such a detestable wretch—that I am not actually your wife!"

"Have a care!"

"Of what? Of whom? Think you I stand in fear of any person, who shall hear this declaration? No, by Heaven I set no value on any of you; I am my own mistress, and will not be restrained—I neither want approvers, nor dread any censurers. Here, among you all, do I exult in my freedom! Here, rejoice that, in acting as I wished, I imposed nothing on myself, but what I can readily discard."

"Dare you," cried Mercia, "dare you affirm that you are not his wife?"

"Aye, noble sir! I dare; I do. His wife! Sink me to nothingness, before you make me so despicable a thing as that. His wife! Oh, I should laugh most heartily, if it were not for the presence of all these well-bred observers. Mercia, you lately said that nature once bound us together, but that we must be now separate and distinct.

Why, therefore, should you presume to question, or look so savagely on one, who can be nothing more to you than any other being that serves to encrease the number of the world?"

"Infamous and disgraceful woman! Fly from me, as far as there can be space between us."

"At present not a step—I will not move a foot to please you. In the morning, however, I shall depart; till then check your savage disposition, and restrain your curses. The discovery of my intercourse with this winterly piece of dignity—this Lord, with a herdsman's soul, was made by you. Could you not see through the artifice I then adopted? Could you believe that my free spirits would long associate with his sordid ones? You, to be so deceived! You! whose wisdom and gravity make you a prodigy in the eyes of men? You, whose philosophy will not be equalled, till the wings of the phœnix shall carry her over our British isle! Oh, let my humour have vent, and pardon me for my mirth."

"Merciful God!" cried Mercia, "why does this woman exist? Wretch! The curses of all the world will follow you to the grave, and hang over it eternally."

"Oh, gentleman, I am accustomed to sleep soundly."

"Be not impiously secure, you most depraved of beings. And you, smiling, deceitful, and damnable villain! how will you atone for the injuries you have done me? Draw forth your sword; you have made a strumpet of my mother, and may murderers and common thieves set their reputation above mine, if I forgive you for it."

He rushed up to Celwold, in whose breast he was lodging his weapon; but Mary and Agatha shrieked in terror; and William threw his body on the raised arm of his incensed friend.

"Hold! Hold!" cried Celwold, "and let the nature of my crime be fairly considered. I robbed not your mother of her honour; there was not a court in either France or Germany, in which she had not previously pledged it. If there was any seduction, it was rather on her part than mine; and though I actually offered to marry her, she was better pleased to become my mistress, than my wife. You have heard the declaration of her abominable principles; it must be evident to you all, that she is as loose as she is savage; and I most heartily repent that I was ever drawn into her snares."

"Spare, vindictive hero!" cried Lady Mercia, sarcastically, "spare this spirited and gallant lover!"

Mercia however still struggled with his detainers; and Celwold immediately left the apartment, and locked himself in his chamber.

"Pursue not the wretch," said the unabashed Lady Mercia, "follow him not, for I confess, he has spoken some truths. My actions you call crimes, such, however, I do not deem them; and I shall extenuate no part of what I have dared to avow. I soon despised the thing I associated with, and could not throw it off by any other means than those I adopted. I am going from you, Mercia, I shall return to some of the countries in which I have travelled since the death of your pusillanimous father. This will occasion no regret in either of us; nor shall I recollect you, unless I see a wolf or tyger, full of ire and savageness—then perhaps, I may say, I have not yet lost sight of my son."

"Away, away! You almost tempt me to destroy you. My blood is on fire!"

"Mount to the ramparts, sir; the air blows coolingly on them. Come, Mary, you shall lie with me to-night; and early in the morning we will depart. Bid adieu to your friend, your Agatha, the intended bride of Mercia; rise, and obey me. What, am I to be insulted by you too?"

"I come, madam," said Mary, faintly. "Farewel, dear Agatha! Farewel——"

"You shall not go with this iniquitous woman!" cried William, throwing his arms around her. "Your innocence must not be polluted. Stay with your friend, your lover——"

"Lover!" exclaimed Lady Mercia, "find a name, boy, before you seek for a wife. Iniquitous woman! Repeat those words, audacious stripling! and I will have you strangled ere the morning. Release the girl; I will pluck her arm from her body, if I am any longer opposed."

She laid her hands on Mary, who, terrified and almost distracted, freed herself from the grasp of William. She entreated Lady Mercia to be less passionate, went out of the room with her, and returned no more. Agatha, exhausted and nearly fainting, was obliged to retire immediately. William perceiving greater danger

in leaving his frantic friend alone, resolved, great as his own afflictions were, to continue with him till the morning. Mercia could
scarcely believe but that his intellects were deranged; and he
endeavoured to persuade himself, that those circumstances which
distracted him were merely imaginary.

It was a night of mental anarchy and horror. Mercia could only
with difficulty be restrained from flying on the wings of vengeance,
to the causes of his tortures; and William believed, that within a
few hours he should for ever be separated from the persecuted
object of his dearest affections.

Early in the morning they heard the servants making a noise
below. Both of them were anxious to see the departure of Lady
Mercia and Mary; and going down with very different feelings,
they waited for their appearance.

Agatha soon joined them. She was pale and languid, and it was
evident that she had been waking and weeping ever since she separated from them. She hid her swoln eyes in the breast of Mercia;
and though she spoke little to her brother, that little related to
Mary, and was extremely affecting.

It was about seven o'clock when the titled harlot, and the lovely
Mortimer, came from their chamber. The former turned her eyes,
filled with pride and indignation, on every person she met. The
latter looked on her beloved friends, and wept in anguish.

Reproving her companion with great severity, Lady Mercia led
her to the castle-yard, where her horses and servants were prepared to take her to the shores of Kent, from whence she intended
to embark for France. Mary went with dread and apparent reluc-
tance. William often entreated her to return to him and her other
friends, and to break with her infamous protectress. Some kind
of instinct, however, seemed to draw her to the vile mother of
Mercia.

William was well acquainted with the nature of Edward. Fearing that he might again be hurried away by the wildness of his passions, all the servants of Celwold were desired to leave the castle-
yard, and the attendants of Lady Mercia were the only witnesses of
the parting. The wanton associate of Celwold mounted her horse;
and Mary, having talked for a few minutes, earnestly, but in a low
voice with her, retired to a little distance, and stood irresolute.

Agatha threw her arms around her; William implored her not to leave the castle; and Mercia vowed ever to protect her. Lady Mercia spurred her horse towards them; and Mary not only shrunk from the fury of her eyes, but also placed herself between her male abettors.

"Come to me immediately," said the enraged woman.— "Instantly mount your horse, and go with me quietly, or dread my future rage!"

"I will not, dare not come to you!" Mary replied.—"Mercia, save me, protect me!—Do not let me be taken hence to be treated with oppression. I am your sister!—And, breaking through a vow, which tyranny imposed, I declare before God, her, and all of you, that she is my mother. Oh, save me!—Do not resign me to her cruelty!"

"Perdition to your perjured soul!" exclaimed the ferocious mother.—"Curses on you, savage son of a most despicable sire!— Thousands on the villain who hides himself within; and not one less on these the private bastards of some pennyless wretch!"

"May infamy blow on you from all quarters!" cried Mercia, holding the bridle of her impatient steed, "and may the waves you are going on, draw you down to their lowest bed!—Fellows, look at this woman, and never hereafter obey or protect her. She is an impostor, a harlot, a nuisance to the air that passes to the breast of virtue. She is no mother of mine—she never bore me. Let her go through the world with vice flaming on her brow; and tho' I would not awaken the wrath of heaven, yet may she have no being after the ceasing of her present functions."

She answered not this speech, but pulling a small dagger from her bosom, aimed it at his side. It did not, however, pierce him, and before he could regain the bridle, she had darted out at the gate, and passed over the bridge. Her men followed. Their horses were vigorous and light of foot, and in the course of a few minutes they bore their riders beyond the sight of the agitated observers.

Mercia stood pale and agonised; his fiend-like mother had nearly crazed his brain, and he almost shrieked when he caught hold of William for support. Mary was the object that recalled his wandering senses.—She prest his hand to her lips—she wept on it; and having strained her affectionately to his breast, he gave her over to her lover, who, as well as his sister, was astonished at her declaration, of being the daughter of the inhuman woman that was then flying from them.

They all went into the castle, and were soon afterwards informed, that Lord Celwold had privately departed from thence at a very early hour in the morning. It was the steward that gave this information to Mercia; who was also told by the same man, that his Lordship, intending to be absent some considerable time, had expressed a strong hope of vindicating his conduct, to the satisfaction of Mercia, before his return.

This intelligence only served to provoke the person who received it. He cursed aloud the cowardly paramour of his mother; and went in search of the lying chaplain, whom he resolved to chastise severely. But he found that the priest had also taken himself away, and, by a secret retreat, evaded the punishment he deserved.

Returning to his friends, he requested Mary to tell him more concerning herself and mother. The lovely girl obeyed.

"Had any other person than Mercia," she said, "urged me on a subject like this, shame and confusion would have restrained my tongue. But I am among those who will judge me by myself, and consider me independently of the actions of her to whom nature once fastened me.

"As an orphan daughter of an Englishman called Mortimer, I supposed myself in my childish days; and those who were around me, taught me to look with respect and gratitude to my preserver, Lady Mercia. She cloathed, fed, and caused me to be educated.— But she treated me with no great degree of tenderness; and frequently absented herself from me for a period of several months. She was continually wandering from place to place; and her rank and beauty gained her admittance wherever she sought it.

"I was not always excluded from society, but ever found myself a subordinate member of it. I had publicly to attend to the caprices of Lady Mercia, and sometimes to appear in a character scarcely superior to one of her menials. Still I counted the sum of gratitude, and attended patiently to her humours. Her frowns were sure to make me tremble; yet her smiles, sparing as she was of them, filled my heart with joy."

"Go on, Mary," said William.

"Lady Mercia was always very private in her correspondence and concerns. At a time when I believed her to be much engaged, I happened to go into her chamber, the key was in her cabinet. Almost without designing it, I raised the lid, and seeing that it contained several epistles, I felt a strong curiosity to peruse them, and gratified my inclination at the expence of my happiness. The letters were written in terms of an extravagant affection. Lady Mercia and a Frenchman of the name of Brecourt, were the correspondents; and it was then I learned, that from their illicit passion I took my existence.

"My astonishment, on that occasion, had never been equalled. I found that I was growing unreasonable, and vainly endeavoured to check myself. My feelings triumphed over my understanding; I screamed aloud, and turning my head towards the door, saw my newly discovered mother, red with rage, and enlarging with resentment.

"The papers were lying on the table; she asked me whether I had read them, my looks openly, and my tongue faintly confessed it. She then shut and secured the door, replaced the letters, and shook me violently for my curiosity and temerity. She commanded me to swear that I would never make known the secret she had so long concealed. I started and refused to comply; but apprehending that she would deprive me of life, at length I took the oath she administered.

"After that day, the few indulgencies which had been granted to me, were considerably lessened; I had found a mother, but also found in her an arbitrary and cruel foe. She made me of still smaller consequence in the eyes of those who were around me; and threatened me with poverty, infamy, and death, if I ever broke the vow I had made. She went shortly afterwards, with some of the french nobility, to the nuptials of the Duke of Burgundy; and as she was absent nearly a fortnight, before her return I enquired concerning my father, of whom I gained some little intelligence."

"Who was he, Mary?" enquired Mercia, with great impatience.

"A man of some family, but very small fortune. He shifted incessantly from one dissipation to another; his uncommon beauty was noticed by the eyes of most women; and his life taken by a Frenchman of distinction, his avowed and former sincere friend. He had pillaged the wife of his opponent of her honour, and he died by the sword for the offence. I need not say any more, I trust that Heaven will pardon me for breaking the vow I reluctantly made in the moments of terror; and throw myself, dear Mercia, upon your generosity and bounty."

"I shall not receive you, Mary."

"Not receive, not shelter me! Oh, whither, then, shall I fly for protection?"

"Into the arms of this man,—of my friend," cried Mercia, "seek refuge there, and seek it instantly. Mary, in me behold an affectionate brother; look on my Agatha as your sister; and regard William as your destined husband. No thanks, dear girl! I am already satisfied, and wish only for your smiles and love. As to our mother— shame on her—let us resign her to contempt and forgetfulness. But no longer will I live under the roof of this defiled place; let us all depart from it, and for a while, claim the hospitality of the virtuous Bartonmere. By the will of my father, I know I cannot yet take my fortune; but next week will I see if it be practicable to wrest it from the hands of my infamous guardian, and place it in others more honest."

His companions agreed to all he proposed. About noon they left the castle, taking with them some things of value; and in the evening presented themselves before Lord Bartonmere, who received them with smiles and open arms. It was necessary to explain to him the particular cause of their abrupt appearance; this was done without hesitation, and their confidence made their host their general friend.

Mercia being anxious to learn whether a change of guardians could possibly be effected, for a short time absented himself from Agatha and her companions. He went to London on the business, having previously enquired of Lord Bartonmere, whether he would be willing to succeed Celwold. His Lordship gave a very ready assent; but when Mercia arrived at the place of his destination, he found that much trouble would precede the alteration he wished to be made.

While he was away from Bartonmere, William, accompanied by Mary, his sister, and host, often wandered amid the rural beauties of the village. When he rambled alone he frequently went to the heath, and mused over the spot where the noble Alwynd had perished, in the cause of friendship and honour.

"Will the spirit of a warrior," he heard a voice one day enquire, "will the spirit of a warrior approve the tears of an earthly being?"

William raised his head, and saw a man of most strange aspect and figure, standing by his side. The person turned towards him, discovering to the astonished youth the wild and expressive features of Martyn of Fenrose.

"By your countenance," cried Martyn, "I perceive that I am remembered by you. I know your thoughts, but fear me not. Go with me where I shall lead you, for I have things most important and wonderful to communicate."

William still considered this man as one lost to reason. The face of Martyn had something both of the terrific and sublime in it; and the person whom he now addressed was preparing to leave him in silence.

"Stay!" he cried, with a voice like the breaking of waves, "stay, and no longer consider me as a maniac. To convince you of my sanity, I could discourse on the actions of providence, and the complicated deeds of man. But let this suffice to take you out of the error into which you have fallen. Follow, I entreat you again to follow me."

"To what purpose?—What can you have to impart wherein I shall be interested?"

"The story of your birth—the names of your father and mother—your fortunes—your friends and foes; in which last description, I shall take in that blackest of all devils, Celwold."

"My father!—My mother!—And do you, indeed, know any thing relating to them?"

"Every thing—from the moment of their births, even to the moment of their deaths."

"And you will speak of them to me?—And you will not betray me?"

"I will tell you all that concerns them. I will guard you with my arm; and, if you require it, bring you again to this spot."

"Oh, what are these sensations!—God's mercies and blessings on you, stranger."

"God's blessings will never come to me!" said Martyn, with a sullen and almost suffocating grief.—"But let us away, for you must go a short journey with me. I could, indeed, tell you many secrets here; still, if you accompany me to my dwelling, you shall see them written by the hand of your unknown father."

"Delay not another minute—take me hence—satisfy the cravings of my impatient soul."

Martyn of Fenrose moved forward, and William followed him. They walked together nearly five miles; and Martyn, though he refused, for the present, to answer those enquiries which related to the topic that he had slightly spoken of, yet his looks assured his companion that his intentions were not unfair.

At length they arrived at the mouth of a cave, into which Martyn descended, and desired William to enter after him. They proceeded along a sloping hollow, and came to the interior of the cavern, where they were received by the wife of Martyn, whose form, features, and manners corresponded with those of her husband.

Martyn took a bundle of papers from a corner of the cave, and having put it into the hands of William, and promised to return when it had been thoroughly inspected, retired with the woman by the passage he had first entered.

The eyes of the astonished William followed them, and a returning fear of artifice for a moment troubled him; but unfolding a paper, which was the narrative that had been addressed to Celwold, he knew the characters of the hand, and, pained and delighted, immediately began to read it. He could not pass over the lines fast enough; and he grudged every moment he lost in removing his tears.

The commencement of the narrative amazed him; but on seeing Alwynd's declaration of his birth, he filled the mocking cave with a single shriek, and fell upon the stone on which he had placed himself. Martyn rushed in, and raising him in his arms, he put his cold hand on the youth's burning temples. But he was almost immediately entreated to retire, and he obeyed.

William read on.—He came to the part where Alwynd spoke of his carrying away the children of Matilda, and took in all the feelings of his father among his own. Having paused awhile he continued the history, by which he was soon led to the death of his mother. This was a point at which he was obliged to stop. His emotions grew more violent—anguish seemed to be wresting his heart from his body—and again he called in Martyn, who tenderly enquired the cause of his summons.

"I am dying," cried William, "surely I am dying!—I am full of mingled joys and woes—amazement and ecstacy are bearing me away from life. Father! father! why did I not know thee before?—Oh, God, these feelings cannot be endured!"

"Taste this cordial," said Martyn, "it will probably compose you."

William hastily took the cup that was presented to him, and drained it of its liquor. A new spirit seemed to be infused into his body. He rose, fresh as the gales of summer; and calmly requested Martyn to continue with him while he perused the remaining contents of the packet.

He finished the narrative, and then broke the seals of the letters which Alwynd had addressed to him and Agatha, on the evening preceding his fatal march to Bartonmere. There was tenderness in every word—and love beyond any that he had ever before expressed.—His counsels were short, but impressive—his language such as must necessarily be heard with the tenderest sensations.

At length, having gone through all the papers, William turned towards Martyn of Fenrose, who stood before him strong in his looks as the eagle, and mighty as the lion.

"I can allow you, at this time," he cried, "to make very few enquiries.—But, here do I stretch forth my arm to heaven, and may it be crisped by elemental fires, if I ever fail to prove your friend. Though, to the eyes of man, I sometimes appear dark as the eclipsed moon, yet if there be brightness in the sun, so is there truth in the papers you have perused. I cannot, however, trust them with you at present. Come to me on the morrow, and bring with you the gallant Mercia, who will return this evening. Shew these letters to your sister and Lord Bartonmere—divulge not the manner in which you attained them—mention not my name to either of them—and be cautious respecting those in whom you may wish to confide."

"Must I say nothing of my birth?—Nothing of the usurpation of Celwold?"

"Yes, say this, and say it aloud—'I have discovered that I am the lawful son of Alwynd; and, by his will, the inheritor of his fortune. This shall be proved ere long—but first shall be discovered the perjury and villainy of him who has seized upon my right.'—Go thus far, but no further. The name of your mother must be secret as the whisperings of death."

"Then, I fear, my fortune will never be amended. Alwynd, however, was my father, and that is enough."

"I cannot answer for the event of every circumstance; but all the good that I can do, shall pass to you, free as the airs that play with the willows which hide my cavern from the eyes of sanguinary men."

"And I believe you have power which——"

"Must not be spoken of now. Oh! the most powerful must, at a certain period, be impotent indeed!"

"Yes, death——"

"Name it not!" exclaimed Martyn.

"Speak not of it!" cried his shrieking wife.

They smote their foreheads and breasts—they groaned deeply, and the responses of the cavern made them cling to each other in agony.

William was amazed, and he trembled violently. Martyn, however, saw the terror of Alwynd's son, and sweeping away the big drops of sweat that had started on his brows, he led the youth from the cave, pointed out the path he was to take, and took his leave of him.

The events of the day had proved of a most uncommon nature. William, as he pursued his way, was often arrested by thought, and hurried forward by passion. His affection for his father he found might still be encreased. He lamented the untimely death of his mother, almost as deeply as if he had remembered her first and only endearments; and, gentle as his nature was, he heaped the curse of injury on the base, ungrateful, and dishonest Celwold.

It was evening when he reached the castle, the owner of which, as well as Agatha and Mary, had been somewhat alarmed by his absence. All of them hastily enquired the cause of it; his cheeks reddened, and grew pale again; and he placed one of his hands on his forehead, the other on his side.

Agatha approached him with great concern, when he opened his arms, took her to his heart, and yielded to the impetuosity of his long restrained tears—the agonizing tears of a man, which flow not on common occasions, or trifling concerns. His emotions created a still greater anxiety, and he was entreated to speak to them. Words not being within his present attainment, he gave one of Lord Alwynd's letters to Agatha, and the other to his friend, the worthy Bartonmere.

They were both read with exquisite feelings, and William, having regained his voice, afterwards spoke in the manner which Martyn of Fenrose had prompted.

Amazement took possession of the whole party, and Agatha, retaining her senses, reclined speechless against the breast of Mary. The assiduities of William, however, soon restored her; she doubted the truth of what William had said; but he first assured her that she was actually the legitimate child of Alwynd, and then retired to another apartment with Bartonmere. To him he related most of the strong particulars he had that day gained a knowledge of, concealing only the name of his mother, and the channel thro' which the almost incredible intelligence had flowed.

The pains and pleasures of Bartonmere were at first nearly equal, at length the latter rose in superior force and number; and while he strained the son of his beloved friend to his breast, he implored Heaven to aid the cause of the orphans, to scourge their vicious despoiler, and place the deserving heir in those possessions, which his ancestor had honourably enjoyed, and honestly bequeathed.

William, finding himself incapable of speaking immediately to Agatha, on a subject so tender and affecting to both of them, requested Lord Bartonmere to go back and relate, to her and Mary, such parts of his story as he should think proper to communicate, and his Lordship complied with a friendly alacrity.

William fell into some reflections concerning Martyn of Fenrose, whose services had already been too great for a limited gratitude to repay, and whose words and actions classed him among the most singular of men. His figure and dwelling were objects that could not be regarded with indifference; and his hatred of the world, his horrid seclusion, and dread of death, gave birth to many sentiments.

When he had demanded a legacy of Celwold, William supposed him to be some wretched lunatic. But on the heath, and
in the cave, he had conversed both with strength and reason, and
sometimes bore himself with a wild and inimitable grandeur. William had read the will of Alwynd, as well as the narrative; in neither of them, however, was the name of Martyn mentioned; and
its omission seemed to cause no disappointment or regret.

There was strong evidence of zeal, but none of self-inter-
est. William recollected some things which Mercia reported of
this strange man; but as they seemed to relate to necromancy,
he would not admit the apparently incongruous opinions of his
friend. He had no belief in events, which were not produced by the
operations of God and nature. All that was said to arise from other
sources, he wholly discredited; and neither the imperfect suggestions of Mercia, nor the many legends and affirmations of the age,
were capable of making him a proselyte.

Still he had to fix some character on Martyn; which was done
by his believing that he was a misanthrope, whose principles
sprung from his misfortunes—whose conduct had been in some
degree criminal—whose singularities were confirmed by habit—
and who still loved to see some of the concerns of the world that
he despised.

William had never been less judicious in his opinions. His
inferences were aberrant, and wide of the causes; there was
more honesty than justness in his thoughts; more virtue than
discrimination.

Mercia arrived that night, and William, without remembering
that his coming had been foretold, received him with pleasure.
Agatha and Mary heaped endearments upon him; and Bartonmere gave him the reception of a sincere friend. Sudden questions
were made concerning the success of the business, on which he
had undertaken his journey; but his countenance confessed that
it had not been complete. He informed his enquirers, that though
his complaints had been attended to, his single dissatisfaction, his
unsupported accusations, and the absence of Celwold, to whom
no abuse of trust could be imputed, would necessarily preclude
the immediate appointment of any other guardian.

He added, that he had employed some eminent agents in the

concern, and that if the retreat of Celwold could be discovered within a limited time, all he wished for might be accomplished. He therefore hoped soon to bring the villain into light, to set him before the eye of contempt, and make him appear as infamous as his actions had been.

William never reserved any thing from Mercia, to whom he was impatient to communicate the story that continued to agitate him. For the purpose of doing so he took him to a private room; and there, with the exceptions only of Martyn, spoke of his birth, his fortune, and the complicated deceits of his crafty foe. Mercia attended to him with wonder and ecstacy; and hailed his youthful friend as the Earl of Alwynd. His rapture abated not; he embraced William many times, and poured forth an hundred sincere congratulations, before he enquired from whom the unexpected and mysterious intelligence had been obtained.

On hearing the name of Martyn of Fenrose, his face altered strangely. He shewed evident signs of terror and distrust, wished the information had come from any other person, and advanced some of his former opinions respecting the being of the cavern. But William entreated him to suspend his judgment till the morrow; and to peruse the narrative and will, if permitted, before he formed any determination.

To this Mercia promised compliance; but the wild form of Martyn, as he presented himself at the battle on the heath, the powers of his sword on that day, and the mystic language he made use of at a subsequent season, were not to be thought of without dread and amazement. Mercia, however, found the tale too delicious for disbelief; he not only felt for the probable elevation of his friend, but was also delighted to think that the lately nameless woman of his choice would become his wife, as the acknowledged daughter of a man whose life had passed in virtue and honour.

To Agatha alone William communicated the appellation and quality of his mother. This he did after the family had gone to rest; and having continued with her during the working of her first feelings, he wished her good night, and retired with the conviction of her secrecy and discretion.

The smiles of morning had scarcely been seen, when William and Mercia went across the forest. As they knew not how long they might be detained at the cave, they desired the servants to inform Lord Bartonmere, that they should probably be absent the greater part of the day. Their discourse on the way related to him they were going to. Though the intricacies of the forest were numerous, William had so nicely observed the path on the preceding day, that he had no difficulty in finding the dwelling of the recluse, who stood at the entrance, and separated the bushes, in order to make their admission more easy.

In walking along the first passage they saw the wife of Martyn. Much of her figure was not to be observed; for she was sitting on an unfashioned ridge of earth, with her pale face partly overspread by her hand, and one of her large black eyes peeping between her extended fingers. She rose not when they passed her. Had she not slightly bent her head to them they might have supposed her to be spell-bound, and fastened to watch eternity without motion.

Martyn led them through the second and third passages, which seemed to be made light only by the matter of his orbs. Soon afterwards they came to the cavern, when he placed them on a seat of stone, and welcomed them as the Earls of Mercia and Alwynd.

"For years beyond the common life of man," he cried, "no human foot has till this time pressed the floor of my dwelling. Fear not the damps of the cave, for there are none. In winter I disperse them with a genial fire; and in summer the airs pass by in succession, and regale me with their freshness. Hail, once more, Edward of Mercia, and William of Alwynd! Friends that are, and brothers that shall be. Githa and Celwold yet live and triumph; still there is a train of black destinies awaiting them, and both of you will exult in your joys and successes, while your enemies painfully grovel in their defeat."

"Then we shall be happy!" cried Mercia, "then none of the miseries you anticipated, when I discoursed with you at the castle, will fall upon us? Your former prophecies will not be fulfilled?"

"Hold, hold, my impatient Lord! There are in life more cares than pleasures; strive not, therefore, to monopolize the latter, lest your ill-success add to the number of the former, and make them more arbitrary and wanton. My former prophecies! What think you of me then? What powers do you suppose are lodged in me?"

"Such as are not awarded to any other person with whom I ever conversed—such as are given by whom I know not, or attained I know not how. Strange, perplexing, incomprehensible! What is obscure to others is to you without shadow or speck. Man is unequal; you neither act nor speak like him. I can compare you only to——"

"To what, or whom?"

"I dare not pronounce—I know you not perfectly; and my suspicions must not be rashly revealed."

"You have not one that is not as familiar to me as my own mind. Look at my face; there, I read you now: I know you, at this moment, most completely. Every thing that is infinite, every thing minute in you, I can determine on. You cannot set up an image of thought, which would perplex me to stamp upon this sand. You cannot pass the swiftest idea, without my arresting it, before the succession of another. I have summoned you both, and you come with different opinions. By one of you I am regarded as a sorcerer; by the other viewed as a mere mortal, peculiar only in his habits and sentiments. Now I open to you, Mercia, I am such as you think me, and gifted as you have imagined."

"Then I have no further business here," cried William, rising from his seat, "Martyn, suffer me to depart, and deceive me no longer."

"I never did deceive you," said the wizard, "by the maker of the world, whom I still regard, I swear I never did. All that I have said to you is true, and in your concerns, I swear, there has been no deception; of which you must now know me to be capable. I have avowed myself, and you judge of me accordingly. But sit, and listen to a few strange circumstances of my life; for I am mortal as you are. What further I am, I will explain to you, if you attend to me awhile."

William wished himself in the forest. But Mercia had more confidence, and a curiosity of great strength; he therefore put his friend again on his seat, and entreated Martyn to speak as he had proposed.

"It is a fashion," said Martyn, "it is a fashion with many, who talk only of common events, and every-day occurrences, to bind to secrecy before they open. This rule, however, I shall not observe, though I am about to discourse of things most strange and intricate—sufficiently so to make the hearer restless in his mind, and impatient of communication. But I regard you both as men of honour, who have obtained a just knowledge of her principles, and will not stray from them. He lives not beneath the moon, to whom my story was ever told; and he exists not whom I should fear to divulge it to, though the hatred of a thousand common enemies centred in him. I am above the malice of man—I am his superior; but, oh, I have obtained the distinction on conditions most horrid, most dreadful!

"My power here is not, indeed, unlimited—still it is vast and mighty. When the creatures of my subjection, however, shall after passing the mysterious ways of death, chant the high song of glory, and sweep the heavenly lyres of ecstacy, I shall take in no sound but blasphemies, and stretch forth my limbs in pain, which will never be alleviated. The sweat of my brow scalds me!"

"Oh, there are vultures plucking at my heart!" were words which came from the melancholy wretch that sat in the darkness of the passage.

Both Mercia and William were awe stricken by the frantic gestures they witnessed, and the horrible groan they heard. Martyn, however, seeing the impression, smoothed his disturbed features, and began, without any other foreign matter, the story he had promised them.

"My ancestors," he cried, "followed many occupations. My father, however, possessing a tolerable large sum of money, on the decease of his parents, went with his wife into retirement, and lived by depasturing a small flock, and his uncommon skill in the chase. His neighbours were few; and he loved not society. My mother's mind corresponded with his; and the village housewife never gossiped at her threshold. He shunned those who sought him. He was somewhat of an enthusiastic disposition—reflective, and much better educated than any of the people among whom he settled. His peculiar humour displeased all of them—and during a residence of several years, he formed not a single acquaintance; and my mother made herself in no degree familiar with the women of the village.

"It was a long time after their marriage before they had any offspring. The first issue was a girl, who died in her infancy; and my mother had reached the age of forty, beyond which my father had gone several years, when I was born. I have been told that the moon darkened at my birth; and that my mother's midwife was a spirit of hell—stories invented by the wicked, and propagated by the idle. Would I had been strangled in the womb, or by the first hand that ever touched me.

"I remember how fond my father was of me in my childhood. He used to carry me in his arms over the mountains; and every morning, in the warmer months, he knit my young limbs, by plunging me into a river that coursed near the house in which we resided.

"My mother seldom went beyond the wicket, for her constitution was impaired, and a pain of long continuance had contracted and warped her body. But her love for me was not less than my father's; and she neglected none of her duties, though her health was so precarious. My father was a tall, muscular man; and the midwife told my mother, that she had brought forth a giant-child. I was, indeed, of an unusual size—I hung not long at the breast, and at a time when other infants are first put upon their legs, I knew my powers, and fearlessly exercised them.

"At the age of seven I went alone up the highest mountains, at twelve I ran with unbuskined feet in the chase, and strangled my prey with a sinewy hand, while my father stood in the valley, smiling on my courage, activity, and strength; and it was alone with me, or my mother, that he ever did smile. He passed the inhabitants of the village without salutation. The Lord and the peasant he alike disregarded; and never spoke with any person, except a man who lived in a neighbouring hamlet, and who was equally singular in his speech and manners.

"As I grew up I perceived that my father's conduct had created him many enemies, and advised him to alter it. I saw that he was always looked on either with dread or scorn; that he was suspected of some crime I truly believed; and the accusation, though suspended, alarmed me as much as the declaration of it could possibly have done.

"My mind reached maturity as soon as my body. When a mere boy in years, I viewed every thing around me like a man; and those only who remembered my birth would have admitted my juvenility. I sported not with the village youth; I was avoided by them; my appearance always interrupted their pastime. I was abhorred merely on account of affinity, and I regarded myself as one who was destined for the curses of society. I expostulated with my father, and warmly told him that his conduct would degrade and ruin me.

"With a calm smile he assured me that my opinion sprung from error; but as I appeared determined, he promised to associate with those whom he had so strangely shunned. He failed in doing so, but the mortification came to me rather than him. Those to whom he spoke either did not reply, or answered him strangely; some with fear, some with contempt, and others with savageness. He held out his hand with amity; but it was put aside with scorn. He hailed the rich and the poor with the unanswered voice of friendship. He provided a feast, and opened his door, but no person stept over the threshold, or ventured to sit at his board. I was provoked, and saw the infelicities attending a being who, actuated by pride or false sentiments, stood aloof instead of joining with his species. He who is once openly contemned by the arrogant will ever be suspicious of the conciliatory terms, which may proceed from whence he met his first degradation.

"My father now secluded himself more than he had ever done before; laughed at my disappointments, reviled at human nature, and attended only to his books. My mother also took up his opinions, and acted on them. The neighbouring villager, whom I have mentioned before, was for a considerable time their only visiter. At length, however, by what means I need not inform you, I introduced to them a man whom I had singled out, and they received him in a manner with which I was well pleased.

"Our new acquaintance had a most honest and respectable aspect. There was energy in his mind and sweetness in his voice; he looked at us with the smiles of virtue, and talked with the tongue of morality. I beheld him with delight, and thought that if the world abounded with men only half so honest, wise, and gentle, I could not too soon go in search of them, and for ever leave the solitude in which I had been reared. I was then but fifteen, my new acquaintance, who had not long resided in the village, supposed me to be eight years older. He gave me his confidence, on the score of moral obligation, and I awarded him mine on the same terms.

"But he had been known to us scarcely two months, when he rifled our coffers, and carried off a bag of gold. My father stormed and raved; I hung my head in confusion, forgetful of the dignities and virtues of man. Afterwards however, my father cooled, and I grew hot on the villainy. I threatened to pursue the deceptious wretch over mountains and seas, and should madly have begun my search, had not my father held me by the arm, and desired me to be tranquil.

"Let the thief go from whence he came," said my detainer, "to the general and every-where corruptions of the world. What I have lost frugality must restore to us; but if you respect my peace bring to me no more men."

"I promised to obey him, restrained the liberality of my opinions, no longer taxed his misanthropy, and again betook myself daily to the hills, the lakes, and the woods. You will say that my actions did not correspond with my years; this I am willing to allow, and to this unusual forwardness are owing many of my subsequent miseries and oppressions. I was, as you may conceive, very ignorant of the world of which neither of my parents could, with any degree of pleasure, converse. I had, however many secret longings and desires, which were quickened and encreased by some conversation I held one evening with an old mariner, whom I fortunately rescued from a robber near the sea-shore.

"I long declined the reward of gratitude, but he insisted on my accepting some part of the treasure I had luckily preserved. He then sat down on the margin of the ocean, and told me such ravishing adventures, that I parted from him reluctantly, and went home full of big resolutions, which were rapidly communicated to my father and mother. To them I bade an hasty adieu; and by the light of the moon that was then shining, left the place of my nativity, strong in body, and determined in mind.

"I travelled in several capacities through many parts of my native country. For my support I neither wandered with a flock, nor hunted the game of the forests. I leagued not with banditti, I joined no savage chief, my means were all honest. A year elapsed before I saw my parents again; and then I returned to them only for a few days. I both found and left them well; they wept at my departure, and though their tears affected me, I wished not to abide in idleness and inactivity.

"In less than a month after this last adieu, I rode on the waves, and was borne by the winds from my native land. My spirits were free as the breezes; my heart light as the cork that sported on the waters. At times however, I was serious and reflective. Unfathomable depth below—immeasurable height above.—My mind was sublimated; it sought for causes and effects, and took in wonder, reverence, and adoration. I passed from country to country, solicited new employers, trusted to new seas, travelled with christians as far as they dared to go, then threw myself without dread among infidels, and afterwards strayed from them to nations, rude, unknown, and savage.

"I went where nature made me appear a prodigy; where the name of my country had never been spoken. Yet even there I established more friendships, and acted with greater freedom, than I had ever done in the dull dwelling of my father. I have lived months under the shade of trees, feasting on delicious fruit, and joining in the dance and song of the negro. I have resided for a long season, without seeing the rays of the sun, where every faintly visible thing is icy, and nature sluggish. I have been where Heaven, ocean, and horrid mountains of frozen snow, were the only things on which I could turn my eyes. I have gasped in extreme thirst under a blistering orb, where my companions grew mad around me, and franticly drank the boiling blood of their murdered fellows. I have revelled in the luxuries of palaces, and wished for morsels which even beggars cast to their mastiffs.

"But I have little cause to vaunt of these adventures; I only take them in with the rest of my vicissitudes. After a wandering of twelve years, and viewing such scenes, and engaging in such actions as none of my countrymen were either familiar with, or would believe, I travelled into France. I had been there before, and from one of the ports of that nation I sailed for the land of my forefathers. I was not returning in poverty—for I possessed a considerable sum of money, acquired in the more prosperous parts I had visited, besides several curiosities both rare and valuable.

"The sea, however, as I came near to the cliffs of England, convinced me of its treachery. It wrecked the vessel in which I sailed, swallowed half of my property, and threw the remaining part of it, and my bruised body, with rage and violence upon the sands. Many of the crew perished, and most of the survivors were plundered by the wretches who lived near the coast, and committed their open depredations when they ought to have acted with tenderness and humanity.

"Though I was much exhausted I had not lost my senses. My only worldly substance was lying by my side, and I saw a gigantic fellow coming to rob me of it. Imploring the aid of nature I started on my legs, and possessing, for a moment, all my former strength, I first took away his reason by striking him with my clenched hand on his sounding forehead, and then, laughing in my victory, hurled his body from the brow of the cliff upon which I had, scarcely an hour before, with difficulty crawled. This was the effort of desperation—the act of one whose limbs were well sinewed; my purpose was accomplished, and I sunk down again upon my unquiet bed.

"It was not long before some few humane souls mingled with the ferocious, and gave succour to the distressed. I was raised from the cliff, and tenderly supported to the dwelling of an old man, whose daughter drest my bruises, bathed my swoln limbs, and did the offices of a gentle nurse. I staid with my ancient host some time, and told him all my adventures. I afterwards married his child, and took her with me to the village in which I believed my parents, if living, still to reside. There I found my father and mother, but they were declining apace to the grave; and I had changed so much in my appearance, that when I asked for their blessings they stared on me as one whom they had never seen before.

"The olive colour of my skin, the strength and blackness of my beard, and the width of my chest, made them almost disbelieve me when I declared to them I was their son. But afterwards they hung upon my neck and wept—they took my wife in their arms, and called her by the name of daughter. I told them my story, which seemed to them marvellous and almost incredible. I shewed them my wealth, which the waves had spared; and satisfied with my past adventures, hoped to sit myself down in lasting ease and tranquillity.

"But in this I was soon disappointed. I found my parents still peculiar in their habits and humours—still prejudiced against society—and visited only by Geoffry, whose residence I was never acquainted with before my departure, and whose company I sought not after my return. I now found that the villagers looked on my father and mother with encreased dread and malice, and that they were suspected of diabolical practices. As I was one day approaching a number of peasants assembled together in a field, with a general voice they exclaimed—'Here comes another devil to ruin and afflict us!—Hasten from the ally of the wizards!—Let us fly from the hell-begotten monster!'

"I went home in anger and amazement. I did not tell my wife the cause of my emotions, but spoke of them to my father, and seriously advised him to go with me in search of some other residence. He knew of the hatred that was around him, but despised those from whom it proceeded, and resolutely vowed never to fly from them.

"His obstinacy I could not conquer. The winds which had blown on me in the regions of the north, and the sands before which I had franticly run in the deserts of the east, might as easily have been directed. The badge of inequality I had never worn upon my sleeve—I allowed no man to be my superior, nor had I till this time ever received an insult with tameness. Perverse as my father was I would not leave him; but I swore to chastise, with extreme severity, the person who should next dare to molest me in my walks. It was not long before I met with another interruption, when I accordingly fulfilled my vow.

"The enemy of the day was not a new one. He was a tall sturdy rascal, of reputed strength and activity; and his renewed attack on me was gross, unfeeling in the extreme, and repugnant to human nature. My breast filled with ire, and I darted on him as a leopard would on its prey. I struggled with the resolution of either conquering or being hardly conquered. The opposition was strong and almost irresistible; however I not only brought him to the ground, but also broke the bone of his lower jaw.

"I left him, roaring with pain and agony, and returning home told my father of my last adventure. Geoffry was likewise there, but I spoke not particularly to him, and he left us within a few minutes. My wife was alarmed and my father pleased by my information. I was gratified by my success, and determined always to act with the same degree of spirit. But soon after this affair had happened, our house was surrounded by nearly thirty peasants, who swore they would demolish our dwelling, and take away our lives. I stood, undaunted, at the door, and braved their fury. None of them, however, executed what they threatened.

"I saw that fear checked the rage with which they had come thither; and they evidently regarded me as a fiend whom they wished to destroy but were too dastardly to oppose. My passions were indeed violent; and my energies in full force. My voice, naturally strong, deepened into thunder; and I brandished my arms, as if I could hurl death and fate among my enemies. They retired pale and agitated, each of them dreading a separation from his fellow.

"On that evening there was a tremendous autumnal storm; much mischief was done in the village; and the operations of nature were believed to be only the machinations of our witchcraft. Those who had been most injured swore they had seen me flying in the darkened air, and directing the lightning. My wife was deemed an accomplice; and even the infatuated and lying priest reported that my father and mother, had, in his sight, worked many of the conjurations of the evening, and afterwards placed a black spirit on his breast, who lashed him with thongs till the morning.

"To fly from these weak wretches, and perjured rascals, was now absolutely necessary; and we all agreed to go from the village as early as possible. My father wished to place himself under the guidance and advice of Geoffry; I had not however any respect for a man, who was feared even more than ourselves, and who always dealt in mysteries. We collected our property, and had provided a conveyance for my old and decrepit mother; but on the evening that preceded the day fixed for our journey, an event happened which interrupted our project, brought agonizing death among us, and doomed me, as well as my wife, to the never ending pangs of perdition."

"Oh, torture! Oh, misery! Oh, hell!" exclaimed the invisible woman. The young men looked towards the passage with affright; Martyn commanded his wife to be silent, and then proceeded——

"I was taking a last view of the village, and ruminating in a

retired spot, on what I called the brutalities of human nature, my
wife was with me; she, at length interrupted me with a sigh, and
our melancholy eyes met each other. We walked on, silent, and
dejected; soon afterwards we heard the groans of some person in
pain, and descending the hill on which we then were, we found,
stretched on the earth, the eldest son of the nobleman who resided
in the nearest castle.

"We raised him softly, and he spoke to us. "I am dying," he
said faintly, "I have been attacked by robbers. If you be charitable
bear me to the next dwelling, tell my poor father the cause of my
death; tell him I blessed him!" I put him gently on my shoulder,
and carried him to my house. There I bound his head with linen,
bathed his wounds with balsam, offered a cordial to his unreceiv-
ing mouth, and left nothing undone, which a commiserating christian could devise, for the aid and relief of an unfortunate fellow
being. He never spoke thereafter, our applications availed not, for
he died within an hour.

"Now I must tell you how the kindness of our actions was
rewarded. The murdered man was sought for, and found in our
house. We were all accused of being accessaries to his death. The
father of the deceased, and the priest of the parish, together with a
large body of men, again assembled at our door; cursed us in terms
most dreadful, and bore away in savageness my aged father, and
miserable mother. They laid hold of my wife; but Geoffry suddenly
appeared, wrested her with ease from four men, placed her across
a horse, on which he mounted himself with the agility of youth,
and in an instant they were beyond our sight. I trusted to the honest Geoffry, but was astonished by his performance. I knew it to be
magical, and though I believed that it would preserve the life of
one, I had reason to fear it would accelerate the death of others.

"I entreated—implored to be heard. I related circumstances as
they had actually been, but there was not a man among them who
did not call me a liar; and the father of the murdered swore he
would have immediate revenge. They could not detain me for a
moment; they would not have been more foiled in attempting to
net a lion. I found, however, that my power could not be extended
to the wretched captives, who were dragged indignantly to a river,
into which my shrieking mother was thrown; and, at the same

moment, my father was drawn, with a cord around his neck, up to the branch of a neighbouring tree.

"Agony and madness!—Alternately I turned to objects horrid and distracting. I saw my mother rise and sink in the water. Her eye-balls seemed nearly reversed—she bubbled the stream in her pangs, and held up her hands in instinctive supplication. On my other hand I beheld my slowly dying father, with uncovered face and unconfined limbs. Oh, spare me the anguish of describing the conflict between strangulation and the exertions of nature!—The cord had been placed indiscriminately, and life was in the writhing man long, long after his first suspension. I was prevented from plunging into the river, and also from approaching the tree, by all of the exulting, deriding, and hellish crew. My mother, contrary to their expectations, went finally to the bed of the river; and at length, the twisting body of my father became as still as death.

"I ran away from the dreadful spot, wild as a fiend, and terrifying every person I met with. I hurried on to a wood at the distance of five or six miles, buried myself in a quarry, tasted no food for two days, and then went back to the spot where I had witnessed the horrors which I last described. It was night when I reached it. The moon was full, but her light often interrupted by gloomy clouds. The winds were sleeping—the trees murmured not—and the waves of the river went sullenly by. Neither beast, nor bird, nor insect, gave any interruption to the general stillness. The body of my father was not yet suspended; a chain had been put around his neck, and his trunk and limbs were encircled by hoops of rivetted iron. I touched him and found he was strait, stiff, and cold as an icicle; when I turned from him shivering, and looked on the muddy waters that went over the corse of my mother.

"Oh! let me burst with grief, and die upon this spot!" I exclaimed, throwing myself under the gibbet. "Let me perish here, and, with existence, cast away my miseries. God! is there no early punishment for those who committed these atrocities?—Oh, that I, indeed, had power to do such mischiefs as my murdered parents and myself have been accused with!—My vengeance should be terrible—my deeds bloody!—Lend me a dagger, some dæmon of malignity, some spirit of evil, that I may lift it high, and strike it deep."

"I heard the trampling of a horse on the other side of the river; and the moon wandering into a clearer path, I saw the steed take to the water and swim towards me. On its back I distinguished two people. It soon came to the bank on which I was standing, when Geoffry dismounted, and put my wife into my arms. She was pale with affright, and wild with ecstacy. Her loosened hair flowed around her waist, and her whole appearance was frantic and confused. She looked at the gibbet, and clung closer to me. The joy I felt on finding her restored was of that nature which sometimes brings frenzy to the mind of man.

"I could not long support her, we fell on the earth in the arms of each other; and for a while I noticed not her deliverer. At length, however, I turned my head towards him, and discovered a most strange alteration in his appearance, such an one as confirmed my belief of his endowments, and put truth upon all former supposed incredibilities.

"Why do you look on me so earnestly?" he cried, "did you never before suspect me to be capable of what I have performed?"

"Never," I replied, "till you took away my wife. But tell me, were the accusations of my father's enemies false or true?"

"False.—Had they been true he had been beyond their malice; and that he was not so, was owing to his obstinacy and rejection of my offers. He should have borne himself as I advised, then he would not have swung over our heads. The moon shines out again—look at his blue swoln face. Was he ever dear to you?"

"I shivered with horror while I looked up to the frightful object.—"Why did you not save him from the agonies of such a death?" I enquired.

"I wanted means. There is no power under the skies but such as is limitable—it may indeed be great, still there are barriers over which it cannot stride. I saved your wife by my skill—the hour was inauspicious, and I could do no more. But the murderers live, laugh, and exult."

"Oh, that I could hurl destruction among them!" I exclaimed.— "Oh, that I could destroy each devil that was busy in these abominable, these damnable deeds!"

"No more for the present," said Geoffry, "your wife is pale and fainting. Put your hand in the river, and moisten her lips.

Yet desist!—The body of your mother grows green beneath, and makes the water impure. Mount my horse, and take your wife in your arms; I will be your guide and lead you from danger."

"I obeyed him, and we travelled with velocity, Geoffry flew before, retaining the bridle. How far we went I know not; but ere the break of day we were placed in a comfortable dwelling, and my wife was soon afterwards sleeping upon rushes. I stood over her and wept. Geoffry put a cordial in my hand—I drank it, it brought instant drowsiness upon me, and I placed myself by the side of my wife.

"When you rise," said Geoffry, "I must have some talk with you in private. If you awake before your bedfellow, disturb her not, but come instantly to me; I shall probably be at the door. Ease to your weary limbs, and quietness to your ruffled mind."

"He went out, and I became forgetful of every thing. I did not wake till noon, and my wife was then sleeping. I remembered the words that had been last spoken to me, rose gently from the rushes, and went immediately to Geoffry. To repeat to you the whole of my conversation with him would be unnecessary. He talked of the injuries of my father and stimulated me to revenge. He proposed means to me which were almost infinite, and at first incomprehensible. He said that I might attain a degree of power which would make all men tremble—crush my enemies like insects—command wealth to the extent of my most extravagant wishes—and live, from that day an hundred years. I was prompted by revenge to the acceptance of these terms. The period he had mentioned seemed an eternity; and I enquired the conditions on which these favours were to be granted.

"Only such," said Geoffry, with a calm smile, "as those to which I have given an acquiescence. To the grand promoter of all your gratifications, your pleasures and longevity,—a surrender of your soul. From him who acts so liberally now, what will there be to dread hereafter? You will only be required to assist him in regaining that eminent station from which he has been removed. If he succeeds, you will stand by his side, a glorious chief with a flaming helmet."

"Who is he that never acceded to an ill proposal, and afterwards cursed his rashness? My adviser was too great for me; his temptations fired my mind, and his sophistry hushed my fears. What I replied I know not; but I have some faint remembrance of a mystic ceremony, and of the entrance of a third, extraordinary person. I remember that Geoffry, within a little while, prest my hand with ecstacy, and said, "carry the sword that lies before you wherever you please, and it shall fall destructively. Wish for whatever thing you desire, and you shall possess it. From this day a hundred years shall pass before death can touch you."

"And my wife?" I said, "how long will she live?"

"The powers of life are faint and languid within her," replied Geoffry, "she will die ere the waning of the next moon."

"Then what to me are lengthened years?" I exclaimed, "I shall not wish to survive her! Are there no means by which her days can be made as numerous as mine?"

"Let her swear as you have done, and you will perish together."

"Swear! Have I sworn any thing? Aye, but she cannot serve the expelled chief. She is too weak, she could not grasp a falchion, and her body would sink under the weight of armour."

"Her body!" said Geoffry, smiling, "as well as your own, is for this vile earth; it is the exhalation that goes secretly beyond it which I have contracted for. True, your wife cannot scour the wide campaigns, where you will be led to battle, nor can she wield the lance before the chest of your imperishable king. Still she can lift the bowl when his lips are parched, and dry his mighty brows with a napkin, when he is in extreme heat. Fly to her—bring her to your purpose."

"Scarcely sensible of my own actions I went to her immediately, raised her in my arms, and found her most dangerously ill. Though it was mid-day I turned my head upwards, and fearfully looked for the moon, before the waning of which, according to the prophecy of Geoffry, she was to expire. I told her of all that I had heard, done, and consented to. The past actions of her preserver had been observed with terror and amazement; she was assured of his power, and trembled at his prediction. She blamed me, she was in agony, and vowed that nothing should induce her to make a sacrifice so great and terrible.

"While she spoke her pangs became fierce, her eyes distended, and her countenance frightened me. The fears of death now assailed her, but Geoffry entered the room, and talked of the joys she might possess during a term which seemed almost endless. I entreated her not to leave me alone in the world, implored her, since my miseries had been so many, to continue with me, and link her fate with mine. She looked as if she would obey me. I threw my arms around her, Geoffry pronounced the vow, she repeated it, and instantly rose in perfect health and freshness from her bed.

"Soon after this Geoffry left the house, and we never saw him again, except as I shall relate to you. All his promises, however, seemed likely to be fulfilled; and those powers with which I had become invested, I determined to put into immediate force.

"The first thing I did was to return to the spot made memorable by my parents sufferings. Invisibility and transformation were two of my peculiar gifts. I went, however, in my proper shape, walked boldly among my fiercest enemies, took the corse of my mother, which was now floating, from the water, broke the chain that fastened my father to the tree, and caused the very wretch who had effected his death, to bury him and my mother in a grave of his own digging. The villain could not disobey me. I made him work till the sweat poured from his brows; I compelled him to pray for the soul of the man whom he had murdered, and then, in the presence of his wife and children, stabbed him to the heart. On that night, I executed my former threats, and dealt out vengeance amply. I terrified and destroyed the marked barbarians, and afterwards returned exultingly to my wife.

"We lived in the cottage of Geoffry about two months, but losing the sense of my late wretchedness, my former love of adventures revived, and my wife promised to accompany me wherever I might wish to go. I gathered together a large sum of money, procured costly habits, and went, in the space of ten years, to most of the cities of Europe. I was too rich to be neglected—I was caressed and flattered in every place I went to.

"It was impossible for danger to reach us, for on land and sea we were equally safe. Neither earthquakes nor whirlpools could swallow *us*, though they might take ten thousand of our companions down to death. I shall not repeat to you many of my adventures, still most of them were extraordinary. I possessed the power of effecting both good and mischief. Authority, however, seldom made me wanton, and I wished to promote happiness rather than misery.

"Fifty years of my limited existence went over, and my wife noticed it to me with a melancholy aspect. Indeed it made me contemplative and serious; the past time seemed only as a single day in a pleasant season, but I shuddered when I thought of the coming period. Geoffry had drawn no terrifying picture when I rashly entered into the covenant; I suspected, however, that he had dealt unfairly with me, and that my avocations in the world beyond me, would be different to those of which he had spoken. His disappearance was a subject that had always surprized me, and now I thought of it more earnestly than I had ever done before.

"I cursed myself for stepping over the ordinary bounds of mortality;—I cursed myself also, for persuading my wife to take the frightful hazard. I pictured the monarch I was to serve, as well as his mysterious dominions; and imagined that I saw my wife acting, by turns, as his slave and compelled harlot. My mind went beyond this, and accumulated horror. One evening I conjured up one of the most potent of those beings who were subject to me, and commanded him to lead me to the place from whence he came. He obeyed, and I grew almost mad with affright. I saw the swarthy king of the regions I was deemed to,—I beheld Geoffry in torments, and was blistered by the hand that he laid on me as I was departing.

"Returning in terror, I informed my wife of my journey. We wept together, and tore our breasts in our agonies. We found we had been juggled with, discovered that our first opinions had been just, our subsequent ones impious; and viewed the unavoidable charm of pain and destruction in perspective.

"Oh, save me!" I exclaimed, throwing myself upon my knees, "if there be mercy in God, I supplicate it now. Surely I have not gone beyond forgiveness. I have indeed wandered widely, but oh, how sorely do I repent my former actions! Hear me, spirits of the good, and aid my cause with tears and prayers. I will humble myself to the dust, remain in this posture during the remainder of my life, fix my eyes on Heaven, and never withdraw them, if the faintest beam of mercy dawn on me. Pray with me, sharer of my miseries! Oh, we have sinned deeply, and must inevitably perish!"

"Be sincerely penitent and devout," said a voice of mildness, "repent, be virtuous hereafter, and hope for mercy and forgiveness."

"Come forth, thou blessed minister of comfort!" I exclaimed with ecstacy. A celestial form stood before me—I prostrated myself in awe and rapture, and my wife did the same. I raised my head again, "Is there," I cried, in apprehension, "any way into which I can turn to avoid the destruction I tremble to think on? Have not our crimes been too many—too dreadful? Oh, tell us, messenger of omnipotence, whether we shall ever receive any degree of pardon, and escape the snares of hell?"

"Creatures of wretchedness and sin!" replied the spirit, "the saints that dwell in paradise have trembled at your actions, and I can give you no assurances of pardon. I wonder not at your misery and dejection; yet hear the advice that I am allowed to offer you. I must begone almost immediately, for I am a guardian of the night to the innocent, and have been drawn hither by your lamentations, from a sick man's chamber. You have many years to live, and will not be deprived of the power with which you were unlawfully invested. This power I would have you exercise; but in a manner which the tyrant Lord of Geoffry will not approve. Do not any despite to the good, and frustrate the intentions of the evil. Sleep not without previously addressing yourselves to him from whom you ought never to have strayed. His mercy stretches wide as the Heavens which canopy the world."

"And will it ever descend on us?" said my mournful wife.

"Strive for it, if you obtain it not. But, oh, I fear you will not be wholly able to appease his wrath, for you have turned from him and leagued with his deadliest foe. Still it will be better to be snatched from, than to pass the gates of hell. You will both expire at one moment; and neither of you will know whether you shall dwell with the blessed, or wander with the accursed. Should you leave any friends, they will be assured of your fate. If your wicked bond be cancelled, your bodies shall shew like those who lived virtuously, and died in purity; but if the fatal deed cannot be revoked, darkness and horror will overspread your faces.—Farewell!—You shall not want my intercessions."

"I had, as well as my wife, been raised to hope; but we were left nearly in despair. After this hour, many times did I call for the presence of the radiant visiter; I called however fruitlessly, he came not. I met with no consolation thereafter, and every ensuing day teemed with fears and horrors. We considered our doom as fixed, irrevocable—still we kept in the ways that had been last pointed out to us, forsaking those which we had long and fatally pursued.

"The dæmon of the shades sent his emissaries to us in displeasure, commanding us not to endeavour to counteract his will. His threatenings however availed not—faintly, and but faintly, hoping for redemption, we turned our means to virtue, did good by engines formed for different purposes; and among the objects of our care and protection, took in you, Alwynd, and Mercia, and all the deserving that belonged to you.

"Your enemies were base and vitious, and in dealing with them I remembered the instructions of heaven's mild servant. Do you not see the wretchedness of those who give the rein to passion—who would impiously grasp the scourge of Omnipotence, and enter into compacts which he knows to be unholy?—What is to me the recollection of my revenge?—There is a hand that would have fallen more mightily than mine. What are my past joys when compared with my future punishments?—What the transient gratifications of vice, to the ever springing pleasures of virtue?—I have no use for the riches I can heap around me. My life is nearly at its termination—within a few short weeks I shall grasp my wife in the agonies of death, and then go down with her to sweat and writhe with Geoffry!"

Martyn's wife rushed into the cave, and wildly clung to him. Their agonies rent their bosoms; and William and Mercia sat in pity, terror, and amazement.

The wizard afterwards recovered, and asked them to retire; but he entreated that they would return in the course of the ensuing week, when he would tell them in what manner they ought to proceed in their different and complicated affairs.

He again assured them of the authenticity of the narrative and will, which he delivered to the heir of Alwynd, charging him to retain it with particular care.

He then accompanied the young men through the intricate passages, to the mouth of the cave, where he took leave of them;

and they saw him return in gloom and despondency, to the destined sharer of his coming punishments.

END OF VOL. II.

MARTYN OF FENROSE,

WIZARD AND THE SWORD.

THE extraordinary story of Martyn of Fenrose caused much conversation between William and Mercia; they thought with pity of his wrongs, and shuddered at his rashness and approaching punishments. It was a most serious and impressive lesson of morality to them; and, the evidences being so strong and palpable, they could not suspect the truth of it. They however kept the mystery to themselves, fearing that the declaring of it would injure both their cause and reputation.

Remembering the appointment of Martyn, they went together once more to the cave, where they found the pale inhabitants in earnest prayer. Martyn requested them to aid the supplications of the contrite; they accordingly bent their knees and devoutly implored of heaven an exercise of its mercies. They then arose—the woman retired, with her arms folded on her breast, and with dejected head; and Martyn welcomed the young men to his gloomy dwelling.

"I ought to make both of you," he cried, "my peculiar care, for, independent of your virtues, I have to admire your fortitude. I live in impenetrable obscurity; no one person is acquainted with this cave, and had either of you, on your first entrance, shewn any deception or malice towards me, you might have wandered for ever in search of me, and yet discovered me not. Oh, how I once loved, how I do still love the confidence of man!—My own suspicions and resentments alone have drawn me into ruin and perdition!"

"You will rise again," said William, soothingly.

"Never!—The world shall rebound out of chaos first. Nothing

can equal the horrors of despair—and no despair can be equal to mine. Oh, where have I to wander, and what to endure!—But let me neither terrify nor afflict you. I wish to talk calmly with you both respecting your rights, and the enemy who at present possesses them."

He sat down, and they placed themselves by his side.

"My approaching dissolution," continued Martyn, "deprives me of much vigor and enterprize. I can no longer curb the spirit-steed—no longer mount, unseen, the guarded rampart; and the sword that slew de Stacey I have returned, with curses, to the giver. I am already contemned by those who were bound to serve me; and when they tell me of the near extinguishment of my power, I am agonized by their frightful shouts and rejoicings. My exertions will now scarcely go beyond those of human nature; and I fear I can bestow on you nothing but my advice. The cause of Alwynd is the last in which I shall engage. And being the cause of virtue, I mourn that I shall not see the termination of it."

"Then I have little to place my hopes upon," said William.

"And I have nothing. Can wretchedness stretch any farther? I will venture to say, youth, that if ever the gifts of your abused father shall reach you, many difficulties and dangers will precede them. I cannot discover the present residence of Celwold, without resorting to means, which, though formerly my sport, are now devilish and disgusting. I cannot clearly see your destiny, but can discover no early good. Yet droop not, son of Alwynd; rely upon the protection of him to whom virtue is ever dear—from whom my fatal vices have for ever estranged me. Had I known you sooner, or rather had the battle of Bartonmere been fought at an earlier period, I would have frustrated the machinations of Celwold, and caused you to be proclaimed the lawful heir of the usurped possessions. But now there is only one short step between me and the frightful grave. William, I can do no more."

"The riches of my father I covet not so much as his name."

"None would respect you for possessing it, unless you could speak without disguise of your mother. And if any one should charge you of illegitimacy, dare you avow yourself to be the son of Matilda? How the resentments of her brother may stand I know not; were I situated otherwise, I would go to his court, and on my return tell you either to cast yourself at his feet, or to shun him for ever. But now I have no time—no strength—I am on the verge of a world of horror, and can think of scarcely any other thing than the next fatal step. Let me, however, warn you to be cautious in all your proceedings. To alter the will would eventually destroy your reputation, and also endanger your personal safety; and as Lord Alwynd unguardedly calls you his son in it, I know not what satisfactory answer you could make, when your pedigree should be demanded."

"I see, I see," cried William, "that caution will ever doom me to penury and obscurity. But if I spurn her, and be spirited in my actions, loyal to my king, and brave in his defence, will he not applaud me for a true soldier, and deign to acknowledge me as the son of his sister?"

"Valour is not rare in Britain, and as the king is grown too old to brave the dangers of war, it is impossible he should witness your courage. Your merits are as likely to be neglected as reported justly, and should the sovereign be informed that the warmest soldier of the day was the long concealed son of the princess Matilda, might not fear whisper to him that you fought for yourself, rather than for England's monarch; and that while you merely seemed to aim at the laurel wreath of glory, you cunningly vaulted to reach the golden crown of royalty?"

"He might, indeed, do so——"

"But he would probably act differently, you would willingly add. Ah, Alwynd! You know not the fears, the jealousies of sovereignty. The king is doatingly fond of the young prince, his grandson, who will ascend the throne, when it shall become vacant. Attempt not, therefore, at least for the present, to step before him. There was a time, when I should have hurried you forward; but now I would restrain you. Leave me to think of your concerns awhile; and I charge you, as long as I live, to carry none of your designs into execution, without making me previously acquainted with them. Adieu, William, for my soul is full of sadness to-day. Farewel, gallant Mercia!"

The young men returned to Bartonmere Castle, but the brow of William was contracted by disappointment. Nothing that he had wished for was accomplished, and the voice of his generous friend could banish none of his anxieties. His ardent spirit loathed to be repressed. On the future agency of the wretched Martyn he placed no hope; he thought of his injuries with indignation, and would have relieved them as valour prompted, had not Mercia's careful friendship, and Mary's apprehensions protested against it. The love of the latter was dearer to him than the riches of his father, and of no less consideration than his unestablished name. If, when he impatiently spoke of going forth to redress his wrongs, she turned her face towards him, he was soothed by the mild expression of her eyes; and if, when he swore to punish the usurper with his sword, she threw herself in fear and sorrow upon his breast, all his resentments were instantly quelled, and his ecstacies dispersed the bold intentions of which he had spoken.

Agatha also dissuaded him from rashness, and Lord Barton-mere calmly advised him not to act precipitately, but to wait till Mercia had, in some manner, adjusted his concerns, before he thought of the more serious arrangement of his own.

"Consider yourself," said the hospitable baron, "as one more distant from necessity and the real causes of unhappiness, than the greater number of your fellow beings. Your birth is pure and honourable. Your virtuous sister will ere long become the happy wife of Mercia, and the lovely Mary is all that man can hope to find in woman, and will come to your breast an innocent and beauteous bride. I loved your father, boy, and you are dear to me. The joys of marriage I tasted but for a short season, and its pale blossom faded with the delicate plant that bore it. I have no wife—no child, and at my death, I shall leave no one to take up my title. This castle, William, and whatever it may contain, from that period shall be your's. Assure yourself of it, and all that I shall require of you will be, to love and respect me while I live, and to protect my poor and faithful servants, after they shall have followed their old master to the grave."

"Oh, my dear lord! This generosity—My prayers shall ever be that God will make your life both long and happy."

The Baron checked the effusions of William, and led him to his friends, in order that the voice of gratitude might be stilled.

On the fourth day after his second visit to Martyn, Mercia was surprised by receiving a letter from Celwold, which informed him that he was returned to the castle, and summoned him to come thither, accompanied or alone, on the morrow, when the office of guardian should be resigned, and a statement of his affairs laid before him.

"I call you to me," it was said in the letter, "merely in the character of my ward, and would not have you presume to term yourself the injured son of Githa, a woman whose name is so infamous, that he who speaks it shall be dishonoured. She at present is lurking near us, and who would not cautiously shun so deadly a fiend? As the creatures of my charity were pleased to fly from it, tell them never more to return to me. Marry the out-cast girl as soon as you please. Her unknown father, though his visage may be thinned by fasting, and his garment formed of the shreds of beggary, will probably declare himself when he shall hear of the elevation of his daughter. I shall have many friends around me, for I know the fiery qualities of your brave spirit and shall treat with you accordingly."

"Tell your Lord," said Mercia to the messenger, "that I shall be with him at the hour he has mentioned." He then went to his friends, to whom he shewed the insolent letter; and it was agreed that Lord Bartonmere and William, as well as six of their attendants, should accompany him to Alwynd Castle at the appointed time.

"The villain fears me still," he said, "in spite of his contumacy, I see he does. But he describes my mother as she is, and I will not interfere in his concerns. Is it possible that she is yet near to us? Let her, however, be cautious in her proceedings; for if she attempt to disturb my quiet, I will look on her with encreased abhorrence, and punish her as the vilest of wretches. I almost forget humanity when I think of her; but I am pleased that Celwold will now perform what I have long wished him to do. You, Lord Bartonmere, will for a few months act in his capacity; you, dear Agatha, must not object to the earliest day I dare fix for our nuptials; and you, William——"

"Will say to Celwold, 'Restore, usurper, to the son of Alwynd, his true inheritance, or your blood shall roll in streams down the blade of his avenging sword.' Turn not pale, sweet girls! And do not overwhelm me with your tenderness. Would you have me

live abjectly and in meanness, crouching for security, and fearful
even of a coward? Does not the blood of Alwynd flow in these
veins, and shall the channels be dried up by apprehension? Let an
instantaneous checking of the languid tide rather make me quiet
for ever. None of you were strangers to the qualities of my father;
none knew him more truly than you, Lord Bartonmere; and that
he had courage, as well as virtue, I have many times heard you
declare."

"He was as gentle as spring in domestic society, but rough and
cutting as the winds in the field. The man that did him good he
loved with sincerity; but he who wantonly injured him was chas-
tised with resentment."

"As Celwold shall be by me! I have been wantonly injured, and
will fill myself with those hereditary spirits which once gave elasticity to the nerves of my father, whose memory would be dishonoured by my quietness. I charge you all no longer to oppose me. I
will tax the guilty villain of his crime—of his abuse of confidence;
but passion shall not master me, and for the present the name of
my mother shall be sacred. I will call aloud for justice, if I obtain it
not, the affection of Lord Bartonmere, the love of Mercia and my
father, and the endearments of my Mary must sooth my cares, and
lessen my disappointments."

The day was passed in anxiety and impatience. The coming of
the morrow was wished for by the whole party, and in the evening
William, without requiring the consent of the solitary Martyn,
read aloud the narrative of Alwynd, which filled the breasts of his
auditors with sighs, and their eyes with tears. They composed an
affectionate family. There was neither a narrow nor selfish thought
in any of their minds; the chain of sympathy bound them closely
together, and all restriction of sentiment, or of feeling, was useless
and ungenerous.

The ensuing morning Lord Bartonmere, and the young men
observed the appointment of Celwold, who received them with
indifference, and with none of the usual forms of courtesy. On
William he fixed his eye, and seemed to consider his coming as an
act of impertinence. The son of Alwynd was unabashed by this
behaviour, but he could scarcely suppress his rage and indignation,
as he approached the vile and contumacious thief of his birth-right.

Mercia had also a fierce struggle with his passions, and though he previously determined on appearing in a single character, he could not banish his detestable mother from his memory, nor restrain the curses that rushed towards the vile abettor of her infamy.

Celwold had many of his attendants around him. His steward was present, with prepared statements of Mercia's property, and two of the nearest residing noblemen were there as witnesses to the transactions. Some considerable time was spent in adjusting the business, on which the meeting had been formed; but at length the accounts were allowed to be perfect, and Celwold, with the consent of a higher power, which had been previously obtained, resigned his charge to Lord Bartonmere. He was then about to retire, but Mercia, stepping forward, prevented his design; and in a speech of considerable length and great animation, taxed him with some of his hypocrisies and vices.

The young Earl was heard by the accused with many changes of passion. Celwold wished to persuade his friends that all the allegations were unjust and petulant—that he could suffer in their opinion only by misrepresentation—and that his endeavours to controul the obstinacy and indiscretions of youth, were the most serious offences the inconsiderate minor could upbraid him with. He moved forward again after this poor extenuation, but was a second time stopped, and William grasped him strongly by the arm.

"Presumptuous!" he exclaimed.—"Who is it that dare to offer me this new insult?"

"Look on me," replied William, "and satisfy yourself. Have you no recollection of me?—Do you not know me?"

"Very well, sir.—I know you."

"Then declare who I am—declare it aloud; and though I fear you have no innate principles of honesty, and will act rightly only by compulsion, yet I will put you to the proof of it, by charging you to relate all that you know to appertain to me."

"Which would amount but to little," replied Celwold, "and which little, unfortunately for you, and though I hastily said I knew you well, would take from your reputation, rather than add to it. I am assured I shall not answer you to your satisfaction, yet I will speak as you are solicitous. Of your name I know nothing—nothing of your family; but, whatever I may have heard you say to the contrary, I should suspect that neither of them would, if truly declared, procure you much respect. Lord Alwynd was a man whose prudence did not equal the charitable feelings of his heart. He was most bountiful to you and your sister; and in his successor, you would have found one willing to administer to your necessities, had your pride been less, and your humility suited to your condition."

"Open yourself more, prevaricating Lord. I am the son of Alwynd—you know me to be such, and it is villainy to deny it."

"I have not yet prevaricated," replied Celwold, with affected calmness.—"I have, indeed, often suspected that he was your father, but I was acquainted with none of his amours; and though I have many times enquired, whether the daughter of any peasant was known to be seduced, at a time preceding your birth, yet I have been able to discover only one poor object, whose ignorance and total deficiency of——"

"Silence, insulting fiend!" exclaimed William, bursting into passion.—"I am the true and lawful son of the man whom you have most villainously deceived. You know me to be such. You have no title to what you possess—this castle and all the demesnes belonging to it are my inheritance, and I will aloud assert my right. My father was incapable of committing so base a crime as you have alluded to; and my mother was honourable and virtuous."

"Indeed!—And her name, sir?"

"Was Matilda."

Celwold started and turned pale, but he recovered almost in an instant.—"Had she no other appellation?" he enquired, "something, surely, should follow, or what does it import?—From what family did she descend?—Who were her ancestors, and what her fortunes?—Besides answering these questions, I could not only wish to see her pedigree, but also to be informed where and by whom the marriage was celebrated. There are many other proofs too, which must be established before I can allow you to step before me. Return to your home, and ruminate on the advantages to which your presumption leads you."

"Have you no shame?" cried William.—"Devils would surely blush at such self-assurances. I have lately read a story, which had previously been in your base hands. You know how I am situated, and would brave me into danger. But let me become despicable to all eyes, if I tamely sit down with my wrongs, or suffer you to retain, without interruption, that which you should yield up to me. I am the Earl of Alwynd—Lord Bartonmere and Mercia can honourably vouch it. Celwold, I have already told you the name of my father, and now declare that my mother was——"

A loud, shrill noise was made at the door, and it seemed to proceed from some person calling an animal. "Fidelity!—Fidelity!" said the voice. A man, with tattered garments and dusty feet, entered the room, and a large, wild looking dog bounded after him.

It was Martyn of Fenrose. William and Mercia instantly knew him; but they saw by his countenance that he wished them not to notice him. He held a paper in his hand, and went towards Celwold, who expressed as much surprise and horror as if the grave had given up the body of his father.

"Why do you start, Baron?" enquired Martyn, "why are the changes of your colours so many?—Did I not tell you I was assured I should return with the papers, the loss of which made you so frantic?—Aye, but I had a long and horrid journey for them!—Nothing under heaven should induce me to go the ways of peril and darkness again. I have lost much time, and my reward must be encreased. My wife and children, if living, are anxiously expecting me; if dead——Come, my reward, my reward."

Celwold would have given half his wealth to be repossessed of the papers; but he was afraid to claim them in the presence of so many people, and looked significantly at the adventurer, as if he wished him to retire.

"What!" cried Martyn, in an impassioned voice, "after all my difficulties and dangers, my weariness and long fastings, am I to be cozened and defrauded of that for which alone I undertook to serve you?—I will not bear such usage! You judge of my soul by the texture of my garment; but you shall find——No, your mind is too poor and sorry for great estimations. I will not be injured twice with impunity; and once already I have been by you—you, who would corrupt on terms which are no inducement to the most abject agents of villainy. If the son of the late Lord Alwynd be present, let him shew himself, and I will put into his hands the secreted will of his father."

"He stands before you," said William,—"he now speaks to you."

"Thus, then, I fulfil my promise. Take it, shew it to the world, claim your hereditary rights, and punish your enemy as he deserves. Having been sent in search of this paper, and after much difficulty found it, I discovered that my employer's baseness was deep as the chasm in which it was buried. I will toil for none such.—But for men like you my feet should bear me over deserts, and my brow sweat during a whole summer. There, there, I have performed the duties of an honest man, and will now renew my journey."

"Villain and impostor!" cried the perturbed Celwold, "your forgeries will not pass."

"Your name will pass to infamy," said Martyn.—"My truths shall be established, and Alwynd's son be no less honoured than his father. Room for my dog, base Lord! he is an honester creature than you are."

Martyn then went out, and William, who, as well as Mercia, had conquered his surprise, shewed the will to all who wished to look at it. Some believed, others doubted; and Celwold trembled with fear and reddened with rage. He execrated all those who had come from Bartonmere, called them villains and impostors; and then, defying their malice, and artifices, rushed out of the room, and refused to come forth again.

Lord Bartonmere reproached him as he departed—Mercia looked at him with contempt and detestation—and William told him to make speedy preparations for yielding all his ill-acquired possessions, and fraudulently obtained riches. They then quitted the castle, and returned to the impatient Agatha and Mary, who rejoiced that the business on which Mercia went had been so quietly adjusted; and hoped that William's affairs, though they were intricate and ravelled, would at some future period be satisfactorily arranged.

The unexpected appearance of Martyn caused much private conversation between the young friends, who had left the papers, which were brought by him to Celwold, in a cabinet at Bartonmere Castle. They went the next day to his cave, but as they could discover neither him nor his wife, they returned in disappointment.

A few happy days succeeded the contention, and Mercia most

truly rejoiced at the alteration of his circumstances. He turned towards Lord Bartonmere with respect and gratitude; and gazed on Agatha with the eyes of encreasing love.

"My vexations are already nearly forgotten," he said to the latter, "and the prospect to which I am looking is rich and smiling. I have no longer any distrusts, for I have done with Celwold and my mother for ever. I cannot believe but that she is again spreading her levities in France. Near or asunder she is nothing to me; let all the shame pertaining to her conduct rest on her alone. He lives not that should twice reproach me with her abandoned actions. To me she first behaved like one who never had humanity, afterwards with all the insolence of vice; and our poor Mary she has not treated with half the tenderness of brute instinct. The insults which she offered to you, would alone cause me to execrate her."

"Pass her to forgetfulness," said Agatha, "and turn to some other subject."

"To the subject of my love then let it be; that I could dwell on for ever."

"Aye, but not without weariness, Mercia. Mary says it is a topic which, though never exhausted, is made fatiguing by its unwearied repetitions and familiarity of images."

"I have nothing to do with her opinions, they must go over to your brother. I confess, however, that I have little novelty to offer you at this time; and though you may accuse me with sameness, you shall have no cause to censure my prolixity. All I wish is now to fix a certain time for the constancy of your lover to meet its ultimate reward; and that, on the day my friends shall come to congratulate me on the ceasing of my minority, you will allow me to lead you among them, and to say,—'Felicitate me also on this my most precious attainment.'"

"The love of Mercia, and the smiles of his friends, I shall joyfully receive."

"Oh, happiness!" cried Mercia, "surely my present knowledge of you is perfect. Agatha, what delight it will be to dwell with you in retirement; what pleasure to shew you as my wife to those who can justly estimate your virtues and beauty. I have an expectation of the most joyful events, and while my debased mother lives without respect, and Celwold frets and curses his foiled ambition in obscurity, I hope to see you smile in the court of my king, and to be regarded by him as the offspring of his departed sister."

"Ah, that hope is fallacious! Think of the fears of my beloved father."

"They were imposed on him by the affection and tenderness of his unfortunate wife. But, admitting that resentment still travels with time, there can be little to dread if we are secret and unaspiring. Whatever may be the fortune of my friend, it shall not separate him from me. We will live, and our children shall grow up together; and when death comes among us, our tears shall be dried, and our sighs suppressed, by the tender consolations of the survivors. But see, Lord Bartonmere, William, and Mary approach us. Agatha! Blessed be the hour in which we first met, and happy all the days that are to come."

William frequently held conversations in some degree similar to the last, with the woman of his choice, whose artless manners were captivating as her beauty. It was agreed that he, whether he succeeded or failed in securing his rights, should go with Mercia and his sister before the priest, and at the same time take the lovely Mary as his wife. He knew the generosity of Mercia's heart, and also that it would never be suspended. The young Earl had not merely promised to bestow on Mary an ample gift, but also made arrangements for her residing with him; and whatever favours he might thereafter grant, William had only to take as the free will offerings of an affectionate brother.

At this time he was assured, that he should feel many pangs, if he were for ever excluded from his paternal home; but hope whispered that justice would interfere in his behalf, and yet obtain for him the former inheritance of his honourable forefathers. Agatha would indulge no such expectations; she thought the villainy he had to cope with, much stronger than it actually was, and one evening they were seriously discoursing on the subject, when they were interrupted by the entrance of a lad, who had been brought up in the castle by the humane Lord Bartonmere.

The boy was about fourteen years of age, handsome and animated. Misfortune had first recommended him to Lord Bartonmere, who regarded him with kindness, caused him to be educated, and frequently expressed an affection for him. A peculiar sort of gratitude pertained to Oswy, and he made it known in terms which were not used by the vulgar. It was augured that his talents were of no common order. Complaints indeed were frequently made by the servants of his pride and spirit, but his patron considered them as arising from prejudice, and was sometimes led into anger, by accusations which he believed to be unjust.

Agatha and Mary had in frolic, called him their page. He loved their society better than that of the men, and was ever striving to obtain their notice. He talked with liveliness and fancy, recited the tales of the bards with spirit and correctness, gambol'd like the son of sport, and sung both with art and simplicity. He came into the room hastily, and was running up to Agatha; but when he saw her brother sitting by her side, he stopped, turned his face towards the ground, and begged that his intrusion might be pardoned.

"What have you to say to me, Oswy?" she enquired, "is it a secret that must not reach my brother?"

"Yes, madam—no, madam—I had something to say—something to shew you—but some other time—when you are alone——"

"Oh, never mind me, young sir," said William, laughing at the boy's embarrassment, "pray make your assignation freely."

"I hope to-morrow evening will be fine," said Oswy, with more confidence, "that neither you, nor a certain lady of the castle, may be disappointed in the proposed ramble through the wood."

"Fairly retorted, upon my honour, William," cried Agatha, taking hold of her laughing page's hand, "but tell me, Oswy, what you were going to say, or rather what you wished to shew me."

"Two shipwrecked wretches," replied the boy, sinking into instant dejection—"two shipwrecked wretches, sheltered in a hovel near the shore on which they were cast. Oh, it is a piteous sight! The old man has lost his only son—his daughter, her lover. I have carried them food from the castle, but when I come near to them, I feel so sad and melancholy, that I stop till my heart grows lighter, before I can enter into their comfortless dwelling."

"And how bears the girl her misfortunes?" enquired the deeply interested Agatha.

"As one, Lady, who has a wandering, but painful remembrance of them. The old man strives to solace her on his breast, and while she lies in his arms, he raises his tearful eyes to me, and says, 'alas, boy, my daughter is mad!' Ah, it is melancholy! I wish you would remove them to the castle."

"They shall be taken care of," said Agatha, "what are the appearances of the wretched girl?"

"You plucked a lily yesterday, while I was with you in the garden; and the rain, you know, had bent it to the earth. I can compare her to nothing but that flower. I took some food to them this morning. In my way I met with Adela, who had strayed from the hovel, and was dressing the fancied grave of her drowned sailor with the green seaweeds. The tide was coming in, and I trembled lest it should sweep her away. I therefore went to her, though I was much afraid, and led her to her father, who, after long watching, had fallen asleep. I awoke him, told him where I had discovered Adela, and received from him the greatest reward he could bestow—a poor man's thanks, a wretched father's blessings."

"Shew us the way, Oswy," cried Agatha, "we will go with you."

"And, if you wait a minute," said William, "I will ask Mercia and Mary to accompany us."

"Oh, I will spare you the trouble," said the page, "I will look for his Lordship and his sister myself, and request them to go with us to the poor mariner."

The boy went out, and returning almost immediately, said, that their intention had been anticipated, and that Lord Mercia and Mary were actually gone to remove the sufferers to the castle.

"But let us walk briskly," he added, "and we shall soon overtake them, for Reginald, the steward, tells me, that they are but just gone, and have taken six of the servants, to bring the poor old man hither in a litter."

Oswy threw on his hat, and went out of the room, followed by those who commended his pity, and were anxious to relieve the objects of it. He said the distance to the hovel was more than a mile, but as two hours had to precede sun-set, and the evening was remarkably fine, Agatha stept lightly over the meadows, anticipating the pleasure she should enjoy with Mary, in affording comfort to the distressed. William talked with Oswy as they went forward, and promised to make him a present on the morrow for his humanity; but the boy looked as if he wanted no reward, and sought for the smiles of Agatha, rather than the commendations of her brother.

The breeze came lightly over the sea, and sported with the glassy locks of Agatha. They were not able to overtake those who had preceded them, and came within view of the hovel, without obtaining a sight either of Mary or Mercia.

"They have been too brisk for us," said Oswy, approaching, "but, in the cause of affliction, who is ever more prompt than the noble Earl? Only point out distress to his notice, and he will hasten to alleviate it. Tell him where misery complains, and he will seem to borrow the wings of angels to fly and solace her. I think I can see him employed at this moment. He presses the hand of the miserable father, stamping on it sweet assurances. He raises the distracted Adela in his arms, imploring Heaven to restore her to health and reason. Excellent Mercia! Enter, Lord William—enter my dear mistress."

He pushed aside the door of the hovel and rushed into it. His admiring companions followed quickly, and while they were looking for the expected mariner and his daughter, six armed men darted upon them. Four of them laid their hands on William, and bound him with cords evidently prepared for the purpose; and the other two secured Agatha in their arms, but offered her not the insult that had been imposed on her brother.

So instantaneous was the attack, that it almost seemed to have been effected by magic. William could not resist the force of his enemies; Agatha shrieked and became nearly insensible, and Oswy ran up to a man, who seemed the principal in the conspiracy, and from whom the unblushing imp received a purse, apparently filled with gold. The surprise of William changed to horror; he strove to seize and punish the early son of vice and perfidy, but his attempt was vain. The urchin laughed at the impotency of his enemy, and sported with the purse that had been given to him.

William was distracted by the situation of his sister, and he entreated her detainers to use her with gentleness and decency. He found, that to struggle with those who had the charge of him, would be an useless exercise of his strength, he therefore did not exert himself; but, with a loud voice and an undaunted spirit, he enquired by whom the base stratagem had been planned, and who was his enemy.

"Let your own conscience tell you," replied the man to whom he had addressed himself.—"Think of the person whom you have most injured, and spare my answer."

"By heaven," cried William, "I have injured no one!—I call God to witness that I have not!—That boy, whose complicated villainies fill me with wonder, must have deceived you. Oh, look upon my sister!—She will die—she will perish!—Release her, and do what you please with me."

"The lady shall not be injured, either by me or any of my party," answered the man; "but I am sorry, young sir, that you should boast of virtue, when you do not possess it. If you were to live with me fifty years, you would not hear me proclaim any of my merits. You are most completely in our power—nothing can release you; therefore I shall not scruple to confess, that your fate, hereafter, will depend on the will of Lady Mercia."

"Indeed!—Is she our enemy?—That fiend, that harlot!"

"Beware—restrain your licentiousness. Should she be informed of this, she would make you writhe in torture."

"I will not retract a syllable—I fear her not. What has urged her to this act of treachery?—What have I and my sister done to be treated in so base a manner?"

"That you must ask of our employer, when you meet her, she has not commissioned us to enter into any explanations. That you have injured her, and basely too, is no secret, for you have heaped calumny on her, and openly leagued with her enemies. She will be revenged for it, and I applaud her for it. Her means are precious. She can, if she please, hide you in the cells of death; and that she will do so is highly probable. But be assured that the lying daughter of Mortimer, and the tyrant son of my Lady, will never behold either you or your sister again."

"Oh, Mercia! Oh, William!" cried Agatha, with unclosing eyes, "save me—stretch out your hands to me—Let me not die for want of your assistance."

"Villains!" exclaimed William, "release me instantly, and give my sister to my arms. What, do you refuse? God strike you all with madness and death! Look at her—there is no blood in her cheeks, no motion in her heart—murderous fiends! Execrable Oswy!"

"Away with them to the vessel, and put to sea instantly," said
the man who was at the head of the conspirators. William and
Agatha were carried to the beach, and placed on board a small
bark. They were both prevented from making any noise, and the
bestower of the purse, having conversed for a few minutes with the
corrupt page, came on board and unfurled the sails. They immediately receded from the shore, and before William was forced into
the cabin, he saw his young betrayer deriding his sufferings on the
strand.

The instructed son of guilt gazed awhile on the vessel, as it
went from the borders of the ocean. He then returned in haste
to the castle, at the gate of which he took up a flint and wounded
his hand. Making an outcry, he afterwards ran through the hall,
drew a crowd of servants around him, and panting and bleeding
rushed into a room where Bartonmere, Mercia, and Mary were sitting in expectation. They raised the frantic boy from the floor, on
which he had thrown himself; and seeing the blood running from
his hand, they enquired by whom he had been wounded.

"Oh, I dread to answer you," he cried, "put on your swords,
Lords, mount your horses, and fly to rescue Lady Agatha and her
brother, or they will be lost to us all for ever."

Mary was almost petrified. Mercia started with astonishment,
and hastily demanded a further explanation.

"Let the grooms, then, prepare your horses," said Oswy, "while
I am telling you, in order that a single minute may not be wasted.
About the business, immediately, good fellows."

"Merciful God!" exclaimed Mercia, "what can be your meaning? Speak, Oswy, or I shall die with apprehension."

"My Lord, I was walking with your friends, about an hour ago,
near their favourite copse. They were going to do an act of charity
at the cottage of the man whose leg was torn by the sickle, and
which they had almost reached, when a party of men came from
behind the trees, and instantly made them prisoners."

"Prisoners!" cried Mary, "oh my bursting heart!"

"The villains fastened their hands with cords, and, with drawn
weapons, bore them to a little distance. I followed shrieking; but
they offered me no harm, till I threw my arms around my beloved

Lady, whose agonies I cannot describe. One of the wretches then
struck me with his sword. My terror was greater than my injury;
and while I lay on the ground, I saw the monsters bear away their
victims, place them upon horses, and ride across the heath, with a
speed almost incredible."

"Give me strength, Heaven," cried Mercia, "and let me not sink
at a time like this. Lord Bartonmere, go with me; Oswy, accompany us to the spot you came from, and point out the road which
the rascals pursued."

"I will my Lord; but as the party consisted of seven or eight
men, it will be dangerous to go without attendants. They looked
not like common robbers. After they had left me, I found this
paper, which probably belonged to one of them; but I had neither
time nor inclination to peruse it. Oh, my sweet Lady! I fear I shall
never more behold you."

Mercia took the paper with an agitated hand. It was addressed
to "Bernard Aubrey," and stamped with the seal, as well as signed
by the hand of the infamous Githa.

"My mind has not changed since I saw you on Thursday," said
the *billet.*—"You will, therefore, convey your captives to the place
I then mentioned, where I will be waiting to receive and punish
them as they deserve. Your reward depends upon your services.
The gold that comes with this may assist you in your journey. I
only want you to deliver to me the objects of my hate; and the station you wish for I will immediately allow you to step into."

Mercia knew the writing of his mother. Almost distracted he
rushed out of the room, accompanied by Lord Bartonmere, Oswy,
and several of the attendants. It was nearly dark. They instantly
mounted their horses, and rode to the spot on which the attack
was said to have been made. Having received the directions of the
page, they set off with velocity, leaving the boy, and one of the
servants, to return to the castle.

The situation of Mary was exceedingly distressing. Her tears
flowed not, but she was sick at heart; the pain of her head was
intense, and almost severe enough to bear away her reason. She
guessed at the motives of Lady Mercia, knew the malice of her
disposition, the cruelty of her nature, and doubted not but the
revenge of this inhuman mother would be full and ample.

She wondered that the savage woman had not also aimed at securing her; and actually wished that she had been taken in the toil, rather than be separated from her lover and friend. She apprehended that neither of them would ever be restored to her. There was misery in the thought; and she shook with encreased violence, while her head lay on the bosom of the sinful page.

"Oh that I could console you!" cried the matchless hypocrite, "that I could place comfort in your fair bosom, and command it to abide there. But my efforts would be only mockery, and I must sympathise in silence. The machinations of your mother will I fear prevail, for there is strength and determination in the instruments she has employed. Oh, heaven! If she should doom the lovely Agatha to death——"

"Oh, God!—Talk not thus, Oswy,—my brain cannot bear it."

"It is, indeed, a horrible subject; but what is there not to be dreaded?—Had you seen them in the arms of their enemies!— Agatha, with a death-like face, was borne before, and her anguished brother compelled to follow her. He could not exercise his bravery. He looked first on his insensible sister, and then on me. 'Oswy,' he said, 'bear my love to Mary. Tell her I will ever implore the God of innocence to protect and bless her; that while I have life and reason, I will pray for her peace and felicity.'"

"Misery and insanity are both assailing me!" cried Mary.—"Boy, send my women after me—I am afraid of myself, of every body. William, Agatha, and Mercia! Where are you all?—Oh, these tortures are too many and fierce for endurance!"

She ran to her chamber, and passed the night in agony. The morning broke upon her, and found her griefs encreasing, for still all was horror and uncertainty. Four days she spent in a similar manner. Almost assured of the irretrievable loss of William and his sister, the absence of Lord Bartonmere and Mercia, led her to conjecture that they also had fallen into the hands of the villains whom they had gone in pursuit of, and been savagely slaughtered by them. To all who remained in the castle, circumstances seemed so desperate, that little consolation was offered to Mary—none however she could have received; she secluded herself in her chamber, refused the attendance of her women, and found herself wholly unable to support a conversation with the boy who had brought to her the last words of her lover.

She often threw her eyes hastily on the door, thinking that some messenger of good news was entering. She looked from her window, across the heath, with the hope of discerning some of those dear friends, who might yet survive; and frequently sat, still as a statue, to take in any sound that should announce the coming of travellers.

In the evening of the fifth day of her loneliness and despair, she was roused from the lethargy into which she was falling, by the trampling of horses over the bridge. The party had gone so far that she could not see it from her window; nearly breathless, therefore, she ran down the stair-case, and entering the hall, saw Lord Bartonmere, with her brother leaning upon his arm. This was sufficient to convince her that they had been unsuccessful, to encrease her miseries, and plunge her in the depths of desperation.

"They are murdered!" she exclaimed, franticly, "they are murdered, and we must be miserable for ever!"

"Hush, hush!" cried Lord Bartonmere.—"Look at this object, your miserable brother!"

She raised her eyes on Mercia, and saw him weak, pale, and inexpressive as idiotism. His features varied not—the wreck of his noble mind was visible. He had a bandage on his head, which, she now perceived, was stained with blood. She flew to him, clasped his senseless hand, and pitying his condition, almost sunk into it herself.

"Oh, this completes my misery!" she cried.—"Tell me, my Lord, what new calamities have befallen my brother?"

"Our search," replied Lord Bartonmere, "has been so totally unsuccessful, that we have not been able to obtain the least intelligence of our betrayed friends. Your brother's afflictions have been many indeed; and I have with difficulty restrained him from acting desperately. He had a fall from his horse; and I fear the contusion, and his extreme heat of blood at the time the accident happened, have seriously affected his brain. Oh, God! our joys of late were many; but the number of our misfortunes is now infinitely greater. Assist me in conveying this creature of affliction to his chamber; assist me, also, in recommending him to the immediate mercy of his Creator."

Mercia was led away; but Mary, as she went with him, was frightened by the inanity of his once noble face.

The castle now became a scene of general distress. The loss of William and Agatha, as well as the situation of Mercia, was bewailed by every person; and even the guilty Oswy felt many a pang, and turned repentantly from the hoarded gold, that had induced him to put his uncommon hypocrisies into motion, and to act with such wanton cruelty and deceit. It was the first scourging of guilt, by the severe lash of conscience; the cords struck hard and sunk deeply, and, to avoid discovery, he, as much as possible, shunned the eyes of those whom he had so seriously and inhumanly treated.

Mercia continued for a considerable time alarmingly afflicted, which caused Lord Bartonmere to dread that the seal of insensibility was fatally pressed, and Mary to fear that she should never thereafter solace or be solaced by her beloved brother. Every one who had any knowledge of his merits and character, sent the kindest enquiries after him; and even Celwold occasionally dispatched a messenger, and twice stopt in person at the castle-gate, to enquire whether there was any amendment in the unfortunate Mercia.

Two miserable months had passed since the disappearance of William and Agatha, before he knew any thing respecting his own situation. The slow return of his senses, however, was witnessed with joy; and when there was meaning in his looks, and calmness in his speech, Mary threw herself on his breast with ecstacy, and Bartonmere addressed his maker with prayers and thankfulness. But Mercia's recollection came tardily back, and, in the conversations which he held with Bartonmere and Mary, a wild and most strange image would often intrude. His strength grew with his reason, and when he could leave his bed, he always took his sister aside, in order that he might freely talk to her of the loss of Agatha, and the wretchedness it had occasioned.

"By your kind attentions, dear sister!" he cried,—"By your watchfulness, care, and assiduities, I believe my life has been preserved. But I feel myself an ingrate; I can scarcely thank you for recalling me from the shades in which I was wandering. What avails it to set up a blighted tree, the untimely blossoms of which have been strewn upon the earth? It may, indeed, look poorly

green for a while, but cannot linger in its disease, till the next mild
and unfolding season. It repays not the generous hand that rears
it—It perishes, sapless in its trunk, and with arms naked as those
of winter."

"And will my brother," said Mary, "sink, without exertion,
beneath the storm that blows on him? Has he survived only to
draw a heavier chain of affliction? Only to give me the blessings of
a few short days, when I had reckoned on those of years, then,—
then to depart from me in silence, which never can be broken,
leaving me the sad memorial of his grave! Oh, Mercia! thus pressing you to my bosom, I conjure you, by God and his angels, to banish your despair, to drive out the gloomy objects of your mind, to
hope——"

"Hope! There is nothing to fix it on. Mary, I shall never hope
again. Where should I place it?"

"See, how sweetly smile the heavens above our heads! Place
it there; for there mine is resting. He who dyes the clouds with
beauty, he who fashioned man, and upholds him in this erring
world, may yet send to us joys, the rapid succession of which will
make them countless. Though I have sought for comfort, let me,
dear Mercia! become your comforter. I will still believe that William lives, that Agatha will be restored to us, lovely and uninjured
as she went."

"Her murdered body," cried Mercia, "may probably be sent to
me! Ghastly, in her shroud, I may still behold her! But with life,
with innocence and beauty——Is not my mother her enemy?
Does not that fiend triumph in her artifices, and have we not assurances of her past vices, sufficient to make us think her capable of
every crime, which those who are more impotent than devils can
commit? Where has she lodged her victims? She has no place of
residence, she is only a wandering strumpet, that would defile the
dwellings of the good. Her assassins have completed their work.
Agatha and William have bled, and an unconsecrated grave has
received their bodies. You grow pale, Mary; you join your belief
with mine, and therefore must partake of my wretchedness."

In such conversations as these, and they were frequent, Mary
could find little consolation. In the presence of her brother, she
attempted to display a degree of fortitude and resignation, which

she did not possess; but when no one was near to observe her sorrows, she endeavoured not to restrain them, and yielded to their pressure. Lord Bartonmere shared their distress; the restoration of the beloved children of Alwynd he no longer expected. He frequently sighed oppressively for their fate, and the return of every messenger he sent to search for the abandoned Lady Mercia brought him only grief and disappointment.

His favourite, Oswy, too, was lost to him for ever; and, as his crimes were unknown, the unworthy boy was sincerely lamented. A sudden and painful death closed his early vices. Attempting one day to pass over a foot bridge, that lay across a neighbouring river, he fell into the swelling flood, and dreadfully lingered in suffocation till he expired. There were many in the castle who scarcely pitied his fate; but his patron deeply lamented it, and caused his body to be buried in a tomb, which recorded the event that occasioned his death.

It was now winter, and the season rigorous. It had been usual to observe the christmas festival, to fill the hall with music, to dance on the foot of frolic, and, with harmless mirth, make the roarings of the December storm, and the bitings of the frost unregarded and unfelt. The annual sports, however, were scarcely thought of by any person in the castle, for the domestics saw the melancholy and dejection of those whom they served, and none of them were inclined to be untimely merry.

Mary grew pale as the falling snow; and Mercia was scarcely more than the shadow of a man. Health and quiet had gone away from him. From morning till eve he gazed around him with the almost rayless eye of grief, and while the undisturbed slumbered in their beds, he frequently sat and heard the patterings of the rain, and paced the battlements, though the blast was strong, and the sky frightfully black and portentous.

He walked his round unconsciously, telling to the rude elements the woes of which he bled, and looking like the unquiet genius of the night. He wanted space to move in. His thoughts were so quick in succession that they bred confusion. It was with a wildness of recollection that he frequently called on William and Agatha, and he often poised in giddiness over the parapet.

One morning his mind recurred to Martyn of Fenrose, of

whom he had for some time ceased to think. He believed that the recluse could not be aware of the situation of William, as he had not evinced any desire to extricate him from it.

He was now accustomed to ramble long and widely, without apprising any person of his route. He therefore told no one of his intention; but, taking a staff to try the depths of the snow, he departed from the castle in search of Martyn's cave. In finding this, however, he had great difficulty. He had no track to guide him; he trod in fear of covered pits; and when, at length, he reached the dwelling of the wizard, it was with no inconsiderable degree of labour that he forced his way through the opposing thorns, which were bending beneath the weight of frozen snow. But he entered the first passage of the cold cavern, and called aloud on Martyn. The echo alone answered him. He spoke again only to listen to mockery, and, with his heart still losing its warmth, went fearfully along the dark and slippery path.

His head often dashed against the crackling icicles, that hung above it, and many times he stumbled over large stones, which were bound to the earth by the frost. When he came to the cave he looked around him, but all was emptiness and desolation. Inclement as the season was, neither bird, nor beast had taken shelter there; and Mercia had walked nearly round the large and gloomy space, when he discovered two bodies stretched upon the earth.

These were the remains of Martyn and his wife. They had evidently died in the arms of each other, and no part of their faces, which pressed the ground, was visible. How long their breath had been suppressed Mercia could not tell; but, on touching their limbs, he found them cold and stiff, as if they had been modelled by the chisel of a statuary.

The previous knowledge he had of them conjured up some fears, which, for a while, were unconquerable; and he trembled lest the dark power that had limited their days, should come suddenly upon him, and shut up the passages of the cave for ever. He wanted to fly from the horrid solitude, but felt like a man who dreams that he is assailed and spell-bound by a demon. The consciousness of innocence, however, soon caused him to be more firm and collected; and he took in the assurance, that wickedness might be embraced, but could not be imposed.

He now looked on the prostrate victims with less dread than pity; and virtue taught him some hasty lessons while he stood over them. A broken sword lay by the side of Martyn; his habit was torn, in a manner that bespoke a struggle with an enemy; and a glass, which had calculated time, stood shattered and emptied of its sand near his head. But there were no appearances of blood; and though death had left behind him the memento of his victory, it seemed that he had treated Martyn, as he had been accustomed to deal with all mortals, since he quitted the distorted body of his mother.

Mercia recollected that part of the wizard's story, which related to the visitation of the guardian of the night, and also what the spirit of good had been reported to say, in respect to the only signs by which the doom of the sinful might be known after their breath had passed from them. It was with fearful hesitation and trembling limbs that Mercia sought for evidences. He turned the body of the woman, and found it scarcely changed; he then looked more confidently on Martyn's, and discovered in it a larger share of serenity than it had ever expressed while he was living.

"Praises to the God of heaven!" exclaimed Mercia, "eternal praises to him for his mercies!"

Believing that, the inhabitants being dead, any person had the power of exploring this recess, he dragged the bodies to the darkest corner of the cave; and then returned, musing on what he had seen, to the castle.

———————

William and his sister were confined three days in the vessel, and the situation of the latter made her brother almost desperate. With those to whose power they had been compelled to surrender they very seldom discoursed; for the men, though not severe, were sparing of their words, and brief when called upon to answer any question. The waves were gentle, but the minds of the prisoners tempestuous; and when they found, on the fourth day, that the vessel was anchored, and were afterwards put into the boat to be taken on shore, Agatha clung still closer to the breast of William, and shuddered with horror when she thought of the vengeance of Mercia's inhuman mother.

Being landed, they were commanded, on pain of eternal separation, to walk quietly, and without making either sign or motion
to any person whom they might chance to meet. The condition
exacted obedience; and they went forward a considerable way,
through meadows and coppices, when they came to a dwelling, in
which they were commanded to enter. Opposition was fruitless,
and Agatha privately entreated her brother not to make any; but
when the gate closed on them, rage swelled the breast of one, and
fear shook the bosom of the other.

They were conducted through several unfurnished rooms, and
at length shewn to one, which, they were informed, would for a
while be appropriated to their use. It was an interior apartment,
which, though somewhat dark, did not seem proper for the purposes of tyranny; and soon after they had entered it, provisions
and wine were brought in, and they were desired to partake of
them.

They had fasted long, and Agatha being faint and exhausted,
William offered her some refreshment; but a sudden fear of treachery entering his mind, he drew the liquor hastily from the thirsty
lips that were going to receive it. This action was observed by one
of the men, who guessing the cause of it, not only took the bottle,
and drank some of the wine, but also tasted the food that was on
the table, in order to give assurance to William that every thing
was fair as it appeared.

Two servants stood behind William and Agatha while they
were appeasing their long neglected appetites, but nothing that
they said in regard to their situation was answered; and after their
repast the attendants cleared the board, and withdrew in silence.
Left alone with her brother, the head of Agatha fell upon his shoulder, and she sobbed as she repeated her fears of their being lost to
Mary and Mercia for ever.

"I entreat you, my sister," replied William, "to dismiss your
shocking apprehensions, and to believe that we shall not long have
any injuries to complain of. As yet we can scarcely speak of violence; and I hope the returning sense of our enemy will, in the
course of a few days, induce her to give us liberty. Why she has
caused us to be brought hither I cannot conjecture; and it seems to
me very probable, that her accessaries have mistaken her orders,

and that they should have secured Mercia and my sweet Mary, rather than us. The anxieties of those dear friends, and of Lord Bartonmere, afflict me more than any thing has done since our separation. If Lady Mercia supposes that I will renounce Mary, she will certainly, and if she expect that you will give up the love of Mercia, she will probably be deceived. I can look to no other views than these. How she succeeded in bribing that smiling imp that led us into her snares I know not. But she has commenced her operations with no great severity; and should she proceed to any, let me suffer greatly, if I do not foil and humble the arrogant harlot of Celwold."

"But think of her means—her power," cried Agatha, "think of the wretches who will wink significantly, and run at her command."

"Think not of them at all, dear sister, at least, banish them from your mind for a little while, and trust that our deliverance is near."

The remainder of the day was spent in a cheerless manner; Lady Mercia did not appear, and at night a woman, the first they had seen since their arrival, came to conduct Agatha to her chamber. The alarmed girl said she would not leave her brother; and in her terror hung upon his arm. Fearful of villainy he also declared, that she should not be separated from him, when the woman retired, and soon afterwards she returned, accompanied by the man who had tasted the suspected viands.

He protested that no injury was designed against either of them, and that their accommodation would be regarded. He offered to shew them the chambers, which had been prepared for their reception, and gave them keys, by which they might make themselves secure during the night.

"At present," he continued, "I command here. On the arrival of my superior I shall not be accountable for any thing that may happen; but while I am in office, I swear, by my God, that I will act honestly with you. I shall like your confidence better than your suspicions; trust me, therefore, and you will not hereafter repent."

Agatha still looked fearfully, but William, who had compared the man's voice with the tones of a natural sincerity, and found no dissonance, asked him to lead on. He followed, with his sister leaning on his arm, and entreated her to believe that their conductor's intentions were such as he professed.

They were first shewn to the room assigned to William, and afterwards to that which was to be used by his sister. They were only a small distance from each other, and nothing appeared in a doubtful light to either of them. William told the attendant that his professions should be relied on; he then took a lamp from the woman, and put it into the hand of his sister, whom he wished a good night, and bending his knees, he devoutly prayed the Almighty to bless her.

The man seemed to enter into his feelings; but he was silent, and, bowing to the youth when he returned to his chamber, he retired with the female.

William closed not his eyes till long after the break of day, but often went to the door of Agatha's room, and to soften her fears spoke soothingly to her. These visitations were most acceptable. After his first coming she sat listening for the succeeding ones, and if she heard him not at the expected minute, she left her bed, and applied her ear to the door, thinking that he might be groaning beneath the daggers of Githa's numerous bravoes. But when morning beamed on her, she fell gently upon her pillow, and slept calmly till the hour of nine, when she arose and flew into the arms of her loving brother.

That day went over, and they saw not Lady Mercia; a month succeeded, and the female tyrant yet absented herself. Their accommodation was strictly observed, but those who waited on them became still more obstinate in their silence. It was from the superior alone that they could draw any thing beyond monosyllables, and even he was evidently best satisfied with his conduct, when his tongue was not called into motion.

William had not expected so long a captivity, and could scarcely solace his sister with a single hope. What Agatha had first anticipated she now witnessed; and what she had feared she now more strongly dreaded. William offered to bribe the man, whose fidelity, he found, was not to be sold. He also silently examined the place of his confinement, with the hope of stealing privately from bondage; but discovered that every attempt which he might make, would be attended by peril, and finally by disappointment.

He saw, with agony, that health was rapidly flying from his sister; he thought she suffered much for want of air, and entreated the deputy of his foe to let her go abroad. This request was not granted. He was told that it could not be done without perjury; but that he and his sister were at liberty to walk in a large room, from which the country might be viewed. William hastily accepted the offer, and ascended the stair-case with the drooping Agatha. The man preceded them, they entered the large apartment, and William ran impatiently to the grated window.

He saw a wide prospect, which even the lateness of the year had not made undelightful. His emotions subdued him, the flood of tenderness was not wholly to be restrained, and, with the tones of sorrow, he exclaimed, "How long shall I be held in this debasing—this undeserved captivity?"

"Perhaps for ever," replied his conductor, "I shall leave you, sir. When you please you may return to the apartment below."

"For ever!" cried William, "did you hear, sister? For ever! Let me banish that thought of wretchedness and despair. Man can be happy no longer than he is free. What joy has it been to me to exercise my limbs in the early hours of morning, and to walk in the paths of nature, while from the breezes I drank the copious draught of health. The hills and valleys of Alwynd—Ah, how delightful!—The friendship of Mercia, the love of Mary—Agatha, I shall grow wild, if I dwell on a theme like this; and yet my mind is not to be diverted from it. Our guard speaks as he has been prompted. His revengeful mistress will command the gate never to be opened to us, and here your existence, as well as my own, will terminate. The eyes of those whom we love took their farewel of us, before the execrable page assigned us to our slowly destructive enemy."

Agatha, fully believing this melancholy prediction, stood by the side of her brother, gazing with deep regret on the wide and unknown scene. They could form no opinion in regard to the name, or locality of the place in which they were imprisoned. It was evident that the building was not small; and though it differed much from a fortified castle, yet there was great strength in the walls; and a bridge and moat defended it. Its situation was retired, no road was near it, and the only edifices discoverable from the window, were two or three poor peasant huts which stood in a distant valley.

To look at the external appearances of nature, was, in some degree, a pleasure to the captives; and though it gave birth to many regrets, they were loath to depart from the window. At length, however, the sun went down, the evening proved cold, and they returned dejectedly to the room in which they had been accustomed to spend the principal part of their time.

Almost every day, during the ensuing month, they spent two or three hours in this apartment; and though the winter was growing sharp, and the prospect dreary, they were unwilling to bid adieu to the only spot on earth on which they were allowed to cast their melancholy eyes. They seldom separated from each other, after they had risen, till they retired to their beds; and one evening, while they were together, and after a confinement of nearly five months, they were summoned to meet the person under whose displeasure they had fallen.

"Is the infamous woman come at last?" cried William, "then I will be satisfied. Lead us to her instantly, friend, that I may try the force of virtue, and see whether her guilty face can turn unblushingly towards mine. Why droops my sister? Take hold of my arm, and go resolutely with me. Think of your recent injuries, and let neither your father, nor your mother be forgotten in a moment like this."

The man conducted them along a gallery, at the end of which was a richly furnished room. They went in, but found it empty; within a few minutes, however, they heard a noise at the opposite side, when a door was thrown open, and Celwold, with six attendants, entered to the astonished captives. William started at this strange and unexpected sight; and Agatha shrieked, on discovering that they had fallen into the hands of an enemy more to be feared than Mercia's mother.

Celwold smiled triumphantly at the confusion of the one, and the terror of the other. He approached them with derision; and William, who was flying, hot with rage, towards his insolent foe, was seized by the guards, and menaced by their swords.

"You see the danger you incur by violence," said Celwold, "your safety lies in quietness and submission; and I charge you on your life, to be respectful in your speech, and tame in your actions. The sword is suspended, and let your own prudence caution you against its fall."

"I spurn the cautions of a villain," said the undaunted William, "and despise him from whom they come, more than the fiend that shall hereafter lash him for his deeds. You have made me a prisoner—but now I call on you to open the gates, and, if you value life, to let me go from hence this very day. I have sinned against no man. On the names of yourself and the strumpet widow of Mercia, shall be heaped loads of infamy, even by those whom the world shall know to be infamous."

"Punish the rude and insolent boy," said Celwold to his men, "strike the audacious stripling!"

"Forbear!" exclaimed the frantic Agatha, "murderers forbear!— Delay your vengeance for a while. There—now proceed as your sanguinary paymaster directs; now, while I hang on the neck of my brother, stab us both to the heart, and give the crimsoned trophies of the action to the wretch that covets our blood—to Celwold—to him whose crimes will ever hide him from God."

"Silence, ungentle girl, and do not provoke me further. Take your hands from them, fellows. I will trust to their discretion. William, you may yet make me your friend; and, by means which I will propose, render yourself free, rich, and happy."

"Name them, name them," cried William.—"Yet stay, first tell me why you have called in the aid of Lady Mercia on this occasion?—Why she assisted in bringing us into this disgraceful condition?"

"She had no concern in it," replied Celwold, "I only borrowed her name, to aid those intentions which I have fortunately executed. She knows nothing of you; and ere this she has sought for her former gallants in France. Oswy was an admirable boy; and without his assistance my projects must have failed. He led you into the snare with a fascinating ease; and he has since sobbed for your unknown fate in the arms of Mercia, and on the downy bosom of his sister."

"Oh, impious!" exclaimed William. "You know yourself to be the property of devils, and would not go singly into perdition. I will, at present, enquire no further—my heart has already sickened at your crimes. Agatha, go with me, and look no more on that mass of vice and sin. Stand off, brutes!—If I remain with you any longer, it shall be in death. Take your foul hands from my innocent sister. See, our tyrant sanctions not your actions, therefore stretch not the poor authority of which you are so proud any further."

"Let them retire for the present," said Celwold.—"William, I shall oppose neither your present desires, nor those of your sister, my lovely captive. But in the morning you must see me again—I will then explain to you the motives of my actions; and I should like it better if you were to come unimpassioned, and to talk amicably."

Neither of the children of Alwynd made any reply; they retired together, and Agatha had so many terrors in her bosom that she resolved not to leave her brother till the morning. Her fears encreased as the night lengthened, and she looked for dangers and unavoidable insults.

"Be more composed, dear Agatha," cried William, "and let not your anticipations distract you. I must, I confess, look with suspicion on our foe; but I cannot think he brought us hither for the foul purpose of murder. What! torture and stain the bosom of my sister!—No, no, I will not believe it. I wonder at the complication of villainies and deceits by which we have become prisoners; but the annals of guilt can produce nothing equal to the duplicity and baseness of our youngest enemy. I can now conjecture why we have been brought to this place.—Convinced of our legitimacy, and just title to what he has unlawfully possessed himself of, he would first alarm us by his power, and afterwards bring us to compromise, in such a manner as shall establish him in the place where ambition leads him to sit. But let me be called the bastard of Alwynd, a villain, by every one, if I be made either to give up any part of, or bargain for, my birth-right. In the morning, however, we shall learn more of him and his intentions."

"In the morning!" cried Agatha, doubtingly.—"God, I implore thee to shield and protect us!—Ah, William! I fear your thoughts do not half meet his motives."

They watched the lamp till the flame faded, Agatha then threw herself on the bed, and William endeavoured to find some repose while sitting in his chair. Both of them obtained a short sleep; and

soon after they awoke they prepared themselves for a second interview with Celwold, whom they met about the hour of ten.

It was evident that he wished not to look like an enemy, for he
received them with a smile, and invited them to the repast that
stood before him.

"This is no time," said William, "for the indulging of our appetites. To business, to business, my Lord—surrounded by mysteries
I am impatient to be extricated, and shall not rest till I hear an
explanation of the conduct which has so much amazed me."

"You are, indeed, most hasty," said Celwold.

"I cannot believe but that the spirit of my father is troubled at
an hour like this. I am glad to meet you alone, as it will remove all
constraint from our discourse. And now, as you hope God to be
merciful to you, I charge you to tell me why you have brought us
hither, what your purposes are, and how you mean to dispose of
us. But first I would have you inform me, who you really think me
to be, and what the world may call me."

"I know you to be the son of Alwynd; but the world shall call
you so only on my conditions. Nay, be calm, sir,—look on my
sword, and remember that you are unarmed. I always esteemed
myself the heir of your father, for he has often declared that you
and your sister were only the children of a deceased friend; and of
his being ever married, I had neither belief nor suspicion. Do you
know what it is to nurse the hopes of years, and at length to have
them snatched away by the hand of disappointment?—When Alwynd died, I thought it would be only a lawful act to take his name
and fortunes;—but, lo! some papers are discovered, which entitle
me only to a paltry benefit,—set you, whom I had considered as a
poor pensioner, in grandeur above my head,—and make the man
of acknowledged truth a most despicable liar!"

"Do you not stand in fear of hell?" cried William.—"Oh, detestable hypocrite! abominable slanderer!"

"Look at my face," said Celwold, "and you will still find it
smooth and calm. Spend not your breath, therefore, in loud words,
but listen to what I would further say. You call me a hypocrite,
such your father was to me, during his whole life; and your other
accusation will not rest, unless you allow that there is slander in
truth. But, to proceed, my manner of losing Alwynd's will seemed

to me most strange; and the means by which it was given to you still more extraordinary:—But of the arts which were practiced I could not long be ignorant, and, were I not merciful, I could punish you for sorcery. Previous to that, or rather to the time at which you absented yourself from the castle, I was well disposed towards you; and, tho' I had determined never to reveal to you either the narrative or will of your father, yet I should have resigned to you a part of——"

"Insult me no longer with language like this," cried William, "you cannot make your cause any better than that of a robber, who should have taken from me a hundred pieces of gold, and afterwards reluctantly restored one of them. Beggary be my portion if I ever listen to such conditions;—I am the heir of Alwynd, and the son of Matilda—let that suffice."

"In the former character what would you do against my opposition, even should I set open the gates and say to you, 'Take your leisure and best opportunities to establish your fortunes?' Who would believe your written evidences?—'They are illegal,' it would be generally said of them;—they are base contrivances, and let those who impudently speak of their validity, be suspended by their necks till they die in agony. I would be cruel only in extremity; but should you dare to aim at what I have in my possession, I will produce men who shall swear that they were witnesses to, and might, had they closed with your terms of bribery, have been assistants in your forgeries."

Agatha hung down her head at this acknowledged capability of wickedness, and her brother shook with passion.

"And then, your vaunted royalty!" continued Celwold, "tell me, what would it avail?—While princes are popular and generally smiled upon, nature must have formed them strangely if they are not happy; but on the ebbing of the tide of applause and favour, they sink still lower than any of their subjects in misfortune. The common man has only to stand against an individual assailant, at most a class of foes; the prince, however, bereft of his authority, suspects every thing he sees,—every thing he hears. His enemies, like bees in summer, swarm thickly around him, and, if they light on him, not one of them will with-hold the sting that contributes to his death. Declare yourself to be the son of Matilda,—some there are who will stare on you, and pass without moving their caps; and others will ridicule a prince who is too poor to feed and clothe a single lacquey. You will be hooted at as a madman,—despised as a bastard,—and should the king get you within his power, he would either cause a dagger to be privately stuck in your heart, or the remainder of your days to be wasted in a dungeon. I know him well,—his rage would even induce him to have the corrupting body of your father torn from the grave, and exposed on high with all its deformities."

"Oh, horrid!" cried Agatha, "this is too horrid!"

"Turn, then, your eyes from the picture I have drawn, and place them, with your brother's, on that which I shall next present. Were my intentions tyrannical, my conduct would have been different to what it has been.—In separating you from the hot-brained Mercia, and from the officious Bartonmere, I wished to be as ungentle as possible; and it was to keep myself from their suspicions that I did not sooner come to you. Since you have resided here, I trust that confinement is the only thing of which you can complain. If any of my fellows have been either insolent or remiss, point them out to me, and you shall witness their punishment."

"He must have deeply offended me, whom I should put to *your* correction," said William, "but proceed, you promised us something more than this."

"Yet I have promised nothing equal to what I am willing to give. William, on one condition you shall take the name of your father, and I will relinquish the larger part of his possessions;—those who have followed me as their Lord shall turn to you, friendship shall again unite us, and eternal amity keep from us the remembrance of all past bickerings and dissentions. For these actions, however, I shall expect a dear and precious reward."

"Name it, name it, if I grant it not."

"The hand, the heart, the person of your lovely and adored sister!—of Agatha!—of the woman who is first in my love, and whom I now press in my desiring arms!"

"Away! away!" cried Agatha, shrinking from the embrace.

"Stand off!" exclaimed her brother, "Celwold desist, or you will make me do something that is desperate."

"What, scorned by both of you?" cried Celwold, "unwilling to believe it I will not remain only half assured. I have before this time declared my love to Agatha, and I now repeat it, in the presence of her brother. I must ever despise the unworthy object of her romantic passion, whose abominable mother drew me into an engagement when my heart was the sole property of Alwynd's daughter. Agatha, I charge you to be not rash and inconsiderate.— Once more I offer myself to you as a husband;—will you discard the fretful Mercia, and accept of me?'

"Never!—I declare, before God, I never will!"

"William," said Celwold, "entreat your sister to recal the vow she has made; for tho' I am most sincere in my present professions, disappointment may soon cause me to be wild and tyrannous."

"If you are jesting with us," replied William, "it is with much gravity; but if you speak seriously, I would have my smiles, not my tongue, give you an answer. You marry my sister!—You supplant the noble Mercia!—Sooner than take benefit from means like these, I would sell myself to irredeemable slavery. This is extravagant beyond my conception, and I blush to hear what folly unblushingly spoke. If Agatha does not become the wife of Mercia—of the friend of my heart, let her die in maiden singleness; and rather than consent to her union with you, whose age, manners, and habits differ as much from her's as autumn does from spring, and as duplicity and vice do from sincerity and virtue,—I would for ever bear the chain of captivity, and grovel till death in the vilest cell you could scoop out for me."

"Base and insolent stripling!" exclaimed Celwold, "your boasted resolution shall soon be tried, and I will speedily humble the arrogance of your sister. Love converted to hatred is fierce and deadly in its operations;—beware of the change to which I allude, and curse only yourself when you shall feel the painful effects of it. To this house your deceptious father brought you in your infancy; and here you both shall perish, before I will be either defeated in my purposes or degraded by your contumacy."

He then retired hastily, and his captives immediately went to their apartment filled with astonishment and agony.

"Enable me, good Heaven!" cried Agatha, "to bear the insolence and oppressions of him whose crimes make him most detestable. Here our father smiled while the tender Neville reared his motherless infants;—here, perhaps, we are both fated to the blow of an hired assassin!—My blood curdles.—Where, oh, where are you, my beloved Mercia? William, let me lean upon your arm,—my forehead beats and my imagination grows wild."

"Sink not, Agatha, for we can hope no longer than we are resolute.—But tell me what the villain meant, when he said that he had before declared his love to you?'

"He took an opportunity, in the absence of you and Mercia, to speak of it, and addressed me in such terms, that I was discomposed till you came back to me, when I again thought myself secure. He renewed the subject only once, and that was soon after the arrival of the partner of his licentiousness. With the knowledge I had of your temper, as well as of Mercia's, I thought it would be imprudent to reveal the cause of my uneasiness; and Celwold's subsequent conduct was such as led me to believe, that I had become indifferent to him, and that Lady Mercia was entitled to the love which I had rejected. But now I find I was deceived—now, perhaps, the life of my brother will be savagely taken from him, and no person will give me aid, while I shriek and implore to be rescued from violence."

"Let the most dreadful punishment of God, come quicker than lightning to him, who shall dare to injure you. Fear it not, my sister. Celwold will never proceed to such extremities; and though I have no present hope of freedom, I trust the time will arrive, when I shall go into it, with a heart unoppressed by a single care. I have now some knowledge of the place in which we are imprisoned, and it may be of advantage to me. Oh, that I could either speak or write a few words to Mary—that I could apprise Bartonmere and Mercia of our situation and danger!"

During three ensuing days they saw not him by whom they were held in bondage; but on the morning of the fourth he came to them, and repeated his offers, which were again peremptorily rejected. While he was renewing his wishes and intentions, he was calm, collected, and conciliatory; when they, however, again assured him that his terms were held to be despicable, and would never be acceded to, his eye blazed and his chest rose with passion.

He vowed that his vengeance should fall on both of them, and that it should not be long suspended. He cursed their arrogance, for turning from an alliance that would have honoured them; and bade them feed no expectation of ever departing from a place, in which they had shewn such an insolence of spirit. After some further and severe menaces he retired. His ferocity terrified Agatha, and alarmed her brother; they more seriously dreaded his power and malignity, and while they were earnestly discoursing on the subject, six of Celwold's men entered the room, and tore them from the arms of each other.

Seeing that four of the wretches were bearing her brother away, Agatha made an effort to throw herself upon his neck, but she did not succeed, and falling with violence on the floor, William perceived that the boards were stained with her blood, and heard her shriek for her brother, her beloved brother!—His attempt to free himself was ineffectual,—his assailants were too many for him,—and they hurried him away, without allowing him to raise up or speak to his wretched sister.

The senses of Agatha wandered for a considerable time, and on their return, she found Celwold standing over her. He endeavoured to console her, raised her on his breast, and spoke soothingly to her, when he thought her capable of understanding him. With a full recollection of her condition, she freed herself from his embrace; and, with indignation beat down the hand that was held out to her. She seized him by the arm, and looking with a wild expression in his face, called and even franticly raved for her brother.

"I know what you mean," she cried, "by tearing him from me. It is his blood you crave; your black soul is impatient for it, and yourself and your murderers are equally ready. But you shall not— dare not touch him. Some counteracting spirit will come upon you, and ere you can perform the guilty deed, your throat will swell and blacken in its grasp. Oh, Celwold! By the true and only God, I implore you to offer no violence to my brother! Send him to me, replace him in my arms, and all my curses will be changed to blessings."

"You know my terms, Agatha—will you accept them?"

"No! Did twenty lives, with my own among them, depend on my acquiescence, I would ever answer thus. No, Celwold! the state of death, however little it may be known or understood, I would go into, rather than the miserable certainty you have proposed."

"Then your brother shall die, unfeeling girl!"

"Virtue never dies; it sleeps for a while, to wake more joyfully than it went to its repose. But when you shall have passed through existence, horrible will be the banishment of your dreams. Heaven will be in your eyes, and hell beneath your sinking feet. My brother! Give me—unnatural murderer, give me my brother!"

She was running in search of William, when Celwold seized her in his arms, and bore her to her chamber. He desired that the woman might come to him immediately; and as soon as she appeared, he put Agatha under her care, and desired her to be watchful over her charge.

Though Celwold had as yet gained but little, he believed that perseverance would bring him much; and though he actually meant not to carry his resentments so far as he had threatened, still he was determined to push them forward, till he attained some of his wishes. Opposed as he was, he did not despair, but that he should yet humble the spirit of Alwynd's son, and succeed in making Agatha such as he wished her to be.

His love was of a strong, but peculiar nature. The time had not long passed since he despised her and her brother alike. But it was in witnessing her sweet gratitude, after the death of her father, and in comparing her modest loveliness with the bold features of the abandoned Lady Mercia, that he took in sentiments, which had been banished during a series of years, or rather, which he then came to an original knowledge of.

Hating Mercia as he did, it was glorious to think, that she might probably be wrested from him; and though he knew that great sacrifices must previously be made to her brother, yet even avarice seemed inclined to offer them quietly. What he might gain by the alliance he had ambitiously calculated. He believed that he possessed policy enough to work himself into greatness; and though his words and actions appeared to his prisoners gross inconsistencies, he knew how their unities might be discovered, as well as the manner in which they would co-operate.

He had always entertained a private vanity in regard to his person, and in spite of the recent remarks of William, he thought it might still stand the test with that of his youthful rival. Previously assured that he should have many obstacles to oppose, he had not expected from Agatha an immediate acquiescence. There was, however, in her, as well as in her brother, more determination and spirit than he could have wished to find, still he believed that they would bend to his purposes; and though Agatha had made a most strong and serious vow, yet he had both heard and read of the same being done by many women, whose perjuries were forgotten by themselves, and unnoticed by the world.

Having placed William in a separate and distant room, he suffered several days to elapse before he renewed his suit. But he made frequent enquiries after Agatha, and desired his fellows to wait on her with attention and respect. His principal agent and ambassador was a man who had not been long in his service, but whose daring spirit and deep duplicity seemed well adapted to his employer's purposes.

This fellow's name was Eustace. He had been in the continental wars, the proofs of which were on his forehead and cheek, though vanity caused him to hide the marks, which valor would have prompted many men to display.

Villany cannot act upon inequalities. A certain degree of familiarity subsisted between Celwold and Eustace; and whatever the one thought or designed, he without reserve communicated it to the other. Eustace was in the habit of visiting both William and Agatha. He sometimes looked on them with a deadly hatred, as if he had received from them a thousand wrongs; and sometimes that part of his face which was visible would not be without tenderness and compassion.

William noticed his apparent qualities, but as his visits were limited to a few minutes he could not try them. Still it was somewhat extraordinary to him, that an uninjured man could look so revengefully; and equally strange that one hired for base actions, and the exercise of oppression, should occasionally call into his face the seeming natural looks of mildness and sympathy.

Agatha found nothing inexplicable in Eustace; she scarcely ever looked up to him, and was always anxious for him to depart. He would not speak of her brother—and of no other person or thing she wished to converse. He refused to tell her where he was, or whether he was well, for which she deemed him a savage, and inwardly execrated him. The horrors of her situation were growing more black and insupportable; and when Celwold visited her again, he found her so greatly changed, that for a moment he was seised by shame and remorse. But discovering that she was still inflexible, severe in her reproaches, and strong in the epithets she placed on him, he again grew into hardiness, and swore to carry his resentments as far as they would extend, if she did not alter her conduct, and comply with his wishes.

She started at his menaces, and her eyes turned towards him with terror.

"Why, why," he cried, "will you force me to severity?—However harsh my actions may seem, I protest that I love you still. Reproachful, obstinate, and insulting as you have been, my passion yet survives, and my heart remains your property. If you consent to my desires, I will lead you forth in splendour to my admiring people, and say to them, 'Observe and reverence my wife.' He who serves you with most diligence shall be best rewarded. But if any one of them disobey your commands, he shall soon meet with disgrace and infamy. Oh, Agatha! your smiles and love——"

"Name them not, but think of Mercia."

"Forgetfulness to the name, and ruin to him who bears it!—Know, tormenting girl, that every minute of your delay adds to the pangs and distresses of your brother. You have driven me into the paths which I now tread—I was compelled to enter them for the want of a middle way. You have no affection for your brother—you would have his life waste in sorrow and captivity—you never wish to see him again."

"Oh, falsehood, falsehood!—Restore him to liberty, and do what you please with me. Once more I will appeal to you—again implore and supplicate.—Let me see and speak to my brother. If, but for a moment, you will suffer me to look on him—if you will only allow me to say, 'God bless you, William!' you shall find that I will——"

"What?—tell me what, my lovely Agatha!"

"Urge me no further now, for I hear the voice of nature calling aloud to me. Lead on, lead on. I conjure you, by heaven and its saints, not to blast the hopes of my anxious and throbbing heart!"

"Follow me, then," cried Celwold, "be timely wise, and do not dally with happiness till the arms of misery are rivetted around you."

He led her down the stairs, and they soon came to the basement floor. Taking her arm, he then directed her through several passages, descended with her another flight of steps, and at length entered a large dull and vapoury place, around which Agatha cast her expecting but affrighted eyes. It seemed to her a spot of horror, and she stood shivering with dread. She looked upon the face of Celwold, fancied that the features of a murderer were turned towards her, and wildly asked whether that was the detestable prison of her brother.

Celwold touched a bell, and within a few minutes a wide dark curtain was drawn up, which discovered Eustace standing behind an iron screen, at the extremity of the room.

"Bring forth your prisoner," said Celwold, "and tell him to be tranquil."

"Tranquil he must be," replied Eustace, "for he scarcely lives."

Eustace withdrew,—Agatha's head was growing wild, she gazed on the grate and soon beheld the captive and heard his chains. She was flying towards him but Celwold detained her in his arms;—she vainly struggled to free herself, stretched forth her hands to her brother, and called on him with a voice broken by agony.

William, viewed at a distance, appeared thin, weak, and sallow; and he rested his head on the bars, beyond which he wished to fly to meet the denied embrace.

"And are such things as these," cried Agatha, "suffered in the world?—Is there no fear of God, and does not his immediate vengeance fall on the perpetrator of a crime like this?—Oh! base and wicked Celwold! what answer will you make to the account that shall be hereafter stated? William! Brother! speak to me;—let me hear your voice, for I begin to suspect that they have only set before my eyes your murdered body."

"Oh, my sister!——"

"Are these the tones of a man?—Misery!—Why did I come hither?—This object will be ever in my eyes, when death has half closed them it will not be excluded!—Attempt not to hold me, barbarian! I must, I will go to my brother,—he appears to be dying;— let me only have the charge of him till his breath is gone."

"If the last agonies were in him," cried Celwold, "you should not move a step. My business at present is to revenge the injuries I have received from you and him, not to wink at further conspiracy."

"You can fear nothing from feebleness like ours;—You can watch and limit our actions. Almighty God! he cannot speak to me!—He falls for want of aid,—he perishes, unassisted, in the sight of his sister!"

"He is only weak and fainting," said Celwold, "and with a little care health might be brought back to him. If you accept my terms, the roses of summer shall not be more red than his face when he spurns the fetters of captivity; but if you reject them, this night, this very night——."

"This night.—What?—What of this night?"

"His heart shall cease to beat for ever."

"Murder!—Your terms.—What are they?"

"That you will now renounce the vow you made.—That you will immediately become my wife."

"And my brother shall be free? And you will give him to my arms?"

"I will take off his irons myself.—I will place him on your bosom, and watch by your side for his recovery."

"Do it then, do it instantly, and let me satisfy humanity. My brother, I shall clasp you yet! We shall still speak comfort to, and smile on each other. Celwold, here is my hand; take it, and make me what you please. Off with the chains of your victim, and lead him forth to me.—Let me kiss his cheek;—let me lay his weakened body on some easy resting place;—then do you call the priest and say to him, 'Make me the husband of this woman.' If I go wild before the morning, take no unfair advantages of my condition, but regard my brother. Open the grate, and send the priest to the altar."

Rushing up to the barrier, she madly strove to tear it down, and caught the cold—extended hand of William.

"Are you sensible?" she cried, "have you heard the accepted conditions of Celwold?"

"Yes, I have heard them," he replied, with all possible exertion, "but now you must swear never to become his wife. Never, whatever may be our fate, to bind yourself to one, whom it is pollution to touch, and disgrace to associate with."

"But, did you hear him? To-night!—Look at him and tremble."

"Let him be as diabolical in his actions as he has threatened; that he will be so I can well believe, but even the certainty of it, should not draw from me an assent to his proposal. We may never meet again—God bless you, Agatha!—He will protect you, sister, if virtue was ever his care. Mary and I are separated eternally! Think of Mercia; and do not, even for the preservation of life, run into perjury."

"For my own sake I would not—But for you—A death of torture, depending on means I know not how horrid; effected by devils I know not how ingeniously sanguinary! It must not be! You shall still be saved. Celwold, Celwold! Take me hence instantly."

The person she called on approached, and was leading her away, when William, growing almost frantic, shook the bars of his prison, and summoned her back to him. She tore her hand from Celwold, and returned to the captive.

"I could wish to bless you in death, Agatha," he cried, "do not, therefore, urge me to curse you. By the reputation of our father, by the virtue of our mother, and by the purity of your past days, I conjure you to dishonour neither yourself nor your brother. I was ever assured of your love; I now read it in your wild countenance. But I most solemnly declare, that if you consent to be united to the villain who stands before me, I will disdain to accept his mercy, and tear out my heart, if I have no other instruments than my nails."

"My noble brother! I have caught your spirit, and will nourish it in my breast. Now, Celwold, hear a repetition of my vow. By every thing that is holy in Heaven, and good on earth, I swear I never will be your wife!"

"Then instant vengeance shall be mine. Eustace, away with the prisoner, and dispose of him as you have been commanded."

The curtain immediately fell. The brain of Agatha seemed to sink into oblivion, and she made no opposition, while Celwold was conveying her back to her chamber. She looked on him as if she remembered him neither as a friend, nor an enemy; but her beauties were still uninjured, and as she sat, without recollection, on the couch where Celwold had placed her, he not only cursed his disappointments, but hellishly desired some present enjoyments to compensate them.

Within a few minutes Eustace entered, and informed him that he had taken William back to the place from whence he had been brought previous to the interview with his sister. He saw that something strange was passing in the mind of Celwold, for his countenance was indescribable—his cheeks were hot and red—an impatient pleasure gleamed from his eyes—and he seemed panting for something, which he was either fearful of possessing or speaking of.

"What ails your Lordship?" enquired Eustace.—"You tremble violently, your face flames, and, though you speak not, I hear a most strange sound coming from you."

"Look at that girl, Eustace."

"She seems a statue of marble—her senses are surely fled. Yet, how lovely! how exquisitely sweet!"

"She is a truly admirable composition; and you know not to what extent I love her. But I fear I shall never conquer her prejudice, unless it can be done by some previous stratagem. She is now in a state neither reasonable nor senseless. Leave us together, Eustace. This moment may decide my fate—now I may perform an action that will hereafter cause her to accept the hand that she has so strongly rejected."

"Why should I leave you, my Lord? What do you mean?—Violence, rape?"

"Love, love, my faithful fellow!—Begone—stay not with me another minute. The project is formed, and eternal joy will follow the execution of it."

"Eternal torture seize, and everlasting damnation bind up your sinews, if you shall ever dare to do the deed on which you have impiously meditated!"

"How now?—Presumptuous wretch!—Beware that you answer me not, and begone immediately."

"If I do may I be snatched into perdition by one of those fiends whose commissions are signed in hell!—Leave you?—What, give you an opportunity to be both filthy and wicked?—Leave you to oppose a strong and brutal will against a defenceless, insensible woman? God!—How she looks at you!—If such a face as that should be near your deathbed, you need not fear the discovery of any thereafter thing more calmly terrible. Is this an object for passion to feed on?—I dare not look at her any longer."

"Well, well, retire. I have been to blame, and you too rude. Retire."

"You shall precede me—here I fix myself—here will remain till you depart. In Normandy, I once cleft the skull of a young Count for rioting in the charms of a resisting but too forceless villager. I have brought my spirit into Britain, but should be loath to exercise it, without just cause and previous aggravation. Nay, look not so disdainfully, for I assert no more than I have done, and am capable of doing. Perhaps you think that I have too much conscience for your employment, still you dare not discard me. I am not in your power, but you are completely in mine. I know the damned treacheries of my species, I therefore am ever ready for my defence; beside this I prepare my own food, and select the hour most secure for sleeping. I would be more deceptive than sanguinary in my operations; and though I am stern to the captives, I will never be wholly barbarous. Let the girl recover her senses; and suffer not the malady of her brother to be neglected. If they continue to oppose your inclinations, do you continue to imprison them. But you shall go no further while I am here. Murder shall never reach William——"

"You know, Eustace, that I never wished it. My sole intent was to alarm and terrify till I found compliance."

"But here you were proceeding further—here you were heating with a design a thousand times more cruel than either the open massacre, or the private murder of a thousand men. This object will speak more forcibly then my tongue."

He pointed to Agatha, who had not uttered a word since her entrance; but Celwold turned away his head, and almost immediately left the room. Eustace now endeavoured to rouse the girl from her lethargy. He addressed her with tenderness, and repeatedly shook her arm; her features however moved not, and finding his efforts unavailing, he locked the door of her chamber, and went to the other prisoner.

"Your condition touches me," he said to William, "by my soul, I am sincere, when I say that I pity you. It was not always thus, my actions will speak to the contrary. Son of Alwynd, despair not, for all may be well hereafter. Here is wine, drink it and revive. I cannot give you freedom, but, by my God, I will protect both you and your sister against the machinations of Celwold, whom I have never esteemed—whom I now despise, abhor, execrate. Should he come to you alone, be upon your guard; if he seek your blood, let this instrument, which I charge you to hide, find the depth of his deceitful breast."

"Blessings, blessings on you, Eustace!"

"Hold! I deserve them not. They cannot make me what it was once my pride to be."

"But will you, indeed, protect my sister?—For myself I care not; but, righteous heaven! For her——"

"I know what you would say. I will protect her—and you may depend on this assurance as strongly as if it were made within the walls of a church, and witnessed by a hundred registering priests. Oh, how noble would be an universal confidence!—But that is a chimera, for we are all, in a great or small degree, corrupt, sinful, and lying. Our fathers will cheat, and our very brothers act fraudulently with us. Down therefore must fall my fabric, the design of which is beautiful, though its materials are unsound and perishable. William be firm, and careful of your health. The events of this day have terrified your sister; and though I have been a petty tyrant, I now fly to solace her."

As Eustace returned to Agatha's chamber, he passed the guilty Celwold; but he paid him no respect, nor in any manner noticed him. He shewed, however, a calm determination in his actions, and went by his angry, but cowardly employer, as if there were no inequality in their conditions.

He discovered Agatha gazing on a bloody handkerchief, which she told him had been stained by her brother's breast. Recollecting that he had left it there, (he having torn his hand, in conducting William back to his chamber,) and finding that she was now roused from her late stupor, he took the cloth from her, and tenderly assured her that there was no cause for her suspicions.

He could not easily make her sensible of what he said; and he supposed murder had so strongly impressed her mind, that it was long before she would believe in his existence. Eustace stopped not after affirming that William was living. Compassion spread over his olive face, and he told Agatha, that if she would be calm and

composed in her actions during the day, and admit him quietly at
midnight, he would conduct her to her brother, and put her into
his unshackled arms. She grew almost mad with joy, she promised
to be soon tranquil and collected, and embraced his knees in her
ecstacy.

Eustace did not disappoint her. At the time he had mentioned
he came to her with a darkened lanthorn, and after exploring with
her several rooms and passages, again she breathed on the joyfully tumultuous breast of her brother. They were left nearly an
hour together.—Agatha now found that William was weakened by
affliction, rather than tyranny; for he had been attacked by a fever,
that raged for several days with an almost destructive violence.

Their conversation at this meeting was both tender and impassioned; sweetly affectionate, and deeply melancholy. They were
speaking of the strange character of Eustace, when he entered,
and told them that they must separate.

"I am loath to part you," he said, "but prudence directs me so
to do. Celwold may yet be waking; and his fellows will watch for
gain. Come—come, lady, let us begone."

"Oh, Eustace!" cried Agatha, "I expected not to find so much
humanity in any person here. Be further merciful, and convey us
privately from this place of sin and danger."

"By Heaven I have no means. The gates are closed on me as
well as you. But I have sworn to protect you, and may the most
dreadful vengeance follow my perjury. If I cannot give you to liberty, I will save you from violence."

"Eustace!" exclaimed William, "let me strain you to my breast.
I am assured, that in some causes, you could be nobly great. I once
marked you as a desperate assassin, but now find the strength of
your humanity. If I ever regain my liberty you shall stand in my
favour; and your fortunes shall not be indifferent to me."

"Hold, hold, hold!" cried Eustace quickly, but his voice
changed, and in a sullen tone he continued, "talk not to me of benefits and rewards;—of favour and fortune. None of them have of
late belonged to me;—none of them I shall claim hereafter. Man
generally walks the paths of life as an idle spectator. The objects
he meets with amuse only as they vary; and the ways, while they
are smooth, seem alike indifferent. His choice of them wastes not

much of his time;—he enters without consideration, goes forward without reflection, and when he comes to the termination, with one single glance he can view the vast tract over which he has gone. The termination!—Well it has been spoken. Sir, I am no such traveller as I have described. I have set up a sanguine mark in a desolate vale, which is visible to no other person than myself. I have said so far, and not a step further will I go; and an hundred times in every day, I stand and gaze on the beacon, till my giddy brain makes me fancy that it moves towards me to mock my tardiness."

"What do you mean?" enquired William.

"Oh, nothing, nothing. My melancholy will pass away without the aid of the lancet. Come, Agatha, you must depart instantly."

"But tell me, good Eustace! tell me whether I shall see my brother again?"

"I will shew myself your friend whenever I have the power. Let us begone."

"Adieu, my brother! God guard and restore you to health."

"Farewell! dear sister, farewell! Eustace, you have a most precious trust——"

"And never will I abuse it. To your couch, young man, to your couch, or your eyes will be open at daybreak."

He then led Agatha back to her chamber. She slept soundly. Relying on the protection of her newly discovered friend, she received Celwold on the ensuing day, and heard his renewed menaces with resolution; and on the following night she was allowed the happiness of seeing her brother again.

The conduct of Eustace was so evidently changed, that his employer began to suspect him. The fellow nicely watched his gestures, he also discovered some of his thoughts, but neither shrunk from scrutiny, nor dreaded displeasure. Though he could use on no occasion only one eye, that seemed to have been borrowed from the lynx; his heart had been large enough for the chest of a lion; and wariness and a daring spirit were his characteristics. He perceived that Celwold repented of having made him one of his instruments. He saw that many doubts and fears crouded into the coward's breast, and believed that his secret removal by murder had been planned.

"Do you suppose," he said to Celwold, "that, because one of

my balls of sight has been raked out of its socket, the remaining one is so drowsy a servant as to wink at my danger? You have mal-ice in your heart;—your designs towards me are evil. As I lay on my bed last night, I heard a noise at the door of my chamber.—Rats, rats, it may be said—No, there were vermin of a different species trying to get in. But I foiled them, suffered them to make their paws weary with scratching, and then, merely by locking my jaws and blowing through them, frightened them back to their stinking holes, and hiding places."

"And what is this to me?"

"Nothing; design and execution are distinct things. Were not your pulses quick at the time I mentioned? And did you not curse your emissaries on their unsuccessful return? Ha! I was tempted to unbolt the door, and to rip the bowels of the unshod rascals. But the night was somewhat hot, considering the season, and I feared their carcases would taint my chamber, and fill it with buzzing flies to the interruption of my after slumbers."

"How dare you talk with so much insolence to me?"

"Pray enquire not into my prerogative. This sun-burnt ethio-pian face of mine, has been shewn in many parts of the world; and I have seen those who were desirous to question me, draw back in silence. What did you think of me when I stood near the road-side, and asked employment of you with my eye, my heart being too proud for the office? Yet answer me not.—I would not demand of others what I refuse to them myself. This only I say, I will not be suspected even by you; and should any attempt be ever made on my life, I will provide food for your kennel, as well as for the crows that hover over it."

"I know not," said Celwold, "of any designed injury; and if you have enemies, I did not cause them to become such. You must remember the terms of our agreement, from which you ought not to run."

"Perhaps there is not a man living who has not entered into some covenant which he wishes to break. We are the tools of weakness and creatures of precipitance;—but I recollect not that I have performed less than I promised. I hated the captives at first as strongly as you did; my resentments, however, have subsided, and I can no longer be cruel and tyrannic."

"You would encourage arrogance and obstinacy;—you would aid no project by which my happiness might be secured."

"A transient gratification may be had, but happiness can never be obtained by means such as you would employ.—The guilty pleasures of life will ever encrease the horrors of death,—this will be confessed by vice, by immorality, and even by atheism. My lord, if you trust me still, still will I serve you;—but Alwynd's son must have only his fetters to complain of, and his daughter's chastity shall be defiled neither by force nor artifice."

He then left Celwold, who had, during this discourse, sent a thousand secret curses to him. Eustace, when first known to him had acted like a man of ordinary intellects, and seemed a person well adapted for the employment in which he was designed to be placed;—but he had now assumed a character greatly different, displayed a mind both strong and in no common degree cultivated, proudly shewn a power superior to that before which it had been expected he would humble, and, from a servile dependant grown into consequence and authority.

Celwold never possessed much valour, and tho' he execrated Eustace he would not venture to chastise him. He found a most determined opposer in an expected assistant, and believed that nothing could be done to his satisfaction while this strange fellow was living and near to him. To remove him, therefore, effectually, he determined should be his principal aim, and he wished for the arrival of some moment when his cup might be poisoned or a dagger thrust into his heart.

———

While the captives were bewailing their fate, and meeting the insults of Celwold, which were tempered only by the private indulgencies of Eustace, their friends at Bartonmere were sinking into grief and despondency; the bursting spring brought to them no pleasures, and external beauty charmed not those to whom the scenes of nature had ever been dear;—the flowery forest and the dull ocean, the sandy unfruitful tract and the fields of verdure were objects of no seeming difference.

Time encreased rather than lessened their sorrows.—Had they had any assurances of the death of those whose loss they lamented, the inevitable event would have been justly considered, and a period arrived when their excessive grief would have faded into regret; but it was uncertainty that most tortured them, they were assailed by the pangs of apprehension and could call in no hopes to oppose their fears. Of all the miseries pertaining to human life, none are worse than those issuing from a sick and despairing heart; while there is activity in our afflictions we do not think them wholly desperate, but when they are stilled and sullen, to brood over our remediless evils is only nursing death upon our breasts.

Lord Bartonmere was a sincere mourner in himself, but he suffered severely indeed whenever he turned his eyes upon Mary and her brother, who seemed to be wearied by struggling against their misfortunes. Half of the anguish that the former experienced she did not speak of; all her care was directed towards Mercia, from whom she feared she should soon be compelled to separate eternally.—To die for love will be ridiculed only by those who have little knowledge of the operations of the passions;—grief and excessive joy have had their many victims, and love becomes either grief or joy according to its disappointments or successes,—the instinct is to be regarded,—the distinguishment is simply a sound.

Mary viewed Mercia as the poor remnant of her happiness, to preserve which she was most tender and studious. She thought there were not many men, situated as he was, who would have acted so nobly and free of prejudice; for he had warmly taken her to his bosom, where he most kindly cherished her as a sister, though his mother was held to be execrable. He had disunited objects with peculiar tenderness and delicacy; justly regarding the one for its perfections, and contemning the other for its impurities.

Gratitude had ever been one of the principal qualities of Mary's disposition, but she knew neither its force nor extent till she became acquainted with the man who had rescued her from shame and oppression.

She now endeavoured to repay some of the benefits she had received with all the kindness of her nature; and though it was only affliction solacing the afflicted, still she kept most of her own sorrows in strict confinement, and rejoiced whenever she saw a faint smile, or colour, spread upon her patient's cheek. It was always her endeavour to raise a hope, and then skillfully build on it. Her simplicity, earnestness of heart, and devout confidence, formed a sweet philosophy, which Mercia, though he feared many parts of it to be fallacious, heard with pleasure, while he held the fair moralist in his truly affectionate arms.

But for no long period could he be detained by her to listen to a tale in which he found more tenderness than truth. The words of Lord Bartonmere were also unavailing; and Mercia frequently broke from them, in order to ruminate without disturbance in places lonely and sequestered, towards which neither consolation sent her voice, nor curiosity turned an eye.

He went not in pursuit of happiness, and therefore took in no new disappointments when he found it not. His expectations were dead—the blood of his heart seemed to have stagnated in grief, and the stilled current shewed no token of renewing its course.

One evening he rambled a considerable distance, wide of those paths where man was to be found, and through fields where the tall corn bent its head in stillness. The daily course of the sun was just over; his rays had been withdrawn, but the western hemisphere was hung with rich and glowing clouds, which were seen to move in slow and majestic grandeur. There was melody, as well as beauty and fragrance all around. The suspended lark seemed to make her last song the longest and softest of the day; the salacious dragon-fly, in its pursuit of love, twittered its green and burnished wing; and the closing sweet-briar roses, and clustering wild-suckles, shed far and near their delicious perfumes.

Whether summer warmed, or winter froze, Mercia had no eyes for nature.—Her severities caused him not to murmur; and her gales and riches were felt without pleasure, and viewed without gratitude. He no longer praised industry, nor encouraged sport. The village striplings could not regain his smiles; and though he with-held not his charity from the aged and unfortunate rustics, he gave it hastily, and ran from their prayers and blessings as if he either did not hear or was offended by them.

He could scarcely turn his eyes towards any object that reminded him not of the happiness which was past, and of the absence of those friends whose return he never expected. In the course of his long evening ramble, he had stopped at the noiseless cave of Martyn of Fenrose; he had also struck his staff on the spot where Alwynd died; and finally he paused over the rail of the bridge that lay across the river in which the sportive Oswy, none of whose artifices were known, untimely perished.

All these persons had a seeming connection with William and Agatha.—Mercia stood gazing on the rippling water, which the moon beams made beautiful; and he thought so strongly on the disappearance of Agatha and her brother, that at length he almost fancied he saw the spirit of the drowned boy rise from the stream, and express anew the distraction he had shewn when he returned to speak of the violence that had been done to those whom he professed so truly to love.

His head was growing wild—his eye traced many images, which he wished to grasp at, in the liquid mirror beneath; and his staff fell from the hand which was almost too much enfeebled to clench the unsteady rail, while he repeated, aloud and despairingly, the name of Agatha.

"Who is there?" said some person on the other side of the river.—"If it be Lord Mercia let him speak, for I am in search of him."

"You have found him, then," replied Mercia.—"If you have been sent by Lord Bartonmere, return, and say that I shall soon be with him."

The man came hastily over the bridge, and stopt on the opposite bank, to which Mercia had retreated, when he assured the young Earl, that he came not from Lord Bartonmere, but that he had something of consequence to impart.

"Let me see you in the morning," said Mercia, "I do not know you, and neither the place, nor the hour, is suited to conversation."

"Though you remember me not, you have seen me before—you enabled me to build up my cottage, which the storm had thrown down—you fed my wife—you cloathed my ragged children——"

"If you have any thing farther to ask, defer it till to-morrow. I assure you my means will reach none of your necessities till then. Good night!"

"Hold!—My Lord, indeed you must not go without hearing me. I came not before you merely to tell you what I have already reported, but to confess myself an ingrate, a villain—one who was too base to receive benefits, and whose life grew worse for its preservation."

"If you have designed me evil," said Mercia, "I forgive you. Let that suffice, and may your conscience be quieted."

"You have taken a load from my heart," cried the stranger, "but you will, I fear, shew me less lenity hereafter. You must listen to me here—I have something to tell which will surprise, agonise, and, perhaps, enrage you. But you have given me your pardon—remember that; and though I ought to suffocate in this stream, I beg you will do me no violence. You are unarmed, take my sword and trust me."

Mercia felt interested. He declined the weapon, and sitting down on the bank, he desired the man to proceed.

"At the time when you, my Lord did me the services of which I have spoken, I was more unfortunate than criminal, and had been so for a considerable time, almost long enough to make me lay down the life of which I was weary. I suffered many calamities.— My case was not reported to you, till excessive distress made me a robber. One night I stopped Lord Celwold in the forest, and took from him all the gold he had about him. The next morning your unexpected bounty reached me, and then my ill-acquired riches were as curses to me."

"Go on," said Mercia.

"I gave comfort to my afflicted wife, food to my famished babes, and again reared my cottage, in which I intended to live honestly. But two months had scarcely elapsed, before Lord Celwold found that I was the man who had assaulted and stripped him. He taxed me with the crime, and I confessed it. I offered to restore his untouched property—bent my knees—made my wife and little ones prostrate themselves and pray for me. The Baron, however, was inflexible, and he swore to hang me for the crime which I so earnestly repented."

"And how did you escape the sentence?"

"Aye, my Lord! there lies all the villany. Oh, I deserve the severest punishment that can be invented. I was long threatened with vengeance, and, in my terror preparing to fly from it, when I was arrested by Lord Celwold, who said I must either submit to fate, or act upon conditions which he should propose. I estimated my life most dearly, when I found it was likely to be lost; and after looking at my wretched wife and family, I promised to become his slave, if, in this case, he would be merciful. He put a purse into my hand, and desiring me to expect him again in the course of a few days, he departed. On the fourth I saw him;—he commanded me to follow him to a hovel near the shore, where I found five other men assembled. I was yet a stranger to the business I had to perform, and after a short stay Lord Celwold mounted his horse, and rode away from us. As my alternative had been dreadful, I could not much repent of my engagement; still I was apprehensive of an evil being imposed on me, almost as great as that from which I had run. About half an hour elapsed, and then a youth, whom they called Oswy, abruptly entered——"

"Oswy!" exclaimed Mercia, "poor lad, he perished here!"

"Pity not, but rather curse the simple imp," cried the stranger, "yet why should I, an experienced villain, wish you to execrate one whose years were so few. Suffice it to say that Oswy was composed of the worst qualities. Celwold bribed the lad, and made him great promises; in return, he cunningly led the objects of your love and friendship into the power of the Baron, whose agents conveyed the surprised captives to the manor-house which once belonged to Lord Alwynd, where they now remain in sorrow and apprehension."

"What!" exclaimed Mercia, "in the power of Celwold? Do you speak truly in saying so?"

"I do, my Lord; by Heaven I swear it!—But your Lordship is fainting. Throw off your hat, and lean upon my arm."

"It is surprise that overpowers me. But I have found them! I have found them, and shall be happy! I will restore them to light and liberty—I will lead them forth with—Oh, this is too great and sudden for my unprepared heart! Mercia, that thou art so near to felicity!"

"You are much agitated, my Lord. Let me lead you to the castle, and there I will tell you further."

"Be rooted here till I am satisfied. Stir not the smallest space till you have told me more. Oh, villany, villany! I will borrow a dagger of revenge, and its qualities shall be tried upon the accursed body of Celwold. But was my mother busy in the plot?"

"It was, I have been informed, so reported to you. I dare swear, however, that she had no concern in it; and the artifice of Oswy, in that respect, has often created mirth among the creatures of his employer."

"God pardon me, then, for my recent words and curses!—But say, what are the intentions of Celwold?—How do my injured friends?—And what were all your purposes in thus seeking me?—Oh, you know not how impatient is my soul!—With-hold not your answer,—speak instantly, or I shall go wild with conjecture."

The purposes of Celwold were well known to the man, who now declared them to the astonished and almost disbelieving Mercia. The lover of Agatha rubbed his brows as if he thought his brain were affected, when he was informed that Celwold hoped to persecute her till he compelled her to be his wife, and that her acquiescence was daily demanded.

Mercia made the man speak it again, lest his ear should have been deceived.—His heart alternately softened at her constancy and fired with her injuries. He implored the aid of Heaven, for her, as well as for her brother; and while he heaped curses on Celwold, he wished for the means of immediate vengeance. He afterwards asked some further questions, which the fellow, whose name was Robert, answered, as they had been put to him, collectively.

"Poverty," he replied, "has been the spring of my worst actions, to soften—to atone for which I am now come to your Lordship as a penitent, who raises his head on shame and scarcely hopes to be forgiven.—Oh, I have witnessed such scenes since I entered into my contract with the wealthy villain, that I shall never pardon myself for becoming the wretch I lately was. Lord Celwold, opposed most vehemently by William and his sister, deputed me and a man of the name of Eustace to watch over your unfortunate friend.—Ah, how great was his misery when he was separated from Lady Agatha! He fell ill, his veins swelled, the blood boiled in them, and the foot of death seemed to be near. Eustace was supposed to be one of the most hardened rascals that ever moved in the world. I had often seen him look with a deadly savageness on the prisoner, but one day, while the unfortunate William was sleeping, I discovered my fellow-guard weeping over him.—My astonishment was great, and I wondered that I had so long been deceived.—Made joyful by the discovery of this commiseration, I threw myself upon my knees, pressed the hand of Eustace, and pointing to the insensible captive, recommended him to his mercy (he being the head of Celwold's agents), and implored him to frustrate the accursed designs of his enemy. But Eustace dashed me from him, and, with a contemptuous smile looked as if he suspected my honesty.

"In the course of a few days, however, his eye softened, and calling me aside, I found that my suspicions had greatly wronged this singular man. 'Lord Celwold,' he cried, 'has sent me to seek for you; he wants you to go as a messenger to his steward at Alwynd, on some pressing concern.—I have examined your face and proved your sincerity,—I first suspected you of being an insinuating scoundrel, but have since taken in some better opinions. I find you hate the wretch you serve as much as I do; and believe that, if wishes could send him to hell, you would readily strengthen mine with your own. When you are at Alwynd, I would have you go from thence to Bartonmere-Castle, find out Lord Mercia, tell him of the past deceits of his enemy;—tell him, besides, that if he will return in privacy with you, I will contrive to put him into the arms of William and Agatha!'"

"God's blessings,—his choicest blessings on this Eustace!" cried Mercia, with transport and energy.

"Eustace left me immediately," said Robert, "and I went to Lord Celwold, from whom I received the letter and many cautions and directions. I begged that he would allow me to spend a little hour with my deserted wife and children, but it was long before he would agree to it; at length, however, he consented, and, in order to make me more prompt in my services, presented me with a piece of gold to give to the wretched mother of my poor babes. I trust I shall be pardoned for my subsequent perjuries.—I have delivered the letter to the steward, I have kissed my wife, and taken my children on my knees. Now, my Lord, I summon you to go with me,—to accept the favors of Eustace, and, with the arms of love and friendship, to raise the objects of Celwold's tyranny from the depths of despair into which they have fallen!"

"You will be honest to me?"

"I will, by my Creator!—By my Saviour, I will!"

"It is enough. I will trust you now, and better your fortunes hereafter. Oh, that on this occasion I had wings to bear me through the air!—The lightest footed horse will seem a sluggard to me. Return with me to Bartonmere. I will stay at the castle only a few minutes, and then away with you. Come, come, let us begone— each minute is now a little eternity."

Mercia stepped hastily from the bank of the river, took up his staff, recrossed the bridge, and, followed by Robert, went over the moon-light meadows till he came to the castle.

Bartonmere and Mary had seen him go out like the hooded genius of melancholy; but he returned to them with briskness in his steps, and with roses in his cheeks. Having told them of all he had heard, he called on Robert to vouch for the truth of his extraordinary story. Lord Bartonmere was transfixed in amazement; and Mary shrieked at the commencement of her sudden ecstacy. Mercia resolved that his journey should begin immediately; and Bartonmere proposed to accompany him, when Robert interposed, and told him that it must not be.

"Think not ill of me," he added, "for objecting to it, but if Lord Mercia has a single attendant our project will assuredly fail. Eustace is a second master to Celwold's small but desperate party; and in a man of his occupation, I never discovered so strange a character. We must force nothing on one who has found the means even of humbling the crest of Celwold. Allude not to his past actions, but treat him as if he were still honourable. He has alleviated the sufferings of those who have so long been placed under him; and, my life on it, he will yet do more. Artifice, my Lord, will be better than force. The house is curiously constructed, and there are such villains in its walls, that the prisoners may be removed, and put away for ever, before any public search can be made for them. I shall rejoice in your successes, by my soul I shall. I love my wife, my children, dearly! yet I could almost sacrifice one of them, if by so doing I could repair all your wrongs."

Mercia embraced his friend and trembling sister, he then rushed out of the room; and he and Robert wasted that night as well as the following day in riding. Their horses were so jaded and worn out that they left them behind, while they went the remainder of the way by water. The breezes blew kindly on the sail; and at length

Robert said to Mercia, "Yonder stands the prison of your friends."

It was evening when they left the vessel. Robert placed his noble companion in the hut of a peasant till he had spoken to Lord Celwold; he then returned, and conducted him secretly to Eustace, who received him at a private entrance, of which he alone had the charge.

Eustace had a lamp in his hand; but his face was concealed more than ever, and his dark eye only once sullenly glanced at Mercia, and then, for a moment, fell on the ground. The young traveller was struck by the little that he saw of Eustace's countenance; gratitude however filled his breast, and he clasped the hand of this new friend, while he poured forth his thanks.

"If you would have me serve you," said Eustace, "pray give me no soft words. I would rather hear the hissing of a thousand arrows in a field of battle than sounds like these. Perhaps in serving you, I gratify myself; and, to speak plainly and with sincerity, no action ever gives me greater pleasure than that."

"I would not, for the world, displease you," said Mercia, "but my heart is warm,—my emotions are quick. Tell me, did I never hear your voice before?"

"Were you ever in the northern part of England, before the age of ten?"

"No, I was not."

"Nor in Palestine since that period?"

"Indeed I was not."

"Then you never saw or heard me till this hour. Five and twenty years I lived with christians, afterwards some ten or twelve with infidels, and by Mahomet! (he will do for my present purpose) I swear I know not in which country villains most abound. Oh, there is a vigorous growth,—a most plentiful harvest of them, under both hat and turban. This, however, relates not to your concerns, nor shall I now tell you why I spurn at the commands of Celwold to gratify a stranger. But I desire you will not offer me the smallest reward; for I am somewhat proud, and susceptible of offence; and I shall like you better, if you give me no more thanks for what I have done. Follow me, and I will lead you to your friend."

"Is he apprised of my coming?"

"How could I tell that you yet existed? We are daily—hourly—

momentarily flying from the world. We make the wing of the swallow seem lazy;—we dart into eternity as quick as the beams of the sun travel to the earth. Neither he nor Agatha know any thing of it. Follow me with a light step, and keep your tongue without employment.—Come hither!"

He took the hand of Mercia, griped it like a man who puts aside hatred, and returns with an impassioned heart to friendship. He then went on, and soon afterwards the impetuous tears of Mercia, rolled down the breast of the astonished and almost incredulous William. The prisoner, thus surprised, grew almost frantic with joy; and he hung delighted on the neck of his friend, while he with ecstacy exclaimed, "is the hour of my delivery at length arrived?"

"No," replied Eustace, "it is yet to come. But why sink you in a moment? It is ever thus with man; he craves, possesses,—craves still more, and loses what were good to be retained, by attempting to grasp beyond his reach or might. These weaknesses will degrade Alwynd's son; let me trace something more noble in his conduct."

"Eustace," said William, "you were never immured in a place like this—you have been allowed to walk in the world, freely and without interruption."

"Have I not told you that I have been manacled, lashed, and despised? Pray, good fellow, do not turn satirist, nor strive to make my love of adventures run before my memory. I have brought a friend to you, and that is more than I could bring to myself, if posted on the brow of the highest hill, that was ever piled up by God's own hand, I were to proclaim the want of one, with a trumpet that should be heard from the extremity of the east, even to the western verge of the earth. Enjoy the present hour, for at the commencement of the next you must part."

"Indeed!" cried Mercia, "must it be so soon? If you would have many and happy days—if the peace of the human mind be dear to you, drive me not hence before you bring Agatha to me. Shall I, Eustace, shall I see her?"

"Perhaps you may—I will go a step further. Be rational, and you *shall* see her within half an hour. Robert, be careful in your watchings, and warn your charge not to be too high sounding in their speeches."

He then retired, Robert stationed himself at the door, and William and Mercia renewed their embraces. They had so many questions to ask of each other, that they both thought themselves not sufficiently answered. Most of their enquiries related to Mary and Agatha; and they were talking of the latter, when Eustace returned, and put her into the arms of her agitated and almost breathless lover.

He saw her pale and nearly insensible.—Her fixed smile created alarm rather than delight, and several minutes elapsed before she could either move or speak.—William endeavoured to recal her reason, Mercia strained her to his breast and kissed her cheek, on which he soon discovered reviving roses.

"Is this illusion?" she cried, "tell me, who is it that now holds me?"

"Mercia! your adoring Mercia!—Let all my past sufferings be forgotten in the felicity of the present moment. Surely I now know how great the happiness of man can be!—By your eyes, Agatha, by the returning colour of your cheeks, I find I am not single in my joys!—But poverty is imposed on my tongue by the emotions of my heart; I feel what I cannot express, and am delighted beyond my own report and your comprehension."

Eustace now allowed them another opportunity for free communication, by retiring to the passage;—the new met friends availed themselves of it, but they had scarcely time to speak of their immediate situation, before Eustace returned hastily, telling them they must separate on the instant.

William's countenance grew dull, Agatha again sunk into despondency, and Mercia implored that he might not so soon be driven away.

"If any of you oppose me," said Eustace, "my friendship will cease and my services be over. Robert, conduct Lord Mercia again to the cottage; and lady, you must creep softly back with me to your chamber. Lord Celwold, I find, has either not been to rest, or is disturbed out of it;—let there be no opposition, for I must be obeyed, aye, and instantly too."

"But when shall I return?" enquired Mercia.

"To-morrow night, if it be practicable. Robert put the skirt of your habit around the lamp. Come, Agatha, come, delay not a minute, lest the beast we sport with should suddenly spring upon and seize us."

"Brother, good night!—Adieu, dear Mercia!" cried Agatha, with a voice of tenderness and sorrow.

Mercia again pressed her hand, but he was denied speaking any farther; Robert hurried him away, Eustace led Agatha back to her apartment and William was left to ruminate on this most unexpected event.

Eustace and Robert, on the following morning, made some arrangements for the evening;—but, during the day, the former conversed nearly an hour with Celwold, respecting Agatha.

"Your eye, my Lord," he said, "has of late been a most stern reprover;—still I rejoice in having prevented an action that would have damned your name and soul for ever. Woman is, perhaps, the richest prize of man, let him, however, in his ventures for her, avoid all black artifices. That Agatha is perverse I am willing to allow; but, considering her sex, the quality I speak of makes her not singular. You love her,—you shall possess her yet,—but you must first marry her."

"To-morrow,—this very day would I do so," cried Celwold, "did her inclinations correspond with mine."

"Not so soon,—it cannot be,—within a month, however, you will have nothing further to wish for; but I must have your confidence or I will not act.—Leer suspiciously and bend your brows at your fellows;—I will be treated differently. They are only dogs with some uncommon instincts; I am a man and will not be abused."

"By my soul you shall not!"

"By my soul I *will* not. I have been accustomed to walk erect and conscious of all my qualities. The brute creation would be nearly doubled were nature merely to transform two of the limbs of those beings, who lie, most darkly, when they speak of their first father.—It is my wish to see you as happy as you deserve to be, and if the possession of Agatha can make you so, it shall not be long before you confess it to me."

"But by what means?—What cause have you for these new hopes?"

"Leave every thing to me, and be ready for the event. I have said it shall be done, and it shall. Yet, my Lord, I must smile at your impatience.—Why did you not marry Mercia's widow?"

"Lightnings singe and vultures prey upon the witch!" exclaimed Celwold,—"I would have a new hell hollowed purposely for the strumpet."

"A pleasant conceit," said Eustace, laughing, "and expressed with a good christian enthusiasm. Were the winds capable of bearing it to the ears of Githa, what a massacre of Frenchmen would there be while her fit lasted!—Good day to your Lordship, for I have business for my hands. If you are averse to solitude, send one of your fellows to the priest who is pricking his lazy mule over the bridge. Mercy, how the storm pelts him!—And what a string of anathemas hangs from his righteous lips!—Were my head not so much like that of an ostrich, this object might draw some conclusions from me. Your Lordship has more capacity, and therefore I leave you to be critical with him."

Celwold was then better pleased with Eustace than he had been for a considerable time before. Though he was a hypocrite himself, and generally awake to the artifices of others, yet Eustace had completely duped him, and he actually expected all that was promised. He now thought of his own reward, and of that to which Eustace would be entitled. His mind grew warm upon the assurance—the images that filled it were bold and glowing; and on the entrance of one of his men, he quickly retired to a more private room, in order that he might receive no interruption in his mental repast.

Mercia, as well as Agatha and her brother, longed for the approach of night; and his heart bounded with pleasure when Robert came to the cottage to conduct him to the castle. He found no obstacle to his entrance. Robert led him immediately to William; and it was not long before Agatha was brought to him. She was, in spite of her captivity, considered by him as a redeemed treasure, which he knew not how to prize according to its value. Her looks were improved. Mercia gazed on her with admiration, but love did not banish his gratitude; and as soon as she had removed herself from his arms, with the liveliest emotions he pressed the hand of Eustace, from whose eye, to his astonishment, he extracted a tear, which however was soon swept away by indignation.

"Be not ashamed of that which is honourable, my friend," said Mercia.—"You have dashed upon the floor a gem more precious than any that all the known mines can produce,—a pearl that would have added to the beauty of humanity's bosom. I wonder, Eustace, while I look on you.—There lives a spirit within your breast that would have suited the noblest of employments, and yet in how different an one do I find you!—There must be some treaty between us; I want to make you my friend. My house, my table, my purse I would have you partake, and that most freely, and in such terms as subsist among generous brothers. I cannot suppose that you have summoned me to a transitory happiness, merely to banish me hereafter into eternal misery;—you must have other designs, and I guess at them. In the name of God, I charge you to take us hence to-morrow night, and guide us in safety back to Bartonmere."

"Mercia," replied Eustace, "that I can never do. Bad as my actions have been, I still believe there is a God—still fear him! I have bent my knees at the altar, pressed my lips upon the sacred volume, and sworn never to open the gates to the prisoners of Celwold."

"Then we are doomed to perish here!" cried Agatha in extreme agony.

"Hold, Lady!" said Eustace, "and let caution teach you to speak with a lower voice. I should not have dispatched Robert to Lord Mercia, had it not been for some words, of which I took particular notice. William, you once told me what your first action should be, if you could obtain your liberty; perhaps you forget it not, and will declare it again."

"I told you, Eustace, that I would remain in uncertainty, no longer than I remained in captivity;—that, after such time, fear should not direct me—that I would go to the king, declare my birth to him, and trust to his mercy, without previously appealing to it."

"Would you have your brother do as he proposed, had he the present means?" said Eustace, turning to Agatha.

"I think I would—yet I know not—oh, I might have everlasting cause to curse my assent to it!"

"And what do you, Lord Mercia, say to the project of your friend?"

"I applaud it; I wish he was allowed to execute it immediately. If the king were to design aught of evil against him, I would, most earnestly endeavour to snatch him from it; and afterwards fly with him and my Agatha, to realms far distant from that in which so cruel a tyrant should wear a crown."

"Alwynd is worthy of such a friend," cried Eustace, "and Agatha of such a husband! Now listen to me, while I declare all that I intend to do—all that I can ever perform. I love to see the blaze of spirit! it is as precious to my eyes, as the radiance of the setting sun is to him who has just recovered his sight. I confess that the children of Alwynd ought not to be immured in a place like this. Last night, in my sleep, I thought their father, bony and erect, came from the grave, and smote me on the cheek with his rattling hand. Lord Mercia, do you return to Bartonmere; take the papers on which your friends build their title, to the king; tell him of the treachery of Celwold, and direct him to the place where the offspring of Matilda may be discovered."

"And what if he should tear them to the scaffold? Answer me, friend?—William—Agatha!——"

"To the scaffold! For what? By the power that gave us all life, I would rather stab them both to the heart then see them so sacrificed. The king loved his sister; once in every year he mourns for her most piously, and I think he will protect her children, not destroy them. Go this very night, and be quick in the business. Till we hear from you, I will continue to act as I have done with Celwold's captives. Your success will, perhaps create the last pleasure that shall ever enter into my heart; but should you be disappointed, I will strive to ward off the blow of danger, and fly with you all from England."

"Go, Mercia," cried William, "for my sentiments accord with those of Eustace. Let us hear from you as soon as possible; and make your friend either better than he is, or eternally forgetful of having been anything. Agatha, be composed, bid adieu to our messenger, and trust to the assurances of Eustace."

After taking a farewel, the tenderness of which was confessed by every eye, Mercia was conducted out of the mansion by Robert.

Early in the morning he began his journey to Bartonmere. When he arrived there he spoke of his designs, which alarmed Mary more than her host; and, having collected the papers, he did not allow himself a single day's rest, but went, without delay, to the court of his sovereign, and entreated a private audience, which was granted to him.

For a few minutes irresolution pained his heart, and bound his tongue. At length, however, he spoke to the king, who started at the name of Alwynd, and confined himself to the treachery and baseness of Celwold. But it was necessary to explain further, and he found himself unfit for the office. In extreme agitation he confessed his love for Alwynd's daughter; he then put the documents into the hands of the king, who retired to peruse them, and whose countenance, Mercia, when next admitted to the honours of an interview, knew not how to read perfectly. Amazement and anxiety were stamped on it. His eyes were red with either smothered rage or grief, and to the great surprise of Mercia, he commanded him to return to the place he came from, and there to wait for him in privacy.

Mercia could discover none of the monarch's sentiments. He returned, filled with alternate hopes and apprehensions, to his friends, whose spirits fell when they were informed that the king was coming to them in person. Agatha, more fearful than any other, again implored Eustace to favour their escape, but she found him still inexorable; and William declared that he would not go beyond the gates, even if they were set open for him to pass.

They all spent a truly anxious night, and to their astonishment, the king arrived on the following day. But their surprise was comparatively small; Celwold was involved in wonder and confusion, and received his royal visiter most awkwardly. Robert was dispatched by Eustace to Mercia, who repaired immediately to the mansion, and concealed himself in one of the remote apartments, in order that he might attend more readily, when it should be proper for him so to do.

The coming of the king occasioned much confusion among the servants; and Celwold could scarcely prevent their instant departure. He knew not what answer to make, when it was first asked of him, whether William and Agatha were yet in his custody. At length however he replied they were; when he was commanded to say who their parents were, and on what grounds he had so long detained them.

At that moment Mercia entered, and the villain, with faulty

pulse and a face despicably pale, recoiled from him. But he was again desired to attend to the questions that had been asked, and after some further hesitation he complied.

"The unworthy objects of whom your Majesty speaks," he said, "are still in my power. Their mother could not be otherwise than honourable, because she was a princess of Britain; but their father sported too freely with his reputation when he seduced Matilda from her duty. Their offspring, my liege, I almost blush to speak of. The pride of the daughter is excessive—the ambition of the son bold and truly dangerous.—Filled with their own greatness, and aided by Mercia, in whom no trust should be reposed, they have designed a conspiracy; and Alwynd's son has often wished his uncle, as well as the young prince, in heaven, and himself upon the throne of England. I thought it my duty to secure this dangerous and misguided youth, and all that I have done in the business was to preserve my sovereign from insult and injury."

"Oh, sinful and accursed!" exclaimed the wonder-stricken Mercia.—"Most abominable slanderer!—May I ever be an alien from God's kingdom, if these are not the foulest of lies!"

"Lord Celwold," said the king, "were all my peers like you, I should be proud of them indeed. Send for the prisoners instantly—let me see the hero that would snatch at my crown. Dispatch! Dispatch!—I am as hot for vengeance as Alwynd's son is for prerogative. Go for them yourself, my Lord; instantly too, and suffer me to remain as short a time as possible in suspense."

Mercia's heart grew cold—Eustace's eye fell on the floor—neither of them dared to speak; and while the exulting Celwold went for his captives, the face of every person he had left behind was marked by fear, dread, and expectation. Soon afterwards a noise was heard, and Agatha rushed into the room at the front of Celwold and her brother.

"Where is the king?" she cried, "where is the king?—Let me kneel at his feet, and appeal to his humanity. Oh, royal sir! I bend distractedly before you!—What have we done, and what are our offences?—I know of none—I never did you aught of injury; and yet this wretch has just now said, that you are come here purposely for our blood. Our blood!—It cannot be—I will not believe it!"

"Matilda!" exclaimed the king—"Surely it is Matilda!"

"No, no, I am her poor and miserable daughter!—A persecuted and heartbroken wretch!—This is my brother—and may heaven deal with you as you shall deal with him. Do any thing with me—drive me naked into beggary—shut me in a cell, and leave me slowly to perish—but spare my brother!—Save him!—Save him!"

"Save him!" exclaimed the king.—"What, suffer a traitor to be at large—a wretch, who craves my honours, and conspires against my life?"

"A traitor!" cried William.—"Conspire against your life!—God of truth and righteousness!—Who has said this of me?"

"Celwold—a man who loves and respects me—the flower of our nobility, that shall not hereafter bloom without great distinction."

"That shall wither and crisp where the sun's body could not cause a fiercer heat!" cried Agatha.—"Is there no fear in man, and serves his maker only for derision?—Shews it like treason, when my brother calls on his king to rescue him from the cruelty and oppression of a private, but destructive enemy—from one, who to robbery would perhaps have added murder!—Rest, rest, my father! and come not on the earth to pine, though fate should ensnare your children."

"Agatha!" cried the king, rising and going towards her, "Agatha, this upright, loyal lord has declared your conduct to be such, that you shall experience——"

"What, what, my liege?—Be merciful as you are great. Oh, tell me what I shall experience?"

"My favour, my protection, my countenance and love!—Thus, taking you to my breast, I swear they are already your's, my Agatha!—they are your's, sweet daughter of the lamented Matilda."

"Are these blessings real or imaginary?—They *are* real, and my ear was not deceived. On my knees will I send forth my gratitude. Oh, royal uncle! how shall my heart repay you?—But my brother?"

"He is now Earl of Alwynd, and shall be greater hereafter. Take my hand, dear boy! as an earnest of it.—My resentments are past—I almost forget that I ever had any. You must love the prince, who is to be my successor; and you shall ever remain in my heart and favour."

"Ever, my gracious sovereign!" cried William, "ever will I be your true, your loyal, and your loving subject.—Your ear has been abused, indeed it has, most shamefully abused!—May I become an object of your scorn, if the allegations of Celwold, of him who now bends his head in shame before you, are not false and abominable. My evidences are but few—they can however come in my behalf to your Majesty, with faces such as honest men should wear. My father loved you, my liege, by my soul, he loved you truly!—and let me never go where he now dwells, if the affections which I have professed to feel are less sincere. Punish me, heaven, as much as man can be punished for sins too great for pardon, if I ever were, or ever shall become a traitor to a virtuous king!"

"Boy! what are you doing with my heart?—You shall aid my counsels, and fight my battles.—Come to my arms again. Agatha, your love must not be wholly given to Mercia; your uncle claims, and is intitled to a part of it. Let all who are now around me, learn that this is Earl Alwynd, and my nephew—this the daughter of my sister, and my niece—and this her approved and destined husband. Now, Celwold, I must turn to you; and never did my eyes encounter a more abhorred object. Before I saw the children of Matilda, I discovered that your soul was black and treacherous. The story of their parents had previously softened my heart, and none of your calumnies could reach it."

The king drew Agatha nearer to him, and continued his speech to Celwold.

"You have been exemplary in vice, and exemplary shall be your punishment. I do not merely say that you shall crave pardon of those whom you have so basely injured, and make restitution of their property—no, that would be stopping much too soon. The name of Briton ought not to pertain to you—you disgrace our country, and shall fly from it. If you be found in my realm at the commencement of the ensuing month, I will not only pardon, but, also reward, any man who shall lay your head at my feet."

"I beseech—I implore your majesty to hear me!"

"Not a word, your crimes are too manifest. You have heard the sentence, and let your own discretion tell you how you ought to act hereafter. Come, my children, for such I must now consider you, we will be gone immediately; our horses will carry us to the castle of Sir Walter Mowbray, which is but a few miles distant, and there we will procure further aid. The day on which I became the king of my noble people, was not more joyful than this. William, lead the way to the gates; and lend me your arm, my girl!"

They then left the wretched Celwold, standing among his fellows, almost in a state of stupefaction. Mercia, who followed his friends, took hold of the arms of Robert and Eustace, and stopped to speak with them in the hall, while the royal traveller and his attendants were mounting their steeds. He put a purse of some value into the hands of Robert, and desired him to return immediately to his wife and children, and to expect a permanent reward for his past services.

Mercia then embraced the late governor of William's prison, and asked in what manner he intended to dispose of himself. The eye of Eustace almost frightened the enquirer, who was not answered for several minutes.

"I cannot tell you," he at length replied, "in what manner I shall dispose of myself. There is a mist before me, and no sun to dispel it. For a while I shall remain here; but for what reason I pray you do not ask me. Mercia, I have sinned against you—I never shall forgive myself, and all I fear is, that you will curse me as long as you continue to live."

"You are deceived. God bless you, Eustace!"

"On your knees, repeat it on your knees. You bend, I hear again your prayer! Now I am satisfied. My heart would burst were I to stay with you another minute. Oh, farewel! From this moment we are lost to each other for ever!"

Mercia could not detain him; he rushed out of the hall, and the young Earl's eyes were filled with tears, when he overtook the party that had preceded him.

After his departure, Eustace succeeded in soothing his passions, and went to Celwold, whom he found almost as cold and senseless as a statue, and surrounded by men, who murmured at their own disappointments.

"What are you," said Eustace, "that thus you stand as if you were formed out of a rock? What, oh! my Lord, why do you not speak to me? Man cannot look upon a sight like this without amazement. You have eyes, and know not the use of them; ears that exclude all sound, and seemingly, a body from which breath has departed for ever. Answer me. What are you?"

"A wretch! A lost—an abandoned wretch! Eustace, let me rest my head upon your shoulder. Oh, I can sink no lower—no lower than this!"

"You are banished, it is true, my Lord, but what of that? There are other places in the world, infinitely to be preferred to this paltry island—this spot of damps and fogs, where a sunny day employs every man in telling his neighbour that such it is. Oh, you should see the plains of France, the lovely scenes of Italy and Spain, and many other parts of the globe where I have travelled with blistered feet. Look up, my Lord. The world is still before you, and something may be attained, better than any thing that you now possess. Revive, and forget not that great capabilities are lodged within you, and that you bear the name of man."

"I am capable of nothing—can attain nothing,—I have already advanced some way into perdition, and there is no retreating. My own vices have ensnared me,—I have gone beyond the mark of redemption, and must encounter ruin whichever way I turn.—Oh, I could do something desperate to free myself from my present miseries! Give me a sword,—a club to dash out my brains,—any instrument that will destroy for ever the sense of my wretchedness."

"You talk franticly," cried Eustace, "and your complaints are puerile—Curse what you dread and laugh at your present distresses;—he who is truly a man would neither heave a sigh nor drop a tear at a fate like your's. Before you will be compelled to sail from Britain, nearly a month has to elapse, and, during that time, you may gather in your fortunes, at least some part of them, and make arrangements for your departure.—France, I think, would afford you the best asylum, and thither would I have you repair. After you have crossed the channel, assume some other name, stick a white plume in your cap, and force the gallic daws to respect you. These men that stand around you, these honest, worthy fellows, will be anxious to accompany you.—I see it in their faces,—their eager eyes confess it, and I beseech you not to turn from their solicitations; they only wish to wait upon you, they will spurn at rewards should you offer them any."

"Flatter me not, Eustace, I charge you. Anxious to accompany me, do you say?—See how they turn from me;—mark their sullenness and dissatisfaction. No, no, the unfortunate have none to page their heels!"

"In faith, they seem to have no stomach for it," said Eustace, "and I fear my own want of discrimination.—Oh, interested rascals!—Self-loving knaves!—While the hand feeds you it shall be kissed, but when it lacks provision you would smile to see the lightnings blast it. Heap a curse on them, my Lord, and turn from them for ever. You shall not go singly into exile; I will be your servant—your slave. The breeze that wafts you from England shall also blow upon me;—I will link my fate with your's, and we will live and die together."

"The passages of my heart are open. Eustace, I thank you, even with my tears I thank you!"

"Then my services are accepted, and I know what I have to perform. I said I would be your slave, but distinctions must not subsist if you would have me act with kindness towards you. I shall consider you merely as a man, while I render you the services of a man.—Open your arms, my Lord, and let me swear fidelity upon your breast!—There, I press you now as I have long wished, and can you not believe in these assurances?"

"Oh, God!" exclaimed Celwold, sinking on the floor, "you have —you have stabbed me to the heart!"

"Once—twice—What! will not the third stroke finish you?— Damnable villain! you surely have a plurality of lives. Before your sight fails for ever look upon me.—See, my eye has an uninjured fellow—my face is unscarred—and I can wipe off this dark complexion with the greatest ease. Do you not know me, fiend?—Oh, yes, I see you do!—Mercia's widow triumphs and is revenged!— There is another blow.—Now, get you to the common hell; and ask, if, according to your wish, a new one has been hollowed for me."

Celwold groaned, writhed, and died. His murderess placed her foot upon, and laughed over his body. The men who were present were filled with horror and surprise, they could scarcely believe that she was the person she confessed herself to be; but after she had thrown off some of her disguises, their doubts were at an end, and they gathered around her. None of them however dared to touch her, for she snatched the dagger from the wound of Cel-wold, and poised it boldly in her defence.

"Those who are wise," she cried, "will not exasperate me. Death has invested my hand; and, though I am a woman, where is the man that shall dare to oppose me in an hour like this?—My story may have been heard by some of you; and were not the rest too despicable, I would myself inform them of it. I know how easy it would be to expiate this offence, and to remove all stains from my name, as well as from the hands that did the deed. Is there any thing that the clergy and gold cannot effect?—The priest may be a precious villain; money is formed out of a precious metal, and if it be dropped here and there, rascals shall rise, as if it were by vegetation. Here is the poniard that ripped open the body of the accursed wretch, who ought to have died sooner. Acting as I intend to do hereafter, all of you will exclaim, 'Oh, sinful deed!—Oh, dreadful murderess!'—But had I resorted to my treasure, saying to the mason,—'Take hence what will be sufficient to build a monastery, in which I will put, and also feed, an hundred holy men, to pray for the soul of him whom I have slain, as well as for my own,' had I said this—seen the fabric reared—placed the hoary cheats in the secretly supplied cells of sanctity and abstinence—had I gone thither only once a year, kneeled at a baby toy, and looked dejected, what had been said of me then?—Oh, I should have been praised and pitied for the remainder of my life; and, after my death, every lying monk would tell the world that he saw me pass the station of Saint Peter!"

"You shall not escape without punishment, impious woman!" cried one of the men.—"Lord Celwold was banished by his king, but not condemned to your inhuman hands; and your blood shall answer for that which you have spilt."

"Pray, sir, stoop, and let me look upon the crown of your head. Where is your badge of office, mighty and venerable judge?—You find I will not compromise, and therefore will abate nothing of your rigour; yet I would stake my life, that there is not a man among you all who would decline my terms of purchase. Well, sir, you are welcome to make whatever use of my body you please; do not however misconstrue my words with indecency, but rather take them up with the sense of a magistrate. Now I surrender myself—give me death, and fix me on a gibbet. Oh, the very grinnings of my parched face would frighten twenty men, whose valor should be twenty times greater than your own."

"Seize on her!—Shut her in the cells!" was the general cry.

"Away, ye nasty villains!" she cried, "and stain a whole river with your filthy hands before you offer to place them on me. Decency and authority should ever go together; but you are alike ignorant and vile. Look on me, and learn administration—observe me well. Was the thing that is called a culprit set in the front of me, and I were appointed to decide his fate, then would I stand, as I do now, calm and erect—my eye, as it is in the present moment, should be strong, but not impassioned—and if the voices around me were to call for condemnation, I would debase the wretch no further, but stretching forth my arm, and making big my nerves, I would silence him for ever by means like these."

Her dagger was instantly buried, even to the hilt, in her body; and she died as soon as it was removed by the fellows.

When the death of his mother was reported to Mercia, he was divided between horror and amazement. He would not believe in what he heard, till he returned to the spot where she had perished; and where he found her cold, stiff, and still in male attire.

Having identified her person, he blinded himself with his hand, and ran from observation. All malice—all enmity was forgotten. He cursed the daughter of passion no more, he threw himself on his knees, and devoutly implored God to admit her into Heaven, and to give her his pardon there.

The softest consolation that he afterwards found, came from Agatha, of whom, before the summer months were over, he became a joyful husband.

William had not long to sigh for the want of happiness. His royal uncle, for a while, opposed his union with Mary, wishing him to seek for an object of purer birth and distinction. But when her qualities were better known, no prejudices remained. Her virtues placed her high in the estimation of her former censurer, and he presented her, as no mean gift, to him who truly deserved her. While the king lived, it was his chief pleasure to be near his sister's children, who, after his decease, were equally noticed and respected by his successor.

William and Mercia still fondly loved the rural shades of Alwynd, whither they frequently repaired with their fair associates. Their bosoms often met the affectionate breast of Bartonmere, who having spent a long and honourable life, died in their arms, and was truly lamented by them.

Connubial love brought forth the sweetest blossoms, and while they were expanding under the sun of prosperity, and visited by the breezes of health, Mercia and his friend were dealing out charities around them, and doing the best of services to the state.

The cave of Martyn of Fenrose was ever regarded with solemnity, particularly by William, who, in his evening rambles, frequently gazed on it, till he thought he saw the wizard, wild in his aspect, and towering in his height, coming through the passage, in order to walk amid the airs that blew over the heath. His story and services were dangerous to reveal, the knowledge of them became singly hereditary, and several centuries had rolled away, before it went beyond the oldest of the family.

THE END.

CONTEMPORARY REVIEWS.

The Critical Review, **Volume XXXIII, p. 112 (September 1801)**

ART. 38.—*Martyn of Fenrose; or, the Wizard and the Sword. A Romance. By Henry Summersett, Author of Leopold Warndorf, &c. 3 Vols. 12mo. 13s. Boards.* Dutton. 1801.

When we had perused only a few pages of this romance, we felt pleased with the performance; and, in spite of our objections to wizards and sorcery, could not avoid bestowing some commendation on the warm imagination of its author. But, before we had finished the second volume, disgust compelled us to throw the book on the floor, and we confess we have never since proceeded to the perusal.

Is it not enough that the English are already condemned by all Europe for the multiplicity of their oaths and blasphemies, that our circulating libraries must furnish their readers with a new set of anathemas?—'May the spirit of my father strangle me in savageness!' and 'By the ruler of the world of angels, I will level all my rage and resentment at these smiling devils!' are the only two instances of our author's invention with which we will pollute our journal. But should any dragoon or boatswain's mate find himself disposed to improve in the delectable science of swearing, he will here meet with whole pages employed, between a mother and son, in curses and imprecations, from which, if he have taste, he may select many precious morsels for the use of the galley or the guardroom. The German dramatists are here absolutely *out-heroded*.

The Monthly Review, **Volume XL, p. 207 (February 1803)**

Art. 16. *Martyn of Fenrose;* or the Wizard and the Sword. A Romance. By Henry Summersett. 12mo. 3 vols. 9s. sewed. Dutton.

Mr. Summersett's fertile and lively imagination hurries him beyond the boundaries of nature into the regions of enchantment, and we become acquainted with the fleet courser which outstrips the wind, with the magic sword which mows down armies, and with the wonderful wizard of Fenrose, who may be intitled "the prince of the power of the air."—Those who can read of such marvellous faculties, without being shocked at so flagrant a violation of the known laws of nature, will find in these volumes several interesting and amusing scenes, characters, well supported, and events related in a manner which displays ability and genius. We might mention in particular the description of the field of battle, the descent of the stranger and his dog Fidelity into the abyss, and the scene of William's imprisonment in the vault.

9 781934 555392